MW01126068

Drysine Legacy
The Spiral Wars, Book 2

Joel Shepherd

ISBN: 1-5330-2508-8
ISBN-13: 978-1-5330-2508-1

The Spiral Wars:

Renegade

Drysine Legacy

Kantovan Vault
(August 2016)

CHAPTER 1

Four hundred meters above the valley floor, there was a strange kind of peace to be found, hanging by toes and fingertips in the mid-afternoon sun. Colonel Timothy Khola clipped his harness onto the next stretch of rope up the cliff-face, and took a moment to look around. The valley was beautiful, filled with tall green trees above which the cliff rose vertically, white and yellow stone aglow against the green forest below. What a joy to climb in this place, after the austere and brutal beauty of his native Sugauli.

To his left, a young officer-cadet was struggling, breathing hard with obvious fatigue as she searched for her next set of hand and foot-holds in the rock above. "Cadet Lo!" Khola called across. "How you doing?"

"I'm..." she gasped for more air. "I'm fine sir!

"Slow and easy, Cadet," he told her. "Slow and easy. Remember, you can't be fast if you're rushed. It's all about rhythm and pacing."

Cadet Lo nodded intently. Beneath her, other cadets were following the rope up, like so many insects slowly crawling up a wall. From this height, it would take at least ten seconds to hit the trees if you fell. *Such* a view. Of course, with proper use of ropes and harness for beginners, falling was impossible. Not like Kulina trainees learned to do it on Sugauli, free-climbing, for that ultimate rush of focused concentration. Free-climbing one learned to lose oneself entirely within the task at hand, and learned that skill and execution, in the moments that mattered, were all the tools one needed to stave off certain death. Of course, he couldn't recommend free-climbing to these marine officer-cadets. His job was to train them, not kill them. But for himself, with the ropes and harness in place, it wasn't quite the same.

To his right, a lean, brown figure flowed smoothly up the rock from one hold to another, as fast as his fellow cadets were slow. Cadet Rohan, Khola saw with little surprise. "Good afternoon

Colonel!" Rohan called across to him with a calm smile as he climbed. "You were right, it is a beautiful climb!"

"You just make sure you stop and *help* the next person you rocket past, Cadet Rohan!" Khola replied. "If you reach your target thirty minutes before the rest of your squad, the enemy will thank you, then kill you."

"Yes Colonel!" Rohan continued to scamper upward, fast but not rushed. Khola shook his head, and followed with fast, easy pulls of his strong bare arms.

Fifty meters from the top, a cruiser howled overhead, black and official-looking, then vanished beyond the lip above. Khola kept his pace steady, giving encouragement to cadets around him. Ahead, Cadet Perris was in difficulty, having been passed by several since the bottom. Khola stayed with him until the top, not telling him where to put his hands and feet, for it was not his job to perform basic skills for these cadets. He simply reminded Perris to breathe and relax, and soon enough, in a better frame of mind, the young man made the top and hauled himself over the lip with obvious relief, and cheers from those already arrived.

No-one gave Khola a hand up, that would have been temerity. Looking around as he unhooked, he found that three-quarters of those who'd started were already here. Now they sat exhausted and took in the view, or took turns helping others up, or put salves on sore and bleeding fingers. Beyond the cadets, the cruiser waited on the rock before the tree line. Nearby stood a man in blue spacer uniform with a rear admiral's stars, talking with two others as they admired the view and watched the arriving cadets.

Khola walked to them, displeased they'd not waited another thirty minutes until everyone had summited. Turning these kids into officers and warriors had been his life's work for the past ten years. Even most admirals knew better than to interrupt him on the job.

The officers saw him approach, and Khola pulled a crumpled cap from his pocket, and yanked it on in order to perform the proper salute. The officers returned it. Beside the Rear Admiral was Major Varika from the Academy, whom Khola knew well, and a spacer captain whom he didn't.

"Colonel," said the Major. "Rear Admiral Bedi, and Captain Cain." Bedi offered a handshake, which let Khola know that the formality-level was low. That wasn't good. When Fleet brass came calling with friendly gestures, usually they meant to ask him something he wouldn't like.

"How are they coming, Colonel?" asked Rear Admiral Bedi.

"They're a good bunch," said Khola. "They're disappointed they're not likely to see any action. I tell them to be careful what they wish for, but they don't listen to me."

Bedi nodded. He was a smallish man, round-cheeked, a little portly. Amazing how fast some former ship captains put on the kilos, once back on station dock or planet-side assignment, with a table full of nice things every day instead of the usual ship food. "Colonel, I've been sent here by the Guidance Council."

Khola took a deep breath. "Yes Admiral." *This* was why they'd come to him. He didn't like it, but he was Kulina, and Kulina made a lifestyle of doing things that most people would rather not. "Why me?"

"It must be someone beyond reproach," said Bedi with certainty. "The group was in agreement. Your service record is exemplary, even by Kulina standards. You hold the Liberty Star. You have repeatedly refused higher promotion in favour of your Academy role. The wider Fleet hold a low opinion of officers who do their superiors' dirty work just to win promotion. You are not that sort of officer, and everyone knows it."

"So this is about appearances, then."

"Isn't everything?" asked Bedi. "Look Colonel, they screwed up. Captain Pantillo was a pain in the ass, but you can't just kill the guy because he gets in your way. Or if you do, at least have the sense to do it quietly. Not court-martialled on Homeworld for millions of people to see, and billions more when the media grab it. And to try to pin it on *Debogande*. Of all the hare-brained schemes."

Khola did not agree with that. People were always wise in hindsight. But Rear Admiral Anjo *had* almost pulled it off. Lieutenant Commander Debogande was the son of one of the most

5

powerful industrialists in human space, and such powerful people attracted distrust. Plenty of people would have believed that Alice Debogande would murder to get her way. They'd been prepared to believe it of her son, when Fleet had accused him of murdering his own Captain.

The reason they hadn't believed it, was Major Trace Thakur, *Phoenix*'s marine commander, and another of the four still-living Kulina officers, along with Khola himself, who wore the Liberty Star. Kulina were known to be incorruptible, and with Thakur on his side, the weight of suspicion had shifted away from LC Debogande, and onto the senior Fleet commanders who'd accused him. And now that Fleet had far larger battles to fight, the whole thing was becoming one enormous distraction they could no longer afford.

"We've got the makings of a full scale insurgency going on with the Worlders," said Bedi, gazing over the exhausted cadets. "Spacers are with us, Spacer Congress is with us... but they have sympathy for Debogande and Pantillo, and the entire *Phoenix* crew. They just don't believe the story any longer, and the more they hear, the less they believe it. It makes us look nasty, and it makes us look stupid."

"It makes us look treacherous," Khola added calmly.

Bedi's mouth twisted with displeasure. "Yes," he conceded. "*Phoenix* got screwed. The more we deny it, the worse we look. It's time to cut our losses on this one. And cutting our losses also means cutting the dead weight that's associated with it."

"You want a scapegoat."

"Three scapegoats," Bedi corrected. "Two Fleet Admirals, and one Supreme Commander. We'll deal with Chankow and Ishmael. But we'd like you to handle Anjo."

"And what happens to *Phoenix*?"

"We'll make them an offer. With the people who screwed them gone, they'll have justice for their Captain, and vindication. We'll ask them to come home, and forgive their crimes." Khola exhaled a hard breath. Bedi raised an eyebrow. "You disapprove?"

"Major Thakur has committed grave crimes, against Fleet and against Kulina. She violated her oath. Amongst our own kind, the penalty is death."

Bedi looked surprised. "She is one of your best, Colonel. You'd really kill her?"

"Admiral, if I had done the things she's done, whatever the cause, the Kulina Council would kill *me*. And I'd deserve it."

Bedi nodded slowly. "Kulina swore an oath to serve Fleet. We'll need you to hold to that oath once more, Colonel. If *Phoenix* accepts amnesty, you will let Major Thakur live. Whatever your custom, and whatever Fleet's standing agreement that we will allow Kulina to practise their custom where ever possible."

"*Phoenix* will not accept amnesty," Khola said grimly.

"Well I think they might. And I know Fleet ask a lot of the Kulina, Colonel, but I must insist again that you forgo your custom in this instance. Should you have Major Thakur executed *after* *Phoenix*'s amnesty, Fleet will not look the other way. The perpetrators shall be punished, whoever they are, am I clear?"

"Very clear, Admiral. But *Phoenix* will not accept amnesty."

"Very well. We will see." Among the trainee-officers, Cadet Rohan was helping new arrivals to unclip, and showing them the finer points of ropes and harnesses. "That lad there looks Kulina," Bedi suggested.

"Cadet Rohan, yes. Since he arrived from Sugauli two years ago, he's been leading his class on half of the disciplines, and is top fifth in the others."

Bedi whistled. "Some effort in this field. Was Thakur that good?"

Khola smiled faintly. "Trace wasn't great at everything. Her classwork and theory were never much better than class average. She coasted. Some assessors thought it could hold her back. I warned her about it, once. She said that obsessive focus on academia interfered with her field performance. She was all about field performance, rarely less than an A-plus on anything field related. I said that some assessors doubted not just her application, but her ability. Her next academic test came in at ninety-five percent, just to prove the point. And then dropped back to her usual eighty-five percent, like clockwork."

"How many years did you have her for?" Bedi asked curiously.

"Just the one." Khola's smile grew broader. "She was more than a good cadet, she was a good kid. Somehow managed to combine real leadership with real empathy for the vast majority that couldn't match her. Many young hotshots don't manage it."

"Yes," said Bedi. "I remember."

"And she remains the single most determined and focused individual I've ever met. Mental discipline like a steel trap."

"And yet despite all your admiration, you'd still rather see her dead?"

"In all the seven hundred years of the Kulina, no serving warrior has ever violated the oath as she has, and been allowed to live." Khola turned to the Admiral, and looked him in the eye. "When the time comes — and believe me Admiral, the time *will* come — I'll kill her myself."

CHAPTER 2

Alone on the bed of her hotel room, Trace Thakur sat cross-legged and meditated. The bed was too soft. It was a joke among her marines, that she refused even small luxuries in favour of things that were tougher, harder, more unpleasant. But in this case it was true — the bed was too soft, and her posture suffered. She couldn't sit on the floor because her full armour suit currently occupied much of it by the door, while her huge Koshaim-20 rifle took up the rest beside her bed.

With much of Phoenix Company crashing about in the hallways, the hotel quarters were the only place quiet enough to meditate in. Usually when she meditated, she focused only on her breathing, making it slower and deeper until all time and space seemed to drift with the gentle rhythm of her heart. When she was younger, that focus had come naturally. In the last few years, however, that peace had been harder and harder to find.

When inward focus abandoned her, she typically thought of clouds. In her quarters at the Kulina Academy on Sugauli, she'd watched them rolling in across the ragged black mountains, building into great, thundering storms. But thinking of Sugauli only made her think of Aran, and how she'd stared out of the dirty windows of the coroner's office at age seven, having just seen his body, and wondering why the clouds looked so unchanged. Didn't they know that her brother was dead? Didn't they care? Her whole universe had changed, yet the clouds rolled on regardless. Like it didn't matter. Like nothing did.

Aran had been an apprentice miner in Sugauli's many pits and shafts, having left home and school early, like so many Sugauli youngsters. The money was good, far better than a more advanced education might earn, but the safety conditions weren't as great. A loader he'd been operating had malfunctioned in an earth tremor, and run off the side of a huge, deep pit. For perhaps twenty seconds, the coroner's report confirmed, the loader had hung upon the edge of that pit, dangling, while Aran had struggled with the unfamiliar safety harness and shouted for help. Men had been near enough to help, but had not. They'd been scared. And sure enough, the loader had fallen, and taken Aran down with it.

Trace had hated those men. She hated their weakness. Like she hated her own father's weakness, in being the violent, drunken oaf who'd driven Aran away at such a young age. And like she'd hated her mother, for caring more about her dreary social life, gambling and drinking than she did about her own children. There had seemed to be so little virtue in the world. People put their selfish needs first, and disasters followed. From then, she'd dreamed only of becoming Kulina. The Kulina were at war with the tavalai, but the true war that Trace had wished to wage was the one within her own heart.

On *Phoenix* she'd found comradeship and love — not the petty, selfish love of a girl with a boy, but the love of people who needed each other so profoundly, for simple survival, that their individual identities began to fuse into a single, greater whole. That love was the greatest happiness she'd ever known, and so she distrusted it. Love and happiness were selfish things. Selfishness had killed Aran. Since becoming Kulina, she'd devoted herself to scouring all selfishness from her soul. The Kulina did not simply want to make one person better — they wanted to make the whole universe better. Selfishness made bad karma, and bad karma would eventually destroy everything good in the world. Thus you could love and be happy, yet actually make everything worse, if you loved and were happy in a selfish way. Her father had been happy when dominating others. Her mother, when gambling with noxious friends. Tavalai soldiers were happy when killing humans. 'Happiness' in itself was no object worth seeking. Selflessness was all.

And so she sat here, alone in the dark, and tried to purge the human attachment from her soul. The more attached she became, the more harm she would do the very people whom she loved. Lately, purging that attachment had become very hard indeed. Some people, individually and together, she simply loved too much.

And it terrified her, that she might live long enough to see her own failings hurt those very people she'd most like to save.

A heroic death was always the most she'd expected and wanted from the war. She'd come very close on numerous occasions. But that happy fate had not been granted, and so she was stuck here, worrying over the consequences of her own selfish failure to die, as so many other Kulina had had the fortunate good sense to do.

Her uplink coms clicked. *"Hello Major,"* came Hiro Uno's voice. *"You promised me a sparring session. Is now a good time?"*

Trace took a deep breath, and unfolded herself from the bed. "Of course Hiro. I'll be right down."

The marines on guard in the hotel lobby did not bother checking Lisbeth's ID — these days everyone knew her on sight. She dressed in spacer blues and harness with Fleet insignia on the shoulders and a *UFS Phoenix* cap pulled tight over her frizzy brown hair, and while she did not exactly feel like one of the crew, she looked the part in every way except for the lack of rank, and unorthodox haircut. Vijay and Carla walked with her, looking like marines in just the same way — except that they weren't. Ex-marines, but now Debogande bodyguards, protecting their charge with the light armour and weapons that *Phoenix*'s officers had allowed them for the task.

The hotel was barabo, like the station, like the entire solar system. But for the last week the hotel had become human, the rented property of the legendary *UFS Phoenix*, one of the most powerful warships in all known space. Lisbeth walked now through the lobby bar, filled with off-duty marines and spacers talking, drinking and eating, but none entirely relaxed and all with weapons close. Barabo staff served them, and were greeted with smiles and chit-chat — all of *Phoenix* were on instruction to be nice to the locals. The humanoid, furry barabo would grin with those big, toothy mouths just made for grinning, and chatter back with the aid of translator speakers.

In the main hall beyond the lobby, military crates and unoccupied armour suits lined the walls, waiting for trouble. Here on this lower level were meeting rooms, dining halls and convention spaces, all filled with more gear, or with *Phoenix* crew in recreation or work. Lisbeth sidestepped traffic, heavily armed marines, spacer crew in animated discussion of some technical problem, bemused barabo staff going about hotel business and hoping the humans didn't completely trash their nice facility with all this gear and weaponry. In the week so far, it hadn't happened, and *Phoenix* was paying twice the usual rate for a full house.

The big open room beside the enclosed gymnasium had also been taken over, gym mats taken from *Phoenix*'s own holds and laid to make an exercise space. Marines now yelled, shouted and heaved in combat drill, or rolled around on the mats seeking a killing leverage. And a few spacers too, Lisbeth noted as she wove between them, game to risk unarmed combat training with some of humanity's most deadly warriors.

Lisbeth spied Major Thakur over by a wall, with the other two of her Debogande security crew, and walked to them. The Major was sweaty in her workout T-shirt and pants, as was Hiro, sitting cross-legged on the mats. Jokono knelt alongside in his good suit, as befitted a former station security chief and current Debogande household security chief. Though back on Homeworld, they'd probably found someone else to replace him in that role.

"Have you two been sparring?" Lisbeth asked, squatting down beside Hiro and the Major. "Who won?"

"It's training," said the Major. "The object is not winning, but learning." She had that effortless way of making Lisbeth feel about two foot tall, her playful comments crashing into a steel wall of dry good sense. "Can we help you?"

Lisbeth realised that she was interrupting. "Oh. Well yes... Romki's annoyed, and..."

"Romki's always annoyed," Thakur said calmly. She had muscles in those bare brown arms that some of Lisbeth's girlfriends would have sniffed made her look like a man. But even short-haired and sweaty, Trace Thakur looked like no man to Lisbeth, and doubtless cared even less what some skinny civilian girl thought of it. "He's made you his errand girl?"

Lisbeth blinked. "Well no, it's just that I was on my way to work out with Carla and Vijay before I head back to *Phoenix* for shuttle sims with Lieutenant Hausler, and I called in on Romki in his Engineering bay and he says you won't allow him any marine guard so he can go and call on his contacts here…"

"I don't trust his contacts here," said Hiro.

Lisbeth looked at him questioningly. Hiro's handsome, narrow eyes gave little expression back. "Really? Stan would never do anything to harm *Phoenix*, he's our friend."

"Stan Romki has more shady contacts than I do," said Hiro. "I don't want him kicking any nests to see what crawls out." Hiro had been a Federal Intelligence spy. The operative kind, who went out in the field and gathered Intel, not the kind that sat behind a desk and analysed. Sometimes he did it very aggressively.

Lisbeth looked questioningly at the Major. Thakur nodded. "It's my call Lisbeth. Off *Phoenix*, I'm in charge. I don't want Romki wandering the station, not even under guard."

"There's tavalai on this station, Lisbeth," Jokono added, in that wise, fatherly manner he had. Lisbeth guessed that with the possible exception of Doc Suelo, Jokono might be the oldest person on *Phoenix*. "And sard too. Romki has a lot of friends among the tavalai. And if he really *has* discovered this huge plot involving our wonderful allies the alo, then he's probably safer staying on *Phoenix*."

They'd all been arguing with Romki, Lisbeth knew. *Phoenix*'s commanders were trying to stop a human civil war from breaking out, between the Spacers in their stations and habitats, and the Worlders on their planets. *Phoenix*'s old commander, Captain Pantillo, had seen that war coming and tried to head it off by running for office on a pro-Worlder platform. Fleet had killed him rather than see it happen, and tried to pin the murder on Lisbeth's brother, Lieutenant Commander Erik Debogande, to shut him and the powerful Debogande family up, and dissuade them from further Worlder sympathies.

But Major Thakur had broken Erik out of custody and sent *Phoenix* running in search of answers... a search that had brought them to Stanislav Romki and his terrible secrets about alien allies that Fleet did not want widely known. Erik and the Major were now adamant that they had to continue the struggle, to prevent a human division that would surely mean doom, in a galaxy filled with aggressive species looking to exploit the weakness of others. That was *Phoenix*'s mission now — to use Captain Pantillo's old contacts and leverage to gather those representatives from Worlder and Spacer factions who disapproved of Fleet's leadership on the issue, out here where people could say what they thought without Fleet constantly looking over their shoulder.

Romki, of course, thought they were all idiots. The true threat to humanity, he insisted, came not from internal human divisions, but from external threats. One threat was the alo — one of humanity's great allies in the Triumvirate for which the just-passed hundred and sixty one year war was named. Romki insisted that the alo were in alliance with an old forgotten remnant of the AI machine-race that had once dominated the galaxy, twenty five thousand years ago. And now he spent most of his days cosseted away in one of *Phoenix*'s engineering bays, examining the remains of an AI queen that the Major herself had killed just three months before.

"Romki says you're putting *Phoenix* in danger by not letting him get out and meet his contacts," Lisbeth tried again. If anything could make the Major listen, it was concerns for *Phoenix*'s security. "He says he knows people who might be able to tell us things that could help."

"That could help *him*," Hiro replied. "He wants us chasing alien shadows across the galaxy. He'll do anything to steer us that way."

"And what do *you* think?" the Major asked Lisbeth, with that calm, dark-eyed gaze. "You've been spending the most time with him lately, studying the dead hacksaw queen."

"Well, I wouldn't say the *most*..."

"Do *you* think we're wasting our time with peace talks?"

Lisbeth was slightly astonished that the Major was asking her. Then she realised — Erik wasn't the only heir to the Debogande empire on the ship. And she *had* absorbed a lot of that big-picture talk, at home amongst the overlap of family, friends and business folks who discussed this kind of thing endlessly. Human politics, human wars and human futures, writ large across the stars. The last ten years, in fact, she'd heard far more of that kind of talk than Erik had.

"I don't think it's ever a waste of time to try," Lisbeth said carefully. "It's just that we're a long way from home out here, a long way from any human space really. And *Phoenix* is a warship. There's a lot of talent on *Phoenix*, but not much experience at diplomacy." She said it a little nervously, but she needn't have worried — the Major never took these things personally.

"It'll take a famous Fleet name to make peace," Thakur said firmly. "Fleet Command may not listen to us, but plenty of Fleet captains will. We've got their sympathy now, given how Command screwed us over, and Worlders will talk to us because we're the only ones with big influence in Fleet who are prepared to listen. The Captain died to give us this opportunity, and I'm not about to waste his sacrifice because Romki finds aliens more interesting than humans."

Barabo had a thing for wooden furniture. Erik ran a hand on the slick, polished surface of the meeting room table, admiring the patterned grain in red-hued wood. Unusual on a space station, given the costs of transport, even from a lush, populated world like Vieno next door.

"Good quality synth," he suggested.

"No, I'm pretty sure that's real," said Lieutenant Kaspowitz, knocking on the table top. "I've seen enough synthetic tables in my time."

"Must have cost a fortune." Erik looked at the leafy green plants along the walls, and sniffed the air — it smelled vaguely floral, the barabo put something in the air filters to make it that way. "But then I guess it fits, barabo aren't big on economic common sense."

He gazed out the windows at the geo-feature — a huge, deep cavern that split through the Tuki Station rim down to a floor far below. Halfway down, the sheer drop was broken by a luxury hotel pool deck, furry barabo swimming or sprawled on recliners. An impermanent-looking roof spanned the floor below that, a transparent awning made to look like jungle vines, but instead alight with advertising. Beneath that, a sea of barabo and other species at market, tiny figures when viewed from this height.

Lieutenant Crozier spoke to one of her marines on coms, waiting by the door in light armour — 'light', of course, being relative only to the powered armour suits that could devastate entire station districts. They didn't wear those around barabo civilians if they could help it. Erik stood by the end of the table, placed his own helmet on the surface and waited, Kaspowitz beside him.

From the outside, Master Sergeant Wong opened the door to the meeting room, and a human man in a business suit entered. Wong nodded at his Lieutenant to indicate he was unarmed. Erik smiled and walked to the new arrival, but their guest beat him to it.

"Lieutenant Commander Debogande!" their guest exclaimed with delight, and strode to clasp his hand in a crushing grip. "Randal J Connor, Major General retired, Ninth Army mobile infantry. An honour and a pleasure!"

"Likewise Mr Connor," said Erik, extricating his hand to indicate Kaspowitz. "This is Lieutenant Kaspowitz, first-shift Navigation Officer. And Lieutenant Jasmine Crozier, commander of Delta Platoon."

More handshakes, and a barabo staffer in the loose but formal robes of a professional assistant entered with tea and snacks. Erik indicated that they sit, and Connor chose a chair up the table end with a view of both the big windows overlooking the geo-feature, and the room doorway. Erik and Kaspowitz sat opposite, content that with Crozier here and First Squad on guard outside, they didn't need to watch their backs.

"So what's the food like?" Erik asked as Kaspowitz poured tea. That felt slightly odd, as Kaspowitz was nearly twice Erik's age. But then, being in command *was* slightly odd. Having fallen into the role three months ago, Erik had concluded that there was nothing natural about it, and he should stop waiting for it to feel normal or he'd be waiting forever.

"Their tea's nice," Connor admitted, taking some nuts from an accompanying bowl and chewing. "Bit of an aphrodisiac. If that's a problem." He glanced at Crozier by the door, and winked. Randal J Connor looked every bit the retired army officer — broad-shouldered, square-jawed, strongly spoken and devil-may-care. Probably well over a hundred, he still looked in the prime of life, and behaved accordingly.

"How about the nuts?" Kaspowitz wondered, setting down the teapot and taking a few.

"Nuts?" Connor grinned, still chewing. "They're beetle-shell. Dried, fried and spiced." To his credit, Kaspowitz ate them anyway. "Bit of an acquired taste."

"Bit," Kaspowitz admitted. "How long have you been on Tuki Station?"

"Oh... going on five years now. The barabo, you know, they're fascinated by humans. So I run a nice little consultancy, telling them everything they want to know about humanity, introducing them to contacts, setting up long-term trade plans for when the day comes, that sort of thing. Tavalai used to be the big cheese around here, but now they've lost their war with us and they don't really have the firepower left to keep the peace out here in neutral space."

"You mean they're terrified the sard are going to take over as the big power here," said Kaspowitz.

"That too," Connor admitted. "Sard are one of the tavalai's most important allies, but with the tavalai surrendering, sard are getting antsy. With sard, you know, that's not a good thing."

"You hear anything bad?" Erik asked.

"With the sard?" asked Connor. "Hell, always. Nasty pieces of work, all six hundred billion of 'em, or whatever it's up to now. You know, you've fought 'em."

Erik nodded. "We have. The talk is that the sard didn't want to accept the surrender. The tavalai insisted."

"Yeah, look," and Connor leaned an elbow on the table, talking with big gestures from broad hands, "you gotta understand, sard don't like anyone but sard. Tavalai they cut some slack, because tavalai discovered 'em, got 'em into space, put a leash on 'em." He munched some more beetle shell. "Tavalai have known how to control them for a few thousand years, and they did all the tavalai's dirty work for them — they're brilliant at maths but stink at technology, if that makes any sense, so most of their tech is tavalai, and they listen to the tavalai because the tavalai are alpha-dog and sard respect alpha-dogs."

"But now the tavalai have lost the Triumvirate War and half their old territory," Kaspowitz finished.

"Exactly. And the sard, they don't respect old alpha-dog no more. So sard start pushing and barabo get nervous, start coming to my office and asking me when human Fleet's going to come and save them." He glanced around. "You know, I was kinda hoping Major Thakur would be here. Always wanted to meet that gal. Beautiful and deadly, just how I like 'em." With another wink at Crozier.

Erik forced a smile. Behind Connor, Lieutenant Crozier contemplated murder. "The Major's primary responsibility whenever *Phoenix* is docked is ship and personnel security. She's kind of busy."

"And she kinda sucks at diplomacy," Kaspowitz added, sipping his tea. As one of Trace Thakur's oldest friends, he was sure to know.

Connor laughed, then gulped some tea. "So," he said, putting the tea down with a theatrical flourish. "You guys! Anyone else, any other ship gets into a fight with Fleet Command, they'd be running off and hiding in some distant part of the galaxy. But you guys come rolling in here trumpeting your message for all to hear —

18

peace talks!" He shook his head in amazement. "In Kazak System, right?"

"Joma Station," Erik agreed.

"Do they know you're coming?"

"They do by now," said Kaspowitz. "Everyone else does." He said it with the edge of someone not entirely happy about it.

Connor heard. "And it's occurred to you that when you run around Outer Neutral Space trumpeting your intentions and your destination to everyone, then all the folks that want to kill you might show up and try just that?"

"It has," Kaspowitz said mildly, with a glance at Erik.

"Because even *UFS Phoenix* isn't indestructible, right?" As though her young commander might not have thought of that.

"Not indestructible, no," Erik said calmly. "Just very determined. You've heard the word from Fleet, it reaches out even this far I'm sure. Trying to kill *Phoenix* just became a very unpopular policy."

"Yeah sure," Connor agreed. "Fleet fucked up big-time with what they did to you guys. Oh, and real sorry about your Captain, by the way. Great man, I was real sad to hear that."

"Thank you."

"But still, you guys... how many Fleeties did you kill when they came chasing after you? *UFS Starwind*, wasn't it? A hundred and twenty lives?"

"About that," Erik agreed. "They were trying to kill a fully loaded *Phoenix* shuttle at the time, piloted by me. Unprovoked."

"Hey," and Connor held up his hands. "No argument here. But still, you guys blew up a Fleet warship, no survivors. Got into numerous shooting matches with non-marine security, the way I hear it... put a warhead through the side of Fleet HQ on Hoffen Station and threatened to blow them all away? Man!" He shook his head with a disbelieving chuckle. "You guys have some serious balls. And they still want to forgive you, so I guess Captain Pantillo really packed some clout, huh?"

"Fleet Command swore the same oath everyone else did," Erik said coldly. "To protect and value the lives of their brothers and sisters in arms. And instead, they murder one of their best, and expect the rest to just lie down and take it. We didn't. It escalated, far beyond what any of us wanted. And now that the dust's settled, the rest of Fleet has had a chance to think about what happened, and have decided they don't like it. If Command can murder Pantillo, then who amongst them is safe? Command is scared now, and on the back foot. We have an advantage."

Connor considered him, shrewdly. "That you do. Anyhow, you didn't invite me here just to chat about current events. You want Worlder contacts. I've *got* Worlder contacts. I'm a Worlder myself, born and bred, like most army brats. You Fleeties all go zooming around in space — myself, I've lived and fought in the dirt. I mean someone's got to take those damn worlds once you get us access, don't they? Army gets the blisters, Fleet gets the glory."

Erik nodded slowly. Kaspowitz leaned forward. "Our information is that you know a *lot* of Worlders," the Nav Officer said meaningfully.

Connor nodded. "I did a lot of business after I retired. Lots of old army buddies... plenty of Worlders, you know the army." Both Fleet officers nodded. They did. "This latest ordinance of Fleet's... you guys have any idea of the lives it's going to destroy? Forcing Worlders to abandon all downworld holdings or assets in order to get any kind of Spacer job? Forcing them to choose?" He shook his head in disbelief. "We're all one species, right? One humanity? Wasn't that what we were fighting the war for?"

Erik thought he might have quibbled — the Triumvirate War had been fought to free humans from alien threat, not to keep all humans equal. But it wasn't the time. He nodded. "The Captain thought so," he said diplomatically.

"Right," Connor agreed, slumping hard back in his chair, nodding with satisfaction. "Right, he did. And he died for it. And for him, I'll tell you what I'd never tell any other Fleetie — damn right I know a lot of Worlder contacts. Big contacts, Heuron Dawn, Worlder Council, you name it. People who would be prepared to listen to you. If you could get some compromises from Fleet? Wind back some of these new ordinances?" He nodded sharply.

"Only *Phoenix* could get those kinds of concessions, I reckon. Worlders might just agree to press pause on their plans if you could get that from Fleet. Now that most actual Fleet officers are listening to you even more than Fleet HQ."

"Press pause on their plans?" Erik questioned. "What plans?"

"Oh Worlders have got plans," Connor said grimly. "Your Captain knew. Fleet thinks we're defenceless at the bottom of our gravity wells — we're not. We have assets. Fleet thinks they can piss us off with no consequences, well, they're about to learn differently.

"Now there's a ship arriving here in a few days. Should jump in any hour now. Human freighter, name *Grappler*. Worlder representatives, knew you were here."

"How did they know that?"

Connor spread his hands expansively. "You guys have only been yelling it to everyone who'll listen! Just trust me that I know, never mind how. Now you're setting up this big meeting in Kazak System, Joma Station wasn't it?" Erik nodded. "And there will be Spacer representatives there?"

"Yes. Can't say who, but senior people."

"Can you guarantee they've come to talk?"

"I can guarantee that if they weren't interested in a compromise deal with Worlders that would avoid a civil war, they wouldn't have come at all."

Connor nodded slowly. "Good enough. Anyhow, keep an eye out for the *Grappler*. Their passengers will want to talk to you in advance, discuss the Worlder position. Then maybe we can talk your Spacer friends into doing something to *avoid* a bloodbath for once."

CHAPTER 3

Barabo stations were unlike anything Erik had seen before. Human station docks were kept clear of clutter, but here the main dock before the station berths was filled with irregular market stalls. Tuki was small by human standards, barely half-a-million population on a single rotating wheel with fifty primary berths, but the markets made it feel crowded.

Erik and Kaspowitz walked in the centre of First Squad, Delta Platoon, Lieutenant Crozier at Erik's side, while about him exotic animals whooped and howled, sellers and buyers shouted and waved their hands, and burly security guards stood by displays of precious stones and eyed the crowds with suspicion. Most here were barabo, some shirtless, some in flowing robes or sleeveless tunics, some with hats or crazy hairstyles, in all different colours and types. Such a varied people, Erik thought in amazement. He knew that before the Earth was lost, humans had been a varied people too, but *Phoenix*'s resident academic, Stanislav Romki, was clear that humans had never been quite *this* varied.

"Pretty clear what Connor's doing out here," said Kaspowitz as they manoeuvred between armoured marines. He stood nearly a head taller than most, gangly in his own light armour. "Worlder resistance told him to see if he could find some financial and political backing out here. Don't imagine he's had much luck, the last thing the barabo want to do is upset Fleet."

"You think he's bluffing with that talk of Worlder battle plans?" Erik asked.

"Probably not," Kaspowitz said grimly. "The Captain thought it would be a full scale civil war if it wasn't stopped. He wasn't some strategic idiot, he must have known the Worlders had something up their sleeve."

"Yeah," Erik muttered. "But what?"

"Guess he didn't get around to telling us that before he died."

Also scattered through the markets were random tavalai, with their broad shoulders and protruding, flat heads and wide-set eyes, and the occasional kaal, like thick walls of grey muscle lumbering through the crowd. All were merchants or other harmless types, and made a clear space for the armed and armoured humans. Tuki had not demanded that *Phoenix* crew disarm when on dock. Barabo military vessels did not stray far from their core systems, and were reluctant to enforce their rule over places like Vieno for fear that someone would take that as provocation.

Barabo were five thousand years in space — new by Spiral standards, and had escaped the AI scourge during the Machine Age. Tavalai had discovered them instead, and given them a helping hand into space. Grateful to be found by tavalai and not sard, whose territory also adjoined, barabo had taken to space with curiosity but no particular drive or ambition. Barabo were lively, chaotic and almost entirely self-interested. Humans found it hard to understand, because barabo were smart, and made good tech when they chose. But they simply found themselves more interesting than the rest of the galaxy, and looking around, Erik thought he could possibly see why.

When the Triumvirate War had begun, human space had been a long way from barabo space. When humans had begun drawing near, some of the more determined barabo had demanded that their tavalai friends and mentors deserved barabo assistance in the war. Ships had been built, and a small fleet sent to help — all largely destroyed in several disastrous actions against the hardened and brutally efficient human forces. Barabo had quickly decided to leave the fighting to the tavalai, in the hope that when humans eventually won, as had probably seemed inevitable, they'd not be too hostile. Tavalai had been the true guarantors of security in this neutral space, but the tavalai conditions of surrender had left them with barely enough ships to maintain security in their own remaining space. Outer Neutral Space was now largely unsecured, and a big, wandering warship like *Phoenix* found no one telling her she couldn't do exactly what she pleased. So far, at least.

"*LC, this is Phoenix,*" came Lieutenant Lassa's voice in Erik's ear. "*PH-4 is on her way up, Lieutenant Jalawi says they have cargo holds full of seafood. Should make a pleasant change for a few days at least. ETA ninety-four minutes."*

"Thank you *Phoenix*, the LC copies." Actually *Phoenix*'s chefs were out securing other sources of fresh food as well, but it was thoughtful of Charlie Platoon to help them out on their brief R&R visit to Vieno's surface. Thoughtful, and self-interested.

"You know," said Lieutenant Crozier, "I think we have a selfless duty to inspect those kebabs."

"Amen," said Private Rai nearby. The kebab stall they passed had a small queue, with spiced meat roasting on open flame — unheard of on a human station. The air pollution alone would have had someone booked... but it smelled delicious.

"Sure," said Erik, smiling. "On your own time." They deserved some nice things, after all they'd been through the past weeks. All the marines carried rifles at casual, muzzles at the deck. Polite but alert was the drill. Anyone who tried to push between them to get through was blocked and coolly instructed to go around, so as not to violate the secure perimeter around the LC.

"So did you check out those volunteer kids?" Erik asked the Lieutenant.

Crozier smirked. "Yeah. They're off a freelance freighter, done some martial arts and weapons training. Doesn't make you a marine, unfortunately." She peered at a cage containing a prowling, cat-like animal that snarled at passers-by.

"Theoretically," Erik asked, "how long *would* it take to train a new marine on the job?"

"Well that's just the problem," said Crozier. "We're not a training ship. Trainees need special environments where they can't make a mess. Everything we do 'on the job' has fatal consequences if you fuck it up. And trainees are supposed to fuck up, that's how they learn. So understrength we may be, but I'd rather keep it that way."

Erik knew what she meant. Training spacer crew on the job was a little easier than marines, but Erik's Academy scores were some of the highest anyone had seen. The regular crew of *Phoenix* were also elite, and did not take well to the idea of welcoming anyone less qualified into their ranks.   With a quarter of *Phoenix*'s spacer crew missing, everyone was working overtime, and sleep, recreation, and sometimes tempers were suffering.   But Erik sympathised when most of them said they'd rather keep it that way than work alongside people who'd do a substandard job.

Marine strength was down more like ten percent than twenty-five, but as Crozier said, marine skills were more exacting and less forgiving.   And then there was the question of augments, the various physical enhancements that all *Phoenix* marines possessed that brought them up to the superhuman levels required.   Augmentations could be had out in these territories for a price.   But for humans, it was unlikely, and probably unsafe and substandard too.

"Though if you could find me a fifteen-year-experience Squad Sergeant to fill in for Third Squad," Crozier added.   "That'd be nice."   Staff Sergeant Kono had recently been Delta's Third Squad Commander, until Trace had lost Command Squad's veteran First Sergeant and taken Kono to compensate.   Crozier understood, and knew Command Squad's priority was higher than Delta's, but still griped about it.   Sergeants like Kono didn't grow on trees.

"Plenty of people lost worse than you, Lieutenant," Erik told her.

"Yes sir.   Well aware."

"If Third Squad needs a Sergeant, promote someone."

"Thinking on it, sir."

"Never let the perfect be the enemy of the good, Lieutenant," Erik told her.   Captain Pantillo had said that a lot.

"No sir.   So when are you going to take the promotion to captain, sir?"   Erik just looked at her, to let her know she'd gone too far.   He didn't have to answer questions like that from marine lieutenants.   Marine majors, on the other hand...

"Yo!" said Staff Sergeant Wong on coms up ahead.   *"We've got spiders, dead ahead."*

"Keep walking," Crozier said calmly.   "Real careful, everyone.   Let's not jump at shadows, but real careful."

Sure enough, amidst the milling foot traffic between stalls ahead, there stalked five thin, spindly shadows.   Back-canted lower legs, elastic limbed, they did not walk across the deck, they flowed like water. Many-eyed heads turned their way, inset mandibles flickering. Creepy as hell, to human eyes.

"Five of them," Crozier murmured. "That's neutral. Don't trust it though."

"They don't look armed," Wong added. *"Merchants, it looks like."*

"They're sard," Crozier disagreed. "Merchants, soldiers, no difference."

Sard socialised in groups. Brilliant mathematicians, their societies were ruled by numbers. The only emotions they appeared to feel were toward those numerical arrangements, not to the individuals who comprised them. Sard had compassion for patterns, not people. Those who deviated from acceptable patterns, meaning most non-sard civilisation, could find themselves subject to 'rearrangement'.

They hadn't been in space much longer than the barabo. Endlessly tolerant of dangerous things, tavalai had found ways to impress and control them, and when Spiral politics turned bad for tavalai, had used them to do the various dirty things that tavalai found distasteful to do themselves. Tavalai were undoubtedly far 'better' than sard, from a human perspective, but when an aggressive dog mauled you, did you blame the dog, or the one holding its leash? If sard had been the first instinctively aggressive and violent species humanity had encountered, humans might have been more tolerant of them. But they were the second, after the krim, and the krim had been tavalai-sponsored as well. The krim had exterminated Earth, and after five hundred years of struggle, humanity had exterminated the krim, down to the very last child. Most humans would happily have done the same to the sard, just as precaution against what most knew was possible, should sard power grow.

These sard passed by in single file, mouthparts flickering as they tasted the air. Taller than humans, though not as strong, even augmented. Individually, Fleet marines handled them comfortably. But the larger their numbers, the more sophisticated and clever sard tactics became, and they would sacrifice individual formations for overall success as humans would never do. Erik heard the whine of their vocals as they passed, like a cicada shrill, with rhythmic chirps at harmonic intervals, creating mathematical code that took human computers to decipher, but sard understood instantly.

"Yeah, keep on walking, bugs," Lance Corporal Kess muttered.

"Is it true they've got eyes in the back of their heads?" Private Haim wondered.

"Watch where you're going or you'll get my boot in the back of yours," Crozier told her.

The entrance to Jigi Trade and Freight was a lobby with green walls and open water displays. Again it violated a bunch of human architecture regulations, but it was increasingly clear that those were anathema to barabo. The effect was an indoor jungle, and as the lobby attendant beckoned them past the welcome desk, inset speakers made jungle sounds and the buzzing of insects.

Lance Corporal Kess's Third Squad remained in the lobby, while the white-robed attendant beckoned the rest into a large office. The office had its own lobby, with a water fountain in the middle, and intricately carved wooden panels on the walls. More attendants gestured them to wait, while one went into the main office, and fetched their contact — 'Ben Guring', *Phoenix*'s computer had insisted Erik pronounce it.

She emerged, a big barabo with a big grin, and a big mop of dreadlocked hair tied in a bunch above her head. She wore big dark brown robes with intricate gold trim, and many bangles chimed and clanked upon her arms as she swept them wide in welcome.

"HELLO!" she declared to the room, with great extravagance. "Hello! Hello!" Erik repressed a grin. Barabo could be... unrestrained. Ben Guring seemed most pleased at the opportunity to use her one human word.

"Hello," Erik agreed, turning the translator mike on. He offered her a handshake, barabo-style, palm flat and fingers locked. "I am Erik. I am in charge of *Phoenix*." The speaker at his collar translated that into Palapu. Surnames and exact ranks were pointless — the translator would mangle them. For all their simple cheerfulness, barabo were not stupid, and could figure the details for themselves. "This is Kaspo, from *Phoenix*'s bridge crew, and this is JC. She is in charge of the marines here."

"Erik De-bo-gan-day, yes?" Ben Guring grinned at him with those big teeth. *"Do not worry, we all know family De-bo-gan-day here."* As the translator took over. *"And JC... another woman marine? I thought that this was rare for humans?"*

"Tradition," Jasmine 'JC' Crozier explained, shaking the barabo's hand in turn. "With technology, there is no reason why women cannot be marines. But there is tradition, and some tradition does not change, even if technology does. Some tradition goes backward." There had been more female marines seven hundred years ago than now. Erik knew it bothered Crozier more than it bothered Trace.

"Ohhh," said the barabo, knowingly. *"It is the same with barabo, just the same. I have five sisters — one of them wants to play the zarp, two make themselves busy with many babies, and one only thinks of colchee and karom. So I am the only one who makes money, yes?"* She boomed laughter. *"So they all ask me for money, and I say no! Come, come!"*

Erik had no idea what any of that meant except the babies and money, but smiled and followed Ben Guring into her main office. Crozier joined him, removing her helmet to reveal cornrow hair and a discoloured top half of her left ear where it had been regrown after shrapnel removed the original five years ago. The other seven marines remained in the office lobby, and accepted tea from an attendant with a tray.

"So," said Ben Guring. *"Your mother ship arrive. Very nice ship. Very good cargo."*

"What cargo?" Erik wondered.

"Oh no!" said the barabo, grinning. *"Mother tell me, don't tell Erik! Better for Erik if Erik not know. I not upset Mother Debogande, so I not tell."*

"Yes that sounds like my mother," Erik conceded. And it did make a certain amount of sense. *Phoenix* was a renegade from all human law. Of course everyone would suspect that Alice

28

Debogande would assist her son, and probably would have sympathy with his cause, having supported similar in the past. But so long as no one could prove it...

"So I sell cargo on market, make you credit with Nari Bank." Ben Guring rummaged beneath some papers for a slate reader. *"I get you best price, I guarantee you find no better. Credit is... see here, sixteen million, and a bit more. So credit to Phoenix is thirteen point six million, and Jigi Trade and Freight get other twenty percent. Commission, yes?"* Big grin. *"So you all good with bank, yes? Much credit, you go around barabo space and pay for things, no problem."*

Because otherwise, they'd have had to resort to piracy. Or whatever you called it when you just turned up at station and demanded all services, and showed them your very big guns when they asked for the cheque. Merchanters had bank credit and built up tabs with stations. Barabo warships would be covered by barabo government, such as existed, as human warships had all expenses covered (within reason) by Fleet and Spacer Congress... in *human* space, or on official human business. Out here, no one picked up *Phoenix*'s tab, and no one took human credit anyway. Thanks to this little bit of blackmarket trade, they now had some reasonable funds in the bank. Not that Debogande Inc was the first human entity to do this with barabo, whose financial governance was anarchic. The corporate joke among humans was that the official symbol of the barabo financial regulator was a shrug.

Ben Guring had some papers for them to sign, all in Palapu of course, and no electronic copy. Having been warned of barabo tricks, Erik scanned the documents back to Lieutenant Lassa on second-shift Coms, who ran them through translation and gave the all clear — they were very vague, no real indication of what transaction had transpired between Jigi Freight and *Phoenix*, but they satisfied whatever requirement Jigi had. Lieutenant Lassa, like all Fleet Coms officers, was legally trained at a high level, and not just human law.

"So now you will be needing transport for sister Lisbeth," Ben Guring pressed. *"Safe transport, back to Mother."*

"We will arrange that ourselves," Erik told her.

The barabo raised her eyebrows. *"Because we can arrange most safe transport! Most safe, yes. Reliable captain, good ship, the very best."* Erik didn't doubt it. Doing business with Alice Debogande was no doubt turning out very profitable for Ben Guring. Delivering Alice's daughter safely to her arms would be rewarded with a *very* tidy sum. But Erik doubted whether the barabo had any real clue of just what the dangers were, and if she'd be quite so helpful if she did. People who worked only for money could always hand over the cargo if offered more... or have it taken from them if they could not or would not defend it.

"We will arrange that ourselves," Erik repeated with a smile. Ben Guring took the hint, and Erik and the marines took their leave with friendly farewells.

"Fun to be young and running loose in the galaxy on mommy's credit," Kaspowitz offered as they refastened helmets, and stepped back onto the chaotic, teeming docks. "Is that trade with your mother even legal?"

"In human space, no," Erik conceded. "Here? Not much that *isn't* legal. I just hope that big girl doesn't get her throat cut."

"You think they'd do that, all the way out here?" Crozier wondered.

"The people who are after us?" Erik replied. "Certainly."

Their next stop was to meet with the Tuki Stationmaster, in a big office near the bridge. The Stationmaster was snow white, with yellow rimmed eyes and long, fine hair strung with beads, most unlike the scruffy, bristle-bearded majority.

"I can assure you," Erik told the anxious barabo, "no human Fleet vessel will hold it against you that *Phoenix* is here. Tuki Station is unarmed, there are no warships here to enforce your lanes. *Phoenix* is one of the most powerful warships ever built. Humans will understand."

"They want kill you?"

"It's unclear," Erik said carefully. "The top leaders want to kill us. Tried to kill us. Those top leaders made a mistake, and now they look bad to the rest of Fleet. We want them brought to justice. Justice for Captain Pantillo."

The Stationmaster nodded nervously, chomping on the smoking cigar between his teeth. He'd offered one to Erik and Crozier, but they'd declined. *"No want human trouble,"* he said. *"Many business here, many people. Want peace, yes? Barabo tried war, war no good. Barabo no good at war."*

"I understand," Erik said sympathetically. He could see the fear on the man. It was understandable. Barabo had been lucky in that their first alien contact had been the tavalai. Humanity had been unlucky, in that theirs had been the krim. Could the barabo have fought back to become the galaxy's greatest warriors, had *their* homeworld been destroyed, as humanity's had? Erik doubted it. Humans had been warriors well before they'd discovered aliens. Barabo knew violence and war, but in forms rare and disorganised. Erik thought that if a bunch of barabo got together and declared a war, a barbecue would break out instead.

"Tavalai used come here," the Stationmaster added, gazing out the big porthole window in the wall. They were on the darkside of Vieno, and there were no stars to be seen. *"Tavalai kept safe. Now only small tavalai come. Most tavalai ships gone to war, war with humans. Only ships here are sard. Sard space close."* He turned back to Erik. *"You think human ship come? Human Fleet?"* Hopefully.

"Probably," Erik admitted. "We've big former-tavalai territories to administer, now that the war is over. But Fleet won't like all this uncontrolled territory off their flank, either."

"When? When Fleet come?"

Erik had to force down a surge of contempt. The Stationmaster wanted humans to save them. Once the tavalai had been the barabo's guardians, and now they needed new guardians. Humans had learned the price of being defenceless. Barabo had not.

"I don't know when Fleet will come," he said. "I'm just a Lieutenant Commander."

"I tell you this," said the Stationmaster, jabbing with his cigar. *"Damn sard everywhere. Merchant ship come, through dark point mass, for jump. They say sard, sard here, sard there. Too many. People here damn scared. Sard once tavalai ally... tavalai gone, sard no respect tavalai no more. Not just barabo scared. Tavalai scared too."*

Erik doubted that — even defeated, the tavalai were still an enormous force in this region of space. And tavalai had known how to deal with sard for millennia, in both friendly and unfriendly ways. "You see tavalai out here too?" he asked. "Big tavalai ships?"

An evasive shift from the Stationmaster's yellow-rimmed eyes. *"Just said. No tavalai, tavalai not come here anymore."*

"Not the regular tavalai traffic," Erik explained patiently. "Big tavalai fleet warships, made to fight humans. Tavalai had to give up fifty percent of their warships in the peace treaty. And all the human talk is that tavalai would hide many ships out here. Neutral space, humans don't come here. Yet."

A shake of the head. *"Tavalai not cunning. Not play tricks. Honest tavalai, yes? You do treaty, tavalai do treaty good."*

"Maybe," Erik conceded. "You don't see any tavalai ships out here? Big warships hiding? Remote bases, built a long time ago?"

The Stationmaster tapped ash into a tray. *"I no see. Maybe human Fleet come and look for them, yes?"*

"He's lying," Erik said to Crozier as they ventured back onto the docks. "That freighter captain the other week was pretty sure, big tavalai signatures on those jump readings. They've had decades to prepare for it, I bet they could hide a big fleet out here indefinitely if they wanted."

"I dunno," said Crozier as they walked past stalls and crowds. "Stationmaster was right — froggies don't play tricks. If Fleet caught them at it, and decided to punish them, lots of tavalai could suffer.   If they violate the peace treaty, technically the war starts again."

Erik frowned.   "Humans will never be like chah'nas. However bad they've been to us, we're not just going to start punishing tavalai civilians indiscriminately."

Crozier looked at him warily.   "Yeah?   Well I guess we'll see."

Erik's com uplink blinked, and he opened it.   "This is the LC."

"LC this is Lassa.   Thought you'd want to know, a human-registered freighter just came out of jump, transponder says it's the Grappler, just like Major General Connor said.   ETA fifty-one hours."

"Thank you Lieutenant, keep an eye on it.   LC out."   And to Crozier, "Our Worlder contacts just arrived."

"Now we see if it was worth listening to that pain-in-the-ass Major General yapping for half-an-hour," Crozier grumbled.   Erik laughed.

Phoenix's main corridor was always chaotic when they were at dock.   With three-quarters of the crew cylinder inaccessible at station-G, most crew were sleeping on station.   That meant a big block of hotel space, accommodation for five hundred and sixty plus, as they currently stood.

But with most of the crew off-deck, all supplies and things they might need had been pre-positioned in the main ship corridor. With marines, that meant a platoon's worth of armour and weapons — the rest was accessible up in Assembly, but that took time, climbing ladders through the stationary core to the marines back-quarter, all of which was now upside-down.   With two platoons of armour in the accommodation block, and one here, *Phoenix* had three platoons of heavy armour ready to deploy on dock at a moment's notice... but it meant a mess of spacers and marines squeezing past each other in the crowded main passage.

Erik left Delta Platoon and headed down to M-bulkhead at the cylinder's rear.   Usually access between the crew cylinder and midships was via the cylinder core down the central spine of the ship.   But with the ship docked and the cylinder no longer rotating, midships access was via an airlock hatch from M-bulkhead that joined the two habitable ship sections.

In that narrow space he was passed by the first marines from Echo Platoon, disembarking from PH-1 now locked to the midships grapples on *Phoenix*'s underside — no small manoeuvre, given *Phoenix*'s current one-G rotation locked into the huge station carry gantries.   PH-1 had been up at the station hub, getting supplies directly from an insystem trader rather than hauling it through the station.

"LC," the marines greeted him as they passed, and Erik played his usual game of trying to recall every name, and where he knew the name, the nickname.   As Lieutenant Commander he'd known all of the spacer crew, but not the marines... though now he was getting better.   Inside midships was an open structure of gantries, cargo nets, acceleration slings and exposed machinery.   It all worked much more elegantly in the accustomed zero-G, but here marines had to climb up from docking operations, where Grapples 2 and 3 held their two assault shuttles.   Their 'borrowed' civilian shuttle, AT-7, was currently locked to Grapple-1, further up the midships side, and difficult to access at dock.

He took a left through the central partition bulkhead, then down a ladder to where Operations crew held position amidst the big, exposed grapple mechanism, amber warning lights flashing. He took hold as the grapples crashed, huge hydraulics plunging and kicking as PH-4 hit them from below, after a sustained one-G burn to chase the moving station rim.   Yells and signals from the crew, then a vibration as the access extended, the docking chief talking to Ensign Lee, the co-pilot on the other end.

Trace arrived at his side, in light armour and a cap.   At this station call, it was policy that she had to put the armour on just to cross the docks from their accommodation block.   "Hope they had a nice holiday," said Erik.   Vieno was supposed to be very pretty, with big oceans and hundreds of thousands of kilometres of sandy beaches.   There were many good arguments as to why it was silly to send a shuttle all the way down to the surface for a load of fish.   But maintaining morale on ship was an even better argument, and Trace had agreed — and put Charlie Platoon on the shuttle for security, with instructions to find a beach for an hour or two while awaiting rendezvous trajectories, and relax.

"Be funny if they got sunburnt, given all the radiation warnings we get up here," Trace said. "I hear they got good fish?"

"That's the word," said Erik, glancing at her. "Brought you running I see."

Trace smiled. "I want to talk to Jalawi about the planet. It's called a debrief."

"A likely story. I'm glad at least we didn't get jumped while Charlie Platoon were working on their tan."

"Kaspo says with the asteroid belt and outer gas giant's gravity well, we'd get at least a two hour warning from most approaches." Trace adjusted her cap to block the glare from a nearby light. Visual augments made marines fussy about such things. "Tif says she could have made it back for pickup in thirty-five, worst case scenario. Hausler says thirty-two."

"Yeah, well." Truth was, Erik always felt nervous when any of his marines were off-ship. If they had to leave in a hurry, marines could get left behind. And he particularly disliked it when *this* marine was off-ship. Thankfully, she hadn't asked to go.

A private clambered down the G-ladder to Trace's side. "Major," Private Melsh said glumly. "LC."

"Private," Erik acknowledged. And looked at Trace, eyebrows raised.

"I gave Private Melsh Furball-supervision duty in the gym," Trace explained. "And he failed to supervise the Furball. So the Private gets to help midships crew unloading all the fish, lucky man." Erik sighed, and gave her an exasperated sideways look. Trace rolled her eyes. Melsh winced. "Private," she said to Melsh, "make yourself scarce for a moment. We're about to have a command discussion."

"Yes Major," said Melsh, just as glumly, and retreated back up the ladder.

"We've really got to do something about that," said Erik.

"So would you rather we aced every menial job and sucked at combat?" she said defensively.

"Shouldn't have to choose, Trace. I mean it's just a menial job now, but what if the Furball really did go missing? What if they just wave someone through on guard duty who it turns out is carrying a bomb? Fail to inspect some random civvie who ends up killing a bunch of us?"

Trace sighed, and didn't argue.

"They've been at war a long time, I get it," Erik pressed while he had the advantage. "Combat is most important. But out here, we're going to have to learn to be good at all the other, small boring stuff too. Because when people look at the size of us, and figure out how little chance they've got in a straight-up fight? They'll figure the best way to kill us is that small boring stuff that our marines find too dull to bother with." A hiss from the grapples airlock, as PH-4 opened it from below.

"I've told the platoon commanders you're pissed about it," Trace offered.

"Well that doesn't help," Erik said with exasperation. "Tell them *you're* pissed about it."

"I prioritise," Trace said stubbornly. She'd lost a bunch of them recently. A bunch more had been badly hurt, and were just now recovering. She only showed temper with them sparingly, when she thought morale could handle it. Clearly she didn't think this was one of those times.

"Well they're your command," said Erik. "Figure it out."

"Aye sir." For a moment Erik thought she was being sarcastic... before recalling that Trace didn't do sarcastic. He'd fallen into conversation-mode, but she'd taken it as a direct order. Well, fair enough. The best thing about arguing with Trace was that she didn't do resentment either. "So when do I get to call you Captain?"

Erik gritted his teeth. Not this again. "You don't."

"Look, don't give me this shit about how you don't have the command authority to give yourself a promotion. I'm promoting Corporals to Sergeants and Privates to Corporals. The rank fits the job, and we need those jobs filled. *You're* promoting Warrant Officers to Ensigns and Petty Officers to Warrants, as you need them. No difference here."

"Not now." There were voices coming up from the grapples airlock.

"When then? This ship needs a captain, not a temp."

"When I say so." Trace's look was skeptical. One nice thing about a promotion, Erik thought, would be that he'd properly outrank her, rather than this vague, technical thing he had over her now. But he didn't think for a moment that she'd give him any more peace for it.

Several Charlie Platoon marines emerged from the floor airlock, stomping and whining in heavy powered armour. Amidst the confusion, a lithe brown blur flew down the G-ladder and darted around several stomping suits.

"Ware!" called the marines. "Furball at twelve o'clock! Hey Furball, careful now, stand back."

"Skah, over here," Trace called, and Skah came. The little boy was kuhsi, tawny-brown furred and golden-eyed with the most impossibly big, wide ears. "Now keep out of the way of the marines, Skah. That armour is very powerful and it could hurt you if you get in their way."

"Not Skah, Furbaw!" Skah insisted. He liked the nickname the marines had given him much better. "Nah-ny on shuttuw?"

"Yes, your Mummy is on the shuttle. She's flown back up from the planet with lots of fish. Do you like fish?"

Skah nodded enthusiastically, big ears flopping. "I catch fish with Nah-ny in Kuchik! Fish good!"

"You caught fish?" Trace asked. Erik watched with mild surprise. Trace's reputation said nothing of being good with children. "How did you catch fish?"

"Wike this, wike... grrr!" and Skah made a stiff-fingered thrust with one hand. Adult kuhsi had lethal claws that would skewer a fish, but like most kuhsi children, Skah's had been clipped. Erik thought that just as well. "And... and then eat wike... wike grrr, and fish aw good, fish taste good!" Miming tearing into the flapping meal with sharp little teeth, all enthusiasm. Trace grinned and ruffled his ears. Three months ago Skah had been sickly and thin, but now he was a bright-eyed, glossy-haired handful. Busy in her new role as *Phoenix* shuttle pilot, his mother found no shame at all in using *Phoenix* marines and crew as her personal babysitting service. Far from minding, the crew had all but made Skah the ship mascot.

"Skah," said Erik. "Did you make trouble in the gym?"

But Skah's eyes widened at the sight of someone emerging from the airlock. "Nah-ny!" he shouted, and ran for Tif, who grabbed him up in her flight suit and oxygen tubes, helmet under one arm and little boy in the other. And he erupted in a torrent of coughs and growls in their native tongue, at which Tif blinked, and somehow managed to free her ears from the scarf that bound them over the top of her head — necessary for kuhsi in helmets.

Then she looked up, and saw both of *Phoenix*'s commanding officers watching. "Skah!" she said accusingly. "You nake troubuw?"

"Only small trouble," Trace assured her. "He ran into a storage crate and spilled some equipment in the corridor." She glanced at Erik. "Grenades. X-4s." Erik's eyes widened. "They're inert until fired, no danger. Just looked a bit interesting, grenades all over the floor. That reminds me... Melsh!"

"Yes Major!"

"Get down here and help unload this fish!" And to Tif, "Is it good fish? I think we could all use some good fish about now."

"Fish good," Tif agreed. "Vieno nice. Pretty. Barabo nice too, we no fight barabo?"

"No Tif," Erik agreed. "We don't fight barabo. I like barabo too."

"Barabo no guns." Tif looked a little worried. Clearly she understood the situation. "Sard aw here, but barabo no guns."

Erik sighed. "Yeah. I don't think that's going to work out for them either."

Lisbeth entered Engineering Bay 8D to find Stanislav Romki at a workpost. He sat with Augmented Reality glasses on, lost hypnotised in that glow of blue light, fingers dancing across invisible icons in the air before him. Integrated into the workbench was a wide transparent cylinder, filled with thick liquid. Within the liquid, held firm with intricate clamps, was the most amazing object Lisbeth had ever seen.

It was a head, of sorts, severed from its mechanical body. The head of a sentient machine, from a race of AI warriors who had ruled this portion of the galaxy for twenty three thousand years, only to then become extinct for another twenty five thousand. Or mostly extinct. This one had a fist-sized hole through its single, big red eye where Major Thakur had put a round through its head. It was not especially well armoured, as rather than being a warrior, this one had been a commander, a higher-sentient intelligence purposed for command and control. A queen, in human understanding, in the hive-like structure of AI society. And Stanislav Romki, since his first moment aboard the *UFS Phoenix*, had found it fascinating beyond description.

"Stan, you should eat," Lisbeth told him as she came alongside.

"Yes yes yes," Romki shushed her. "In a minute."

"No look, I brought you some stir fry," said Lisbeth, holding the container for him. Romki peered past his glasses, then abandoned his control icons for a moment to take the container and fork.

"Thank you, thoughtful girl." Romki's detached fascination for AIs and aliens, and his relative disinterest in human beings, had become something of a joke among *Phoenix* crew. But confronted with something like an AI queen, Lisbeth sympathised. She bent to peer into the big, dead eye behind the curved glass.

"She is completely dead, right?" she asked. "I mean, the size of that hole..." On this angle, she could see right through the queen's head. The primary rifles used by fully armoured marines were enormous.

"Well yes and no," said Romki past a mouthful of stir fry. It was a *Phoenix* kitchen staple, and quite tasty too, but became repetitive for every second meal. Recent rumours of fresh fish had everyone excited. "Functionally she's quite dead — much of the neural processing core has been completely annihilated. She simply lacks the hardware to create a conscious thought.

"But this... this... entire brain structure is something..." he trailed off. Lisbeth had an advanced engineering degree from one of the best colleges in human space. It was specialised in starships more than computers, but she still had enough knowledge to know why Romki couldn't complete the sentence.

"I know," she agreed. "It's incredible."

"Beyond incredible. All the literature on hacksaws says molecular-level processing, quantum computing, but... well, maybe someone in Fleet or in tavalai labs somewhere knows how it works. I'm struggling. There's at least twenty different kinds of brain structure here, but the main data-retention seems to be almost crystalline. It's like it *grows* memory and data, and somehow feeds sub-molecular level storage into these incredible crystal matrixes. And I mean, they're *beautiful*. So beautiful."

"Maybe the reason we find it so hard to figure out how it works is that we're organic," Lisbeth murmured. In the thick fluid submerging the queen's head, shimmering swarms of dust seemed to swirl. Like a billion microscopic animals, turning together in unison. "The first machines were just server droids when they rebelled against the Fathers. Then over twenty thousand years they evolved into this. Maybe it takes a machine to make another machine this advanced."

"That's quite possible," said Romki, barely listening as he ate.

"Any more ideas about *what* she is? Which branch of AI civilisation she belonged to?"

"Oh god no," said Romki. "It's hard enough just trying to figure out how she works. And there were hundreds of branches. That was actually a very complicated civilisation — I mean imagine, twenty three thousand years, spread over so many hundreds and thousands of star systems.   How complicated did humans get in just a few thousand years on one planet?   But it's all so long ago now, they were extinct so long before humans even got into space, and all the species that were around at the time would rather forget."

"And you've got her in the nano-tank," said Lisbeth, looking at the thin veil of swirling metallic dust.   "Any chance the micro-machines could actually complete a full circuit?"

It was what the nano-tank was designed to do.   You put damaged electrics into it, and the micros swarmed and analysed and figured out which pathways needed to be completed in order to restore function.   And then, in human tech at least, they set about joining themselves to create those pathways.

"No, dear girl, look... our queen is a work of art.   Such advanced synthetics, almost beyond belief.   Our own technology, including those micros, is so primitive by comparison... using them to make her work again would be like trying to restore function to a supercomputer with an elastic band and a couple of paper clips."

"But you said yes *and* no," said Lisbeth.   "You mean... she's *not* completely dead?"

"Well this is pure conjecture on my part... but I see no reason why these crystalline neural structures should not retain complete data sets long after the neural mechanism itself has long since ceased to function."

"You think she's still alive in there?" Lisbeth breathed. "Waiting to be revived?"

"Well beyond *our* technology, I'm quite sure.   More's the pity."

Lisbeth gazed at him.   "You think we should do it, don't you? Wake her up?"

Romki raised the glasses for the first time, and looked upon her.   His head was bald mostly for shaved convenience, his eyes dark and intelligent, his brows arched like an owl.   It was a face that did intelligence and enthusiasm well, and condescension and disdain even better.

"Ms Debogande," he said with angry amusement.   "Which do you imagine is more important?   Attempting to make peace

41

between two groups of humans who are hell bent on trying to kill each other due to factors entirely beyond our control?   Or researching the true nature of our alo allies?   Because if the alo did indeed absorb some portion of the deepynine hacksaws all those thousands of years ago... well, it would explain why their technology is so advanced, for one thing.   The most advanced species usually became that way after interacting with other species, but the alo just popped up two thousand years ago, refused to talk to anyone but the chah'nas, refused to let anyone travel in their territory, and were already more advanced than the tavalai.   Fishy doesn't begin to describe it."

He pointed at the queen.   "She might know.   She might even tell us, if we asked her.   In that synthetic brain may lie the clue to exactly what threat humanity allied itself to, at the beginning of the Triumvirate War... but no, your brother and his muscle-headed Major are still so tied to Fleet's apron strings that they can't imagine looking outward toward what's most important."

·   "Well..." Lisbeth blinked, wondering how to explain it to a man like Romki.   "Well they'd like to go home," she said lamely. "Everyone here would like to go home."

"Exactly," said Romki, exasperated.   "Humanity has been in space for over a thousand years, yet still we look to answers amongst ourselves.   One day, Lisbeth Debogande, we will have to grow up. There's an entire universe out there."   He waved a hand expansively at a wall.   "And until we learn to cast off these childish things, and venture forth as a truly grown up species, a species that *belongs* in this galaxy, we will always be in terrible danger from the many things out there that we refuse to understand."

CHAPTER 4

Colonel Timothy Khola's cruiser landed on the pad within wide, pretty gardens on a hill. He left the cruiser, presented his ID to the marine guard who came to check it, then walked with his two officer companions toward the mansion. The neighbourhood was wealthy, as all neighbourhoods were on these green hilltops that overlooked the gleaming city of Shiwon. The city and ocean view were partly obstructed by tall, green trees, and the gardens stretched downhill to patios, swimming pools and flower beds, surrounded by high walls.

Fleet personnel bustled about, mostly officers on business. They were moving a lot of files and boxes, and furniture piled on the pavings beside big French doors. The mansion was Shiwon Fleet Administration, the personal residence of Fleet Admiral Paul Anjo. The third-most-senior officer in Fleet, even Anjo's own home was filled with staff, on full-rotation service. And these staff looked like they were preparing to move house.

Khola entered the downstairs living room, wide and spacious, where civilian removalists were considering the furniture. A middle-aged black lady in expensive clothes fretted with them beside a sofa. An adult daughter held a grandchild nearby, chatting to a Fleet officer Khola didn't recognise.

Khola went briskly upstairs, down a hall past more officers carrying boxes, to some big double doors guarded by marines. Both marines came to attention as Khola approached. He wore full dress uniform today, with medals. He didn't do that often. The Liberty Star had an effect on all who saw it, even civilians. After one hundred and sixty one years of war, few humans didn't know what it was. There were rumours of rare ones on the blackmarket fetching fortunes, for collector value alone. To serving personnel, they were worth far more than money.

The marines let him in unasked, and the two officers with him. Fleet Admiral Anjo was talking with several Captains and Commanders. About his office, more boxes, filling with files, pictures, framed commendations. Several shelves were approaching bare. Against the wall behind his desk, the twin flags of the Fleet Arrowhead on Crescent, and the United Forces Starburst about a blue sphere. The blue sphere was Earth, and rising above the northern-most point of the star, the silver wings of a Phoenix. Humanity, rising from the ashes.

All turned to look at the new arrival. "Colonel Khola!" exclaimed the Fleet Admiral in surprise. "This is an honour. To what do I owe it?" In Fleet seniority, Anjo was a whole five ranks above Khola — a stratospheric O-11, where Khola was merely an O-6. Yet while Anjo might receive more salutes, no one in Fleet was under any illusion who got the most respect.

"I have some special business, sir," Khola said simply. "I would be gratified if we could attend to it immediately."

Anjo's eyes went wide. Special business, coming from Khola, could only mean the Guidance Council. Much of Fleet thought the Guidance Council was just a rumour, a tale to be told late at night. The administrative version of a ghost ship story, told to frighten junior bureaucrats into good behaviour. Select very senior officers knew better.

Anjo nodded to the officers about him, who left with respectful haste. One of Khola's companions followed them out, and shut the doors behind him. Khola glanced at the boxes. Anjo smiled nervously. "I've been informed that the security standards in this neighbourhood are no longer up to scratch. You know, with things as they are."

Khola nodded. Anjo had upset the Debogandes. The Debogande Family was known to employ some very serious muscle, much of it ex-Fleet. Anjo had pinned a murder on Alice Debogande's son, then tried to kill him too when it all went bad. Worse, he'd tried to kill Major Thakur, and Thakur wore the Liberty Star just as Khola did. Many marines were furious, and Anjo, whatever his rank, was no marine. Anjo had set a precedent, of top officers murdering, and attempting to murder, their own. No one was especially surprised that High Command could do such things — one hundred and sixty one years of war had demonstrated that the

44

universe, and Fleet Command, could be equally dark and dangerous. But even so, such behaviour could be catching. No doubt Anjo was nervous, and moving somewhere safer.

"Colonel, what kind of drink could I offer a Kulina that you might accept?" Anjo asked. Anjo was dark and portly. His uniform belt was let out several notches more than Khola thought seemly, even on a spacer.

"No drink, thank you Admiral." He fixed Anjo with a calm stare. "I'm here to inform you that the Guidance Council has deliberated, and found the present situation intolerable. Fleet must maintain Spacer dominance over Worlders, but instead of uniting behind you, your actions have divided us. One of our most powerful industrial families, a family with a record of great service to Spacer causes and a great friend to Fleet, has now been made our enemy. Spacer Congress representatives are upset. My fellow marines are upset. Some Spacer captains involved in the initial pursuit of *Phoenix* from Homeworld were then, and are still now, on the verge of mutiny. Even many who were in the greatest disagreement with Captain Pantillo's politics cannot accept on principle that one of their own could be dealt with in this manner."

"Look," Anjo said shortly, temper and fear rising as one. He jabbed his finger at Khola. "I was given *specific instructions* to deal with Pantillo. Immediately, that was the word I received. I know many of the Guidance Council were in agreement at the time, and only now, in hindsight..." He broke off, and strode to stare out a window at the green gardens. "I mean what did they think would happen? The war was ended, Pantillo was going to run for office from Heuron, where he'd probably win, and then a man with his war record, organising on behalf of the Worlders... well, only a matter of time until the Worlders gained full democratic rights at the top of our political system. Unacceptable, I was told. And so I dealt with it, *exactly* how I was instructed, only now does everyone see the impossibility of the situation I was placed in!"

"I quite understand," Khola agreed. "But that does not change the present situation."

"And how the hell did that *girl* get loose in the detention cells?" Anjo demanded. "I'm telling you, this was an inside job. I think I was set up, Colonel. And I'll not take the fall for this alone, I can assure you."

"There was no inside job," Khola said calmly. "Major Thakur is Kulina, like me. Others may have her combat skills, but very few possess the calmness of mind to utilise them as she does. She was my student for one year at the Academy, and while her decisions have surprised and disappointed me, the outcomes once she made those decisions have not." He paused. "And you will take the fall for this."

Anjo turned to look at him. Lips pressed tight, trembling with hard emotion. "I will not," he retorted. "I was placed in an impossible circumstance."

"That is irrelevant," said Khola. "We battle for human survival. Our own individual survival is unimportant. And fear not, Fleet Admiral Ishmael and Supreme Commander Chankow will meet the same fate as you."

"I will appeal!" Anjo retorted. Khola had been warned of this, and it did not surprise him. Anjo had been climbing this greasy pole most of his life. Like so many of Fleet's highest officers. "I will demand a full accounting of the decision making process behind my dismissal! It will not be pretty, Colonel. You go and you tell your Guidance Council that, before we take this any further."

"There will be no accounting, Admiral," Khola told him. "You misread the situation. Fleet needs a clean break from its current leadership. There can be no dispute, no ongoing proceedings leading to further debate and acrimony. It must be fast, and it must be final."

Khola pulled his sidearm from its holster. Anjo paled. "Oh no no no," he murmured. Tremors began in his hands, and he stumbled back a step.

"For the human cause, Admiral," Khola said simply. "The only cause that matters. It must be by your own hand. You will leave a note admitting your responsibility and regret. Humanity's future depends on it."

"I won't." Anjo stumbled back against the wall for balance, face blank with terror. "I won't, I won't."

"You will."

"Please." Begging, as his eyes filled with tears. "Please, my family is downstairs. You can't do this. Think of them."

"I'm thinking of us all," Khola said calmly. "And I shan't do it. You shall."

In sudden fury, Anjo drew himself up. "I am a Fleet Admiral!" he yelled. "I have worked my whole life to achieve this position, and I will not be intimidated by some lowly Colonel with jumped up delusions of grandeur!"

The yelling would not help him, Khola knew. This was a secure room, and largely soundproof. Lieutenant Abrahms, who had departed the room before, had moved the marines on guard outside at the same time. No one would come. He nodded to Lieutenant Parrikar, who walked around Anjo's desk to the drawer, and pulled out the Admiral's personal pistol, just where intel had said it was. Parrikar handed it over to Khola.

Anjo grabbed a chair and tried to heave it at the window, but the chair was heavy. Khola grabbed it with a hand, then broke Anjo's grip to make him drop it. Anjo lashed at his arm, but that merely gave Khola the leverage for an armlock that dropped Anjo to his knees. Anjo screamed, but Khola took a handkerchief from his pocket he'd kept for the purpose, and stuffed it into Anjo's mouth. He then dragged the man, with Lieutenant Parrikar's assistance, kicking and flailing to his desk chair, and put him in it.

The pistol was a snubbed K7, standard Fleet officer's issue, and would not make an especially loud noise in a secure room. With augmented strength Khola locked Anjo's left arm behind his back, forced the K7 into the right hand that Parrikar held ready. Parrikar then bear hugged Anjo to the chair to hold him in place, while Khola locked the arms, and forced the pistol hand around and stuffed the muzzle into Anjo's mouth. Anjo tried to thrash his head, and Parrikar stopped that with a steel grip. The muzzle went in, to Anjo's muffled shrieks.

"Clear!" Khola instructed, and Parrikar removed her hand from the top of Anjo's head, just before Khola blew it off. Bits of skull and brain went flying, then stillness. Both marines dropped the Fleet Admiral, as the pistol fell, then a hand. Blood dripped thickly, and Khola removed the bloody handkerchief.

Lieutenant Parrikar looked at their handiwork, and surveyed the blood spatter on her hands. "Fuck," she summarised.

Khola nodded, scrunching the handkerchief and scanning his uniform for blood. "Always messy," he said distastefully. "The dishonourable always are."

The doors opened, and more spacer uniforms walked in. They carried medical bags, and pulled on rubber gloves even now. "You two," said their leader, "the washroom's in there, make sure you're clean before you leave. Anderson, go with them to be sure. We'll take care of this."

"Yes, forensically we won't fool anyone," Khola said drily, handing one of the new arrivals the bloody rag. "Do a good job or Lieutenant Parrikar and myself will meet a similar fate in some prison cell, I'm sure."

The man opened his bag on Anjo's desk, revealing an orderly arrangement of cleaning agents, cloths, magnifying lenses and tweezers. "Oh I'm sure they'll know exactly who did it," he told the two Kulina marines. "We're just betting that at this point, they'll understand the necessity."

Alice Debogande was not particularly impressed by the sight of Rear Admiral Bedi. He was a little round man with a twitchy little face, who clearly had not seen any recent combat during his service. She had met Erik's dear Captain Pantillo while he was still alive, and even at thirty years older than Bedi (her intelligence people told her) he'd looked far more spry and fit than this.

Alice stood beside her chair in the mansion's lower sunroom, surrounded on all sides by glass, and beyond them, wide green gardens. Bedi's accompanying captain was invited to wait by the door from the gardens.   About Alice, ten personal security, well armed with weapons prominent.   In the gardens outside, many more. The Debogande family house had aerial radar and defence mechanisms.   If she'd been allowed, she'd have had anti-aircraft installed.   But Fleet, of course, said no.

"Rear Admiral," she said coolly, and indicated the chair opposite.

"Madame Debogande," Bedi tried, and offered her his hand. Alice ignored it, and took her seat.   Bedi recovered well enough, and sat also.   As serving Fleet, he got to keep his uniform pistol, and even Alice's security could not by law argue with that.   But if he was armed, they would be too.   Bedi ran his eye across the wall of holstered weapons around him.   It was unsubtle of her, but Alice was well beyond caring about subtlety, with men such as these. "You've heard the news then?"

"I heard," said Alice.   "Fleet Admiral Anjo is dead. Apparently there's even a note."   With dry amusement.

Bedi cleared his throat.   No doubt he would benefit from a drink.   None was offered.   "He did show an appalling lack of judgement.   Your son was an unfortunate casualty of it."

"Not yet he's not," Alice said coldly.   It terrified her, what had happened to Erik, and to Lisbeth.   Yet on a level that she knew was most unwise, it made her proud beyond words.   Family Debogande had once stood for proud and principled things. Following Earth's destruction, when humanity had been reduced to a hundred million Spacers squeezed into overcrowded accommodations on stations or bases, a man named Junwadh Debogande, an ordinary stationhand originally from an African place called Burkina Faso, had emerged as a brilliant organiser of desperately needed industrial activity.   When the Chah'nas Continuum had funnelled money and technology into those desperate few colonies, Junwadh had quickly risen to prominence, and been granted responsibility for a huge swathe of activity.

When humanity began to win victories against the krim, humanity's war footing had loosened enough to permit traditional capitalist enterprise once more, and Family Debogande had thrived.

But they hadn't just made money, as human interests expanded. They'd taken political stances that had at times cost them dearly — stances aimed at what the family perceived as humanity's best interests at the time. The family had spent enormously of its wealth to promote those interests, and continued to do so today. At times Alice feared that her attempts to drum this legacy into her children had failed, with their unavoidably soft and comfortable lives. But they had not failed, at least, with Erik. Nor it seemed with Lisbeth.

But always, with the pride, came fear. She was the family statesperson, presiding over empires and principles, but she was also a mother. And she wanted her children safe, and desperately.

"Mrs Debogande," Bedi tried again. He leaned forward in his chair. "Let me be plain. What that fool Anjo did to the *UFS Phoenix* has been an enormous embarrassment to Fleet. It has divided us against ourselves. Fleet against Fleet, and Spacer against Spacer. Now there will be a new leadership, and a chance to wipe the slate clean.

"*Phoenix* will be granted a full pardon, along with all her crew. Captain Pantillo, and the others who lost their lives in Homeworld orbit, will be given heroes' funerals, and their names etched into remembrance walls with all our other fallen warriors. Now believe me, this will not be easy for us. *Phoenix* was forced into a corner, and she fought very hard. Harder than many of our senior officers believe was proper... I know, easy for them to say, but instead of retreating to deep space and waiting for Fleet to sort out its own command problems, *Phoenix* went to Heuron, for reasons yet not fully known to us, and did a lot of damage there."

Alice frowned. "From what I hear, Heuron was already a mess due to the declaration." The declaration was all they were calling it now, humanity-wide. The ordinances that relegated Worlders to second-class status in all human space. Fleet might be condemning Anjo, Chankow and Ishmael for *Phoenix*, but they weren't condemning them for the declaration. Evidently that hadn't been just their decision.

"They did a lot of damage at Heuron," Bedi repeated, refusing to be drawn. "But *Phoenix* is currently dividing Fleet, and so we shall grant them pardon, so that Fleet can unite once more behind the new leadership."

"Now that Captain Pantillo is conveniently dead and you no longer have to worry about him running for office," Alice said drily. "How lucky for you."

"Mrs Debogande, I must press upon you that if you have any contact with your son, you *must* convince him to accept Fleet's pardon. Fleet will only make the offer once, and it comes with conditions."

"What conditions?"

"That *Phoenix*'s crew must all retake the oath of loyalty, and swear alliegance to the new leadership. They will be allowed to remain together as a crew, they will have our word on that. But they must commit to the Spacer cause, and abandon any of this foolish nonsense their old captain was toying with, supporting Worlders to upset the existing order. *UFS Phoenix* must once again commit to being one of us. And not one of *them*. I can't put it any plainer than that."

"And should *Phoenix* refuse?"

"Then their renegade status will be reinstated. And Fleet will commit to do what we do to all renegade vessels. Hunt them down and destroy them."

And wasn't it just like Fleet, Alice thought, to turn an apology for trying to kill her son, into an attempt at blackmail. Make your son agree, or we'll go back to trying to kill him. Some choice.

She took a deep breath. "I will do what needs to be done," she said heavily.

CHAPTER 5

"Well this doesn't feel inconspicuous at all," Stanislav Romki complained as he hung on a strap in the thrumming train carriage. About him were four *Phoenix* marines in light armour and weapons. About *them*, the train was crammed with colourful barabo, plus a few tavalai, all staring at them.

"You know, you complain a lot," Lieutenant Tyson Dale remarked. Beside him, a barabo lady in a big green robe clutched a game bird of some kind that squawked and clucked. "Howdy," Dale told her. The barabo blinked. "Dinner?" Looking at the bird.

Romki rolled his eyes. "She's a diji-do, the bird is a sacrifice, she'll be taking it to a chan-chala in the hope it will grant her family good fortune." Lights flashed by as the train hummed past steel grey gantries. "And instead, she ran into you."

"Good fortune right there, I reckon," said Dale. He was bigger than most of the carriage's barabo, save for a group by one door who towered over the others. Like his three marines, he wore glasses beneath his helmet, earpiece in, rifle pointed at the floor in one fist.

"She's a diji what?" asked Private Tong.

"There are more than three thousand recognised religious forms on the barabo homeworld," Romki said through gritted teeth. "Diji Ran is the third biggest, as you'd know if you read the basic material I provided for the ship-net before we arrived. They believe in fortunes and sacrifices, and they wear a figure-eight symbol around their necks." He nodded to the woman's necklace.

"I was busy reading my latest Juggs & Ammo," said Tong.

Private Reddy leaned close, mouth open and staring at Romki like a drooling fool. "Gol-ly. You mus' be some kinda real smart guy, huh?" Gunnery Sergeant Forrest sneezed laughter. Dale grinned. Romki fumed.

"Now now boys," their Lieutenant said. "Marines are taught to handle explosive materials with care."

The train arrived at a dark, crowded station with lots of bright overhead lights and flashing displays in various scripts. Barabo were carrying things everywhere, loads of garments, bangles, various arts and crafts, a load of wooden poles that Dale had no idea about. They hustled to get onto the train before it left, heedless of the marines' rifles, and Dale used his armour to block one impact. When he looked about to make sure Romki was following, he found Romki had somehow edged ahead and was sliding through the chaos more easily than the heavy marines.

Dale hustled to catch up, halfway between annoyed at the lawlessness, and reluctantly intrigued. Stations were not ships, you were allowed a lot more loose items on the former than the latter. But in human space, the rule still remained that on stations, things had to be more or less bolted down, and loose clutter was kept to a minimum. If human station inspectors saw this crazy mess, they'd have had an aneurism.

The humans went with the flow of the crowd, as screens flashed odd messages that might be advertising, and live music thudded from just ahead. A group of barabo were busking on the platform side, mostly drums and other percussion... and damn good too, dancing and jiving with the typical barabo lack of restraint. Then they reached the upward stairs, as Gunnery Sergeant Forrest managed to get back in front of Romki with a stern look that the professor ignored. Romki wore his usual civvie pants and sleeveless vest with many pockets. He was far from a soldier, but as Dale was learning, he was also far more accustomed to this environment than anyone else on *Phoenix*.

The station stairs opened onto a big steel canyon between apartment sides. Upper windows and advertising displays looked down onto a teeming market that made the stalls up on dock level look meek and organised. Products overflowed on all sides, cloth and silk, jewellery expensive and simple, exotic spices, honeys and other foods Dale couldn't identify. A shouting barabo trader showed him a truly awesome set of stainless steel knives with curved blades. Another offered to spray some scent on him that smelled like tree moss. And always there were animals, from little long-armed things that shrieked to little four-legged things that shrieked, to jars of colourful insects to bouncing amphibians.

"You see Lieutenant," Romki shouted from amidst it all, "if someone really wanted to kill me from within this crowd, there isn't actually a lot you could do about it. So I asked specifically to come alone because alone, I can blend in and avoid notice. But with four big steel monsters tramping after me, I make a much more obvious target."

"Yeah, well that sounds all nice to your exotic, alien-wandering ears," Dale replied. "I bet you'd like to believe that. But you've never been hunted by the kind of folks now hunting you, so you're not actually qualified to make that judgement."

Dale still wasn't sure what had happened that Romki was suddenly allowed to leave the ship. Word was that neither the Major, Hiro nor Jokono wanted him wandering, but now, suddenly, orders came that he was allowed to visit a tavalai contact who might have useful information. The Major had told Dale to stick with the professor like glue, and Dale didn't think it was entirely Romki's safety that concerned her.

Romki stopped by a stall selling precious stones, surprising a tavalai who was haggling with the owner. Romki chatted easily in Palapu, while the tavalai blinked in astonishment at the sudden appearance of this human — the demon race that had eaten half of all tavalai space in the last hundred and sixty one years. Possibly he'd never seen one in person before, and had least expected to see one out here, in Outer Neutral Space. Then he turned, and found four armed human marines standing behind and around him.

"Gidiri ha," Dale told him. The tavalai just stared, halfway between bewilderment and defiance. Had to hand it to tavalai, Dale thought — they didn't scare easily. He'd always found their expressions hard to read, with their big long heads and eyes so far apart, it was hard to know where to look. Alongside the tavalai, a barabo security man looked on, massive within a big leather jacket, like the little cluster on the train. One of the big mountain races, from the barabo homeworld.

"Man," said Private Tong, looking at the same. "What do you think he lifts?"

"Whatever he wants," said Forrest, still watching the crowds.

"Just up here on the left," Romki told them, and thanked the stall owner. "Let's go marines, double time."

"No one says that," said Reddy as they followed. "Do you say that Sarge?"

"I don't," Forrest admitted. "But I could if you'd like."

They turned left between stalls, and up a hallway past a flashing display. On the right was a barabo hair salon, animated displays showing the latest styles, while in the main room, barabo women gathered in ecstatic clusters to examine the latest crazy-beaded and woven arrangement being tied into another woman's hair. Their yelling conversation and shrieks of laughter were deafening even from the hallway. Beyond that was a smoking den, where barabo men reclined on chairs and puffed on water pipes, and the haze was so thick it rolled in waves across the hallway ceiling.

"How the hell do these people ever get anything done?" Tong wondered. "If they're always stoned or putting things in their hair?"

"That's why we run the galaxy now," said Dale.

Romki smirked. "Is *that* what you think, Lieutenant? Well well."

A corner, then on the left a big glass wall with turnstile pressure doors, and images of lake reeds and lilies on steaming water. "Hey, tavalai baths," said Forrest, quite intrigued. Ahead, tavalai were entering with small bags of bathing gear. Inside, the air looked steamy. Tavalai preferred the pressure and humidity much higher, and loved the water. Dale had been on their stations newly captured, with the environmentals set to tavalai preferences, and if you removed your helmet too quickly, it was agony on the ears, and breathing felt like mouthfuls of soup.

"Just here," said Romki, indicating past the baths, no doubt reading the Togiri script on the windows. On the right was a restaurant. Peering through the windows, Dale saw a tavalai layout — a smorgasbord of pots, lots of watery-looking things in rows, and big bowl seating where diners would sit in what looked to humans like uncomfortable proximity.

"It's empty," said Dale.

"It's the wrong time of day," said Romki. "Tavalai stick to routines, even on station time." He went to the door.

"Wait!" Dale barked. Romki paused. Beyond him, the next cross-alley showed the grand market resuming, bustling crowds and shouting hawkers. Dale peered through the glass once more. Beyond the reed-mat partition, where the chefs would be, he saw nothing. "There's no one here at all. I don't like it."

"Lieutenant," Romki said with exasperation, "I can assure you that..."

"Woody," Dale interrupted, "check the door." Forrest went to do that, as Romki rolled his eyes with impatience... and the world went sideways as the restaurant blew up, glass and debris crashing over them, Dale's ears ringing and lungs full of smoke.

'Up', he forced himself with effort, as thirty years of combat reflexes imposed themselves and guessed what was coming next. "Up!" he yelled, scrambling dizzily back to his knees and a firing crouch, unable to see a damn thing through the smoke...

"Contact!" Tong yelled, opening fire on something, and...

"Down!" yelled Forrest, as return fire came from the market end, red tracer ripping through the smoke.

Dale threw himself at the hallway's opposite side, where glass surrounding the bathing house had collapsed, and sheltered behind the end wall. "Get cover!" he yelled, but his section had already done that, none as experienced as him but close enough. Rapid fire hit the wall and he ducked back, hoping one of them had grabbed Romki... and saw half-naked tavalai behind, shocked, crouched and staring, and too close to the line of fire. He gestured hard at them to get back and get down, and was uncertain as he did it that it wasn't a tavalai shooting at them, and now he had a room full of them at his back.

Fire redirected, and Dale put his rifle around the corner, sighted, and saw a dark shape advancing, movements flowing but clearly mechanical, heavy weapon swivelling from one marine cover position to another as it came.   He put a burst on it, saw it hit but immediately swing his way, and ducked back as more rounds tore at his wall. "Droid!" he shouted. "It's a fucking droid!"

In heavy armour he'd have his Koshaim-20, twice the calibre and many times the hitting power of this light P-8.   The Koshaim would tear a droid in half with a few shots, he'd even seen them kill hacksaw drones with accurate fire. The P-8, not so much.

"I got him flanked," came Reddy's voice in his earpiece. *"Fire in three, two, one, mark."*   A hammering burst, Dale waited a moment for the droid to spin, then popped out and fired on full auto. The others joined him, and the droid staggered, lost pieces, then exploded in a fireball that demolished every surviving bit of glass in the hallway.

More fire cut past, but they were already in cover, and the bullets hit only walls — a second droid.   Again Dale waited until someone else fired, then popped out to fire himself, as another marine opened up as soon as the fire came at him.   The droid seemed averse to taking cover, and after repeatedly taking fire from whomever its weapon was not pointed at, it turned and ran.   Dale ran after it, and cleared the smoke in time to see it racing into the near-deserted market, a long civilian coat flowing out behind.   It moved fast, and Dale knew it was pointless to follow.

"Damn thing's wearing civvies," he said, backing up with rifle levelled in case it or a friend came back. "Everyone okay?"

"Good," Forrest agreed on coms.

"Good," Tong echoed.

"Yeah okay I guess," Reddy muttered.   He was pulling himself out of the ruined restaurant wall, amidst broken tables, pots and food.   Everyone else had gone left, away from the explosion — Reddy must have gone right, straight into the residual flames and smoke, because he knew he had to get the droid flanked on both sides.

"That was good stuff Spots," Dale told him.   "How's Romki?" Everyone looked. "Fuck. *Where's* Romki?"

Trace was late, and not happy about it, having been in the *Phoenix* gym when word of the attack came in. Two squads of Bravo Platoon were already at the scene, amidst a bunch of red uniformed barabo police, and other station security. They clustered about the entrance to the hallway by the market, far too many to be useful, while stall owners packed away their wares, sensing there would be no more sales for a while and wary of leaving things unsecured.

Bravo's commander, Lieutenant Alomaim, was arguing with a barabo police chief, firm and no-nonsense to the barabo's hand-waving exasperation. "Major," Alomaim said as she approached.

The chief saw her, and his translator-speaker squawked as he let fly. *"This my station! This not your station! I get access to crime scene! Tell your man let me access crime scene now!"*

"Not a crime scene," Trace replied to her own translator. "Act of war. *Phoenix* is a warship, weapons of war were used, military action ensued. You'll get access when we're done with it."

That upset the barabo chief further. *"War, crime scene, no difference! This my station, this my scene!"*

Trace held up her massive Koshaim-20 in her suit's armoured grip. With power-assist she barely felt the weight. "This says it isn't," she told him, and walked past the armoured *Phoenix* security line.

Lieutenant Dale was standing in his light armour, as Corpsman Rashni dabbed at the small cuts across one side of his face. Glass fragments, Trace guessed. "Why always you?" she accused him with affection.

"Been asking that for years," said Gunnery Sergeant Forrest, who looked much better, but had a hand wrapped. Privates Tong and Reddy were nearby, talking with Jokono and Echo Platoon's Heavy Squad commander, Corporal Barry, who was probably *Phoenix*'s best explosives guy and had been summonsed for the purpose.

"I'm sorry about Romki," Dale said in a low voice, obviously ashamed. "I just couldn't go chasing after him, I had to secure the scene, we've some light injuries and he's pretty damn good at moving in these crowds…"

"Don't worry about Romki," Trace told him calmly. "We're on it."

Dale frowned at her. "You're on it?" Trace nodded. "Who's 'we'?"

"We're on it," Trace repeated, and went to where the others stood in the ruins of the restaurant. There wasn't much left, all the internal fittings had been torn down in the blast, or set aflame thereafter. What survived was the steel frame, pipes and wiring, to which the decor had been attached to create the illusion of a more pleasant indoor setting than a steel cage. Some ceiling attachments were hanging precariously, blackened and now wet from the sprinkler system that had since been deactivated.

"Major?" came the LC's voice in her ear. *"What's it look like?"*

"Here, I'll put you on conference," Trace told him, and linked the coms of those around her so he could hear. "LC's on conference," she told Jokono and Barry as they talked amidst the mess. "What's up?"

"Well it's not sophisticated," said Corporal Barry, holding several twisted metal bits in his hand that had once been a bomb trigger. "Could be just that they used local materials, or maybe they were covering their tracks. Who do we think it was?"

Trace looked at Jokono. "We've got a list," Jokono said wryly. "Tavalai, maybe. Sard, less-than-maybe. Alo, likely. Fleet, also likely. Given what Romki knows about the alo and deepynines."

"Any forensics that might narrow that list down?" Erik asked. Trace could hear the frustration in his voice, mostly, she thought, at being stuck on the ship while others roamed. When he'd been third-in-command, he'd sometimes tended to on-station situations, usually where some crew or other had gotten into trouble on station leave. But as Acting-Captain, he was far too valuable to risk roaming the station, and hadn't taken any leave on Vieno either.

"Well there's not an awful lot left," Jokono replied. "The advantage of using a simple bomb, as Corporal Barry says, is that there's not very much we can trace. I mean, I'd think half of *Phoenix*'s marines, and any spacer in Engineering, could have assembled this from simple store-bought parts in a day or two. We'll hand what we know to the local cops, but they don't like us very much right now, and even if they did like us enough to tell us what they find, I'm pretty sure they'll find that there's hundreds of people buying those parts every day. And barabo being barabo, lots of purchases aren't even officially recorded."

"What about the explosive?" Trace asked. "Surely you can't buy that off a shelf, even here."

"Would you like me to list the number of things on space stations that make explosives?" Jokono asked wryly. "Sublighter fuels, engine components, mining stores? Chemical supplies, hydroponics fertilisers, paint mixtures?"

"Gas filtration," Corporal Barry added, sniffing a piece of debris.

Jokono nodded. "Before we even get to the blackmarket weapons. We could probably find out what it is, but good luck learning anything from it, out here. I'm much more interested in those attack droids. You've all got far more military experience, but to me it looks like the droids were the primary weapon. Whoever or whatever detonated the bomb saw that Lieutenant Dale was suspicious, so blew the charge before he could get really suspicious and withdraw, expecting the robots to handle the marines once they were down. But *Phoenix* marines are very hard to kill."

"Who do you think?" Trace asked.

"Someone who knew Romki's connections with tavalai?" Jokono ventured. "This tavalai in particular. Lieutenant Commander, if you can get *Phoenix* database working on station records from your end, that would be a start. Mr Romki said the tavalai's name is…"

"Yes, he's given us all that information, we're tracking it now."

"Someone's watching us," Jokono said thoughtfully.

"Everyone's watching us," Trace replied.

"Someone who's not just curious.   Someone who knows our interests.   *Phoenix* is concerned of potential enemies, like tavalai. Like sard.   We haven't seen their warships since we've been in Outer Neutral Space, but I'll bet that's about to change."

"No doubt," Trace agreed.

"But we're also concerned with our own politics," Jokono continued.   "Spacers versus Worlders.   I called Major General Randal Connor through a neutral coms ID Hiro had set up when we got here.   Can't be traced to *Phoenix*.   Got no reply.   Connor's often busy, I take it he goes out to drink a lot with his contacts, but now I'm thinking we might want to go check on him."   Trace frowned.

"We're trying direct uplink right now from this end," said Erik.   *"Personal uplink, not his office or remote construct. Nothing."*

"You have a location?" Trace asked.

The ride on the station train was even stranger amidst fully armoured marines with Koshaim-20s, interlocked grenade launchers and full helmets.   Trace kept her helmet on for convenience, visor popped for local vision, as even curious barabo stayed well clear. Powercells whined and hummed, and armoured limbs occasionally rattled with feedback tension, making a combat suit an intimidating thing even without the weapons.

They rode with Jokono two stops before the station nearest to Major General Connor's office, on Jokono's insistence that he had a fix on Connor's location.   How Jokono could do that, on an alien station using strange network protocols, Trace did not particularly want to know.   It wasn't in a police officer's usual repertoire, but since he'd left public security, Jokono had been spending a lot of time with the likes of Hiro Uno in the Debogande Family's personal security.   Spies like Hiro had crazy network skills, their skulls crammed with the latest cybernetic interface that allowed him to break down com routines in his head.   Jokono, Trace knew, had some of the same.   If he said he knew where Connor was, Trace believed him.

The rail station was dark and ugly with none of the life and vibrations of the market stop.   Seedy neon flickered upon dark platforms, and some torn posters flapped in the foul-smelling warmth of a ventilation grille.   Jokono took them left down some stairs, then a dingy corridor where barabo nervously made way for thumping, armoured marines.

Trace dropped her visor as her squad did the same — she'd left Command Squad behind for a change, as half of them were still recovering from months-old injuries, and hadn't been positioned to respond to this call anyway.   She'd brought First Section of Second Squad, Alpha Platoon, instead — with four plus herself, five made an awkward number, but it hardly mattered.   Tacnet propagated, blue dots upon her visor map, plus Jokono... though how an unarmored civvie showed up on marine tacnet, she also had no idea. Network skills indeed.

They turned again, onto a steel mesh walkway above a canyon drop of at least five levels, onto pipes and other utilities. More walkways ran the length of the canyon above and below, lined with grimy doors.

"Budget accommodation," Sergeant Hall remarked, looking around with distaste.   Something eight-legged and insect-looking raced away from an armoured boot.

"Just up here," said Jokono, also on coms, the only way he'd be clearly heard now that the marines all had their visors down. Another stairway down, and the walkway canyon ended, replaced with wire gates and security doors.   One asked Jokono for a clearance, which he somehow provided.   Lights flashed green, and he led them inside.

Inside was very dark.   Jokono tried the lights.   *"No lights."* Trace flipped to IR, and saw storage, rows of stacked pressure crates on old runners, some wheeled loaders sitting idle in the aisles. Condensation dripped from the ceiling.

"He's in here?" she asked Jokono, with skepticism.

"That's my reading. No more than twenty meters. Can't pinpoint it, too much interference."

"My audio just read movement ahead," said Private 'Benji' Carville, nervously.

"Yeah, I vote we go in quietly," Corporal Barnes suggested. *"Something's in there, I read it too."*

Trace's sensors weren't reading anything. All these tight spaces were asking for trouble. "Jokono, you might want to stay here."

"Alone? No thank you."

"Okay then, stay between us." Jokono pulled his pistol, and Trace wondered if his plain eyesight was augmented enough to see in this dark. No doubt he was a good shot with that pistol, but it would barely scratch a suit.

Sergeant Hall went first, then Carville, then Trace with Jokono just behind, with Barnes and Private Tuo guarding the rear. Moving quietly in a suit was a challenge, and the aisle between stacked crates wasn't wide enough for a proper stagger pattern, so they were blocking each other's field of fire. But dividing to move down separate aisles was poor craft in a built-up space, as it increased blind spots while decreasing the firepower response.

Hall put up a fist, and they paused at a gap in the crates. *"Through there,"* said Jokono, and Hall ducked under, stepping through the supports. And stopped.

"Son of a bitch." Tacnet gave Trace the feed from Hall's helmet-cam. Slumped against the neighbouring crate in the storage rack, was Randal Connor. There were bits missing, and lots of blood. Death had not taken the fear from his eyes.

In the dark about them, there started a low, insect-shrill, like rainforest cicadas after a downpour. The shrill grew, and spread, from neighbouring aisles and dark spaces, echoing off the cold steel ceiling.

"What is that?" Jokono asked, staring about with pistol ready. A policeman might not have heard it before. All of *Phoenix's* marines had.

"Sard," Corporal Barnes muttered. *"Lots of sard."* The shrill reached a throbbing shriek, pulsing in time. Jokono looked frightened. Trace didn't blame him. If she'd been unarmored, she'd have been frightened too. As it was, she couldn't keep the chills down.

"Everyone cover," she advised them, crouched beside a container and keeping low with a good view of the container tops, and the spaces up near the ceiling. "Sard are light and like to climb. They'll be up by the ceiling. Everyone load frags and prepare to manoeuvre. Jokono, stay low. If you have earplugs, now is the time."

The shrill began to wind down, interrupted by sharp cackles. No one knew why sard did it, except that their brains were all 'hive' and 'group', and rhythmic harmonics told them all where everyone else was. And possibly they had some idea that it freaked most non-sard species the fuck out. But now tacnet was giving her an estimation of numbers, programmed to do that from sard harmonics.

"Tacnet tells me about twenty," she said. "Let's see if we can reduce that a bit. Fragmentation ready, rapid fire. Now."

Four launchers spat grenades toward the ceiling, which exploded in a row of pyrotechnics and raining shrapnel. Shrieks and clatters as sard took cover. Free grenades replied, bouncing off the crate sides to hit the floor.

"Out!" yelled Trace, and dove the other side to roll and cover against the far crate wall. Explosions flashed, then movement up high and she hammered that spot with her Koshaim, thundering a series of holes through the ceiling as spent casings clattered away.

"High!" she heard Hall shout.

Then, *"Low straight!"* as the others spotted targets, rifles hammering in the enclosed space.

"Hall! Displace and run straight for new cover! I've got your tail, go!" Hall ran, Trace saw them all moving on tacnet without needing to turn. She ran backward at a zigzag, no easy feat in armour, and blasted at something down the far end that fired a quick shot. Ahead, Hall reached his new spot, with Carville and

Jokono close behind… but here to the side was another missing crate. "Beatle, hole on your left, take it!"

She dove in after him, and gestured Private 'Beatle' Tuo to silence, pressed against the crate wall.   More fire tracked toward Hall and Carville, who returned it.   "Porky, displace another three crates up, draw them after you."

"Got it.   Let's go Benji."   They left, and Trace looked at Tuo with a finger to the visor where her lips would be.   Sard hadn't seen them come in here, they were following Hall and Carville.   Trace crept to one side and peered upward.   There against the ceiling, IR showed her a slender, stalking figure, big rifle in its hands, keeping low and peering over the edge in search of a shot.   On the other side, Private Tuo also peered up… and indicated to her that he saw another one.   No, two, as he raised two fingers.   And now to Trace's left, up the aisle adjoining Hall's, the light scrape of approaching weapons.

Trace fired a frag around the corner, then stepped out and mowed them down as the grenade blew others tumbling into steel. The one above her shot at her as she kept going across the aisle and pressed her back to the crate.   The sard above leaned out to get a shot down, and she pointed straight up and blew its head off.

"Benji, Porky, get up top and knock these bastards down."   A short pause, then heavy fire streaking beneath the ceiling as Carville and Hall leaped quickly to the top crates, and put down fire.   Trace hadn't sent anyone up before because they were out-numbered and possibly out-manoeuvred up there — but after a nasty surprise, sard weren't expecting it.   Another one hit the ground nearby, and Carville gave a yell of triumph.

"Get some!   Get some!"   As he hammered burst after burst at running, leaping sard.   One more tumbled further up Trace's aisle, rolling as it avoided fire, and staggered back to its feet in a daze. Trace blew it in half.   Carville and Hall's fire stopped.   The red 'enemy' dots on Trace's tacnet display were gone, replaced only by two 'doubtful' greens, somewhere vaguely among the crates.

"Can't see any more, Major," said Hall.

"No, me neither.   Jokono, you okay?"

"Deaf," he replied. *"But thanks for asking."* Trace walked to the nearest of the four she'd cut down in the ambush. Sard bled red, just like humans. They didn't look like they ought to, with long, skinny-straight arms, clawed feet and multiple glazed eyes. A complex series of throat-parts extended down to the chest, where serrated edges vibrated in place of a vocal box. Some sard races made that noise from vestigial wings on their back. These wore no armour, but their rifles were powerful enough to hole even marine armour at close range.

"Holy fuck!" Carville was gushing, thrilled at the outcome and frantic with adrenaline. *"How'd she know? How'd she fucking know they'd fall for that?"*

"Benji!" she said sternly.

"Yes Major!"

"Get down off the stack, form up and get over here. We're not secure yet." And she flipped channels. "Hello Lieutenant Dale, where are you?"

"We've been listening Major, we're on our way. What's your situation?"

"Bunch of dead bugs and a dead Major General. Looks like they tortured him to death."

"Dangerous to be a friend of Phoenix," Dale remarked.

"Certainly seems that way."

CHAPTER 6

Erik met Trace on the *Phoenix* dock. On orange alert this portion of dock was filled with fully armoured marines, and transiting dockside traffic was obliged to take an inner-wall route to pass both *Phoenix* and her accommodation block directly opposite.

Trace stood with her Lieutenants Dale and Alomaim, visors up and discussing deployments. Normally Erik would rather discuss command matters in *Phoenix* and away from prying eyes and ears, but Trace rarely allowed herself to be separated from an ongoing situation. In command matters, she was old school, and liked to talk to her deputies face-to-face wherever possible, and see what they described with her own eyes.

"I have seven ongoing deployments," she told Erik without being asked. "We've got a group at the sard shootup with Jokono, he's trying to get details before station security clean it up completely, station security's not happy. Then there's the first bomb explosion and droid ambush, a few of Corporal Barry's people are gathering evidence but again, station security issues.

"I've got another group checking with people at Randal Connor's office on Jokono's instruction — they're pretty distraught, but a few are being helpful. And I've got two more securing the last of our food resupply, now that it looks like they could use an armed escort."

"Any idea where Romki is?" Erik asked.

"Hiro's on it."

"Because if the sard have him…"

"Hiro's quite sure they don't," Trace said grimly. She didn't sound any happier for that news.

"If he planted that damn bomb himself just to lose my marines," Dale growled, "he's going to wish the sard did grab him."

Erik blinked at Dale. Then at Trace. "You don't think…?"

"It's a possibility we've been discussing," Trace said flatly. "Romki's too damn smart for his own good. He's certain we're wasting our time with peace conferences, he thinks aliens are really the problem and should be our focus. So naturally he's gone to talk to aliens, minus our oversight."

Dale didn't look at either of them, and past the gel-smears on the little red scars on his face, he looked generally more pissed than usual. He'd let Romki get away. Meaning Romki hadn't been fooled for a second into thinking that his 'protection' was only that, and at his first opportunity had given his marine escort the slip. Erik recalled his recent discussion with Trace about *Phoenix* marines being less-than-brilliant at things that didn't involve actual combat. And thought further that if Romki were so desperate to wander Tuki Station on his own that he'd risk further attacks without any marines to protect him... hell, it was impressive enough that he'd retained the sense while under fire to grasp his opportunity. Impressive, and deeply suspicious.

"Be useful if we still had some friendly tavalai aboard the ship," Erik thought aloud. They'd had a group of them, rescued from the research base at Merakis three months ago. But traumatised, homesick and desperate to report events to their respective institutions, those had all disembarked at the first neutral station, and caught the first ride back to tavalai space. "To translate for us at least, independent of Romki."

"Yes, well we don't," Trace said shortly. "Lieutenant Alomaim thought it might be a smart idea to put a shuttle off station to keep an eye on the three sard ships we've got docked."

"The Major doesn't think those sard were warriors," Alomaim added. He was the youngest and least experienced of Phoenix Company's five lieutenants, but Trace rated him as high as any on pure ability. "They were caught off guard and they died too easily. More likely general crew off one of those ships — they're sard so they can all fight, but the aptitude varies significantly."

"I'm not sure what a shuttle on surveillance would achieve," said Erik. "Aside from make them more jumpy. We can't see anything from outside, and if they break loose we'll have warning, it takes a while to fire up those engines." He glanced across the dock, where some marines were waving down a dock transport, shouting loudly for it to find another way. Agitated barabo station workers shouted back, no doubt saying that the only 'other way' was to drive all the way around the station rim in the other direction.   "It all depends on why the sard killed Randal Connor, and whether the bombing was also them, or someone else completely.   It's not like we're short on people who might like to kill us."

"Jokono says the sard definitely tortured Connor for information," said Trace.   "They wanted to know something.   He's not sure they actually intended to kill him, it'll take a medical examination but station's claiming jurisdiction."

"Next of kin?"

Alomaim shook his head.   "No, Connor was here alone. Some friendly staff but most of them are barabo, just a few humans. Nothing to overrule station jurisdiction of the body."

"We could grab the body anyway," Trace suggested, with clear-eyed calm.   With Trace, that could mean blowing holes in people who got in the way.   Erik wasn't prepared to push that hard yet.

"No, Connor's registered at Tuki Station," he said reluctantly. "Even on a barabo station that counts for something.   Does Jokono have any ideas what the sard wanted?"

"Jokono doesn't guess," said Trace.   "Says it's unprofessional.   But I don't work in his profession, so I can guess that someone wanted to find out what Connor talked about with us. Because the odds that he was tortured to death for information just after speaking to us, and it having nothing to do with us, seem pretty astronomical."

Erik nodded.   "That follows.   But we discussed the peace conference at Joma Station.   Why would sard be the slightest bit interested in human politics?"

"Sard have been known to work for money," Trace reasoned. "It's all resources to them.   Fleet's got lots of money.   And Spacer Congress."

Erik's eyes widened.   "Assassinating our Worlder contacts? Using sard?"

Trace made an off-handed gesture, with a whine of armour servos.   "Sure, why not?   After all else they've done?"

It made sense. Fleet considered themselves at war with the more militant Worlder elements. And doubtless they were very interested in knowing what *Phoenix* was up to with its upcoming peace conference. Sending human agents out this far was impractical — humans were rare out here, and could not operate covertly. Employing common non-human local species was far more practical, and the most ruthlessly efficient of those were the sard.

And yet...

Trace sensed his discomfort. "You've got a better idea?"

"No," Erik admitted. He just didn't like Trace's idea. Trace's command style was to demand that anyone who shot down a good idea replace it with a better one. 'Don't give me problems', he'd heard her say more than once, 'give me solutions'. Erik didn't have one here, and so kept his opinion to himself. "I just feel like we're missing something. I want all off-duty crew moved back to *Phoenix* for the time being, just in case we have to move. Pity we don't have some friends among the barabo station security, it would be real useful to have someone else keeping an eye on sard movements on station."

"The real pity," said Trace, "is that we don't have another ten Jokonos. Hiros too. You tell Phoenix Company to take this station by force and we'll do it easy, but these investigations and cat and mouse games aren't what we're designed for."

"Learn," Erik suggested. "Next available opportunity, select marines with the best aptitude and pick Jokono's and Hiro's brains." He headed back to the main airlock ramp. "Never too late to start learning new skills, Major. Good job here, keep me informed."

Stan Romki sat in the tavalai bathing pool, warm water up to his chest as mist sprayed from hidden nozzles amid surrounding green plants. A tavalai waiter extended a long mechanical arm to place new food on the central table, and Romki smiled thanks.

"Milidana gudiji-nah," he said, and the waiter bowed her wide, smooth head, and moved on to the next pool.

Opposite him, his guest tried the vegetable dish in one of the small bowls. "It is passable," he said, also in Togiri. Romki understood it well, though today that was harder, with his ears still ringing from the explosion. Thankfully he was uninjured, Gunnery Sergeant Forrest having taken most of the flying glass on his armour. "So difficult to get good lily-fry in the Neutral Territories."

Romki tried it, and found it crunchy, mixed with salted fish and something much like vinegar. An acquired taste, very sour and thin, like most tavalai food. "You tavalai have been in space for forty thousand years," he said, "so long you barely remember which of your many worlds is your homeworld. But still you manage to get homesick for it, whichever it is."

The tavalai made an odd gesture, a tavalai shrug. He wore the light mesh shirt that tavalai wore in water settings, now slick and sticking to his mottled brown-green skin. Romki wore one similar — provided by the restaurant. "We are creatures of habit," the tavalai said about another mouthful. "I hear you have a new human ship approaching station. Human ships are rare at Tuki Station, but this has a human-space ID, very unlike what we would expect to find in any alien space. More human politics?"

Nearby, some tavalai children splashed and yelled. Insects and butterflies flittered from broad leaves to water lilies. A thin mesh enclosure overhead held in the insects, and while it was too porous to increase the air pressure to tavalai preferences, it did capture the humidity. Beyond it rose the sheer steel wall of a geo-feature, soaring up to the station rim ceiling high above. Tavalai liked their familiar pleasures, and this recreational establishment took advantage of one of the best exposed views on Tuki Station. Losers in the Triumvirate War or not, tavalai still had money — often far more than barabo. Tavalai money had built many barabo space stations, including this one.

"More human politics," Romki agreed. "I'm disinterested."

"One notices," said the tavalai with amusement. "What does interest you?"

"You know exactly what interests me. Tell our mutual friends that if they are also interested, they should head for Joma Station in Kazak System."

"The human peace talks? Our mutual friend will be just as disinterested."

"More happens there than peace talks. Whether the young fools who command *Phoenix* are aware of it or not."

"Fools, you call them?" His guest sipped a tall, charcoal-coloured glass with a straw. "Are they really?"

Romki sighed. "No, not really. But they are soldiers, and their vision is narrow. In narrow military matters, I'm sure that I'm the fool, and they're all geniuses. Humanity has spent all its one thousand plus years in space running from one war to another, avenging one catastrophe after another. The 'human cause', we call it. It is a filter, it blinds our view of everything. The filter must be removed before one can see clearly."

The tavalai chewed thoughtfully. "Our mutual friend could probably assist in that. Your ship's political situation with human High Command is fascinating. An opportunity."

"Joma Station," Romki said firmly. "Immediately, or you'll miss it. *Phoenix* is a fast ship."

"Oh I'm aware of that, believe me. Alo-powered. The real new power in the Spiral, whatever your human High Command thinks about it."

"And I am most aware of that," Romki assured him.

"Our mutual friend may still require another reason to be interested in Joma Station," the tavalai pressed.

Romki nodded. "I have one more very good reason."

After the meal, Romki stepped from the water and onto the dry-pad, where sonic vibration rid him of much of the wet. He put the mesh shirt into the bin provided, and was rubbing off the rest with a towel when he heard loud voices, shouts in Togiri and Palapu, and the crash of something being overturned. He peered through the green fronds that divided the many dining pools, and saw commotion near the entrance, hands waving, people running. Then he heard the shrill cicada-shriek, rising from one, then multiple sources, and glimpsed a stalking black figure, dodging past attempts to block its path.

Romki swore with real fear and struggled quickly into his clothes. He was unarmed of course — *Phoenix* marines were hardly going to trust him with firearms, and the restaurant would not have held a gun for him anyway. He pulled shoes on quickly, without time for socks, and as he turned to go was abruptly grabbed from behind and spun down against the base of a garden feature. He tried to fight the grip, but one attempt showed him the futility

"Don't move," said Hiro Uno in his ear. "Keep very still."

Peering through greenery, his face pressed to sweet-smelling moss on false rocks, Romki glimpsed shiny black legs, like stilts. The sard moved silently, three-clawed feet upon the floor. Sard never wore shoes, he recalled... or not outside of combat armour or pressure suits. He gazed up, heart thudding in his ears, and saw that multi-eyed face, black beads arranged about grasping mandibles, looking this way and that. There were no restaurant staff yelling at this one, or trying to herd it. The other noise was a diversion at the entrance, he realised. This sard, and perhaps others, had snuck in some other way, while attention was elsewhere. Sard hunted in groups, and coordinated with effortless synergy. Individually they weren't especially effective at anything, but together they were brilliant.

It stalked silently onward. "There's five," Hiro whispered in Romki's ear. "Seven at the door for a distraction, five penetrating within. Five is a hunting party, seven is a command group." Because sard loved prime numbers, and assigned different primes to different tasks. Hiro seemed familiar.

"Are you armed?" Romki murmured.

"Is a black hole black?"

"Are they armed? Who are they after?"

"Yes, and you." Hiro waited a moment longer. "Very quietly, stay low and follow me precisely. Let's go."

He released Romki and moved off, low and crouched between the green partitions. Romki followed, trying to imitate Hiro's effortless glide. They emerged onto a new pool, wider with several low tables and half-consumed food, filled with children and some adults who peered anxiously in the direction of commotion and shouts beyond the greenery. Several looked at Hiro in alarm as he passed, and Hiro made a motion of forefinger to lips, shushing them. The tavalai only looked confused.

"They don't understand what that means!" Romki whispered harshly, then gave them a more familiar, calming gesture with both hands as he passed. Beyond the pool, Hiro immediately crouched, pressed low and motionless against a tree fern trunk. Romki copied, and ahead a tavalai staffer shouted angrily and waved his arms at something out-of-sight... and leaped back in fear at a torrent of rattling clicks, and the swipe of a long black arm. A knife flashed in that clawed hand, and the staffer yelled for help and retreated. The sard looked about, Romki ducking down just in time.

A moment passed, then Hiro was beckoning him on, and Romki went to find the sard departed. Another pool, this one empty, and some stairs beyond, leading down into the floor. A sard stood astride the stairs, peering down into the room below. Rather than scampering for cover before it turned, Hiro kept moving forward, drawing a silenced pistol from his jacket. He shot the sard point blank in the back of the head, caught the body as it fell, and lowered it soundlessly. Beckoned for Romki to follow him, and moved quickly down the stairs, leaving Romki to pick his way over the splayed limbs, one still twitching.

The callousness horrified him. Sard or not, this was a living, sentient, highly intelligent being. And Hiro had dispatched it like swatting a fly. Romki followed Hiro down the stairs and into a spotless kitchen with gleaming steel benches, and several tavalai and barabo chefs huddled warily in a corner, some brandishing knives.

"Come on," said Hiro, moving rapidly down the next corridor.

"Stay here," Romki told the chefs in Togiri, and followed. "Hiro. Hiro!" As Hiro paused in the corridor to glance back, thinking Romki had discovered something important. "No murder! Not for me, I won't allow it!"

Hiro frowned incredulously. "Murder? That was a sard."

"Yes, murder!   Just because we've been at war with them does not give you the right to go around killing them at your pleasure!   They're intelligent beings and humans should have standards!"

Hiro gave a humourless smile.   "You think you know them because you've studied them?   You're an ignorant fool and you understand nothing.   If you really understood how *they* think, like you're always proclaiming you do, you'd favour genocide, like I do. There's an access hatch ahead, now move."

CHAPTER 7

"Hey there guys!" Lisbeth said brightly, holding a food tray she'd brought from the hotel restaurant. Here on the second floor there wasn't as much traffic in the accommodation block, nor were there the crates and armour lining the walls. But here beside the elevators were Privates Dagan and Katta from Echo Platoon, in light armour, guarding a door. "I brought you some food, I figured you must be hungry by now."

"You can't come in," Dagan said apologetically. "Sorry Lis." They didn't really know her — there were about two hundred marines in Phoenix Company, and Lisbeth hadn't been on the ship long enough to get to know more than a handful. But gratifyingly, word had spread amongst the marines that Lisbeth Debogande was a good sort, and most treated her like a familiar friend.

"Oh come on, it's been a whole day!" Lisbeth protested. "Look, at least let me update him on..."

"His information updates are being restricted too," said Katta. "LC's orders."

Lisbeth sighed. "Have you heard anything? Has he asked to speak to anyone?"

"Couldn't tell you if he had."

The door opened, and Jokono emerged, immaculate as ever with neat hair and lean, brown features. Seeing him in a *Phoenix* spacer jumpsuit took some getting used to... though probably not as much as it did for him, looking at her. That had been a recent change — typically he preferred civilian suits.

"Hello Lisbeth," said Jokono with a frown. "Something I can help you with?"

"Yes! I just wanted to see Stan, thank you..." and she moved to step past him. He stopped her.

"I'm sorry Lisbeth, your brother's orders were quite specific."

Lisbeth looked at him in disbelief. "Hang on, you work for me! You're the head of Debogande family security!"

"And the senior member of the Debogande family present is your brother," Jokono said calmly. "And actually…"

"Erik's the senior member of the family?" Lisbeth retorted. "Says who? He's not primarily serving the family interests out here — he's the commander of *Phoenix*! The only family member out here entirely on family business is me! So that means *I'm* the senior Debogande here!"

"And actually," Jokono completed his previous sentence, "my contract is with your mother. How best to serve that contract is up to my discretion, not yours. I'm sorry Lisbeth — this is a *Phoenix* matter, and your brother commands *Phoenix*. He's ordered that no one sees Romki. That's final."

Lisbeth glared at him. Anger was not usually her style. And the last time she'd tried to boss around family employees with the 'don't you know who I am?' routine, she'd been five, and her mother had scolded her so harshly that she'd cried. But the lesson had been learned — in the Debogande family, you respected people according to how well they did their jobs, and not whether their job performance personally benefitted *you* in any way.

But she'd worked with Stan Romki a lot in the past three months, helping him with his analysis of the captured hacksaws. And perhaps it was her mother's insistence on respect for ability above personal charms, but she didn't find him half as aggravating as some of the regular crew appeared to. And she couldn't stand seeing him locked in solitary like this for doing something that surely, *surely* had some kind of reasonable explanation…

"Hello Lisbeth," came Romki's voice from out of the still-open door behind. "Please don't worry about me, they're treating me very well, and I did violate their rules so I have only myself to blame."

"Stan!" she called past Jokono's shoulder. "Stan, do you need anything?"

Jokono hit the door-close before he could reply. Lisbeth gave him a genuinely angry stare. Jokono looked pained, not having seen that expression many times before. But he did not apologise.

"There you go boys," Lisbeth told the marines, handing over the food tray. It was a barabo nut fudge, in tasty squares. The crew had taken a liking to it, and the chefs said it was healthy. "I don't blame *you*, you're just doing your jobs."

She gave Jokono a final glare and departed toward where Carla and Vijay were waiting for her at the end of the hallway.

"I'm less concerned with Romki being an ass than I am with the sard trying to kill him," said Erik, chewing his thumbnail.

Just because *Phoenix* was docked, that didn't mean the bridge crew shifts were any different. In fact, it meant that Lieutenant Draper, *Phoenix*'s second-shift commander, was getting a lot less sleep whenever Erik left his usual first-shift post to go attend to some matter on station.

"Tried to kill him twice, maybe," Trace added. "The bomb might have been sard too." The full first-shift crew were in their seats, watching scan, listening to coms, the same as they would in deep space. Trace had joined them, with Jokono and Lieutenant Dale, who had the most combat experience of any marine, including plenty against the sard during the war. They gathered about Erik's command chair, holding to low overheads and screen supports in the crowded bridge. Standing was always uncomfortable on the bridge — seated was the only way to feel like you had any room, with all your screens and displays arranged about you. "If Romki didn't arrange that himself to get away from his escort."

"You seriously think that?" Kaspowitz asked her, a skeptical eyebrow raised.

"I might."

"No you don't." Kaspowitz was one of the few on *Phoenix* who'd dare contradict her so openly. He thought she was starting to take her disagreement with Romki personally, and had told Erik so. She liked to pretend she was unemotional, Kaspowitz insisted, but in truth she was quite raw, and wrapped herself in thick Kulina armour to hide it. She'd broken the Kulina oath of unquestioning service to

Fleet because she'd come to care about one man, and one ship and its crew, more than the oath that insisted she should have betrayed them. And now she was determined not to let that one man's legacy — Captain Pantillo's legacy, the father she'd never truly had — fade and die. Captain Pantillo had given everything to prevent civil war between Worlders and Spacers. Now that was Trace's cause too, and she didn't take kindly to Romki's provocations.

"So what *does* Romki have to say for himself?" Erik asked Jokono.

"Oh, that conversation didn't get much beyond him explaining to me how stupid I was and that I couldn't possibly understand." Jokono's was the dry humour of a policeman who'd learned long ago to be amused by infuriating behaviour because that was easier. Erik thought he might be nearly as even-tempered as Trace. "But I don't believe he's capable of blowing anyone up, least of all people standing directly alongside himself."

"I thought you didn't make guesses?" Trace accused him.

"Getting a good read on a person's character has a way of allowing you to narrow the possibilities," Jokono replied, unruffled. "Romki's no coward, he's a very brave man considering he's not a fighter beyond some chah'nas martial arts training. But he does value himself and his personal safety far too highly to attempt anything that reckless. Reckless acts are beneath him. He's not one to leave things to chance."

Trace listened with her nose wrinkled in distaste, but did not protest the analysis.

"So do the sard have it in for Romki?" Lieutenant Shahaim wondered from her Helm post at Erik's side. "Or for *Phoenix*?"

"They killed Randal Connor," Jokono reminded her. "Tortured him for information. Connor had no connection to Romki that we know of. As far as we know, they'd have done the same to Romki — tortured him and killed him. Which suggests that their interest in Connor and their interest in Romki is the same, and the only thing that links them is *Phoenix*."

Erik frowned. "You're saying they didn't kill Connor to find out about his role in our peace conference?"

"Well who can say for sure?" said Jokono, with an expansive gesture. "But Romki certainly has nothing to do with the peace talks…"

"The sard don't necessarily know that," Trace interrupted.

"Yes, but attacking a tavalai recreational facility, evidently in search of one human occupant, seems a very public disruption even for sard. Sard have served the tavalai, and though tavalai influence here has reduced, the tavalai still built this station and have great status. Which indicates that the sard place great value on Romki, as a target, if they're willing to upset the tavalai to get him. You don't cause such a big disruption for someone who just *might* know something of what interests you. You cause it when you're absolutely *certain* that person knows something of what interests you.

"Romki is quite well known for his knowledge of alien civilisations. He's very disinterested in human politics by comparison. Even sard could discover this, with basic research, especially amongst the tavalai. Romki is particularly well known to the tavalai. Even famous, in some small academic circles."

"So what's your theory?" Erik pressed.

"No theory," Jokono said calmly. "Just deduction. Sard are known to be very unsubtle in pursuit of their interests. If their interest was *Phoenix*'s role in human politics, then Romki was a very poor target. It seems unlikely. Which if true could mean that Connor was also not targeted for his interest in human politics."

"What then?"

"I don't know. Something concerning *Phoenix*. Something about us that interests the sard. Probably not about human politics, something else."

"This ship was built by the alo," Dale said grimly. "That might interest them."

It was Romki's pet theory — the alo having a hacksaw connection. Alo were on the human side of the Triumvirate War, sard on the tavalai side. Many tavalai found alo expansionism almost as worrying as the human kind, and speculated that the humans were really only puppets in the war, while the alo were the puppet-masters. Romki more or less agreed with them.

"It might interest them," Erik agreed, glancing at his nav feed as Kaspowitz flashed the latest automated approach routines from the human ship *Grappler*. It had arrived twenty-one hours ago, its transponder stating its previous location as Cyranis, and clearly the ship that Randal Connor had told them about. The one carrying senior Worlder representatives, an advance party to discuss matters before the peace conference on Joma Station. "But if the sard had wanted to get information on *Phoenix*, they'd have been better off targeting our crew, not a passenger. I still feel we're missing something. Something big. If you're trying to run calculus without half of the data, you're in real danger of getting misled by false conclusions. We need more data, I'm wary of too much guessing." He glanced at Dale. "You've seen sard up close Lieutenant, more than any of us. Anything to add?"

"Don't be fooled by sard," Dale said grimly. "I've told all my marines when we fight them — they can seem stupid and primitive sometimes, but don't believe it. Their maths are better than ours, for one thing."

"Way better," Kaspowitz agreed. "I've seen some of their navigation calculus off a captured ship. It's insane. Their computing tech is the one indigenous technology they rock at."

Dale nodded. "Sard play chess. Individual moves in isolation look reckless and suicidal. Only when you step back and see the whole game do you see how it all makes sense. They love maths and prime numbers, and they love patterns in those numbers. Everything is tactical, and everything we've seen them do so far is with some kind of big plan in mind. That's not my prejudice — that's just how they think. They can't help it."

"Excuse me, LC?" Erik looked to the speaker — it was Lieutenant Shilu on Coms, peering back past his heavy headrest. "I've just put in a second request to talk to *Grappler*'s captain, and again I've had no reply. The last request was thirty minutes ago."

"What's their range?"

"Now at thirteen seconds light, ETA on current approach path another seventeen hours. I'm getting an automated response, it just seems odd because according to Randal Connor, they're here to see us, right?"

"Right," said Erik, equally puzzled. "Maybe they're worried about someone listening. Keep trying, if they don't want to talk I suppose there's nothing we can do. But keep an eye on them."

"Aye sir."

"And Major? Since we've got a situation on docks, it might be an idea to think ahead of time how we're going to arrange our greeting party."

Trace smiled at him benignly, like an adult to a small child who had just mentioned something obvious. Erik rolled his eyes and dismissed them.

Lieutenant Wei Shilu repressed a yawn as he stood on the late off-shift dock opposite Berth 30. On the berth display besides flashing lights, some barabo writing scrawled, then flipped unexpectedly to English text — Alberta Freightlines, *Grappler*, then its human-space registration.

"Hey look," Shilu said to Lieutenant Alomaim alongside. "English. I didn't know Tuki Station had any English."

"They all think the humans are going to come and save them from the sard," said Alomaim, glancing up-docks to where Second Squad were deployed in sections against inner and outer walls, watching dock traffic with weapons at ease. "They might make English compulsory next. Rather than learn to fight sard themselves." He murmured low commands into his com, advising one of the sergeants.

Shilu felt very exposed out here, on the cold dock with no armour or weapons. Being surrounded by Bravo Platoon helped, Second Squad to his left, Third to his right, and First with their Lieutenant about and behind him. Even Heavy Squad was out, with full scary weaponry, chain guns and autocannon, in pairs against the inner-rim wall between barabo shopfronts. With three sard ships at dock, no one was taking any chances.

"Lieutenants, Grappler is at thirty seconds," came Second Lieutenant Abacha's voice in Shilu's ear. Second-shift were still on duty on *Phoenix*, the LC and the Major supposedly asleep, though knowing them both, probably awake and watching from their quarters. With second-shift needed on the bridge, it had fallen to a senior but not *too* senior first-shift officer to forego sleep and greet their Worlder 'friends' from *Grappler* in person.

"Copy *Phoenix*," said Shilu. Somewhere out there beyond the massive steel wall, the huge freighter was rotating into a one-G barrel roll in pursuit of its moving berth. Shilu repressed another yawn, and glanced at Alomaim. The man hadn't yawned yet. How was it that marines always managed to make spacers feel inadequate? "Any guesses how *Grappler* just happens to be given a berth two from *Phoenix*?"

"We asked?" Alomaim suggested. He was a young man, barely mid-twenties, a brown face, serious and impassive. "Not many stationmasters out here would say no to *Phoenix*."

"LC never asked," Shilu said smugly. "It was just assigned. Someone knows, up in station bridge. Everyone's watching us, and now they're watching *Grappler*."

"Right," said Alomaim, watching some passing barabo civilians, trailed by a rolling luggage bot. "That's why I'm not in bed."

A siren wailed, then a crash of grapples, and the decking shook and squealed as enormous supports caught the freighter's weight. Shilu noticed some barabo open cars careening across the dock, at speeds that would have gotten them arrested on a human station. They pulled up alongside Shilu, Alomaim and First Squad, some workers in orange jumpsuits, and some officials in the robes of barabo formal attire. Several listened on coms to station workers outside, working the grapples and umbilicals that fastened *Grappler* to station. Outside would be a scene of frantic activity, but here on the dock below the entry ramp, all was serene.

Finally, with another siren and flashing light, the main airlock door atop the ramp opened. The barabo waited for someone to emerge, seeming more interested in the heavily armoured marines, and the *Phoenix* bridge officer. Shilu smiled at them and nodded, and they grinned back with those big barabo teeth. Customs officials, station inspectors and the like. Not a weapon amongst them.

A minute later, they were still waiting. The head barabo in robes looked impatiently at Shilu, as though he might know the reason for the delay. Shilu returned a mystified gesture. It seemed to translate, for the head barabo barked instructions and several jumpsuited workers strolled up the ramp to investigate. They moved as unhurriedly as barabo always moved, chatting casually and chewing on something that on a human station would probably also get you arrested.

The workers arrived at the main hatch and waited, peering inside. One looked back at Shilu, as though wondering what he could call out in English.

"Hello Lieutenant Shilu," came his uplink. *"This is the LC, is there some kind of delay?"* So of *course* the LC had been up and watching.

"I'm not sure sir," said Shilu. "The hatch is open but no one's coming out. I can't go up there myself without being in breach of station protocol."

"Barabo will take all day if you let them. Make some haste."

"Yes sir." Shilu made his way over to the group of puzzled barabo, and Gunnery Sergeant Brice and Private Cruze thumped with him in close protection. The head barabo saw them coming, with some alarm, and waved a hand at them to stop. Shilu and the marines stopped, and the headman yelled and waved his long arms. More barabo scampered up the ramp, with more urgency than the first pair.

"LC, I think they've got this," Shilu reported.

"So how many barabo does it take to change an LED?" Cruze wondered. Atop the ramp at the hatch, more argument erupted, hands waving, exasperated gestures down the tube… where were the damn humans? And who was going to go and get them?

"Twenty," Sergeant Brice replied. "One to change the LED and nineteen to make it unnecessarily complicated."

After much heated discussion, the first two workers were sent into the access.

"You think they could have just done that first?" Cruze wondered. "Without ten others coming up to tell them?"

"Knock it off," Alomaim told them. "Eyes open, watch your sector."

More waiting. The new bunch of barabo clustered at the hatch and peered within, talking on coms. For the first time, Shilu began to feel it. Cold discomfort. What if…? But he couldn't act on what if, he had to wait for something concrete. But, what if…?

"Lieutenant Alomaim?" he said cautiously. "I think this might be trouble."

He'd barely completed the sentence when the barabo at the hatch all began shouting together, and staring at the one robed official with the com. His eyes were wide, and he looked alarmed. Then he began shouting, but one of the two workers returned at a run dashing through the mob of his companions and straight down the ramp. He ran fast, legs wobbly, eyes wide with fear.

"Yes I think you might be right," Alomaim said grimly. "First Squad, prepare to move in. Second and Third, watch our backs."

Shilu took off striding once more toward the barabo headman, and arrived just as the worker did and began gibbering in terror, hands and arms waving. Shilu activated his belt speaker, and blinked the icon for Palapu translation… but the earpiece gave him nothing but static, unable to make sense the worker's fearful rush.

"What?" he demanded finally of the headman, and the speaker made that into a harsh Palapu demand. "What does he say?"

The headman stared at him. *"Gone,"* the speaker translated. *"All gone."*

Shilu turned to look at Alomaim, but the marine lieutenant was already moving, First Squad jogging with a crash and rattle up the ramp as barabo wisely made way.

"No Lieutenant, you stay," Sergeant Brice advised, still at his side with Cruze as he made to follow.

"Like hell," Shilu growled, and ran up the ramp, his guard in tow.   Into the bright-lit, freezing access tube, armoured marine backs ahead of him and only too conscious of his utter vulnerability. His breath gusted white, and then came the main *Grappler* hatch, unmanned and unguarded.   A big primary corridor, airlock controls and interior lights all active, marines moving fast and fanning out ahead, coordinating in tight groups.

Shilu turned a corner at the A-bulkhead, and found Lieutenant Alomaim and several others stopped, staring at a wall. Across it, a shocking red blood spatter, a hosing spray like some horrific artwork.   Beside it, a bloody human handprint.   Shilu shouldered past the marines, and saw on the floor beyond another bloody trail, like a body being dragged.   Long marks on the deckplates, where blood-soaked fingers had clutched for anything to stop that progress.   No one said a word.   The cold discomfort Shilu had felt on the docks had well since turned to dread.

"Hello LC," he said quietly to coms.   "Are you seeing this?" He had no mounted camera, but the marines had plenty.

"I'm seeing this.   Phoenix is on red alert, the Major is deploying with Echo Platoon.   You are to secure the ship, Echo will be on your six ASAP."

"Copy LC."

"LT, this is Amal.   We're on the bridge, there's no one here. It's a ghost ship, it docked on automatic.   We didn't get any coms from it on approach because there was no one to talk to."

Alomaim swore.   "First Squad, do not touch anything.   I repeat, do not touch anything, we have forensics on the way and we'll want to know what happened here.   We will commence a total sweep of the ship including all off-access sections around the cylinder — we'll use grapples and climb it if we have to.   Third Squad and Second Squad will join us as soon as Echo Platoon arrives, Heavy Squad will remain on dock and assist Echo in providing cover. Be damn careful — whoever did this might have left boobytraps, or there might even be one or two of the bastards still aboard. Let's get it done."

Movement around a corner, and marines swung weapons into line… but it was the remaining barabo worker. He carried a small backpack, the kind of thing a freighter crewman might wear. It was torn and bloodied, and the workman handed it to Shilu as he approached. The tears in the bag were in parallel lines, as though made by claws. Sard claws. Within, working items, mostly electrical tools, all secured to the bag with fastenings, professionally arranged. On the bag, a stencilled name — T. Rodwell.

"*Phoenix*, I've found belongings marked with the name T. Rodwell, check to see if that's *Grappler* crew."

"*Phoenix copies.*"

The barabo workman looked upset, hands trembling as he kissed an amulet around his neck, and glanced around in fear. Many barabo were animists. This one was afraid of dead humans haunting him.

"Thank you," Shilu told him, and the translator spoke. "All humans thank you. Now go, *Phoenix* will take it from here."

"*No,*" the translator earpiece replied. "*I stay, I help.*"

"No, this is a human ship. *Phoenix* will look after human ships. Tell your people — this is now *Phoenix* business."

The barabo stared at him. "*Sard do this? What you do sard?*"

"Well," Shilu said grimly, "I'm sure we'll think of something."

CHAPTER 8

The borrowed dock jeep and trailer thumped across the deckplates, concerned civilians getting hurriedly out of the way. Both the jeep and the luggage trailer were loaded with heavily armoured marines, driven by an unarmored spacer who could still fit behind the steering wheel. Trace sat behind the driver's chair in the lead vehicle amidst a cluster of armoured bodies, and talked on coms as the driver smacked the horn and marines waved for crowds of staring barabo to clear out.

"Jokono says his contact can confirm the sard who killed Randal Connor were from X1575. He says they've matched IDs on the bodies off the ship's manifest." X1575 was the sard ship at Berth 24. Sard gave their ships numbers, not names, with the station adding an 'X' to identify a ship as sard.

"And Jokono trusts this contact?"

"He says she seems reliable. She's senior station security, and she's very scared of increasing sard presence on station. Apparently she and some other barabo station security would like to see us do something about them."

Which meant there was a chance this sard vessel wasn't responsible at all, Trace reckoned. But station would like *Phoenix* to think they were, to suit station's purposes of warning the sard. No matter. Trace would never have risked hitting any other species' ship unless certain of individual blame, but with sard she was past caring. Sard were a collective anyway, and disdained individuality. It wasn't like they'd protest individual rights.

The jeep rumbled and thumped past dockside markets, barabo and other species pointing and shouting, a few cops talking urgently into coms. Trace was confident no one was going to try anything. There probably wasn't enough firepower on station to oppose a single *Phoenix* squad, let alone a full platoon... to say nothing of the entire company that would descend on anyone who tried.

Before the ramps and protruding wall hydraulics of Berth 24, however, there emerged a cluster of squat, green-uniformed figures with light rifles, looking their way. Tavalai. Trace surveyed the dock ahead — shopfronts on the left inner wall, market stalls before them, separated from the rest of the dock by patches of garden green amidst the deckplate. Light transports were parked against the outer wall by some protruding umbilicals. It added up to reasonable cover.

At sixty meters she called it. "Spacer Ellis, halt here! Turn us ninety degrees across!" As the driver did that, turning sharply as marines leapt off. "Marines, spread and cover! I want a good field of fire! Command Squad on me!"

She leaped and ran for the right wall, accelerating to a sprint nearly as fast as she'd manage unarmored, but with six times the mass and a hundred times the noise. Ahead the tavalai were falling back in bewilderment, some aiming rifles, others shouting for orderly retreat, no one apparently in charge. Trace found cover behind a parked vehicle and saw the unfolding position of her marines on tacnet, the upper-left portion of her vision, an inverse curve of clustered blue dots across the dock. Civilians ran aside, some in the markets picking up all the wares they could carry first. Trace raised her Koshaim for a sight at the lesser-armed and armoured tavalai, and her visor highlighted a convenient row of exposed targets. If she ordered it, they'd all be dead in seconds, cover or no cover. One did not confront United Forces marines on open ground unless one was similarly equipped.

And yet, from the tavalai ahead, there now walked a small group — five individuals, all with light rifles, all striding defiantly with weapons at cross-arms and not even bothering to aim.

"Okay," Trace said conversationally to keep the tension low. "This does not appear an imminent threat, but I want all guard up. Echo, get me a forward flanking position on the left, I want them encircled. Watch your spacing and keep every position double-faced with those shopfronts at your backs."

Lieutenant Zhi gave sharp orders to Echo Platoon, and marines jogged forward up the markets on the left. Facing Berth 24, they were going to be exposed from the shopfronts at their rear, as Trace had said. It meant only half could watch the direction she wanted, and they were in danger of getting scissored in a counter-attack. Which meant she couldn't push them all the way out to encircle Berth 24 — without overwhelming numbers, most berth-encirclements were in truth only quarter-circles.

She gave a signal, got up and started walking toward the approaching group of tavalai. Command Squad formed up around her, Privates Rolonde and Terez ahead on either side — it restricted her field of fire and vision, but it was protection, and if she'd demanded her forward view cleared they'd probably have ignored her. If Command Squad hated anything she did, it was this — walk in full view on an open dock with no cover. Even in full armour, snipers could be deadly if the weapon were big enough.

The five tavalai stopped before her, visibly alarmed as she came two steps closer and halted right on top of them. The suit made her tall, or taller at least, and though broad, tavalai were on average no taller than humans.

The lead tavalai activated his belt speaker, and spoke in Togiri. *"We are Taglinium,"* the speaker translated. *"You are trespassing on this dock. Turn around and go back to your ship."*

Trace opened the coms channel back to *Phoenix*. "Hello *Phoenix*, are you listening? I understand that they are local tavalai fleet presence, but what is Taglinium?"

"Hello Major," came Lieutenant Shilu's voice in her ear, back on the bridge as first-shift took over from second. *"Tavalai have so many fleet factions and special units, and much of it is political. I think all you need to know is that this is what's left of the tavalai military presence on Tuki Station after everyone else withdrew."* In other words, Shilu had no idea.

Trace activated her suit's own speaker, translator set for Togiri. "Sard from this ship have murdered a Tuki Station registered worker, a human. His name is Randal Connor. We have proof, provided by Tuki Station security."

"It does not matter," the tavalai retorted. *"Tavalai fleet guarantees all security on Tuki Station, and tavalai treaty alliances*

have priority." Sard, that meant. Sard were tavalai allies, and this tavalai was protecting his alliance partners. Either someone else on station had tipped them off that *Phoenix* was about to move on the sard ships, or they had a station informer. Or they'd guessed.

"Sard attacked the human vessel *Grappler*, newly arrived at station," Trace continued. "All crew are missing presumed murdered in cold blood."

"Prove that it was this sard ship," the tavalai dared her, head high and eyes defiant. All marines who'd dealt with tavalai reached the same conclusion — the amphibious buggers had some truly giant balls. Utterly outgunned and facing every tavalai's worst nightmare — angry UF marines — this one was prepared to spit in her eye and die on principle. *"Prove that it was this ship that attacked your human vessel, or go away."*

"All sard look alike to me," Trace replied with deliberate menace.

The tavalai's nostrils flared. *"And this is human justice? No wonder your own Fleet cannot stand the sight of you, Phoenix."*

Trace nearly smiled. She flipped up her visor, and looked upon the tavalai with unimpeded vision. "They'll turn on you next. You know that, don't you?"

The tavalai blinked, as though a little surprised to be still alive and arguing. *"Sard have been our allies for a long time. They died for us in the war, in their millions."*

"Sard die for no one but themselves." Past the tavalai's shoulder, his troops were spread in moderate cover, rifles ready but not aimed. Beyond them, about the berth ramp, a dark and spindly cluster — sard, creeping and flowing like oil. Watching with beady-eyed interest. "They've got their eyes on this space, on this system, on this station. The barabo are terrified. Our information on the murder of Randal Connor came from barabo security. You have two allies out here, sard and barabo. You will protect only one?" The tavalai's eyes darted, and for the first time he looked uncertain. "And the one you choose to protect is *this*?"

She pointed past him, at the dark sard cluster. The tavalai did not look. *"We have orders,"* he replied. *"The sard alliance will remain strong."*

"And the barabo won't fight, so you'll just leave them to the sard? You laugh at human justice, but humans know all about tavalai justice. The tavalai justice that left humanity to die at the hands of the krim. Given two species to defend, you'll pick the one least worth saving."

"You are the bringers of genocide," the tavalai retorted. *"You will not be allowed to murder innocent sard here, like you did to the krim. Not on a station protected by the tavilim."*

"There *are* no innocent sard," Trace retorted. "Just like there were no innocent krim. Knowledge of that fact is how the tavalai learned to control them in the first place. But now you owe them, and you're scared and vulnerable, so you've forgotten." The tavalai blinked. Whatever he'd expected from the murderous armoured humans of tavalai nightmares, it surely wasn't this. "Now stand aside and let us deal with this horror that the tavalai have let loose on the galaxy."

"We will not stand aside. You will have to kill us all."

Trace took a deep breath. She switched channels, and deactivated the translator. "Hello *Phoenix*. LC, any ideas?"

"No ideas, Major," came Erik's reply. *"You know the tavalai. An asteroid is more flexible."*

"They've enough firepower here that we can't do it peacefully. I can't personally see how killing them will further our interests here."

"Me neither. And I'd never ask you to." That's what you think now, Trace thought drily.

She reactivated the translator. "What is your name?"

The tavalai drew himself up. *"Tibrotilmanium."*

"Tibro. Humanity holds you responsible for the deaths of Randal Connor, and for the human crew on *Grappler*." The tavalai stared, as though suspecting he was about to die. "You will have to live with that on your conscience, and I want you to contemplate whether the protection of murderers is any better than the murdering itself.   In the meantime, I suggest that you request some reinforcements from your command, because these sard ships are clearly just forward scouts for a larger sard force lying somewhere out in the deep lanes, sard who appear to have taken an unhealthy interest in my ship, and in your station."

"*We have no reinforcements,*" Tibro retorted.   "*Your Fleet destroyed them in the war.*"

Trace gave a short, humourless bow.   "You're welcome," she told him, and turned to go.

Romki blinked awake against the pillow.   Lisbeth Debogande stood before him, a steaming cup in one hand, calling his name.

"Lisbeth?"   He hauled himself up and rubbed his face. Lisbeth presented him with the cup.   It was coffee, and he sipped — black, no sugar, as he liked it.   The hotel room door was open. Outside in the hall, *Phoenix* crew were moving with purpose, shouting, carrying things.   Evidently his guards were gone, as previously they'd not been allowing any visitors.   "What's going on?"

"*Phoenix* is leaving."   Lisbeth looked about the room.   "Is this your bag? Is this all you have?"

"Well yes.   I wasn't here for long.   I don't suppose there's time for a shower?"

"Departure is in fifty-two minutes, lockdown in thirty-five, so no, I'd say not.   Come on, better get moving.   I'll wait outside while you dress."

"Lisbeth?   Why are we moving?   This is earlier than scheduled, did anything happen?"

"I'll explain on the way."

Five minutes later they were leaving the hotel lobby amidst crazy activity, armoured marines using their suits as loaders, carrying heavy crates across the dock amid streams of crew with bags, weapons and other, miscellaneous gear.

"If *Grappler* made it into the system," Romki said with concern as they walked, "and wasn't seen to be intercepted by any sard vessel, then where did it happen?"

"No one's sure," said Lisbeth.   One of her bodyguards, Carla, walked ahead with rifle and light armour, while the bigger one, Vijay, watched their rear.   "There's some speculation that it might have happened back at their midpoint jump on the way here, that the sard took all the crew then sent the ship along on autos.   All of *Grappler*'s records and navlog have been erased, so there's no clues there."

"But they're certain it was sard that did it?"

"Quite certain."

"Then the sard are making a move for power in Outer Neutral Space," Romki concluded, sipping the coffee she'd brought with one hand, hauling his duffel bag with the other.   "That's *very* cocky of them, it's well understood that the tavalai are the power in this space."

"Were the power," Lisbeth corrected.   "They lost the war."

"Indeed."   They sidestepped a commandeered flatbed as it trundled by, loaded with bags.

"Stanislav?" asked Lisbeth.   "What were you talking to those tavalai about?   When you snuck away?"

"I didn't 'snuck' away Lisbeth," said Romki around a sip of coffee.   "I got blown up and was lucky to escape with my life, let alone uninjured.   I was always of the opinion that I'd be safer alone, and I made it so."

"To go and talk to a tavalai other than the one you were supposed to be meeting with," Lisbeth retorted.   "Where did the first one go?   You were supposed to meet him but his restaurant blows up and you go to another one instead... and it turns out you weren't any safer because the sard turn up and cause a major disturbance, and probably would have killed you like they killed Randal Connor if Hiro hadn't tailed you."

She sounded plaintive and upset.   Romki sighed and rubbed his head.   And realised somewhat belatedly that it was concern in Lisbeth's voice.   He wasn't quite sure what he'd done to earn it...

though perhaps she was as much concerned that he'd somehow betrayed her.

"Look," he attempted. "I'm sorry but I won't reveal my contacts. Just be assured that I'd never do anything to put *Phoenix* in any danger. I believe that this ship has inadvertently found itself on a very important mission. A mission that I will do everything in my power to assist."

"And that just happens to not be the mission that its commanders believe it's on," Lisbeth jabbed.

Romki glanced at her. And nearly smiled. She was quite like himself in some ways — infinitely better with people, it was true, though that was mostly not because he had no talent, but because he'd stopped trying decades ago. But she also had a high intellect, was very perceptive, and possessed a dogged determination to call a fact a fact when she saw one, no matter whom it upset.

"There may be some truth to that," he admitted. "But not, I hope, as much truth as you think."

"Why did those sard try to grab you, do you think?"

"I'm really not an investigator, Lisbeth. Why don't you ask your man Jokono?"

"He's not my man any longer," Lisbeth said grumpily. "He's found a higher calling."

"On this voyage, I feel he may not be the only one."

CHAPTER 9

They pushed away from Tuki Station and Vieno orbit in late first-shift. Erik wanted to be in the command chair for undock, given those three sard ships at station, but those did not twitch as they powered away. They ran at a one-G push for two hours, the ship effectively turned on its end for the purposes of the crew, who walked on the walls instead of the floors as *Phoenix* gained position up Vieno's gravity slope.

Kazak was next, by way of an intermediary stop at Chonki. Vieno's current orbit about its M-class star placed them on the wrong side, meaning a long haul across the star's zenith until they were clear of the solar gravity well and ready for jump. In combat conditions they could have done it far faster, but it put unnecessary stress on any ship, let alone one recently damaged and patched like *Phoenix*. A United Forces ship in combat could rely on friendly docks in which to repair any incurred damage. Out here, *Phoenix* had none, and Erik was not prepared to take any unnecessary chances.

It gave them a three day cruise after a jump pulse through the thickest polar intensity of the star's radiation, with all magnetic shielding maxed and corpsmen distributing radiation sensors throughout quarters just in case. Erik left the chair to Lieutenant Draper at the shift change, while Second Lieutenant Dufresne took Shahaim's post and Second Lieutenant De Marchi took Kaspowitz's. All three retired to Erik's quarters, just a few paces off the bridge, and Kaspowitz made them all some coffee at the little brewer, while Erik showed Shahaim the latest simulation results.

The sim chair was back in Engineering where it could still be used at dock. Erik had used it to run a full combat simulation of *Phoenix* being attacked by seven enemy vessels in a difficult system. He'd made them tavalai, partly because the computer knew how to simulate that well, and partly because it was very possible, out here. It kept reflexes sharp, and gave *Phoenix*'s little gang of starship pilots something to talk and bond over. Typically there'd be six of them, Commander and Helm for each of three shifts, effectively pilot and co-pilot. Now the Captain was dead and Commander Huang had remained behind by her own choice on Homeworld. That made Erik, previously third-shift commander, the acting-captain. Shahaim retained her role at first-shift Helm, and Draper and Dufresne, second and third-shift Helms respectively, were now Commander and Helm of second-shift. And now the arrangement was becoming problematic.

"Two minutes seventeen," Shahaim announced, sipping coffee while watching the wall screen of the sim that Erik had seen five times already. "He misses that evasive by, what, twenty degrees? And doesn't burn hard enough, which... yeah, look here. Ordinance incoming, he's having to waste energy and headspace going extra-evasive."

"Draper's conservative," Erik agreed, looking over crew reports that had accumulated while he was sitting the chair. Shahaim had had other duties at Tuki Station, she hadn't had a chance to review the sims yet. "He misses nothing, but his responses are sometimes below optimum."

"Good recovery here," Shahaim added. She was sixty-four, and had the longer curls that Fleet regs allowed women to get away with if they chose. No such luck for men, and some complained about it. Erik's tight curls gave him the option of not caring. "Good pattern of fire. Nice V-boost, good position."

"His spatial perception is great," Erik agreed, grimacing at a report from crew systems at how air ventilation units were now well behind maintenance schedule due to lack of manpower. It was the same all over the ship. "His biggest problem is he gets behind in the count. But he always recognises it immediately, and recovers well."

"Hmm," said Shahaim into her coffee cup. "Simulated opponents are more forgiving."

"Sims are for learning, and you don't learn much when you're dead all the time."

"I learn plenty," Kaspowitz offered, settling his lanky frame into the chair bolted to the lower desk. "I learn I'd rather not go into combat with him commanding."

"Most situations I think he'd do okay," Erik said charitably.

"Of the last three firefights this ship was in," Kaspowitz said drily, "which would you categorise as 'most situations'?" Erik did not reply. His Navigation Officer made a good point, as usual.

"And a good escape," Shahaim observed as the sim concluded. "Sim ranks him eighty-four percent. I think that's a bit generous, I'd say high seventies. Erik?"

It was formality to rank these things. Though out here, there was no formal review procedure, and no official records to send back to HQ. No doubt HQ would have been even more interested than usual to receive them if they had. "Seventy-five," said Erik.

"A harsh marker," said Kaspowitz.

"The Captain always was with me. Check out Dufresne."

"Good?" Shahaim wondered, changing over to Second Lieutenant Dufresne's sim recording.

"Interesting," said Erik. And waited, reading more reports as Shahaim watched the recording. Kaspowitz watched too, but as a non-pilot had little directly to offer. Five minutes later, Shahaim paused the screen.

"Well," she said with emphasis, a thoughtful frown on her face. "That *is* interesting."

"I marked her at eighty-five," said Erik, finally looking up from his slate. "She's not always that much better, the difference is usually more like three or four percent. But it's noticeable, and it's consistent."

"Dufresne's better?" Kaspowitz asked.

"I gave her eighty-eight," said Shahaim. "But then I mark a little higher than Erik."

"I've been stepping up her difficulty too," Erik admitted. "Small increments, and I haven't been telling her. She's twenty-six, Draper's twenty-eight, and Draper's had the more operational experience, thus the higher rank. Draper also had the better Academy scores. But you know, some people only really blossom once they get out on duty."

"Hang on, I thought the consensus was that Draper's a gun?" Kaspowitz asked.

"It was," said Erik. "And he is. But Dufresne's better."

"The thing with being a hotshot all through the Academy," said Shahaim, "is that sometimes you start to just take your greatness for granted." She glanced at Erik, meaningfully.

"Don't look at me," Erik said mildly. "Everyone thought I was getting a free ride on Mommy's name. Every time someone read out my sim scores it was with this note of disbelief in their voice."

"That's *why* I'm looking at you," the older woman said shrewdly. "Some people are too secure, while others are insecure."

"Gee, thanks." But he was smiling. They were all friends here, and even the ship commander could take some gentle ribbing from those most closely ranked. But not all of the ship's officers were on such good terms.

"So we've got the wrong person in command of second-shift?" Kaspowitz summarised. A brief silence.

"Hmm," said Shahaim. "Awkward. And then there's Justine's politics."

Erik scratched his jaw. "Yeah. And she's as stiff as a board."

"We used to say that about you," Kaspowitz told him.

"Great," said Erik, with humour this time a little more forced. "And thanks again."

"Don't mention it. Draper's got an ego on him. Won't take it well, and then they have to work together."

"I don't know if I want to do it yet," said Erik. "Suli, you mind going to relieve Justine for a moment?"

"Now?" Shahaim asked in surprise. Erik nodded. Shahaim looked impressed at the decisiveness. "Certainly. If my dinner arrives, please keep it warm."

She got up and left. With the bridge just meters away, it wouldn't take long. Kaspowitz remained where he was, reclined with long legs stretched, and confident that if Erik had wanted him gone, he'd have said so. In truth, Erik wouldn't have had Kaspowitz anywhere else. He'd been on *Phoenix* the longest of just about anyone, and had an uncompromisingly dry view of people and human nature that Erik found valuable.

Soon the door opened, and Second Lieutenant Justine Dufresne stepped inside, freed from her post now that Shahaim was occupying it at Lieutenant Draper's side. Dufresne was slim with short, dark hair and no apparent sense of humour. Kind of pretty, but pinched and tight, as though something were clenched up inside. It wasn't just the current situation that did it, either — she'd been like that since she'd first come aboard ten months ago, after Lieutenant Perot had been promoted to LC on another ship. The crew were calling her 'Giggles', with great irony, and she had few obvious friends. She'd been Erik's Helm on third-shift for most of that time, but despite spending eight hours a rotation on duty together, Erik still could not say he knew her particularly well.

"Sir," she said to Erik precisely. "Permission to enter."

"Permission granted Lieutenant." She came in, and Erik gestured to the unoccupied part of his bunk — in tight quarters there weren't many seating options. Dufresne sat neatly, knees precisely together, hands on thighs. She may have held the same rank as Kaspowitz, but in the unofficial way that so many things worked on a warship, everyone knew better than to believe she held effectively the same authority.

"We've just been looking at your sim-scores, Lieutenant," said Erik.

"Yes sir?" Expectantly.

"Very impressive. You and Lieutenant Draper both." She nodded shortly. Clearly she wanted to know how she'd done. "Lieutenant, how do you feel about this current situation?" She blinked at him. "*Phoenix* being declared a renegade vessel?"

"It's unfortunate, sir."

Erik waited a moment. One of Kaspowitz's eyebrows furrowed slightly, watching her. "Only unfortunate?" Erik pressed.

"It's very unfortunate. I don't think anyone likes it."

Another time, Erik might have rolled his eyes. It wasn't exactly revealing. "Your family has a long record of service. You're known to the crew as a vocal Fleet patriot."

Dufresne stiffened, and her lips tightened. "I'd like to think that patriotism is a common condition among the crew, sir."

"Indeed," said Erik. "But we've had people on this ship lately who felt so patriotic toward Fleet, that they could not stomach our actions against Fleet Command. No matter what Fleet Command did to Captain Pantillo."

"Sir, am I being accused of something?" Three months ago, three *Phoenix* spacers had tried to kill Erik. All had been casual friends of Dufresne. Given how few friends she had, it had raised considerable suspicions, but ultimately she'd been saved by the fact that like with most people, she hadn't known them very well.

"Not at all. But the situation may arise where you find yourself in effective command of this warship." He paused to let that sink in. "And before that happens, I'd like to know your view of our current situation, vis-a-vis the Fleet. Candidly."

The young Second Lieutenant thought about it for a moment. Calculating what she wanted to say. "Sir, I feel that Fleet Command has done very poorly by us. But I also feel that Fleet Command are only human, and capable of mistakes. We should not write off the entire institution because of the mistakes of a few very senior officers."

"I agree completely," said Erik. "I hold great hopes that the rest of Fleet will come to see reason."

"Do you think they might grant us pardon, sir?" It was the closest thing to eagerness, or raw emotion, that Erik had heard from her.

"I think that's entirely possible," Erik agreed. "But not with Supreme Commander Chankow, and the likes of Fleet Admiral Anjo in charge. We have to keep the pressure on them. If Fleet sees that the current commanders have screwed up, as you say, then their replacements may view our situation differently."

Dufresne nodded shortly, but with real feeling. "You're looking to confirm my loyalties to *Phoenix* sir. If we're fighting for a full pardon? And for Chankow and Anjo to be brought to justice for what they did to the Captain? I'm all for that sir. One hundred percent."

Erik glanced sideways at Kaspowitz. Kaspowitz didn't look convinced.

"Listen," said Trace as she spotted his bench presses. It was unnecessary, because the machine held no free weights and worked on adjustable resistance arms. But accidents had been known to happen on ships that manoeuvred at 10-Gs, and this particular machine had once broken an unlucky spacer's ribs when the safety height had failed to engage. "Take the damn promotion. Make yourself captain. If you don't want to pin the damn wings on yourself, I'll do it."

"Doesn't exactly solve my problem, does it?" Erik retorted beneath the bar, straining as he completed his set.

"You have too many lieutenants," Trace spelled out for him, as though he were a little slow. "You have a great fucking logjam of lieutenants, people all of whom are one tiny little rank below you. It challenges your own authority, and it means the ship has no clear second or third-in-command. Worse, it means that you can't establish a clear authority of rank in your little pilot problem. If you're the Captain, then Suli's Commander, then you make either Draper or Dufresne the LC and get that tension sorted out for good. No one has egos like pilots — you get the command ranks sorted out for good or people will start killing each other."

"Gee thanks," Erik gasped, and hung up the bar with a thud. About them, weights crashed, treadmills whirred and music played. "What's the single greatest motivating force driving this crew?" he asked her. "What holds them together in the face of everything? Justice for the Captain. He was a living legend. I've shown I'm a good pilot and a passable commander, but they're not going to go to hell and back for me. Not yet.

"If I declare myself captain, then suddenly we have two captains on the ship — the current one, and the ghost of the legend they served under for all those years. And you can't have two captains on a ship."

He slid out from under the bar, and Trace took his place. She dialled back the weight resistance on the bar to something lighter, and began lifting. Being considerably smaller, and female, Trace's marine augments did not allow her to maintain the power required to lift weights as heavy as an augmented man could. What her augments did allow was the explosive release of power in short, athletic bursts for activities that required it. Her bench-press was only two-thirds of Erik's, but in sparring she had to hold back in case she broke his bones.

"On that sim you all did," she said as she strained against the bar. "What was *your* score?"

"About ninety-five."

"Right. Which as much as I understand the details of warship piloting, is pretty much inhuman and insane. But still you don't think you're up to it."

Erik gritted his teeth, standing over her with hands beneath the bar. How could someone he liked and respected this much be so consistently aggravating? "I do think I'm up to it."

"So act like it."

"Crew morale in a ship is not such a simple thing as mind over matter!"

"You can't allow other people to dictate your actions to such an extent that your own free agency dissolves amongst them. For all practical purposes you *are* the captain. So be the captain. People can't follow what doesn't exist. Make it real, and they'll follow you." She finished with a hiss, and hung up the bar.

"And then there's the politics," Erik insisted. "Fleet will paint me as the egotistical rich boy with delusions of grandeur. If I promote myself to captain, it will look awful and play straight into Fleet's narrative."

"And again," said Trace, sitting upright on the bench and adjusting her gloves, "you're letting others make your decisions for you."

"You don't do politics by telling everyone else what their opinions are," Erik retorted. "That's how you start wars."

"And you don't convince anyone to take you seriously by putting more value on their opinion of you than your own," Trace said firmly. "Come on, your turn." As she got up and gestured, impatient that his rest breaks took too long.

"So I'm not supposed to take anyone's opinion of me seriously except yours," Erik said sarcastically, sliding back under the bar.

"To be in command is to be alone," Trace said firmly. "In this sense at least. It's all on you. You have to know that, bone deep, or you can't function." Erik began lifting, Trace spotting. "On my first posting, I was sent to some crappy little industrial station in Diri System, the kind of place they send Second Lieutenants straight out of the Academy to boss some leadfoot marines around for a few months before a combat command." Leadfoots were what ship-company marines called station marines, or marines posted to guard space facilities. It was important work, but it lacked the prestige of ship-postings.

"They gave me my first platoon, but my company commander was a cynical prick, overlooked for promotion lots of times, no surprise to me. He didn't like some shiny Kulina lieutenant taking one of his platoons from a previous lieutenant he'd liked much better, and he didn't like that I wouldn't drink with the boys. Probably didn't like that I wouldn't fuck with the boys either, we still get a few men like that in the marines. Two more, push!"

As Erik gritted his teeth and heaved against the bar, finally finishing with a gasp and loud clang as the bar locked in place.

"So he started riding me," Trace continued. "Extra duty, insults and jokes in front of the men. I think it made him feel bigger to boss a Kulina around. Maybe he thought he could make me cry, I don't know." Knowing Trace, Erik found the prospect preposterous. "There's not a lot to do on station duty, just endless drills, every now and then you get an interception on a station warship. Lots of opportunities for idle hands to make trouble."

Erik nodded, sitting upright and sipping his water bottle. "I know, that was my gig before *Phoenix*. Helm on *UFS Firebird*, station defence duty.   Our marines got into more fights with each other than the tavalai, I hadn't seen a shot fired until I came here."

Trace nodded.   "This Major's name was Langdon.   I put up with it for two months, figured it was character building... plus the guys in my platoon were okay.   Then I got my first boarding credit, intercepted a smuggler, it was a good haul and the local cops were pleased.

"And so with my first commendation under my belt, I figured enough was enough and filed a formal complaint against Major Langdon."   She slid back under the bar as Erik vacated the bench. He'd heard this story before, but not from Trace herself — something about some nasty proceedings in her first station posting, not the kind of blood-and-guts tale most were accustomed to hearing about Major Thakur.   In retrospect it all seemed a bit anti-climactic. "Which became a total mess, of course.   He hated me, his friends hated me, and I had another two months of nasty bullshit from all sides.   A few times I got death threats, you know how marines can get if you piss on their boots."

She started lifting hard, as Erik spotted.   "So what did you do?"

"Well Langdon made the mistake of going off-the-record, so he could threaten me.   I told him I'd put a bullet in his head, and I didn't care what happened to me after that because at least I'd have improved the Corp by his removal."

"Seriously?"

Trace nodded, face strained as she pushed.   "I meant it.   And he saw I meant it, and that bought me a little space, because he at least realised Kulina don't bluff.   Never go off-the-record against someone who's less scared and more violent than you.

"The point is that I could have tried to be nice.   I could have kept my head down and put up with it.   But I was raised to put professionalism above everything.   I can forgive any number of sincere fuckups, but I won't tolerate unprofessional behaviour, above or below my present rank."

She heaved the bar one last time with a clang, and sat up.   "I have my standards.   They cause conflict with others, sometimes.

That's okay, it's not personal, but I know myself and I know what I do well. And if I abandon those standards in order to make other people less upset with me, then I betray myself, and I betray every marine under my command who relies on my standards to help keep them alive. Out here, standards are life and death. As officers, we don't just enforce standards. We *are* standards. It comes from here." She pointed to her hard midriff, eyes firmly upon him. "Now you're a nice guy. You're much nicer than I am. But that means compromising with other people, because that's what nice guys do. I'm telling you you can't afford it."

Erik leaned forward on the bar. The gym was too noisy for anyone to overhear, and they were close enough to keep their conversation at lower levels. But he lowered his voice a little more, just in case. "Trace. I appreciate you think I need my butt kicked to get me into shape to command this ship. I appreciate that the jump from third-in-command to first is a big one, and I appreciate that you've genuinely helped me make that transition. But I don't need a personal guru. Seriously."

She barely blinked. "Yes you do." He shouldn't have expected anything else, Erik thought with a sigh. "You know why?"

"Because I'm too nice, too soft, too coddled and too inexperienced, and I need you to put some steel in my belly." Sarcastically.

"Yes," she said, with only a hint of humour. "All of that, but mostly this — your current level is here." She held up a hand, flat and straight. "I think you could get to here." She raised her hand up a considerable margin. "The further you have to go, the harder the push you'll need to get there. You're already one of the best warship pilots in the Fleet, but there's more to commanding a carrier than fast hands and fancy moves."

"*You'll* never know," Erik retorted.

"Sure," said Trace. "But if you don't think that commanding marines through ten years of combat has taught me a little more about this than three years as LC has taught you, then I've got news for you."

"Fine," Erik conceded.   He was getting much better at arguing with her without getting upset.   It was all business to her, and she could say cutting, personal things and mean nothing at all by it… except what she always meant, which was one or another variation of 'get your shit together'.   "So how did you end up on *Phoenix* after that mess on station duty?   People don't make those complaints mostly because it leaves a black mark on their record, and people with black marks have trouble getting postings like this one."

"Oh that was always fixed," Trace said dismissively.   "The Captain knew my Academy instructor, Colonel Timothy Khola, and got recommendations from him.   I was at the top, and that Langdon bullshit didn't put the Captain off — he asked a few questions and found that Major Langdon really *was* an asshole, didn't affect my progression at all."

"Ha," Erik teased.   "And people accuse us Debogandes of nepotism."

Trace frowned.   "Is it nepotism when the best people get promoted?"

"My point exactly.   What happened to Langdon?"

"Retired a year after I got the Liberty Star.   Went into business, used to throw my name about to improve his contacts. Said he used to be my commander, was like a father to me, taught me everything I knew."

Erik smiled broadly.   "Aren't people great?"

"When I found out I put out a statement saying Langdon was the biggest prick I'd ever served with and the exemplar of everything a marine shouldn't be.   He threatened to sue.   A visit from a Kulina rep with a JAG lawyer dissuaded him."

"Friends in high places, Major," Erik said with dismay. "Where would you be without friends in high places?"

Trace fought back a smile.   "Come on, stop yapping and lift. I've seen old ladies who take less time between reps than you."

CHAPTER 10

Phoenix crashed out of jump in Chonki, a sparsely inhabited red dwarf system whose elliptical ring contained more rubble than planets. The astronomers said a major planetary collision billions of years ago had wiped out a few of Chonki's main worlds, which had in turn pulverised the remainder with debris that had failed to re-coalesce into new worlds. System entry from zenith or nadir was safe enough, Kaspowitz insisted, but anything faster than a mild push along the elliptic would run you headlong into a rock.

"Scan, report!" Erik demanded as they dumped velocity, his forward visual filled with the dull red light of Chonki's star.

"Feed looks clean," said Second Lieutenant Geish at Scan. "I'm getting rocks, nothing too close, standby."

"Nav-buoy signal is coming in clear," said Shilu from Coms, routing that through to Nav.

"Yeah I got that Coms," said Kaspowitz, watching navcomp compile a growing picture of their position. "Looks like we're in the slot, give me thirty seconds to lock it down."

"Everyone keep their eyes open," said Erik. "Lots of rocks means a good ambush…"

"Pulse up!" said Geish, and Erik's heart skipped a beat. Navcomp showed him a position, but couldn't fix the distance…

"Range?" he demanded.

"I can't get a clear reading! It's close, heading 310 plus 68!"

Too close, Erik thought. "Evasive!" and he kicked the attitude thrusters sideways, then slammed on the mains at 6-Gs building to 8 as scan searched for a clearer read. And switched to uplink vocals as the massive weight of Gs made breathing hard and speaking impossible. *"Orange alert! Someone tell me who just pulsed and where he is!"*

When you came out of jump, and someone was cycling their jump engines right next to your position, that was generally bad news. It was possibly a fluke, and they'd emerged right next to some bewildered freighter... but commanding a combat carrier meant taking no chances.

"*Second pulse!*" Second Lieutenant Jiri announced from Scan Two. "*Heading 100 by minus 170!*" All over the place. Like *Phoenix* had come out of hyperspace right in the middle of them.

"*Red alert! Arms, full lock and prepare to fire!*"

"*Arms has nothing!*" Second Lieutenant Karle retorted. "*Come on Scan, get me a feed!*"

"*Incoming fire!*" Geish replied. "*Heading...*" Erik didn't hang around to find out, killed thrust, swung them back in the direction of travel, and pulsed hard. *Phoenix* emerged travelling a significant fraction of light faster than she had been. No doubt their pursuers would now do the same.

"Arms, full engage!" he told Karle in a brief moment of zero-G, as the crew cylinder ceased rotation for combat.

"Full engage aye!" Thud thud thud as *Phoenix*'s cannons opened up, armscomp laying down its best statistical guess on where that pursuit might be following them. At this heightened speed, Chonki's rocks were suddenly the same threat that ordinance was. Scan showed Erik a whole field of rocks, big and small ahead... currently none were intersecting with their course, but any one of them could be hiding a new ambush, and he swung them sideways and burned hard to give them more room.

He could see three red dots on scan now, as Geish finally got a feed on who had ambushed them — warships of some kind by the way they were thrusting hard to pursue, pulsing even now to match their racing velocity. If they were smart, they wouldn't come out of a pulse too close, or their excess velocity would bring them right into *Phoenix*'s killzone before they could correct.

"*I'm only counting three,*" Erik told his crew, already calculating ahead for the course needed to hit Kaspowitz's next jump to Kazak, and escape. "*If they know where we're going they'll be blocking our next move.*"

"*I'm getting more ahead!*" said Jiri. "*Two marks 350 plus 20!*"

Their spacing was too wide, Erik saw. Against a less powerful ship the trap would have caught them in a crossfire that increased the statistical likelihood of a hit to near-certainty. But *Phoenix* accelerated faster than nearly anything else in space, and could string jump pulses together tight, without risk of overload.

"Course shift, hold on," he announced, and dumped velocity with a massive pulse, flashes on scan as pursuing ordinance overshot. A massive 10-G burn to change course three degrees, then realign and pulse up once more as pursuing warships closed the gap fast. *"Arms, target Mark Five, we're going fast and hard."*

"Aye LC, Mark Five targeted!" Mark Five was what Armscomp was calling that blocking ship ahead, nearly close enough now to be on max visual, a tiny racing dot against the starfield, tail aflame as it burned hard for position.

"Pulse up in five, Helm feed the course." As Shahaim put that projection into Navcomp, which in turn told Arms where the shot was going to be... and *Phoenix* shook from a near detonation, defensive arms intercepting something too close for comfort.

"Mark Four is pulsing, tangential intercept!"

"Fire field is red!" Shahaim yelled, as Navcomp calculated all the converging fire from five ships, and suggested they were about to get slammed.

Erik powered them at 11-G, main engines protesting red from overheat, then hit the pulse once more... and threw them forward at huge acceleration...

"We can't pulse again on this tangential to solar mass!" Kaspowitz yelled at him as they raced toward the target Mark Five.

"Arms acquire starboard!" Erik instructed.

"Arms acquire starboard aye!" said Karle, as Erik turned them side-on for evasive burn, all *Phoenix*'s weapons blazing. Huge flashes as incoming fire was intercepted, then outgoing fire simply overwhelmed the opposing ship's defences and it vanished. *"Mark Five destroyed!"*

"Copy Mark Five destroyed," Erik said calmly as he swung them again to miss a rock looming ahead, and throw off pursuing fire. The ship designated Mark One pulsed hard to chase... and

came out a little closer than was wise, trajectory curling outward on the solar gravity slope. Scan showed its fire cutting across *Phoenix* from that angle, aiming to intercept somewhere ahead of them, and Erik swung them evasive once more with a thundering roar from the mains, blurring vision and a gasp for more oxygen. "*Mark One predictive*," he formulated, and tumbled them abruptly end-over-end to brake hard in their direction of travel, as Mark One was suddenly paralleling them to one side.

Weapons thudded as rounds went outgoing on a pattern spread ahead of Mark One, acceleration 20-Gs with self-correcting guidance, the warheads would hit just about anything they were fired at within their cone of vision, so long as nothing intercepted them, or the target didn't abruptly move elsewhere... which in FTL combat it almost always did.

"*Marks Three and Four just pulsed up!*" came Geish's formulation in his ear. "*Parallel course heading...*"

"*I see them,*" said Erik. Getting into a one-on-one shooting match with *Phoenix* was a very bad idea — *Phoenix* simply had too much firepower and would intercept or dodge nearly anything a single lesser warship could throw at them. But if he let three warships bracket them on parallel course simultaneously... Jump lines read green and he dumped velocity abruptly as the chasing ships raced by, and once-distant ordinance came racing up real fast. But once he hit the 11-G corrective burn, as everything shook and crew gasped and hissed upon the edge of unconsciousness, none of the other vessels could change direction as fast. Two-degrees course change and he pulsed once more, racing up on the far side of Mark One as his two friends struggled to swing across and cover.

Having dumped velocity as well, Mark One realised the mistake and pulsed up, but not as hard and lacking traction upon the solar gravity slope, and now found himself isolated and without friends in the kill-zone of a warship that outgunned him by four-to-one.

"Get him now!" Second Lieutenant Harris was shouting, but Karle was already firing as scan showed the jump field attempting to reestablish about Mark One, but too many pulses too close together and a smaller warship would find the jumplines struggling to recharge in time.

Several small flashes from interceptions, then a big one, and Mark One's signal broke apart to become several.

"Burning on intercept," Erik announced, swinging them once more and roaring the thrust as he set off toward Marks Three and Four. Mark Two was now well behind, and the third and fourth warships saw the human battle carrier thundering toward them with more blood on its mind, and fired up their jump fields.

"*They're leaving!*" Geish announced as he saw it first, and then Mark Three dumped hard and went evasive, attempting to correct course toward some preset escape route. Mark Four followed, then a pulse arrived from far behind as Mark Two jumped, having already set off on an escape run up the gravity slope.

For a brief moment, Erik considered pursuing. But there were large pieces of their second victim still roughly parallel to their present course, and a reasonable chance some of the crew quarters would still be intact, and perhaps even a few live crew left to question.

"Helm, lay me an intercept course on Mark One," he announced, swinging them once more and laying on the thrust. "We're going to go and see if anyone's still alive over there."

"Aye LC," said Shahaim. "I'll get you a final course just as soon as we're close enough to see which is the crew quarters." If the crew quarters still existed at all — they'd hit it pretty hard, and *Phoenix* ordinance was not merciful.

"Major Thakur, I have an intelligence mop-up for you," said Erik, watching the course indicator projected onto his irises edge around by fractions of a degree with every few seconds of thrust. "Give me status and a boarding plan as soon as we have a visual, if you please."

"*Copy LC,*" came Trace's voice from midships, where she typically rode out combat jumps in full armour with the rest of her marines, strapped into an acceleration sling. "*Delta Platoon is on standby, Lieutenant Crozier will handle this one directly, Echo and*

Command are reserve." Meaning Trace was not going to take this one herself for once. About damn time, Erik thought.

"I copy that Major, give me an assessment ASAP." Marines were the experts on how to get aboard wrecked ships, and in guessing how long it would take, and what the dangers were. "Scan, keep your eyes peeled for more contacts, lots of rocks about and places to hide."

"Aye LC."

Three minutes' hard burn brought them up behind the tumbling wreckage, then Erik flipped them end-over-end for a slightly softer decelerating burn, as scan finally identified which part of the ruined steel had been the crew quarters.

"Scancomp says it's likely a dekanur-class, probably an X-5," Geish announced, as Erik eased the thrust back to a gentle 4-Gs on approach.

"That would match their performance," Shahaim affirmed. "Mains reading within parameters, systems flush in progress." After a huge series of burns, the engines needed to take a gasp and refresh themselves, and the boarding would be their chance.

The remains came clear on Erik's screen for the first time — about thirty large pieces and countless small ones, a cloud of independently moving debris, with some big, further-flung bits tumbling in the distance. Less than half the original ship, and clearly this bit had been the crew cylinder, though one side was largely stripped away, exposing inner corridors all mashed together like tin foil.

"Yeah, his ammo blew," Geish observed the obvious. His voice was grim, and not at all triumphant. It was always a sobering reminder, to see the mess that modern weapons could make of a warship. *Phoenix* was more than a weapon to its crew — it was a home, a fortress, a place of life and character, and had perhaps even a soul. No doubt this ship had seemed the same to its crew, also. And in the blink of an eye, had been turned into this.

"Helm, get me a docking angle," said Erik, easing thrust back further. "We're going to have to give it a nudge. Major, you looking at this?"

"I see it. I figure there's probably survivors on the far side of that crew cylinder. Are we on full recovery, or intelligence gathering only?" Anyone they left on this wreck was going to die, and slowly. Its transponder was dead, the only possible rescuers were those who had seen the fight, and knew where to look. Anyone else, entering blind into a vast solar system of any scale with no idea what had happened, had as much chance of spotting a single moving shipwreck as a golfer had of hitting a hundred holes-in-one in a row. Spacer code typically dictated that randomly encountered vessels in distress must be rendered every assistance, regardless of species or politics. When that vessel had just tried to kill you, discretion was allowed.

"We've got fifteen minutes on site, maximum. If you can get all of them off in fifteen, we'll do it. Less time is preferable. Anyone still aboard after fifteen gets left behind. I want particular attention paid to possible prisoners — if this is a pirate or other freelancer it's not impossible." Remembering Tif and Skah, whom Trace had grabbed personally off a chah'nas warship to the total surprise of all.

"Fifteen minutes, copy. Any idea what species they are?"

"Major, this is Shahaim — if it's a freelancer, out in this space, it could be anyone."

Erik timed the final thrust precisely, *Phoenix*'s mains sending smaller bits of debris scattering, other parts bouncing off the armoured hull. Combat carriers were designed to withstand thrust loads that would tear lesser vessels in half — *Phoenix*'s spine was parallel columns of load-bearing alloy of similar molecular strength to diamond, and its primary armourplate was the same. Nothing stopped high-V rounds, but it provided reasonable protection against medium-V, and low-V debris impacts in docking manoeuvres were insignificant.

At one kilometre he cut thrust completely and spun them once more, end-over-end, then engaged bow thrust at a much more gentle negative-Gs. Still they felt unpleasant, pulling everyone forward against their straps, necks suddenly straining to keep heads upright. Erik's main screen flashed with a new course — Shahaim's feed for the docking intercept, calculating the direction of spin and where *Phoenix*'s armoured nose would need to nudge the wreck to stop it tumbling and engage combat grapples.

"Lieutenant Crozier, this is the LC. First contact in twenty seconds, stand by for combat dock."

"Aye LC, Delta Platoon ready and standing by." In midships, forty-four armoured and pressurised marines were wrapped in their acceleration slings, waiting to pop them open and move into the main airlock. This one would not be as scary as boarding a hostile vessel where crew would likely shoot back, but even on disabled wrecks, things could go wrong. On Delta's private frequency, Lieutenant Crozier would be warning her marines of the target's damaged layout, and what formations to progress in.

"Priority," Second Lieutenant Jiri announced tersely from Scan Two. "I have a jump pulse at 23-by-268. Cancel that, I have *two* jump pulses at those coordinates. Cancel that, *three* jump pulses at those coordinates. Range six seconds light. Doppler pattern indicates inbound, I repeat, pattern indicates inbound."

"If they're combat and have pulsed up full, they'll be here real quick," Shahaim added.

Crap, thought Erik. Had they seen them? Jiri's scan feed came through on his third screen... these were jump pulses to accumulate V, the angle was all wrong for hyperspace arrival from another system. Meaning these three new targets were already here, sitting and watching, unnoticed until now. If they'd been using transponders, as all innocent civvies were supposed to do, *Phoenix* would have noticed it by now.

He hit bow thrust and halted their approach to the wreck. "Lieutenant Crozier, we are on hold for boarding. All hands standby."

"Delta Platoon copies LC."

"Command copies LC," Trace added.

"Sir?" said Jiri, a little cautiously. "I'm... the computer's reading those pulse patterns in a combat stagger. It's... the range intervals are twenty-one K by offset twenty-one K, degrees 339 between first and second mark. Between second-and-third mark the same pattern, only sixty-three K, degrees also 339."

Which was a precise geometrical pattern if ever there was one, distances between all three ships at multiples of twenty-one kilometres, offset from each other's trajectories by twenty-one degrees short of the straight three-sixty.

"Fucking sard," Shahaim announced. "Can we take three?"

"Computer gives me no indication of ship class," Jiri added. The best sard warships were a concern, they did not do combat carriers, but their main strike cruisers were nearly to human and chah'nas standard. In about thirty seconds, Erik knew he'd have to make a decision to stay and fight, or boost up and run.

"Be real nice to get some intel on who they are and why they're coming after us," Kaspowitz suggested.

"Main cannon down to thirty-one percent ammo," Karle warned from Arms.

"Triple pulse!" Jiri shouted.   "That's all three together, that's..."

"That's far too big!" Geish warned at Scan One.   "No way that's sard... sir, they just boosted up like fucking alo, they're coming..." And Erik saw the numbers screaming in red on his main screen, and hit the thrust from zero to nearly 10-Gs with no warning at all.   About the bridge, crew went from intent on their screens, to plastered back against their chairs and fighting to breathe, braces engaging to keep arms locked to their chairs in useful position. Erik hit attitude thrust with little movements of his fingers on the lower, G-grip parts of the chair-arm controls, skidding them sideways in a great spray of thrust and tumbling debris out behind.

"Fire incoming!" Geish warned, as Scan One's feed showed intercepting rounds tearing in at ridiculous velocity.   It wasn't possible that any sard ship should pulse that deeply into hyperspace, and come back out with this much V.   Sard were mathematically brilliant but struggled to apply the maths to complicated real-world solutions like starship engines.   Tavalai tech was universally superior to sard, and tavalai were often reluctant to share their best stuff with their troublesome insectoid allies. Sard ships were simply

not this good, or not that any human on record had ever seen. But now Erik's screens were showing him fifteen seconds to incoming fire intercept, at speeds that they simply wouldn't survive if accurate...

"Arms! Full defensive spread!" Watching the jumplines charge up, the FTL drive struggling for purchase on the gravity slope as *Phoenix* fought for position. Defensive armaments thudded to intercept incoming rounds, and still they had nothing like enough speed... scan gave him a brief glimpse of three ships' worth of incoming fire like a hailstorm, and he threw them desperately into a corkscrew as scan broke up in interception impacts, massive flashes thermo-nuclear in scale from the sheer kinetic force of incoming V...

Jumplines flashed green and Erik pulsed... a stomach-lurching flip into a semi-alternate dimension... then back out and racing at three-times-again the previous already-high velocity, incoming and outgoing rounds now far behind but still catching up. Navcomp showed his blurred and vibrating vision the course he needed to get them on to make the next jump to Kazak... a thirty-eight degree deviation from their current course. There was simply no way he could make that course change at these velocities, he'd have to decelerate first and the moment he did that, they'd all die.

"Nav! Alternate jump coordinates now! Get me something close, we have to leave!" The thing was, *Phoenix* simply didn't know this region of space very well. Galaxies were big, and stars swarmed by the dozen in every direction you pointed a spaceship, but they had to be close enough to reach in a jump. *Phoenix* maxed out at about thirty lightyears — more than that was possible in one jump, but increasingly dangerous due to physics that even the people who made these engines didn't pretend to entirely understand...

His main screen flashed with new coordinates, four degrees off their current course, and Erik angled *Phoenix* as far in that direction has he dared without sacrificing forward thrust angle. The burn increased to 11-G, beyond even *Phoenix*'s engine parameters, and warning lights flashed on the Engineering panel...

"New pulse!" Jiri managed weakly, struggling to even formulate on uplinks in this heavy G.   If he passed out, drug implants would shock him awake again.   *"New pulse, three marks at..."*

"I know!"   The sard had pulsed again and were racing up behind.   He was going to run out of room.   Four degrees, he thought as he watched the current heading edge one agonising fraction of a degree across at a time.   Four lousy degrees!   If he jumped too early, or without proper alignment, they'd shoot off through the galaxy missing every gravity well along the way, and never come out the other side with nothing to pull them out of hyperspace.   He needed to pulse up again, to get more V to hold off the sard, but the jump lines were still charging from the last pulse, and pulsing for V right now would postpone the desperately needed jump.

"Fire pattern!" came Geish's uplinked voice.   *"Incoming rounds, real fast!"*   He was going to have to let them intercept, Erik realised.   They'd have to survive five seconds of interception from the incoming hailstorm, because the arrival time, and the jump time, did not intersect.

"Arms!   Everything you've got!"   He couldn't dodge, he couldn't line up the jump if he was flailing around, and evasive manoeuvres would put off the defensive gunnery anyway.   Weapons thudded again, and a series of massive flashes erupted behind, and then to the sides, and then the line was creeping across, three-point-eight, three-point-nine... come on Navcomp, sync it in first time or we're dead... four!   Nav flashed green, and Erik hit pulse on full power...

CHAPTER 11

And they arrived in a crash-entry, alarms shrieking as nav protested it didn't know this system well enough to be tearing in at these speeds. But jumplines charged green almost immediately, and Erik dumped velocity with a hard shove into alternate-dimension... and back out, nav still squawking red but no longer panicked. Across the bridge, someone was heaving up their lunch.

"Scan, watch our tail!" Erik rasped, his voice dry and hoarse. His head was pounding and he desperately needed a drink. If the sard had followed them through jump, which seemed quite possible with ships that high-powered, it seemed almost preferable to let them kill him rather than have to manoeuvre again. His heart felt exhausted from hammering so hard for so long, and he couldn't tell how much of his current consciousness was actually the augment stims keeping the blood flowing to his brain well beyond when he'd normally be out. He pulled the drink tube at his collar, and took a long sip. "Nav, where the fuck are we?"

"It's called Gala Eighty-Eight on the barabo charts," said Kaspowitz. "It's a rock, gravitational yield one-point-seven-three standard, just big enough to drag us in." Thus explaining why there was no light in Erik's forward scan, this wasn't a sun at all.

"Good work on the course. I'd like a new course to Kazak if you please."

"Copy LC, it'll take a few moments to get Navcomp to recalc from this position."

"Engineering, systems report please," Erik requested. He'd thrashed the damn ship getting it this far, and wanted to know everything was okay before he tried it again.

"Copy LC," came Rooke's voice. "I'm running it now, everything looks good at first glance."

"Major, everyone okay down there?"

"Lieutenant Crozier is pissed she missed out on another boarding credit. Other than that, all good." Erik usually felt some amusement at Trace's humour. Now, nothing but cold dread.

"Arms," he continued his roll call.   "How's the ammo looking?"

"Well we're down to..."

"Contact!" called Geish, and Erik's heart leaped again. "Incoming jump!   It's mid-range, it looks like it's on the same course!   Second incoming jump, looks like a formation!   Third, that's all three!"

They were too far away to be an immediate threat, Erik saw with desperate relief — at least one minute light.   But it was clearly the same three sard ships that had nearly killed them back at Chonki. Evidently they hadn't navigated the jump as accurately, and had come out of hyperspace too far away to pose an immediate threat. That they had gotten here at all on the precise same timeline as *Phoenix* confirmed what he already knew — that they were of a far higher level of technology than most sard vessels.   He'd never thought he'd be commanding *Phoenix,* and be so scared of three sard ships.   Usually three sard warships against *Phoenix* would be a slight advantage in *Phoenix*'s favour.   Not so here.

"Okay, they've missed their entry," said Erik, and dumped velocity once again — a groan across the bridge as whoever had lost their lunch failed to appreciate it.   "Nav, give me a rough course while you line it up."

"Copy LC," said Kaspowitz, and a rough course-change appeared on Erik's screen — a full hundred and nine degree shift.

"Bugger," someone muttered as they saw that, and Erik slammed on the thrust at 7-Gs.   It would take a good eleven minutes at this thrust, but the sard would take the same, and were too far away to make an intercept so long as Kaspowitz could get him that new course to Kazak on time.

"*Phoenix this is the LC,*" Erik formulated as they burned and shook, gasping the tight little breaths that many years of heavy G experience had taught him.   *"That last jump was an escape jump to an uninhabited system.   We are currently ten minutes of burn time from a new course to Kazak.   We are being pursued by three sard vessels of very high technology, and it will be very ill-advised to engage them.   We will find better circumstances at Kazak.   LC out."*

He hoped.   No one aboard had ever been to Kazak, and knew only that it was another barabo frontier system with no inhabited planet and just a few moons and stations to its name.   It had quite a bit of ship traffic, including some barabo military and security freelancers that the stations employed... but what security freelancer would stand a chance against whatever was chasing them?

He couldn't even think about who they were or why, or the difference between these three sard and the first five unidentified ships who'd ambushed them at Chonki.   The possibilities behind all the people who might have been trying to kill them were just too much right now, with his head full of numbers and the Gs pounding his brain to mush.   The biologists said that sard didn't handle Gs any better than humans, but then these sard hadn't had to manoeuvre anywhere near as much as *Phoenix* had.

After eleven of the longest minutes of his life, the lines finally matched.   The sard were still chasing, or scan showed that they *had* been chasing a minute ago, when the light wave reached them.   It was far too far back to be a threat... but if the sard were as advanced as it seemed, there was no guarantee they couldn't pass *Phoenix* in hyperspace and arrive at Kazak in front of them.   How the hell had sard gotten such powerful ships?

"Phoenix, standby for jump."   He pulsed once, accelerated to racing speed, and had time to hope that Kaspowitz had lined everything up in this alien part of space...

...the shiny new Lieutenant Commander had walked the docks of Reva Station straight off the transport from Homeworld. His uniform was pressed and neat, in contrast to the rough working blue jumpsuits and jackets of passing spacers, and black-clad marines.   One blue duffel bag carried all his personals, and when he approached the berth, he saw the display reading the words *UFS Phoenix* and his heart had skipped a beat.

The marines on duty at the airlock had barely raised an eyebrow at their new LC, and informed him that the command crew were currently out to dinner, of all things, and given him the name of the restaurant where he might reach them. But they'd see his bag taken to his quarters if he'd like?

The restaurant had not been far, a walk along thriving bars and pounding music, establishments filled with marines and spacers, and no few MPs to keep an eye on things. Grizzled veterans of the Triumvirate War had barely glanced at him as he'd walked, feeling very out of place in his spotless blues, his shoes polished like twin mirrors upon the deck, single bronze leaves impossibly bright and heavy upon his shoulders where just weeks before, Lieutenant's bars had rested.

The restaurant had been Chinese, quiet and low-key, and in a corner he'd found them, lounging like old friends around several tables they'd dragged together in a corner, nursing the single beers that station leave away from the front lines entitled you to. He'd approached, hat beneath his arm, and they'd all slowly glanced and noticed him... and his heart had nearly stopped, for here was Lieutenant Kaspowitz who had helped rewrite formation navigation practises... and there was Commander Huang with chopsticks in hand, laughing with Lieutenant Shahaim over some private joke that surely no outsider would ever comprehend... and there, dear lord, was the legendary Major Thakur herself, younger and smaller than he'd expected, first to notice the shiny new LC's approach and oh-so-unimpressed with her dark and somber stare.

But Captain Pantillo, the even greater legend and the man whom Erik most desperately wanted to emulate in all the universe, had gotten to his feet with a broad smile and welcomed him into their little family like a long-lost uncle...

...Kazak, navcomp was blaring at him as he blinked his eyes wide on his main screens, brain overloading from trying to take in too much information at once.

"Good entry!" Kaspowitz was calling with calm authority. "Kazak System, deep entry, Rhea dead ahead, range seven minutes light." Kazak was a hyperactive G-class star, too hyperactive for close-in habitable worlds, but supporting two big gas giants further out, each with multiple moons. The smaller was Rhea, where most of the development was, and the system's largest station.

"Scan, I want proximity positions now!" With every reflex jangling in the expectation of another ambush. But exact jump entry points were impossible to predict, and that last bunch at Chonki must have just been lucky. If someone here were going to try and kill them, they'd surely get some more warning this time...

"Proximity scan shows nothing," Geish replied. "No rocks, no hiding spots. There's a whole bunch of insystem traffic, and FTLs coming and going from Rhea, but otherwise we look clear."

"Well they haven't jumped in ahead," Shahaim observed. "Hard to believe they'd be *more* advanced than *Phoenix*."

"After what we just saw I'll believe anything," Erik replied. "Everyone stay alert, they could be coming in behind us any moment. I'm not dumping V for a while yet. Coms, contact station and tell them we're coming in hot with hostile sard ships on our tail. Confirm with them that our intentions to station are entirely peaceful."

"Aye LC," said Lieutenant Shilu from Coms.

Three hours later *Phoenix* command was crammed into the captain's quarters, which was barely big enough for three people to gather, and became very tight indeed with five. Joma Station's two security vessels were approaching fast, and Erik had instructed Lieutenant Draper to keep close eye on them — tavalai-model cruisers but barabo-crewed, they didn't seem likely to prove a threat and their captains were courteous when contacted. Joma Station was less so, their Stationmaster decidedly displeased to see them... and of course, unable to do a damn thing about it.

Erik had only just handed off to second-shift, wanting to be certain they were out of jump-entry range for any incoming threat, and that Kazak System itself had no further surprises lurking. He'd given them all fifteen minutes to shower and change, which was harder for some as delta bulkhead water mains had ruptured in the manoeuvres and taken local recycling systems with it. The Systems crew were taking apart several corridors to repair the break, with Warrant Officer Krish reporting it would take most of the run into station to fix, with everyone sharing bathrooms in the meantime.

"Seems logical to me that Chonki was two separate ambushes," said Shahaim, exhausted as they all were, sitting on Erik's bunk alongside Kaspowitz and the nervous Second Lieutenant Karle. Erik sat on his little desk-side chair, and Trace leaned against a wall, insisting that marines didn't need a seat. All were either eating, or just finishing a meal, save for Trace who had already finished her food having less to do after jump than the bridge crew. "The first bunch knew exactly where we'd emerge, it's easier to guess in a transit system like Chonki where nearly everyone is turning toward Kazak... though they still got lucky. And still couldn't finish us, so I'd guess they were poorly informed about the threat we'd pose."

"Which suggests they don't have much contact with humans," Kaspowitz added. "Human freelancers or mercenaries would know exactly who we are."

Shahaim nodded. "Their tactics appear to rule out sard, their coordination was nowhere near sard standard and lacked their numerical fetish. Tavalai don't do mercenary stuff..."

"Much," Kaspowitz warned.

"...and neither do barabo."

"Much."

Shahaim gave him the tired look of a mother in no mood to bother with unruly kids. Fortunately for Kaspowitz, Suli Shahaim was one of the most patient people Erik had ever known. "The ship layout didn't seem to have the heavy-gravity rotation we'd expect with kaal, so anyone's guess is as good as mine as to who they were."

"There are Fleet reports of mixed-species freelancers out this way," Erik told them. "The weakness of the barabo military creates a vacuum that freelancers move in to fill. The word is that a lot are outside human-sphere."

Glances among the officers. The human-sphere was shorthand for those alien species whose space directly adjoined human space. In the past hundred and sixty years of wartime expansion, human space had increased quite a bit, and human-sphere aliens now included chah'nas, tavalai, kuhsi, alo, sard and kaal. Barabo were right on the fringe and only now being added to that list, and krim had once been on the list, before humans had removed them from all lists, for good. Hacksaws, of course, didn't quite count as a 'species', and were not extinct despite everyone's best efforts, and also lacked a contiguous region of space.

"On review, their ambush was competently executed," Shahaim continued. "But they failed to allow for *Phoenix*'s power and mobility, and got their spacing too tight... which is always the temptation in an ambush against a larger vessel — to concentrate firepower. Which our intrepid commander immediately recognised, of course, and quickly killed one in busting out of their crossfire, forcing the others into a parallel pursuit which is always bad news against the combined firepower and mobility of a combat carrier, and allowed the LC to isolate the second target and put him into a one-on-one contest that he was always going to lose."

"Hell yeah," Kaspowitz affirmed, to nods and general approval from the others. "And some sterling work from Mr Karle and Ms Harris on guns." With a whack on Karle's arm, which pleased the young man.

Erik did not join the enthusiasm. His hesitation at the near-boarding of the wrecked ship had nearly gotten *Phoenix* and everyone aboard her killed, and he was in no mood for backslapping. No one else seemed to see it that way, but Erik knew what he'd done, even if they did not. Only Trace seemed to notice his mood, watching him sombrely.

"Which brings us to the sard," Shahaim continued. "I've never seen anything like it. Their tech is never that good, as we know, and tavalai don't share their best stuff with them."

"Those ships were better than anything the tavalai have," Erik said grimly. "Either they stole them, or they bought them, or were gifted them... whatever. They came from somewhere else. Who else makes ships as good as *Phoenix*?"

"Sard aren't alone in other people giving them technology," Kaspowitz cautioned. Meaning humans, of course, as *Phoenix* was alo-tech.

"Sure," said Erik. "But we were only behind in the technology because we were so new in space. When the krim hit us, humanity was barely beyond the pressurised bathtubs of the early space age. But we internalised every technology given to us, we even started taking some of it in new directions that its inventors hadn't thought of. I mean, humans went faster-than-light on our own. Not many species in the Spiral did that, most had it given to them by someone else. Sard in particular."

"Weird that a species so good at maths is so dumb with tech," Trace pondered.

"Maths isn't science," said Kaspowitz. "Science is a cultural institution of asking questions and using reason and experiments to challenge established norms. Sard are a hive mind, they're internally uncompetitive, they don't ask questions or get into debates, they just harmonise. It doesn't produce great tech." Trace nodded thoughtfully, no doubt thinking about that cicada-shriek in the cargo bay where they'd found Randal Connor.

"Anyhow," said Erik, "it doesn't matter how the sard got those ships. Or it doesn't matter to our immediate situation. My guess is that the first ambush at Chonki were mercenaries, probably employed by Fleet Command, since Chankow and Co are having such trouble killing us themselves. The sard probably saw that ambush being set up, and came in quietly to stand off nearby and pick up the pieces. *Why* they came after us, I don't know, and even our resident genius alien expert hasn't a clue."

"Do sard need a reason?" Trace wondered.

"Our main takeaway is that lots of people are trying to kill us," Erik continued. "So what's new?" Dry smiles from the group. "Now, there's a few interesting ships on Joma Station. *Europa* is a

Regelda Freightliners vessel, that's of course a Debogande Incorporated company, or sixty percent owned by DI anyway." Everyone nodded. Regelda Freightliners was well known to all Spacers. In any busy human system their ships would be ubiquitous on scan or station docking lists. "Station lists say she arrived fifteen standard days ago, which is a very long stay for a commercial freighter. We've also got no record of DI trading ties to anyone in Kazak, or regularly passing through Kazak... though I'll admit our records are sketchy. Lisbeth agrees that she can't think of any family interests here."

"Looks like she's waiting for us," Shahaim surmised. "Or for you, more precisely."

"Or better yet, for Lisbeth," Erik added. Oh good god he hoped that *Europa* would check out as ultra-reliable, so he could put Lisbeth on board and kiss her goodbye. He'd miss her terribly, their time together on *Phoenix* had reminded him of just how proud he was to have her for a sister, but that last action had nearly gotten all of them killed. He could not protect Lisbeth out here, not even with all of this huge warship's firepower and technology. Having the lives of everyone on *Phoenix* at the mercy of his mistakes was bad enough without having her here as well. "Also at dock we've got... what's the Heuron-registered ship?" He clicked his fingers at Shahaim.

"*Edmund Shandi*," said Shahaim. "Shandi was a founding father of the human settlements on Apilai. She's registered to a Heuron Starfreight, which was heavily Worlder-owned before the ordinances. Don't know what's happened to it now."

Erik nodded. "Right. So a Worlder civvie ship. She got here five standard days ago... now we lost about six real-time days on our little detour, but aside from us all being six days younger on this date than we would have been, I don't think we've lost much."

"That's it?" Trace asked with concern. "We did all that advertising to everyone to come to Joma Station, and we only get two ships?"

"So far," Erik cautioned her. He could not deny it was disappointing. He could see it on Trace's face — rare for her, to let those feelings show. This was the Captain's legacy at stake, and she took it personally. "Remember it's dangerous to come out here. Fleet doesn't like it, for one thing. And Randal Connor got *Grappler* to come out to Tuki Station, and look what happened to them."

"We still don't actually know who was on *Grappler*," Shahaim reminded them. "Aside from the long-term registered crew, but we've no idea about passengers. Connor said it was senior Worlders. Maybe someone at Joma Station can tell us."

"Right," Erik agreed. "Everyone knew we were coming here. But getting here early could be real dangerous, given everything else that's going on. Much safer to arrive late, and be sure *Phoenix* is already here, to give them some protection. And look — sure enough, we did get here late, thanks to our little sard encounter. Anyone who got here on our advertised date would have been ahead of us, and exposed. The others will be along in due time."

Trace looked somewhat mollified at that, but still unusually anxious.

"Be nice if they did actually turn up," Kaspowitz murmured. "Given what we went through to get here."

"We all knew the risk," Erik told him sternly. "We all discussed what might happen. We all signed off on it. You too, Kaspo."

"I know that," Kaspowitz said evenly. "But if we have to do it again, and tell everyone we're going to some new destination to do more diplomacy, then given what's now chasing us we'd probably not survive it..."

"LC's right Kaspo," Trace cut him off. "You agreed, and pointing out the obvious now seems like needless point scoring. Leave it alone."

Kaspowitz took a deep breath, and said no more. Knowing Trace so well meant knowing when to cut your losses.

"So what we're going to do here is much the same as we did at Tuki Station," Erik continued. "We're going to dock at the rim and set up a station rim presence. Lieutenant Shilu will be in charge of accommodation, he'll be coordinating with Major Thakur as to exactly what's needed and what station will give.   Lieutenant Shahaim will be in charge of the money — spend it wisely please."

"I'm the only one who would," Shahaim said wryly, with an accusing look at Kaspowitz.

The Navigation Officer smiled.   "No special requests Suli?"

"None."

"Now," Erik continued, "Second Lieutenant Karle will be responsible for finding us some more ammunition."   As understanding dawned upon the young man's face.   It was Karle's first command meeting that Erik could recall, typically only the very highest officers were called.   Karle had been second-shift prior to all this mess, but Lieutenant Paulson from first-shift hadn't come up from Homeworld to meet them.   Thus Karle was even more a stranger to first-shift than Erik was.   "So, Rhea is a very large multiple-moon system, there are some quite sophisticated-looking fabrication plants on and around a few of them, and even a small shipbuilder out near the fifth moon, I forget what it's called…"

"Dada," said Kaspowitz.

"Thank you."

"Barabo names are easy to remember," Kaspowitz added. "Dada, Papa, Gigi, Poopoo."

"You made that last one up," Shahaim accused him.

"I might have."

"And I want you to contact each of them," Erik continued still without humour, "and find out if anyone can fabricate what we need."

"Yessir," said Karle, nodding as he thought about it.   "Sir, our armaments are kind of secret, or at least the specifications are…"

"We only want ammunition.   The ammo's not secret, we've fired enough of it in the war to make a small moon.   Plenty of specimens for study and reverse engineering, not all of them detonate."

"But viper rounds always detonate sir," Karle persisted.

"Not always," Erik said firmly. "You think Fleet will punish us if we share those tech specifications with aliens? Maybe declare us a renegade vessel and try to kill us?"

Karle fought back a nervous smile as he grasped the point. "Um, yeah. I get it. I'll tell them."

"Vipers aren't even the best missiles in service," Shahaim added. "Tavalai use better. And we don't need the guidance heads, we can do them ourselves. Just hull, engines and warheads."

"You think private companies out here will sell us warheads?" Karle wondered.

Erik forced an encouraging smile. "Ask nicely. We're still in barabo space, a smile and a drink goes a long way."

CHAPTER 12

Two hours from dock, and Lisbeth was doing Skah's maths lesson. She took it in the quarters she shared with Major Thakur, a necessity because Skah was easily distracted. Even now she had to flick his ear to stop him playing with a stylus, and concentrate on the puzzles she'd set him. Today it was simple multiplication, about what she figured a human child would be doing at the same age. Skah was plenty smart, but like a lot of little human boys would much rather have been running around with the marines and watching preparations for dock.

The Major interrupted them by entering with a meal, and sat on Lisbeth's lower bunk to eat it. "Najor Thakur!" Skah announced brightly.

"Hi Furball," said the Major with affection. "What are you learning?"

"Naths." With a kuhsi's sharp teeth, 'm' was a problem. 'L' wasn't much better.

"Do you like maths?"

Skah shook his head, big ears flapping. "Boring."

"Oh come on," Lisbeth scolded. "Maths isn't that boring. You're very good at it."

"I know," he said. "Stiw boring."

"Your Mommy's very good at maths," the Major told him around a mouthful of noodles. "She has to be good at maths because she's a pilot. Would you like to be a pilot one day?" Skah nodded enthusiastically — he'd learned that gesture around humans, but his mother had to force it. "Then you need to study your maths, and you need to listen to Lisbeth. Is Lisbeth a good teacher?"

Another enthusiastic nod. "I rike Risbeth. Risbeth good teacha."

Lisbeth laughed, and ruffled his ears. "Thank you Skah, I like you too."

"Not Skah!" Skah insisted crossly. "Furbaw."

"Come on then Furball," said the Major.   "Tell me your times tables. Do you know your fives?"

He was onto his seven-times-tables — and considerably more focused when performing for the Major, Lisbeth noted — when his mother entered in her blue pressure jumpsuit, pilot's helmet under one arm. She went to Skah and put an arm around him, asking rapid questions in their native tongue, with many guttural coughs and growls, looking at his maths-work. Skah answered reluctantly, the very picture of a boy being told to be good and work hard even if he didn't want to.   The two humans smiled as they watched. And smiled more broadly still when Tif licked her hand to plaster down some unruly fur, while Skah squirmed in discomfort.

"Tif," the Major asked her. "You go flying?" Indicating the flight suit.

"No," said Tif.   "Pre-per...no.   Pre-par-a-tion."   And smiled, pleased she'd gotten it right.   Tif's health was as improved in the past few weeks as her son's, her scratches and scars now fading beneath a healthy sheen of tawny-brown fur. Lisbeth thought she was quite gorgeous, with big golden eyes and dark highlights. Lithe and quick, she was a shade shorter than the Major, and moved with the fluid grace of a dancer. "Ship dock, we sit shuttew cockpit. Watch systen. Naybe quick go, if probren."

"Yes, good idea," the Major agreed.   Lisbeth thought that must be procedure for all combat shuttles, docking at a station they weren't sure was safe.   But then, Tif was not a regular combat shuttle pilot — was not even military, in fact.   Utilising her in military procedures was surely an issue.

"Najor, rook," said Tif, and bared her teeth.   Usually when Kuhsi did that at you, it was bad news, but not this time. One of Tif's two big incisors had been missing since they'd recovered her from chah'nas custody. Now it was back, sharp and white, to make a full carnivorous grin.

"Prosthetic!" said the Major.   "Doc Suelo does good work, yes?"

"Good work yes," Tif agreed, and showed Lisbeth. "Nissing

tooth bad for kuhsi.   Rook bad.   Kuhsi wonan with no teeth, no good."

Lisbeth nodded — it made sense, given the size of them. For a young kuhsi woman to lose her teeth would be like a young human woman losing her hair.   "Excellent Tif!   You must feel normal again."

Tif nodded vigorously.   "Thank you.   Thank awr *Phoenix*. And for ny boy.   Snaw trobuw, yes?"   Ruffling Skah's ears.   She looked emotional.

"No trouble at all, Tif," Lisbeth told her.   "Everyone loves Skah.   He's part of the crew."

Tif looked more emotional.   She leaned for a quick, playful nip at her son that between kuhsi passed as a kiss, and then left on her business.   Lisbeth and the Major glanced at each other.   There were many things unsaid about their kuhsi guests, mostly because no humans on the ship were expert on kuhsi, not even Romki, and also because with everything else that was going on, no one had the time to think about it.   How Skah was an heir to Koth, the eighth biggest nation of the kuhsi homeworld, whose leader had been murdered, Tif insisted, by kuhsi who did not want the social changes that exposure to all these new aliens was creating.

It was dangerous for Tif and Skah to stay on *Phoenix*, but they were under threat of assassination anywhere else... or so Tif insisted.   Tif seemed to feel safer here, and having three shuttles but only two full-time pilots, *Phoenix* was in dire need of her skills.   For now, Tif appeared to have made the decision that the dangers here were worth it.   Lisbeth wondered if the young mother had enough talent for scheming to figure that *Phoenix*, and perhaps even Family Debogande, might one day prove a very useful ally in reclaiming Skah's rightful inheritance.

"Her English is improving," the Major remarked.

"Ny Engrish better," Skah said smugly.   "I rearn Engrish fast."

"I know, Jessica has been teaching you."   Private Jess Rolonde was in the Major's Command Squad.   No one had suspected she had a teaching bone in her body until she'd volunteered.

"Jessica a sowjer."

"No, not a soldier," the Major corrected. "A marine. All marines on this ship, not soldiers."

Skah frowned. "Narines not sowjer?"

"Similar, but different. Marines fight on ships. Soldiers fight on planets."

"Who better? Narine or sowjer?"

The Major smiled broadly. "Marines, Furball. Always marines."

Joma Station was under construction. It had been under construction for the last fifty years, a near two-jumps from recognised tavalai territory. Kazak System was rich with potential, filled with joint barabo-tavalai mining and industry, and a busy transit point between barabo and tavalai space. Fifty years ago, the tavalai had begun to build Joma Station to replace all the minor stations that decentralised Kazak's logistics industry, and local barabo government had put some funds in also.

But with the war going badly, the tavalai had progressively withdrawn scarce funds and manpower to the point that Joma Station was largely a barabo project... and like all barabo projects in Outer Neutral Space, it was now only three-quarters finished, and messy. *Phoenix* was assigned Berth 18, alongside the unfinished superstructure where Berths 17 to 8 crackled and sparked with ongoing welding and construction. The barabo were finishing the rim while the station was under rotation, which was the much more expensive and dangerous way to do it — zero-G was much more simple for moving huge, heavy components into place. But for *Phoenix*, being stuck up against an unfinished portion of dock had its advantages, from a security point-of-view.

Erik let Shahaim power them in, underside thrust rocking them at a simple one-G while sideways thrust sent them chasing the station's rolling motion. A crash as great underside gantries caught the carrier's enormous weight, and then thrust cut while gravity continued, only with three-quarters of the crew cylinder now inaccessible.

Erik and first-shift stayed on the bridge, as in the main-quarter corridors, chaos reigned with all of *Phoenix*'s crew crammed into one quarter and slowly disembarking. Marines went first to secure the dock and keep safe all the spacer officers and crew who would check the umbilicals before *Phoenix* would accept station air, water or anything. Then there would be station officials to deal with, including customs and finance, though on a barabo Neutral Space facility, perhaps not so much of the former. Erik had supervised the process many times as third-in-command, and was quite glad to now sit on the bridge and let others handle it, while the bridge crew performed final systems checks, and kept an eye on incoming communications.

"Sir," said Lieutenant Shilu from Coms. "Message from *Europa*." That was the Regelda Freightliners vessel. "Welcomes *Phoenix* to Joma Station, and invites us to a dockside meeting, Berth 26. Requests a time of our nearest convenience."

"Sounds very formal," Kaspowitz remarked, still scanning over the Rhea local system. Gas giant systems were always a fascination for navigators, with all their lunar orbits and gravitational intersections.

"Run it past the Major," said Erik. "Get her most convenient time, then send it back to them, with compliments." Gatherings on dock were a security issue, and security issues were Trace's domain. Erik wondered what *Europa* had in store to warrant a formal dock meeting. He turned back to the more pressing matter of the station docking list. That one, he always reviewed with Shahaim, before dock, after dock and during dock. Particularly when two of the ships at dock were sard. "Those sard were already here when we were attacked. They couldn't have been in on it."

"Sard are a hive mind," Shahaim disagreed. "They're all 'in on it'."

Erik chewed a thumbnail, not willing to argue the semantics at this time. Hive mind or not, sard were not telepathic. "We'll keep an eye on them. I've told the Major to tell the marines not to pick fights. This is a barabo station and we'll only fight sard if attacked."

Joma would have a hundred and twenty rim berths once completed, but only sixty were currently operational. Forty-four of those were presently occupied, most by barabo freighters, and seven by tavalai. The central hub held nearly a hundred smaller insystem vessels, and like all gas giant stations, Joma did most of its business transferring freight and people between the big FTL ships and the little sub-lighters.

"Sir," said Shilu, "the Major reports no customs on dock, only a light local security presence and a few civvie spectators. Most barabo, but several kuhsi. Local freelancers, she thinks."

Erik blinked at Shahaim. "Kuhsi do travel," Shahaim reasoned. "If they wanted to go adventuring, this is one region of space that accepts species from anywhere."

"Coms, make sure Tif is aware," said Erik. "No telling who they'll report to, if anyone."

"Aye sir," said Shilu.

"Not like we've been keeping her a secret," Shahaim said. "She's said she doesn't want to stay on ship, either."

"Yeah, I think she's happy to fly the flag and tell all her enemies back home that she's alive with Skah, and she's teamed up with *UFS Phoenix*," Erik murmured. "That's what worries me."

"Order her to stay aboard?"

"Too late now. A ship like this can't hide, we're too visible and Tif is a functioning member of the crew. We need the extra pilot, we have to wear whatever consequences come from pissing off various kuhsi. It's not like we're anywhere near their space anyway."

"Aye," Shahaim said warily.

"Sir," came Shilu again, "*Europa* is requesting Lisbeth attend the dockside meeting also." This time most people glanced at Erik. *Europa* was a Debogande Inc-owned ship... it raised possibilities.

"Sounds like someone might have come to meet you," Kaspowitz suggested.

"Us," Erik corrected with an edge. "Someone might have come to meet *us*."

"Of course," said Kaspowitz, in part-apology.

"Sir," said Shilu again, sounding harried. Upon docking, the Coms Officer was always the busiest. As soon as a ship's nose touched station, suddenly everyone wanted to talk. "Message from *Edmund Shandi*, the Worlder ship from Heuron. Request for a meeting with you personally, earliest convenience."

Erik nodded — it wasn't unexpected. "Confirm with compliments — earliest convenience yet to be determined."

"Aye sir." And almost immediately, "Sir, Stationmaster is messaging. Stationmaster wishes to meet with the commander of *UFS Phoenix*, at earliest convenience."

"Repeat last reply," said Erik.

"Aye sir. Sir, station media is reporting our arrival, I'm getting requests for interviews, Lieutenant Alomaim says there are some journalists out on dock and the number of civvie onlookers is growing." That hadn't happened on Tuki Station, by request to the Stationmaster. A bottle of fine Homeworld whisky had helped convince him to keep the dock clear.

"Might have to bump the Stationmaster up the meeting schedule?" Shahaim suggested.

"Gonna run out of whisky," Kaspowitz muttered.

"Second Lieutenant Harris," said Erik. "You're going to assist Lieutenant Shilu on Coms for a while, help him shuffle through that backlog."

"Yessir," said Harris from up the far right end of the bridge, where the floor was starting to lean. "Sir, only... I've never worked coms before, I'm a gunner."

"Oh you're gonna love it, Bree," Shilu told her drily. "It's so much more fun than blowing stuff up."

Phoenix main-quarter was a mess of ongoing repairs to the broken water system, spacer crew hauling duffel bags to on-station accommodation, and main corridors filled with stationary armour, weapons and ammo so marines could access it in an emergency. Erik walked with Shahaim, Kaspowitz and Second Lieutenant Geish, their bridge posts filled by second-shift, and emerged from the crowd of *Phoenix* comings and goings onto Joma Station dock.

To one side of Berth 17, the dock section seal had closed, making a giant steel wall. The inner wall opposite the berth, where shopfronts, hotels and other establishments would typically welcome tired and thirsty spacers, was a mass of construction beams, clambering workers, power tools and showering orange sparks. The intervening dock was grey, unpolished steel, and covered in construction vehicles. Amidst them stood various barabo civilians, some talking, others taking vision with recording devices.

At the bottom of the berth ramp, before protruding hydraulics from the inner part of the docking mechanism, Lieutenant Alomaim waited with Bravo Platoon's First Squad. "No station officials, Lieutenant?" Erik asked.

"No sir." Alomaim was in heavy armour, but his helmet was replaced by a cap, as was customary in places not yet proven unfriendly. Erik and his first-shift crew wore the same, with light, unpowered armour. "There were a few here earlier, but they left." He nodded across the dock. "Journalists over there have been trying to ask questions. There's no station security here at all."

"Say no to the journalists," said Erik, descending the ramp. "Be polite but firm."

"Aye sir. That's what the Major said. We're heading to Berth 26 sir?"

"Yes."

"Bit of a hike from here, we could commandeer a vehicle I'm sure."

"I'm sure you could too, but I need the walk. And I'd like to take a look at this place."

Alomaim nodded at the thin crowd once more, dissuaded from coming closer by the line of well-spaced marines. "There's kuhsi over there sir. We've had a mike and translator on them for a while. They're talking about our shuttle pilot and her kid, so I guess word is out. It's nasty talk sir, lots of rude jokes, talk of rape."

Erik looked where the Lieutenant was looking, and saw the kuhsi — four of them. "Fuck they're huge," Kaspowitz observed. Kuhsi males, probably local security for some company or other. No visible weapons, dark jumpsuits and jackets. Big ears and massive shoulders, arms folded and watching with golden-eyed contempt.

"I want you to frighten them," said Erik. Alomaim raised his eyebrows. "Don't harm, just frighten. No one talks about our crew that way in our presence. Make sure they know why."

"Yessir," said Alomaim, and gave some orders. Bravo First Squad formed up about the bridge crew as they set out walking up the dock. On their left, several marines casually broke formation to confront the big kuhsi. Marines in armour were imposing, but they were barely larger than these unarmored kuhsi. Words were exchanged, tinny and harsh on translator speakers. Kuhsi snarled back. The marines levelled weapons large enough to turn big kuhsi into red puddles, as surrounding spectators backed away in shock. The kuhsi retreated, slinking away with ears down.

"Makes you proud to be a man, doesn't it?" Geish suggested drily as they walked on.

"They're one beautiful, sexy, fucked up species, that's for sure," said Kaspowitz.

"I want Tif and Skah under armoured escort on station," Erik told Alomaim. "We don't even know if that's political or not. More likely it's just the usual messed up males insisting women don't belong off their homeworld."

"And flying shuttles," added Gunnery Sergeant Connie Brice from Alomaim's side.

"Exactly. Women get murdered for less on the homeworld. If these guys try anything, kill them. No one threatens our crew or our guests."

"Aye sir." Lieutenant Alomaim was the least experienced of *Phoenix*'s marine officers, but Trace had told Erik he might one day be the best, if he stayed in long enough.   He was certainly the hardest to read, deadpan and businesslike even by Trace's standards.

"Poor Tif," said Shahaim.   "Imagine being stuck in that gender system."

"Imagine being out*sized* like that," Gunnery Sergeant Brice added.   "Augments remove much of the performance difference for us, but no amount of augments could let a kuhsi woman equal *that*."

"Those guys were Scuti," said Kaspowitz.   "Southern continent, everyone's bigger down there, males especially.   But yeah, even your typical kuhsi male will have fifty percent bodyweight on little Tif."

"Smaller always means faster," said Shahaim above the thumping of many armoured boots on deckplate.   "Tif's reflexes are insane. What if her old boyfriend the ruler of Koth was running that pilot school for women precisely because he figured women would make better pilots?   I mean, given that size difference, the women could be a *lot* faster, and better with the Gs too.   That would threaten a lot of the old boys, I'd reckon — piloting's a high prestige job on Choghoth."

"Yeah," Kaspowitz said grimly.   "Could have helped get him killed, too. Imagine if women started flying starships — the single most important technical profession of the age, and kuhsi men can't get near their women for ability?   Would turn the whole status of kuhsi women upside down. Lots would kill to stop it."

Ahead on the left, against the inner wall, *Phoenix* marines and spacers were gathered about a hallway through the construction work. A familiar figure in armour strode out to intercept them.

"How's the accommodation?" Erik asked Trace as she fell in beside him, huge rifle racked over one shoulder.

"It's fine," she said.   "The construction's just on the lower levels, once you get the elevator up it's all finished and good.   Of course, having everyone on upper levels will reduce our response time between here and *Phoenix*. Wasn't Lisbeth invited to this thing as well?"

"She's helping Romki with his hacksaws again.   She said she'll grab a vehicle and catch up shortly."

"What's the schedule for *Edmund Shandi?*"

"We need to talk to everyone else first," Erik told her. "Let's leave the Worlders until we're certain of our footing here. We can't get any kind of talks going unless we're sure no-one's about to pull the rug out from under us."

Berth 26 took nearly half an hour to walk, as shopfronts resumed along the inner wall, and the dock level became thick with stationers, mostly barabo mixed with occasional tavalai. Vehicles cruised amidst off-duty construction personnel in fluro worksuits and hard hats — interior workers, an advantage of building a station while it was operating, not everyone needed an environment suit. But there were no markets on the dock, unlike Tuki Station, probably a result of station management deciding that with construction everywhere, vehicles needed the space to drive and stalls got in the way.

There were non-human-sphere species here too, the occasional strange and barely recognisable face amidst the more familiar. One was reptiloid with a bony snout, while another pair walked hunched over with massive shoulders to fight a much heavier gravity, flat heads thrust forward and low. The humans tried not to stare, while exchanging remarks about which species they might be — kratik and shoab respectively, it was agreed, probably attracted to Kazak due to its spacer trade. Tuki had been centred more about trade from its big, inhabited planet below, Vieno. Such trade was perishable, non-industrial and of less interest to distant aliens making long trips. Also, Kazak was politically central in a way Tuki wasn't, and aliens on long trips could make contacts here that Tuki would not provide. But for all its greater importance, Erik found himself preferring the warmth and bustle of Tuki's markets and lively traders. Joma Station was cold, half-built and lacked the colour and smiles.

Approaching Berth 26, Erik looked back to find a vehicle approaching behind — an open-topped buggy with fat tires, four heavy-armoured marines piled into the back with two more light-armoured — Lisbeth's bodyguards Carla and Vijay — compressing the suspension. Lisbeth was driving, and Erik repressed a smile to see his sister in her borrowed spacer jumpsuit and harness, *Phoenix* cap on her head, driving these marines around like she was their CO. But it was sensible, because if they were to guard her they had to have hands free to shoot, which they couldn't do while driving. Plus, in heavy armour it was nearly impossible to fit behind the wheel.

"*Sorry I'm late*," she said on coms, hanging back so she didn't break up the formation. The marines had trained her well. "*Erik, why are you walking? I saw another couple of vehicles back there you could have borrowed.*"

Erik smiled. "Borrowed? You're a Debogande and you want to 'borrow' things?"

"*Well okay, 'rented'. And why are you walking anyway?*"

"It's called exercise, sis. You might try it." Grins from the surrounding crew.

"*Isn't a half-hour stroll a little light to qualify as exercise for a Fleet officer?*"

"Yes," Trace agreed, with a pointed glance at Erik. "Yes it is."

"I'm instating a new ship rule," Erik told both women. "No nagging. Effective immediately."

"You need to be ranked captain to do that," said Trace. Erik gave her an unimpressed stare. Even in casual conversation, she was relentless, and always returned to the sore spot.

Ahead amidst the dock crowds, a screen alongside the wall umbilicals announced Berth 26. Some spacers stood on the ramp before their hatch, watching the *Phoenix* crew approach. One raised a hand in greeting, and Erik raised his in return.

"Eyes open," Alomaim told his marines, who fanned out as they walked. Recently the paranoia had been well earned. Two spacers approached from the ramp, and Erik squinted, thinking one looked familiar.

"*Phoenix* ID says the one on the right is Captain Houli," said Trace, matching face recognition on her visor uplink. "His last ship registry was *Europa*."

"And the one on the left is my uncle," said Erik as he finally recognised the face. And said to his mike, "Lis, get up here, it's Uncle Calvin."

Uncle Calvin was brown, slim and handsome, and spread his arms wide with a broad smile as he approached. Erik grinned back, and embraced him. "Didn't expect to see you here!" he said with feeling.

"You look good, kid," said Calvin, parting with a slap on Erik's armoured shoulder.

"Cal, you'll have heard of Major Trace Thakur?" And to Trace, "Calvin's my mother's little brother. He runs Debogande Inc's legal wing, was a judge first for... what was it, twenty years?"

"Around that," Calvin agreed, shaking Trace's hand. "But I got tired of being impartial and came home to the family. A pleasure, Major."

"We could use a good lawyer," Trace suggested, and Calvin laughed.

Lisbeth interrupted with a shout and came running to hug her uncle hard. "Oh my god, what are you doing here?"

"Your mother sent me on a company legal mission," said Calvin, hugging her back. "Captain Houli here commands the fastest ship that DI has, and we got word from our sources that *Phoenix* was heading to Kazak. Great to see you kids well, just wonderful. The whole family was so worried."

"So how did your sources hear we were coming here?" Erik asked warily.

"You're really going to ask that?" Calvin replied. "I thought everyone knew by now." Erik glanced at Trace. Trace actually grimaced, a rare expression for her. "Before we get into that, I've got something to show you." He turned and beckoned back to the ship ramp. A spacer there signalled inside, and some people emerged. They wore spacer and marines uniforms, blue and black, and carried standard duffel bags like they were going somewhere.

Erik recognised one immediately. "That's Jersey! That's Lieutenant Jersey... where did...?" He grinned in astonishment, recognising several other faces as well. Lieutenant Regan Jersey was the pilot of *Phoenix*'s missing shuttle, PH-3. PH-3 had been on Homeworld when Trace had busted Erik out of Fleet custody. They hadn't been able to use her to escape, opting for Lisbeth and the private AT-7 instead, lest Fleet or Commander Huang get wind of what they were attempting... and at that thought, his heart almost stopped. Was Commander Huang here as well?

But he couldn't see her, as Jersey stopped before him with a grin and saluted. She was only a small woman, and was once Lieutenant Hausler's rival for hottest shuttle pilot on *Phoenix*. Erik saluted back, and shook her hand hard, not knowing her quite well enough for a hug. "Lieutenant, how the hell?" Looking at the others gathering on the dock behind her.

"You left me behind, you bastard!" she said cheerfully, and those crew laughed. "I know why you did it, but still, some of us don't take rejection well. A few of us who got left behind were scheming how to get back to *Phoenix* when some Debogande people suggested they might have a ship that could help." She shrugged. "So we got on board. And we even picked up a few volunteers — figured you'd be a few hands short and came to help. Hoon... where's Hoon?"

A black-clad marine came forward, scarred and weathered, and saluted Trace and Erik. "Master Sergeant Peter Hoon, *UFS Walker, UFS Claymore, UFS Five Junctions*. Thirty-three years active duty, six years retired, volunteering for service."

Trace saluted back, smiling. "I've heard of you. Kresnik's Feint, Horsehead System?"

Hoon smiled grimly. "That's the one, Major. I've heard of you too." Laughter from those behind. "Condolences on your Captain, he was a great man. What they did to him stank. I had several buddies who fought beside you and *Phoenix* in the past, never had the honour myself but they said you'd never steer a good marine wrong. Figured you might need some new grunts, so I and a few of the guys started rounding up others..." he gestured to those behind him. "Lots of grey hairs and old knees, but we still remember how it's done."

Trace's smile grew broader. Behind her, Bravo Platoon were grinning with delight. "Can always use some more wise heads," she said.

"We brought PH-3 back too," Lieutenant Jersey added. "She's grappled to *Europa*, rode her through jumps real easy."

Erik blinked. "You did?" Wow. One large tactical disadvantage, solved just like that. In one stroke, he now had enough shuttles to deploy all of *Phoenix*'s marine company at one time, if needs be. "But Fleet had PH-3 in custody, surely? How did you get her back?"

"Got granted a favour," Jersey said cautiously.

"A favour from who?"

Europa's main corridor was not nearly as large as *Phoenix*'s, and Trace had to take care her Koshaim didn't catch its muzzle on the ceiling. She followed Erik's Uncle Calvin down the corridor, Erik between Lisbeth's borrowed Bravo Third Squad guys behind, just in case. Lisbeth, Lieutenant Alomaim and the rest remained out on the dock, getting to know the new recruits, and hearing the tales of the long lost *Phoenix* crew.

Uncle Calvin took a left off the main corridor at C-Bulkhead, and led them into a recreation room of the kind *Phoenix* lacked — a few nice bolted-on chairs, a central holodisplay for games, even a small bar with a drinks fridge. Paying passengers demanded more luxuries than enlisted ones. Standing before the table, neat and perfect in his black marine dress uniform, stood a very fit man of approaching middle age. Brown skin, pronounced cheekbones, effortless poise. Trace stared.

"Major," said Calvin Debogande with some caution. "I'm told you two are old friends."

Lighter footsteps behind as Erik entered. Colonel Timothy Khola's dark eyes flicked to him, deadly focused. "LC, get behind me," Trace commanded, taking a step forward and across to interpose herself.   Almost without realising it, her close-quarters automatic came to hand from her right thigh holster.

"Major, who…"

"Get and stay!"   Erik silenced, and stayed.   Trace's eyes never left Khola's.   He appeared unarmed.   Even in full armour, it only made Trace feel marginally safer.

Khola smiled.   The expression never reached his eyes. "Svagata mitraharula, Trace bahini."   It was Nepali, today mostly lost, like so many of Earth's once-common languages.   The settlers of Sugauli had returned to it in part, as the natural language of a mountainous world whose primary inhabitants were Buddhist and Hindu, once the krim had been removed.   Trace was not exactly fluent, but as Kulina one always knew the customs.

"You address me by my rank," Trace instructed her old friend.   "Or I swear I will kill you where you stand."

Khola barely blinked.   Beside them, both Debogandes stood very still.   Lance Corporal Kamov attempted to move to Trace's right for an angle, but Trace's raised hand stopped him.   Finally Khola nodded.   "Major.   To see you well is… unsurprising."

It was praise, Trace knew.   She also knew that given what Colonel Timothy Khola was, and had devoted the whole of his life to being, that his sole personal purpose for being here was to see her dead.   But if that was his purpose, this was an odd way to go about it.   "State your business."

Khola took a long, reluctant breath.   "I am here under the direct orders of ranking Fleet Command."

"And who would that be, these days?"

Khola did not miss a beat.   "Major, your actions deserve death, and as Kulina I am honour-bound to kill you.   But the Kulina's primary honour is in the service of Fleet, and Fleet have commanded me specifically otherwise in this instance."

Trace smiled.   "I can see it eating you.   What have they ordered you to tell me?"

"Not you."   Khola nodded at Erik.   "Him."

"And his name," Trace said with measured patience, "is Lieutenant Commander Debogande."   Kulina were disciplined and professional, and that meant always following protocol in formal settings.   Kulina only did otherwise to people for whom their contempt was so great, killing would likely follow.   Trace knew very well what formal disrespect from the Colonel meant, directed at her or her commander, and she would not allow it.

"It's alright Major," said Erik, and stepped to one side from behind her.   Trace prepared her automatic for quick fire, knowing that Khola would read her posture.   If he had a hidden weapon anywhere on his person, he only needed a split second to kill any of them.   "I'll hear what the Colonel has come all this way to tell me."

"Fleet offers you pardon," Khola told him.   For all his discipline, Trace could see the words caused him pain.   "The leadership has been split on the *Phoenix* question.   The leaders saw the difficulties that their mistakes in handling the *Phoenix* question caused.   The captains would not unite under that leadership, so the leadership decided to remove themselves from the equation."

Erik frowned.   "Remove themselves?"

"Fleet Admiral Anjo has committed suicide.   He left a note, accepting all responsibility for the fallout from his actions, and admitting to ordering the unlawful killing of Captain Marinol Pantillo."   Trace heard Erik's sharp intake of breath at her side.   "He personally requested clemency for all those involved, including the crew of *Phoenix* and those Fleet personnel whom he ordered to kill your Captain.   I do not know the fate of Fleet Admiral Ishmael and Supreme Commander Chankow, though it is believed that they may have entered into a pact to end their lives together if this point was reached.   Whatever their mistakes, they are all intensely brave and patriotic men, and will receive full military honours."

Erik said nothing, utterly stunned.   Trace felt blank.   She'd imagined this resolution, had fought for it — punishment for those who had murdered her Captain, and justice for him and all the crew of *Phoenix*, alive and dead.   Yet this felt like no resolution at all.   It was stunningly obvious to her what had happened, knowing the man before her, and seeing how it all fit together.   And this justice tasted like ashes in her mouth.

"You killed him," Trace pronounced very clearly, as though to dispel her own lingering disbelief. "Fleet Admiral Anjo. Didn't you." Khola just looked at her. "You don't know what happened to Chankow and Ishmael because you've come from Homeworld directly. This ship comes from Homeworld, as does Calvin Debogande. Chankow was in Heuron, and Ishmael in New France, it's not a straight line from Homeworld to here. You think they're dead because Guidance Council ordered them killed, otherwise you'd have no way of knowing."

"Major," Erik said in disbelief, "the Guidance Council's just a ghost ship tale..."

"It's absolutely real," Trace corrected him. "The Captain told me. Admiral Anjo was an intensely selfish man of no personal courage whatsoever. He's as likely to kill himself as I am to start drinking. If Guidance Council wanted it done, they would have turned to their most trusted operative on Homeworld. Fleet Academy's on Homeworld. *You're* on Homeworld." To Khola. "You stuffed that gun in his mouth personally, didn't you. And pulled the trigger to end the Fleet Admiral's screams." Khola's stare gave her nothing. That alone let her know she was right. "You couldn't just let them retire because they knew too much, and had such big egos they wouldn't go quietly, and wouldn't stay quiet once deposed. Who replaces them now? Some spineless wet rag who'll bend whichever way the Council blows?"

"Fleet Command has offered you full pardon," Khola repeated blankly. "I have been instructed to give you one hundred standard hours to decide whether to accept it or not. It comes with conditions."

"Wait wait wait," said Erik, with more skepticism than Trace had feared. If ever there was a time to be skeptical, it was now, with Fleet assassinating the politically inconvenient left and right. "Fleet Command has authority to grant us a full pardon, but you don't know who occupies the top ranks of Fleet Command at present? How can I accept the authority of Fleet Command when you can't tell me who they are?"

"The constitutional authority resided, at the time I was given my orders, in the hands of Rear Admiral Bedi," said Khola. "I have those orders in writing, with signatures, and your Uncle has seen them."

"It looks okay to me, Erik," Calvin said cautiously. "I reviewed the books as soon as I saw it, of course. It... it looks good. Erik, you won't be defenceless once you come home, without *Phoenix*. The family is with you. Your mother strongly advises you accept this offer, as do I."

A pause as Erik thought about it. "What are the conditions?" he asked finally.

"That you abandon the Worlder cause," Khola said simply. "That you re-swear your oaths to Fleet, that you follow all orders from that point on and cease this politicking for the Worlders. *Phoenix* will be allowed to remain together as a crew. I've allowed the rest of your crew to reunite with you out here as a token of Fleet's good will. The ship crew will not be broken up, and no hidden or surreptitious punishment will be handed out after the fact.

"And finally, that none of *Phoenix*'s crew, following retirement in the years ahead, will engage in politics on the behalf of the Worlder cause, or pursue any course that could be detrimental to Fleet, and the human cause. Should *Phoenix* fail to accept this offer within one hundred standard hours, *Phoenix* and all her crew shall be declared once more renegade, and an enemy to the human cause. All suitable actions against her shall then resume."

CHAPTER 13

Joma Station's transit line ran around the upper side of the station rim. The enormous rim supports moved slowly past the windows now, massive alloy steel beams, curving slowly about the station wheel. From them extended a huge latticework of additional supports, becoming impenetrable chunks of new station in parts, all crawling with robotic beam constructors and welders, like enormous stick insects, showering orange sparks from their multiple joining arms. Suited workers moved amongst them like ants, walking on atop the beams with nothing but an endless drop into empty space if they fell.

Beyond the maze of ongoing construction, the starfield turned as the station spun, currently in daylight from the distant star. Rhea loomed near, bright orange with brilliant blue rings. Why they were that colour, Erik hadn't taken the time to learn.

"Fleet are here," he said to Kaspowitz. "I can smell it. There's no way they sent Colonel Khola into an unprepared battlespace. They're watching us."

Kaspowitz looked grim. "You think they've got spies on station?"

Erik nodded. "They already paid one bunch of people to ambush us on the way here, they can pay others to watch us now."

"We don't know they did that," Second Lieutenant Dufresne corrected. Erik had invited her to join them, figuring that one of the two reserve pilots should be getting some experience in the off-ship side of command. Lieutenant Alomaim and Bravo First Squad provided security, filling the entire first car of the transit train, as wary locals kept their distance. "Or at least, if it was Fleet, likely it was Supreme Commander Chankow. Who's not there anymore."

Erik considered her. "Does that make you feel safer, Second Lieutenant?"

Slim and pale, Dufresne looked uncomfortable in her bodyarmour. Erik didn't think she'd worn it much before — junior pilots rarely got station duty outside of sitting in the accommodation block. "It's not a question of feeling safe, sir. But they've given us a pardon." Erik glanced at Kaspowitz. Kaspowitz made a wry grimace. Dufresne looked back and forth between them. "We *are* going to accept the pardon, aren't we sir?"

"Out of curiosity," Erik asked her, "how bad would Fleet's behaviour have to get before you decided to call them on it?"

Dufresne frowned. "Sir?"

"They just killed their own commanders. For becoming inconvenient. Before that, they killed Captain Pantillo, and tried to kill us."

Dufresne shook her head. "Supreme Commander Chankow and Fleet Admiral Anjo did that. And Ishmael, the big three."

"You think their replacements will be better?"

"Colonel Khola says they give their word, sir."

"They already gave their word, Second Lieutenant. It's right there in the oath, loyalty and devotion to our uniformed brothers and sisters. But we've seen that for the High Command, Fleet oaths can become optional at any moment."

"Sir, can you blame them?" There was anger in Dufresne's voice, followed by the uncertainty of a young officer who wondered if she'd just overstepped.

"Go on," Erik said calmly.

"Sir, Earth was destroyed. Ninety-nine percent of us were killed, nine-point-nine billion men, women and children. Humanity nearly ended. Never again, sir. My family raised me with those numbers drummed into my head. Never again. It's a dangerous universe, and we have to do whatever it takes. No one likes war, no one likes killing, everyone would love to do the right and proper thing all the time if they could, I'm sure. But we don't live in that kind of universe."

Erik nodded slowly. It was a very good answer, he could not deny it. "It was a very long time ago. We number nearly five hundred billion now. Does one event a thousand years ago justify *everything* we might do out here?"

"Sir," Dufresne said stubbornly. "If you don't think it could happen again, why did *you* join up?"

Erik nodded slowly. It was another very good answer. And a very good question that he wasn't sure he had a reply to. The transit train slowed as they approached a completed station section, then burrowed into a steel tunnel. Then halted, as the airlock doors behind closed and the tunnel about them was flooded with air. Ahead the inner doors opened, and the magnetic train accelerated once more, regretfully without the magnificent view.

An uplink light flashed in the lower corner of Erik's vision — it was Second Lieutenant Karle. "Go ahead Second Lieutenant."

"*Sir, just to inform you that PH-1 is loaded and we are about to depart.*"

"Very good Mr Karle. Just remember, Lieutenant Dale has thirty years of experience at this. On all security matters, I want you to do exactly what he tells you, when he tells you to do it."

"*Yessir. I get the feeling he wouldn't leave me much choice anyway.*

Erik smiled. "You're exactly right. Please tell Lieutenant Hausler not to frighten the local traffic too badly."

"*I'll do that sir. See you soon.*"

"Good hunting Lieutenant."

And, "*I heard that LC,*" Lieutenant Hausler added before the coms cut. PH-1 was headed for Vola Station, where several shipyards had been very interested in the job offer when they'd heard the money on offer. The Vola moon was a closer orbit to Rhea than Joma Station and its Joma moon. Closer orbits were always faster to reach, but any emergency rescue from *Phoenix* would mean plunging deep into Rhea's gravity well. Erik decided that he'd *never* like having his people away from *Phoenix* on shuttle missions.

"It'll take a lot longer than one hundred hours for any local fabricators to make us some new vipers," Kaspowitz remarked.

"Pardon or no pardon," said Erik, "I'd like our magazines full before we head anywhere. Human space included." Kaspowitz was studying him, as though wryly curious. "What?"

"When all our missing crew came out of *Europa*. Did you think for a moment maybe Commander Huang was on board?"

Marines doing security for senior officers usually did a good job pretending not to listen to these conversations. But now, many eyes glanced his way. Erik shrugged, pretending unconcern. "It crossed my mind."

"Curious dilemma," Kaspowitz suggested. Erik understood the unasked question too well. Would you be pleased, or relieved, to relinquish command at this time? Commander Huang had been on *Phoenix* for seven years, all of them as Pantillo's second-in-command. Prior to recent events, she'd held infinitely more respect on the ship than Erik had.

And for a brief moment on *Europa*'s dock, he'd been terrified. Terrified that Huang would come down that ramp in person, declare herself to be *Phoenix*'s true commander and here to finish her old captain's work in his name, and that all the crew would flock to her in preference to him. Which was insane, because in this situation he should have been thrilled to have someone infinitely more experienced in charge. *Phoenix* would certainly have been the better for it, and all her crew, Lisbeth included, would have been that much safer. He thought again of that terrifying instant when the three sard ships had jumped, and he'd realised that they were coming at him far, far faster than he'd expected, and that he should have left thirty seconds ago. Everyone had nearly died in that one lazy, presumptuous mistake, and his nails now dug into his palms as he recalled it. Huang would never have misjudged it that badly.

"Wouldn't have mattered if she had come down the ramp," Lieutenant Alomaim said coolly. "Lieutenant Jersey got left behind by mistake — Commander Huang did it on purpose. Crew wouldn't have her back, sir. More to the point, the Major wouldn't have her back."

Which made him feel a little better. But only a little, because while the approval of marines was nice, they weren't any more qualified to know who the best pilots were than he was to know who the best marines were.

The transit car came to a whining halt at what Erik's uplinks told him was their stop. Bravo Platoon exited the train first to clear the platform... and immediately weapons came up, with yells and warning shouts over coms. Stationers on the platform shrieked and ducked, scampering out of the line of fire as two privates grabbed Erik and pulled him down, crouched on the train floor with weapons ready.

"You get down right now you bug motherfucker!" someone was shouting. Sard on the platform, Erik guessed.

"Hold it!" came Alomaim's voice over the top. *"Everyone just hold it! They're not armed that I can see, no shooting with the civilians on the platform!"* The train's doors began to close once more, but someone hit the override and everything froze, an emergency alarm blaring with red lights. *"Everyone cool it, just back away! Translators on, just back away!"*

Erik wanted to see, but couldn't past his bodyguards. He pulled his pistol from its holster, his only personal weapon. If he ever had to use it, marines would consider themselves failed in their task of protecting him. Past the yelling civilians and confusion on coms, he could hear a high-pitched shrill, like cicadas in rainforest, only much louder.

"Okay, up! Kamov, move the LC now!" And Lance Corporal Kamov gestured Erik, Kaspowitz and Dufresne up, the other two also with pistols drawn, eyes wide with alarm. They came out onto the transit platform, now mostly cleared of civvies. Marines stood in several groups, massive rifles levelled at the tall, thin figures of sard. Insectoid faces turned Erik's way as he exited, multiple beady black eyes tracking him, and the cicada-shrill rose several pitches.

"Yeah, you turn that shit down!" someone snarled — on coms it was impossible to tell who.

Erik and the officers were quickly whisked down a side corridor, one group of marines pulling off the platform ahead, the others falling in behind as they moved. He'd only counted seven sard on the platform, none of them armed.

"Lieutenant Alomaim," he said. "Was that an attack?"

"Just an encounter, sir," said Alomaim on coms from somewhere behind him. *"Taking no chances today."*

They emerged from the access corridor onto the station concourse, an open floor with big information screens flashing colourful scenes at passing crowds. Now those crowds were staring with uncertainty at these thumping, armoured humans who came surging through their midst. Station security in dark-red uniforms moved to confront them, one of them shouting in Palapu as his translator-speaker joined in harsh, metallic English.

"You no point guns at peaceful sard guest! Peaceful sard guest want to catch train too! This not human station, this barabo station! You behave like civilised person!"

"Move asshole!" was Gunnery Sergeant Brice's reply, and the security got out of the way before they were run over.

"Not a human station *yet*," another marine corrected the security man with passing contempt. Erik wondered if it were possible that humans on Joma Station could outstay their welcome.

"I don't think they were tracking us," Kaspowitz said at Erik's side as they strode, breathing hard. "That looked like an accident."

"No chances with sard," Erik replied. "Sard aren't real sneaky, it's not like they can follow us unnoticed, on this station. Manufacturing an encounter like that could be the only way for them to see where we're going. And test our responses."

"And then report everything they've seen to some other sard ship waiting out beyond the system rim," Dufresne agreed close behind them. "I reckon we watch for any of those sard ships leaving the station, fair bet they're going to report on us."

And they still had no *real* idea as to why those three super-advanced sard ships were trying to kill them. More than any chance encounter on a train station, *that* put Erik's nerves on edge most of all.

Joma Station bridge was on the upper rim on the far side of the station from *Phoenix*'s berth. Directly above it, with an elevated viewing level above the main rim, was the Stationmaster's personal quarters.   It was spacious, with the earthy decoration typical of barabo — a thick floor rug, wall hangings of what looked like decorated tree bark, and lots of leafy green pot-plants.

Erik, Kaspowitz and Dufresne sat in deep reclining chairs across a low table, while Lieutenant Alomaim remained standing with Private Cruz, armour tension tuned down to minimum so the whine and rattle wouldn't be distracting.   Out the wide viewing window, the huge upward curve of the station rim ended barely five hundred meters away, replaced with an intricate mass of scaffolding, crawling with robots and workers.

Opposite them were the Stationmaster, and the Captain of a station-defence warship, the *Rai Jang*.   His name was Jen Fan, and he was concerned.   "You not know why sard want kill you?"   He spoke English quite well, and with great skepticism.   His black beard and hair were neatly trimmed, and he had odd shaving marks in his neck that Erik hadn't seen before.   His uniform was black and grey, also most restrained for a barabo.

"We don't know," Erik replied.   "We thought maybe our own commander, Supreme Commander Chankow, had paid them to kill us.   Sard are sometimes mercenary."   Frowns from the barabo. "Mercenary… um, soldiers who fight for money."   Comprehending nods.   Erik was not surprised to find senior barabo here speaking English.   Everyone in this space was just marking time until the human Fleet arrived.   "But now we hear that Supreme Commander Chankow is not in charge anymore, and might even be dead.   So maybe he did buy those sard, and maybe they aren't aware yet that he's gone.   I don't know how that affects a contract, in the sard mind."

Captain Jen nodded, intensely serious.   Erik had not yet met a barabo quite so intensely serious.   He didn't see any harm in telling him this much of *Phoenix*'s affairs — everyone knew *Phoenix* was renegade from human command, even if the exact details of the dispute eluded them.   And they would shortly know, if they didn't already, that UF Fleet's command had now changed, in highly-questionable circumstances.   This much honesty would cost him nothing, and gain him a little trust at least.

"But you say sard ship are advanced?" Captain Jen pressed.

"Very advanced," Erik agreed. *"Phoenix* was challenged."

Captain Jen blinked. "Three sard ships not normal to… to challenge *Fee-nix?"*

Erik shook his head. "No. Not normally. Do you have any idea how the sard might have such advanced ships?"

"Not know," Jen muttered. "Very bad, this news. Tavalai… ten years ago? All this, tavalai everywhere." He waved a hairy, long-fingered hand at the station view. "Tavalai ship, big warship. Sard come here, sard space close, but sard scared tavalai. Fear tavalai, yes?"

"Yes," Erik agreed. "Tavalai gave sard ships, guns, everything. Tavalai understand sard, no one else does."

Jen nodded vigorously. "Yes, this. Just this. But now, tavalai go. No more tavalai, tavalai lose war to human." With an accusing stare. "And now, sard here, sard there, sard everywhere. Now you say advanced sard, big sard ship. This very bad. If human no come here? No come to Kazak? Sard take Kazak, you bet. Bad news for human too, yes?"

"You're barabo fleet?" Erik asked. "Barabo military?"

Captain Jen nodded without enthusiasm. "Am that. Soldier."

"Why can't *you* fight sard? This is barabo space, but barabo don't fight for it."

The barabo's wide mouth turned down in a jaw-grinding frustration. "Because barabo like party," he said bitterly. "Barabo like fun, like good time, barabo no like fight. Some barabo fight — me, friend captain, friend crew. Few barabo, only few. Other barabo not come. Barabo government give us no money, yes? We three ship here, Joma Station base. Good ship, tavalai ship. But not big ship. Fast, but small gun — you see."

Erik nodded. He had seen — they were tukala-class cruisers, agile and fast, and relatively cheap to produce in large numbers. But even all three on Joma Station weren't a serious threat to *Phoenix*, and most tukala-class captains they'd run into in the war had had the sense to stay clear where possible.

157

"You know," Kaspowitz said conversationally, "there are humans who say that if history had turned out differently, humans could be a lot like barabo. Not fighting much, mostly self-interested. Earth was very self-interested, lots of old civilisation that found itself far more interesting than anything else out in space."

Captain Jen nodded solemnly. "But Earth destroy."

"Yes. You had the tavalai for neighbours, so you never had to fight for anything. We had the krim." He shrugged. "And so we never stopped fighting, one thousand years and more. And with all our old roots destroyed, we had nothing to look back at, we could only look forward. Expansion and conquest became how we measured our progress. Military success, defeating our enemies. That's all our history. So don't be sad that you're not like us. A strong military is good, but we had to pay a terrible price to get one."

"And barabo going to pay bad price without one," Jen replied. There was real fear in his dark eyes. But not cowardice, because this fear was not for himself. "I sorry 'bout Earth. In my culture, we speak of great sorrow, we drink to ancestors or they get angry with us." He raised his teacup. "Earth, ri-jen guhar ari-jen."

He drank, and they all copied. Erik was touched, and saw his fellow officers felt the same. He indicated to Kaspowitz's bag with his eyes, suggestively.

"Oh, speaking of drinking," said Kaspowitz, and unzipped the bag. He pulled out one of the bottles they'd been saving for these situations, and presented it to Stationmaster Rang Gan, who had been quietly listening. Rang Gan leaned forward to peer at the bottle from within bristling dreadlocks and thick beard. In many barabo cultures, a head like a giant bird's nest was a sign of dignified age and learning, for men at least. And sometimes for women.

"What drink?" asked the Stationmaster.

"It's called whisky. It's made from grain, very old recipe, it goes back to an Earth-place called Britain, one and a half thousand years ago. The grains were brought into space with us, and this one was made on New Punjab in William's System, by the same old recipe."

Rang Gan's eyes lit up, and he clapped his hands and spoke on coms. Quickly some drinking glasses were brought, and the whisky poured for all. *Phoenix* officers were not supposed to drink on duty, but sometimes foreign customs demanded that rule be slightly bent. A sip, and Rang Gan's eyes lit up even more. Barabo did love a drink, and this tale of an ancient drink from long-lost Earth was irresistible to those who considered themselves cultured. They talked for a while of human drinks and barabo drinks, and all agreed that this could be a great luxury trade between human and barabo.

And then, once the level of the bottle had dropped a little more, Erik leaned forward in his chair, and smiled at the older man. "Now, Stationmaster. We have noticed that on *Phoenix*'s portion of the docks, there are currently very few security personnel. Do you think we could see this situation addressed? Better that your people keep the civilians away, with their small guns, than we do it with our big guns."

"Rang Gan good man," said Captain Jen as they left the office through the lobby of busy barabo at big display screens. A work crew were noisily discussing ongoing station work on a huge technical hologram, hard hats and safety vests amidst more formal barabo office robes. "But quiet man. No push hard, no make trouble."

"Hmm," said Erik, eyeing the activity as they walked. "Could be a problem in a station like this? I notice construction is far behind schedule."

Jen smiled humourlessly. "Everyone notice. Station damn scared. Big business here, big money, but with tavalai gone, no defence. Saying among my people — when tree branch bend, smallest person seem biggest weight. Many barabo sitting on tree branch, see? Hungry animal below. Big barabo want throw small barabo off branch, make branch not break, even though small barabo make small weight.   Big barabo hope hungry animal eat him last, yes?"

His gaze fixed on Erik with hard meaning.   Erik nodded slowly. "I think I understand. Thank you for the warning."

"And you have more that whisky?   My ship take donation." With a very barabo grin.

Erik grinned back.   "Make you a trade.   You give me a bottle of your best barabo drink, I get you whisky."

"Good," Jen agreed.   They shook hands, barabo-style. "Good travel, *Fee-nix*."

"Good travel, *Rai Jang*."

They left the main lobby heading opposite ways, into a heavily-trafficked hallway with busy barabo offices on all sides. "I'm not sure I understood that warning," Dufresne said cautiously, as Gunnery Sergeant Brice and half of First Squad took position in front.   "He was warning that the Stationmaster would toss us to the sard?"

"Worse than that," Erik said grimly.   "Joma Station wants humans to take over protection for Kazak where the tavalai left off. That means Fleet.   If Fleet wants us dead, Fleet could pay the Stationmaster, and he'd facilitate that however he liked."

"Wait a moment... Captain Jen *works* for the Stationmaster, doesn't he?"

"Now you see what he's warning us."

"Damn," Dufresne murmured.

"Everything's 'damn' out here," said Kaspowitz.

"*LC,*" came Second Lieutenant Abacha's voice on com override.   "*I have priority scan, jump entry, one new signal, looks like combat velocity.   Trajectory is straight for Rhea, looks like it came from Sector-Q18, Navcomp says about nine marked possibilities in that direction, Nav is processing them now.*"

"I copy that Scan," said Erik, not breaking stride.   Alomaim gave the signal for everyone to walk faster, listening as they all were. "Tell me the moment you have firm ID."

"*Yessir.   Sir, Scancomp says ninety-nine percent match, tavalai combat carrier, ibranakala-class.*"   And Erik's heart skipped a beat.   If there was one class of ship in all the galaxy that could nearly match *Phoenix* ton-for-ton, it was the tavalai's major combat carrier.   In the war, the appearance of an ibranakala-class on scan would send a cold shiver up the spines of any human crew watching.

"Lieutenant Alomaim!" Erik called ahead.   "Priority recall now, let's get to a shuttle berth!"   And they broke into a run without Alomaim even needing to order, heading for the nearest express elevator cluster.   "*Phoenix* I am on priority recall, get me a shuttle to the nearest berth immediately, Lieutenant Alomaim is coordinating."

"*Copy LC.*"

"*LC, this is Draper.   Incoming mark is retaining V for the moment.   Estimate that at current V it will reach minimum attack-response distance in five minutes.   I've sounded full available crew recall.   Please advise further.*"

Erik knew he could order Draper to wait until he and all *Phoenix* crew were back aboard.   The actual minimum response time was twenty-two minutes, but that was only if they were going to run away.   To actually hold this position, to turn into the attack and engage it, put the five-minute minimum into play.   Joma Station's position on the Rhea gravity slope was strategically poor, and any defending ship had to use those extra seventeen minutes to burn hard for position clear of the gravity well.   If *Phoenix* were going to run, they could all do that together, falling into Rhea's gravity well for a slingshot escape.   But if they were going to fight, Lieutenant Draper would have to do that alone.

"Five minutes, I copy Lieutenant."   Giving life-or-death orders while running wasn't easy.   "We're not going to make it back in five minutes.   If that mark does not dump V, you are to break dock and make a circular flank.   Get in contact with Joma Station defensive cruisers, see if they'll come with you."

"*Aye sir.   Request permission to retain second-shift crew, minus Lieutenant Dufresne.*"

They arrived at a big bank of elevator doors, marines forming a cordon around the largest and simply pushing waiting civvies out of the way.   "It's your ship Lieutenant Draper.   Use whomever you want." As *Phoenix* spacers and marines stood before the elevators and watched impatiently for the next car.

"Come on, come on," someone muttered, watching the approaching elevator. The smaller one arrived first, but it wasn't express, and would stop at too many floors. They were at the top of the rim, and the shuttle dock at the bottom was a long way down. Wary barabo got on, pleased to be away from armed and alarmed humans.

"PH-4 is incoming," Alomaim reported. "ETA two minutes. She's going to have to wait." That was Tif, probably she'd been on midships standby, with PH-1 off on its mission to Vola Station.

"Draper shouldn't try to take an ibranakala-class alone," Dufresne muttered. "Even with our barabo friends as support... sir, we've no guarantee they'll even help, tavalai have always been their friends and protectors."

Erik nodded. "I know." No one even bothered to contemplate that the tavalai might not be hostile. It was entirely possible, but the consequence of complacency in this case was certain death, and they had no choice but to assume the worst. The elevator arrived and some alarmed barabo got off, sidling between the armoured marines. Other barabo who had not been intending to get off were convinced otherwise, and the *Phoenix* crew got on amidst shouts of barabo displeasure.

"Sir, I think he should wait for us so we can run," Dufresne added amidst the tight crush in the elevator. Erik was not keen on running. They'd all worked so hard to get here, and to run before they'd achieved any of their goals would hurt.

"Watch your resistance guys," Alomaim warned his marines, meaning that the light-armoured officers could get accidentally hurt by sudden movements from powered-armour.

"We don't have to make that decision just yet," Erik told Dufresne as the doors closed. But preferably very soon, and while *Phoenix* was still nose-to-dock. Once she left, Draper would be undisputed commander-on-deck, and could do whatever he wanted. Erik resisted the temptation to glance at Dufresne. Never had the matter of who sat the second-shift command chair seemed as urgently important as now.

The elevator hummed downward, skipping a whole bunch of minor floors as it headed for the dock level. *"Sir, it's Abacha. Mark just dumped V."* An audible sigh of relief within the elevator. To Erik it felt as though a 10-G burn had just ended, that sudden gasp of wonderful lightness. *"Scan now has firm ID — ibranakala-class confirmed. Still no transponders, it appears to be on high alert... sir... sir one more dump, they've slowed right down."*

"*Phoenix* this is the LC," said Erik, trying hard to keep the relief from his voice, for Draper's benefit. "Maintain orange alert status, I will be returning to *Phoenix* aboard PH-4 ASAP. First-shift will then resume command, and I want all spacer crew on-ship and prepared for undock."

"Aye sir," said Draper.

"Major Thakur, do you copy?"

"The Major copies LC."

"I want three platoons on-ship, I want two to remain on station for now to secure our holdings here. Joma Station has value to the tavalai as well. If we keep it occupied, we may dissuade hostile action toward *Phoenix*."

"Aye LC, we are mobilising now." Because two platoons of marines were probably enough to capture this station's bridge and other keypoints, given the total lack of serious military force here. Erik did not like to hold a station hostage in the face of a threat, but it was a common enough tactic with carriers. In strategic and economic terms, warships were expendable, but space stations were not.

"This is kind of like Talyrai Station," Kaspowitz volunteered. "Were you on *Phoenix* then?"

"Yes," said Erik, mildly offended that Kaspowitz had forgotten. "I rode the whole thing out in quarters, as usual."

On that occasion, *Phoenix* had docked and occupied a minor station in a tavalai outer system, only to be ambushed by a group of tavalai ships, including one of their less-manoeuvrable but enormous fleet carriers. Ordered not to surrender the station, *Phoenix* had left four of her five marine platoons behind, then took off to lead the tavalai ships a merry chase about the system, while the tavalai carrier had docked and disgorged karasai — the tavalai marines. One rotation later, *Phoenix* had returned to Talyrai Station having destroyed several ships and sent the rest to flight, to find Trace's marines had fought the tavalai to a standstill despite being outnumbered three-to-one. The remaining tavalai had boarded their carrier and run before *Phoenix*'s return.

"That was just before I arrived," Alomaim recalled grimly. "Lieutenant Dale gets furious when he talks about it, because Fleet concluded from the result that the karasai quality was weak. Dale says they were elite, Fleet just didn't want to give *Phoenix* more credit."

"There's no such thing as weak karasai," Gunnery Sergeant Brice agreed. Brice was a twenty year veteran, and had seen significantly more combat than her Lieutenant. "They're slow, like all tavalai, but they're tough as old boots."

There was real respect in her voice. A lot of marines hated tavalai, but none who'd fought them failed to respect them. Fleet propaganda for the civilian world liked to make big claims about human superiority, but in truth, that superiority was limited. *Phoenix* was alo-tech, and more advanced even than ibranakala-class, plus she'd been commanded by a captain who was a genius — but a lot of human warships weren't that lucky. And while most Fleet marine units were slightly superior to equivalent karasai units, a lot of the fighting had taken place on planets, and planets were the domain of the army, not the marines. Human army units varied wildly in quality, reflecting the organisation and nature of the worlds they'd come from. That variant quality had caused many political scandals during the war, when some army units had been neatly annihilated by their tavalai equivalents. And on those unhappy occasions when human army had met tavalai karasai, even the good human units had been mauled.

What had won humanity the war, most capable analysts agreed, was what Gunnery Sergeant Brice had alluded to — tavalai slowness. In reality, tavalai's physical speed in battle had little bearing, though they weren't exactly lightning. They were just too conservative, lacking whatever killer instinct humans and some other species possessed to go for the jugular, and to take risks and be aggressive. Chah'nas were often over-aggressive, and against them tavalai discipline under fire served well, meeting brash chah'nas gestures with calm and unrelenting firepower. But the best human units combined both discipline and technology with calculated aggression and unnerving risk. Against that combination, tavalai had lost system after system across a hundred and sixty one years of war, until half of their previous territory was gone.

The elevator reached the lower rim berths after several stops where stationers were refused entry, then Gunnery Sergeant Brice led them at a fast walk along the busy berths, through incoming and outgoing crowds of mostly construction workers. At PH-4's berth they found Charlie Platoon marines aboard and guarding the entry, then made a quick embark into familiar harnesses. Tif cut them loose with a jolt, turned the shuttle contra-spin and hit thrust until the station's rotation had brought *Phoenix* back around to their position. Another series of fast burns and building Gs culminated with a crash of grapples.

"Two minutes seventeen," one of the marines remarked, having timed their pilot from undock. *"Hausler can do it in one fifty."*

And must have said it on open mike by mistake, because Tif replied from up front, *"Hausrer die young, I die awd rady in bed with thousand grandchyrd."*

Alomaim gave Private Lo a whack on the helmet as they unharnessed. *"Don't be an asshole on an open mike,"* he said.

"Sorry LT."

Erik reached the *Phoenix* bridge to find first-shift had already taken their places in anticipation of the change-over. Only Lieutenant Draper remained in the command chair, unbuckling now as Erik approached. "LC on the bridge!" The relief was plain on his face, where usually there would be faint frustration at having to relinquish command. And when he'd helped Erik finish the final buckle, "LC has the chair!"

"I have the chair," Erik agreed, and gave Draper a whack on the arm as he left. "Status please."

"New mark is still cruising LC," said Geish from Scan. "ETA thirty-one hours." Which was a vast improvement on the thirty minutes they had been approaching on. "Unremarkable approach."

"One communication with station," said Shilu from Coms. "We can't decrypt it, but it wasn't long. I'd guess basic docking request. And we got one message from barabo cruiser *Rai Jang*, coms officer tells me, and I quote, 'this guy no trouble. Good tavalai, hunt bigger fish than human', unquote."

Erik glanced at Shahaim, who'd been here all along. "That the guy you met at the Stationmaster's office?" she asked.

"Yes, Captain Jen Fan. Impressive, as barabo military go."

"You trust him?"

"Well, he warned us the Stationmaster might order him to kill us at Fleet's behest," Erik explained. "So yes, and no."

CHAPTER 14

The tavalai combat carrier was named *Makimakala*, and Joma Station helpfully assigned her to Berth 28, two places beyond *Europa*'s berth and ten away from *Phoenix*. Erik felt no need to undock for safety — *Phoenix* was actually safer nose-to-station, as it was impossible on the approach angle for the tavalai to fire on *Phoenix* without hitting station. Firing on station was an evil offence in most territories, and tavalai were more principled than most. Additionally, *Makimakala* was approaching squarely along Joma Station's axis, and being docked would not stop *Phoenix* from shooting back to equal effect.

Erik did deploy both of *Phoenix*'s remaining combat shuttles, however, sitting stationary in close proximity with weapons trained, just in case. Typically an ibranakala-class's defensive weaponry would neutralise incoming shuttle fire, but at these ranges the reaction time would be minimal and the threat very real. *Makimakala* responded by deploying all seven of her combat shuttles, weapons trained on both human shuttles and *Phoenix*, while Joma Station control looked on and fretted, and civvie ships of all types stayed well clear from the crossfire.

"This feels kinda strange," Trace admitted as Erik met her on the dock opposite Berth 23 — midway between the human and tavalai warships. Behind Erik and Trace stood Charlie Platoon, in casual formation that just *happened* to be offset to allow everyone a forward line of fire. Behind them and out of the line of fire was Delta Platoon, a ready reserve to rush forward if the shit hit the fan. In their accommodation reserve to the left and well behind, Echo Platoon — not combat deployed through the corridors in a flanking move, as that would be openly hostile and sure to be reported to approaching tavalai by barabo locals. But it *was* their accommodation space, and they could use it to deploy in a flanking move through the back corridors if they wished. Bravo Platoon, and those Alpha Squads that had not gone with PH-1 on Lieutenant Karle's rearmament mission, remained on *Phoenix*.

"Have you ever met a karasai formation that hadn't surrendered, and not opened fire on them?" Erik asked.

Trace shrugged faintly. "First time for everything." And glanced back across her formation of tense, heavily armed marines. "Anyone know any songs?" Trying to lighten the mood, Erik thought. *He* was tense, but for marines it had to be on a whole different level. These men and women had spent a good part of their lives fighting bloody battles with tavalai in situations just like this — on stations, in armoured formations.

"Wouldn't it be a good idea to order them to keep their safeties on?" Erik asked.

"Sure," Trace deadpanned. "I could order them not to fart in their suits, too. Doesn't mean they'll listen."

Erik blinked a lower-vision icon that opened a channel to Lieutenant Jersey in PH-3. "Hey Regan. What's it like out there?"

"Oh you know," said Jersey. *"My first day back on the job and I'm in an armed standoff outnumbered three-to-one. Same old same old."*

Erik smiled. "How about you, Tif?"

"Guns," said Tif. *"In-tes-ting."* Meaning her front-seater controlled them, and she didn't particularly like them.

"We're a warship, Tif," Erik said lightly. "Perhaps you noticed?"

"I nake note." Erik laughed. The reports of Tif's growing popularity with the crew were clearly true. Now she was even funny.

Trace was looking at him with approval, not having heard that conversation, but no doubt thinking it was good for her marines to see the LC laughing right now. "How are the new marines?" Erik asked her.

"Good," said Trace without hesitation. "A bit rusty, a few wouldn't pass the physicals... they've got time to work on it. Considering their combat records, I'm in a mood to be flexible. A few of them are behind us right now, in Charlie." Alpha and Charlie had taken the biggest hits, on the rock in Argitori System, in the hacksaw ambush. Erik wondered if Trace had put Charlie in the front rank behind them on purpose, so her most trusted veterans could observe the old new guys under pressure. And decided that of course she had — Trace didn't do anything without purpose.

A dull metallic rumbling drew his attention up the dock. Beneath the lowest curve of the ceiling, the feet of many armoured soldiers became visible, advancing in a solid wall of steel and guns. As they came closer, the whine of many alien power units began to drown the clatter of armoured boots. Karasai powered armour sounded different to human — slightly louder and lower-pitched, pushing a heavier weight with solid tavalai frames. Their weapons were every bit as deadly-looking as the human kind — huge main rifles, shoulder-mounted launchers, protruding secondary weapons on thigh and stomach-holsters, armoured storage webbing for grenades and other gear. Arms and legs mounted the small holes of thrusters for zero-G operation, and their helmets were low, wide and flat, to accommodate tavalai heads. They looked hunched, to human eyes, a powerful, rolling gait of broad shoulders and thick legs. No one could look upon this formation, and believe that those Fleet propaganda tales of outclassed and terrified tavalai were anything other than the steaming piles of manure they surely were.

"No. Sudden. Movements." Trace spelled it out loudly on coms, just to be sure everyone understood. "This is a meeting, not a confrontation. If anyone gets jumpy, everyone here will die. If you can't hold your nerve, tell me now and we'll send you back to *Phoenix* to cuddle your safety blanket."

No one spoke. The alien horde advanced across a dock not-so-mysteriously free of civilians, and Erik noted two tavalai sporting only light armour in the middle. Those two seemed to see Erik, and aimed straight for him and Trace. In full armour, Trace nonetheless wore only her cap — a reminder to her troops, Erik thought, of just how dead she in particular would be if shooting started. Erik suspected that whatever her suspicions of tavalai, she didn't think the shooting would start from *them*. Tavalai didn't panic, even when they probably should. Marines admired that about them, even as they thought them slightly nuts.

The armoured line halted, and Erik could clearly see their formation arrangement — fifteen-man squads in five-man sections, karasai preferring fives where marines preferred fours. Erik wondered what the sard would make of it. The two lightly armoured tavalai strolled forward, their gait still rolling, making it obvious that it wasn't the armour that did it. Trace indicated to Erik, and together they walked forward to greet them.

In the middle of the empty dock, twenty paces each way from the opposing lines, they stopped. The tavalai had insignia on their chest armour, strange markings in some script far older than Togiri... Erik recognised one as the captain's mark. No doubt tavalai found the bronze leaf of both spacer LC and marine major very odd as well.

Erik extended his hand to the tavalai captain, and activated his translator. "Hello," he said. *"Gidiri ha,"* said his belt speaker. "I'm Lieutenant Commander Erik Debogande, of the *UFS Phoenix.*"

The tavalai captain extended a thick paw, gloveless, and grasped Erik's hand. The fingers were slightly webbed, the skin smooth and leathery. More war propaganda said that tavalai were slimy, but this grip felt warm and tough, like an old leather glove. And immensely powerful, too. Tavalai weren't any taller than humans, but their homeworld had one-point-two times what humans chauvinistically called 1-G. Humans called tavalai 'froggies' to belittle them, but the reality was far more imposing than that.

The tavalai spoke in the staccato vowels of Togiri. *"I am Captain Pramodenium,"* said the Captain's translator speaker. *"This is my next-in-command, Commander Nalbenaranda. My greetings to you."*

The oddest thing about talking to tavalai was not knowing where to look. Their heads were so different, long, wide and flat, with widely spaced eyes and a big, flat mouth. Humans were accustomed to gazing upon faces with eyes, nose and mouth all conveniently close together, so expressions could be read without difficulty. But with tavalai, Erik felt he had to almost step back a bit, to get both eyes into the same field of reference.

"This is my marine commander," he added, indicating Trace. "Major Trace Thakur. She is my second-in-command."

Trace shook the Captain's hand in turn. "Captain," she said respectfully. "What brings you to Kazak System?"

"You do," said the Captain, without need of the translator. His big, dark eyes swivelled inward to focus on Trace, then Erik. "*Makimakala* is Dobruta. You have heard of us?"

"It's familiar," Erik lied. In truth, no one had heard of *Makimakala* at all, and the name did not appear on any *Phoenix* database. Given how extensively every ibranakala-class ship was traced by Fleet, that was slightly astonishing.

"We are the oldest unit in all tavalai military forces. The Dobruta were formed at the beginning of the First Free Age, to police the Spiral of AI technology — what you call the hacksaws. We've been performing that task for more than eight thousand years. It has come to our attention that you have acquired some of that technology after you destroyed an AI nest. We are here to see those acquisitions destroyed."

"Wait," said Erik. "You came all this way because you heard we had... dead hacksaws aboard?"

"That is correct. It's what we do. It's what we've been doing for eight thousand years. The leaders of your civilisation and mine are united in thinking that the AI wars were over twenty five thousand years ago. But in truth, they never entirely ended. The machines will return, if we are careless enough to allow them. The Dobruta have been entrusted to ensure that it never happens."

"*Romki,*" Trace's uplink crackled in Erik's ear, a silent prompt. "*Romki went to talk with his tavalai friends, on Joma Station. He must have ratted on us.*" Because aside from some Fleet officers at Heuron three months ago, they hadn't told anyone else. Unless some of the crew had been loose-tongued on station with civvies... but they'd been instructed not to discuss it, and in Erik's experience, officers weren't the only ones with information discipline. And the language barrier had meant it wasn't the kind of thing easily discussed with non-humans.

"Are you in possession of this illegal technology?" the Captain pressed.

"I don't discuss *Phoenix* matters with non-*Phoenix* crew," Erik said calmly.

The tavalai captain tucked his big thumbs into his belt. "Then that is going to cause us a problem. My information was quite specific."

"I'm sure it was," Trace uplinked with displeasure.

"What kind of a problem?" Erik enquired.

"An armed kind of problem," said the tavalai. "Please understand that we bear you no ill will. But destroying old AI remnants where ever we find them is our entire reason for existence. Either you will offer your ship for inspection, or we will find ourselves at odds." He glanced about and behind them, at the masses of heavily armed marines and karasai. "It does not seem a safe situation. Please consider your position, and what you hope to gain."

Erik sat in Romki's Engineering bay, and stared at the head of the AI queen in its nano-tank. The single big red eye stared back, silently clamped in place amidst a silver swirl of micro-machines.

Lisbeth entered, headed for Romki's workbench, but stopped when she saw her brother. "Oh. Erik!"

"Hi Lis. Just taking my three minutes a day of alone-time to think." He didn't mean it to sound bitter. It was only the truth — being in command meant that everyone wanted a piece of him, and he rarely had any time to himself. It was more than a personal resentment. Sometimes he genuinely felt that he was missing things, thoughts and revelations he might have had if only he'd more time to think, instead of being rushed all the time by needs and schedules and other people's problems.

"Oh, well in that case I won't bother you, I just wanted to check some data and..."

Erik shook his head and patted the adjoining chair beside him, at the opposing work bench to Romki's. "No come, sit. I don't value my time alone as much as my time with you." He'd have been embarrassed to say something so openly sentimental, just a few years back. To his *sister* no less. But something was different now, and he found he had no patience for dancing around things as he once had.

Lisbeth smiled, genuinely touched, and came to sit beside him, and take his hand. "So what's bothering you?"

"Everything."

"Sure, but what in particular?"

Erik sighed. Lisbeth was one of the few people on the ship not technically within his chain of command. Commanders weren't supposed to share worries and frailties with those beneath him, but Lisbeth was hardly that.

"I think I might have made a mistake," he said sombrely. "Coming here."

Lisbeth gazed at him with concern. "Well I don't recall it only being your decision."

"Sure. But I'm in command. Everything *Phoenix* does is my responsibility on principle."

Lisbeth thought for a moment. "Are you going to accept the Colonel's offer of pardon?"

"Well I can't see how it's entirely up to me," Erik said helplessly. "There's six hundred people on this ship who want to see their families again. It has to be their decision, doesn't it? But then, if there's so much at stake, how can I just leave it to a popular vote? Big stakes require leadership. I should lead. But what I think we might have to do... I mean, what we *should* do, will likely get everyone killed."

Lisbeth gripped his hand more firmly. "Erik. The Major doesn't talk about you directly with me, she's too professional for that. But it's obvious she values your opinion. And it's also obvious that she thinks you should have more confidence in yourself than you do."

Erik smiled. "Oh yeah. And she has this odd way of trying to encourage it by second-guessing me at every turn."

"Well you know the Major. Everything's a test. What *do* you think we ought to do? I mean, Colonel Khola's offering a full pardon, and justice for the Captain. That's what you wanted, right? To clear his name? They've admitted they were wrong, the guilty have been punished, and we can all go home if we want to, yes?"

"It didn't achieve anything, Lis. A turnover in the top leadership... so what? The top leadership changes every few years anyway, Chankow had only been in the job eighteen months, Anjo two years. They're all disposable. Fleet lives are supposed to mean something, we have all these memorials to the glorious dead and we go on about the terrible loss, but in truth Fleet's command culture has made us all disposable. Even their own top commanders.

"I know the Captain hated it. He was all for personal sacrifice, but choosing to sacrifice yourself is a very different thing from having some bunch of faceless bigwigs deciding to sacrifice you without asking you first. I think that's what attracted him to the Worlder cause in the first place. It's not that he had any great sympathy for Worlder politics, it was just the lack of personal choice that bugged him. The lack of democracy. I heard him say something like it a few times — what's the point of saving humanity from alien slavery if we have to sell ourselves into human slavery to do it?"

"Do you think the new Fleet Command would leave *Phoenix* alone once we return?" Lisbeth asked quietly. "Do you think they'd keep their word?"

"Oh probably," Erik said dismissively. "For as long as it suited them, anyway. That's not the point. We haven't *won* anything, Lis. Fleet didn't concede to us. They're just playing their politics, their numbers games, same as they always do. And they're asking us to shut up and forget everything that's happened to do it.

"And the more I think about what we'll lose if we do play along and shut up, the more I found myself thinking that the real tragedy won't be Worlder politics and trying to find some new deal between Spacers and Worlders to avoid a civil war. I mean we're dealing here with a Fleet that will assassinate its own leadership in order to achieve its objectives. It's a faceless mob, I'm not even sure who we'd talk to if we could, who could make things stick with Fleet.

"No, the real tragedy would be this." He nodded at the queen's head in the nano-tank. "Human politics will always be there, and will always be hard. But this. This is the first time any powerful human force has tried to get to grips with the big history behind all these human wars. And if Romki's right about the alo… how would we find out? The alo won't tell us. Fleet won't tell us. If we go to alo space ourselves, the alo will kill us — *Phoenix* is alo-tech, they're not scared of us, they've got a hundred ships this good. More probably."

"Erik?" Lisbeth asked carefully. "Do you think that maybe Stan was right?" Erik considered the queen. He wasn't quite prepared to go *that* far. "I'd like to ask her some questions," he said of the queen. "I did tell Trace not to shoot her. I wonder if it's not too late."

"Wake her up?" Lisbeth's eyes were wide. "I'm not sure even Stan thinks that's a good idea. And these tavalai Dobruta want her destroyed."

"You know, I never did entirely understand that," Erik confessed. "If we want to know how to fight them, or even to understand the size of the threat, surely we should study them? Not just destroy everything on sight?"

"You heard the tale of McCauley's Rock?"

"Everyone has. But I did some checking on the name, and there was never a research base on McCauley. I think it might be just a story, made up to scare people."

"No." Lisbeth shook her head. "Stan says it's real, they just changed the name for secrecy. Some researchers really were activating hacksaw brains to learn more about them, and some of those hacksaws really did take over the base by remote and kill everyone there. They can take over foreign systems by remote if they learn them well enough, Stan says. Hack into a marine armour suit and open fire on the other marines, that kind of thing. It's seriously scary stuff, and I doubt we could guard against it because even with all our most advanced tech, hacksaw tech still basically shouldn't exist. None of *Phoenix*'s techs really understand how the queen works. It may as well be magic, for all we can explain it."

"All the more reason to study them."

"Erik, the tavalai were nearly exterminated by hacksaws. All organic sentient life was. The slavery, the genocides... I mean we humans had it rough, but we're not the only ones who said 'never again'. Tavalai think the technology's seductive, and that they have to resist temptation. The Fathers didn't resist the temptation, and it destroyed them completely. Tavalai just refuse to make the same mistake. And so they created the Dobruta."

"You've heard of them?"

"No, but I'm sure Stan has. And they make perfect sense when you think about it. I mean, *Phoenix*'s database has never heard of *Makimakala*, when Fleet track every tavalai warship of that class. So *Makimakala* wasn't in the Triumvirate War, despite how desperately the tavalai needed every ship. It was off doing other stuff. Which tells you how seriously the tavalai take that mission."

"Yeah," Erik murmured, staring at the queen. "I bet they'd know a thing or two about her."

"You think they'll attack us to get her?"

"It's not impossible. Probably not if we're ready for it, tavalai aren't usually that brutal, and Captain Pram seems like a civilised guy."

"A civilised guy given the task of preventing hacksaw armageddon," Lisbeth reminded him. "Don't underestimate how determined he might be."

"No, I won't. But with the sard after us too, there might be some benefits in having an ibranakala-class right alongside us at dock."

"But tavalai and sard are allies," said Lisbeth.

Erik shook his head. "Not *this* tavalai. Tavalai factions do their own thing, they're not a very cohesive people. Dobruta strike me as obsessive in their task, they'll take that very seriously.   They won't care who gets in their way — human, sard or barabo."

CHAPTER 15

The dock jeep thudded over deckplates, weaving between pedestrians and other vehicles. Trace sat on the rear amidst several from Command Squad, a *Phoenix* spacer behind the wheel where marines would not fit. Joma Station locals gave them alarmed looks as they passed, three jeeps loaded with human firepower. It was hard not to imagine that most stations would get sick of *Phoenix* quite quickly, attracting trouble and stomping all over their territory with armoured boots. Already the locals' expressions upon seeing them had shifted from curiosity to wary disapproval.

They zoomed past *Makimakala* at Berth 28, with a casual wave to the tavalai karasai on guard across the dock, weapons pointed unthreateningly at the ceiling. Similar waves came back, tavalai wondering what the crazy humans were up to now. It had been ten hours since *Phoenix* and *Makimakala* commands had discussed matters on station dock. Now she'd been pulled from her bunk in the middle of *Phoenix*'s night-shift — now synchronised to station night-shift — on yet another urgent call.

A berth past *Makimakala*, they stopped, the jeep rocking as marines leapt off. Staff Sergeant Kono took the lead with Privates Arime and Rolonde, the other half of Command Squad behind her, sick of being left behind when she went out on station. Not that they didn't understand her need to share herself around — more that to be in Command Squad meant that the company commander's safety was your responsibility above all else. Compared to that priority, everyone else could go jump.

An elevator took them to the upper rim, then into an open garden square, synthetic sunlight from the high ceiling, thick green trees and simulated flowing streams. Such 'natural' designs on stations made nice open space for hotel frontings, and Kono lead them into one such, hotel staff talking with Joma Station police, looking agitated. Another elevator, and a corridor with several marines guarding it, standing by an open door.

Trace ducked to make sure her Koshaim didn't catch on the doorframe, and found herself looking at a crime-scene. Directly inside the door was a body, shot twice in the chest at close range. Human. Not one of hers, or anyone she recognised from *Phoenix*. The corpse wore a once-nice suit, and a pistol remained locked in his cold hand.

"Major," said Jokono in the room beyond. Trace was not surprised to see Hiro with him. *Phoenix*'s own terrible twosome, some called them. Running off on their own at each station stop, not sleeping in *Phoenix* block accommodation, but renting their own rooms, making their own friends, talking to all kinds of people. Last she'd heard, Jokono had been having dinner with Joma Station security chiefs and getting a guided tour of the place. Doubtless the barabo were all intrigued to meet a human counterpart with such high connections as Family Debogande, and Lieutenant Shahaim was keeping Jokono well financed, so everyone could be suitably wined and dined.

"Hello boys," said Trace, stepping carefully past the body, as Command Squad added their security presence to the hallway outside. Into the main bedroom she saw another body on the floor by a bed. There was a bloodstain on the bedcovers, and a big pool of red on the floor. So he'd been shot from about where she was now standing, had bounced off the bed and fallen to the floor. The shots were again precise, and tightly clustered, suggesting professional work. "Your room Hiro?"

"One of two," said Hiro. "My actual room is across the hall. This is the one registered in my cover name."

"Ah," said Trace, dialling down the armour tension now that she was standing near unarmored people. "A trap."

Hiro nodded. He looked calm as ever, but the calmness was slightly forced, his breathing elevated, his eyes more active than usual. He'd done the shooting, Trace reckoned. No real surprise. "I was looking for other humans on station. There's about four hundred, most of them on business, looking for opportunities once Fleet starts moving this way. A few government, obviously. These were Fleet Intel, operations branch."

"You found that out when they tried to kill you?"

"No, I knew already.   I ran into these guys a lot in my previous job.   I had dinner with another of them last night — we were both pretending to be businessmen, we talked bullshit for most of the evening, we both knew exactly who the other really was.   If you've been in the game long enough, you can just tell.

"And then these two came into my registered room, not knowing I was actually sleeping just down the hall."

"Sloppy," Trace suggested.

"They thought I'd drunk the drink my dinner guest drugged. I faked it. I should have been out cold in bed, it was slow-acting."

Trace nodded thoughtfully, looking at the second bed — pillows had been piled beneath the covers to look like a person sleeping. It had evidently held their attention for long enough. The pillow-man had two holes in him, and the dead man by the bed had a silencer on his pistol. Hiro must have come in the door behind them so fast they'd not realised their mistake until too late.

"Their IDs are very good," said Jokono, holding the men's wallets. "The kind of top work you'd expect from Fleet Intel. The thing is, I managed to trace them to the ship they came in on."

"You did?" Trace was astonished. On an alien station, with no access to central databases, that seemed impossible. "How?"

"Never you mind," said Jokono with a faint smile.   "The thing is, they arrived just yesterday off a ship from Lucient."

"Same place *Europa* came from," Hiro added.

"It's the closest human system," said Jokono, "so it makes sense.   There were thirty-six humans on that ship.   A very, very disproportionate number of them being very fit, youngish, male, etc, etc."

Trace blinked.   "You think they're Fleet Intel Operations too? All of them?"

"Not *all*.   Statistically, maybe half?   Most of the businessmen I meet aren't quite that fit and well dressed, like they've all had their civvies chosen for them by central casting." With a skeptical eye at Hiro's nice suit. Hiro rolled his eyes.

"Well that's not too surprising," said Trace. "The LC said himself he'd bet Colonel Khola wasn't here alone. Obviously Fleet were going to be keeping an eye on his mission. Maybe positioning themselves to intervene violently." She'd have to boost security again, she thought. Increase the minimum numbers in which marines could patrol, and make extra certain no spacer crew went unaccompanied.

"Here's the thing," said Hiro. "*Phoenix* has been advertising she was coming here for a while. Far too loudly, and for far too long."

He'd made that complaint before, Trace knew. But the priorities of spies, and the priorities of *Phoenix*'s commander, were at present two very different things. "Go on," she said.

"So if you're going to move a covert force to Joma Station to support Colonel Khola's mission, you do it *before* he arrives. Prepare the ground. Khola's been here for sixteen days, but these guys just arrived."

"Hmm." Nothing pleased Trace quite so much as the company of people who knew more about certain specialities than she did. In jobs like this, you never stopped learning, and never stopped encouraging those with specific skills to feel free to do their thing. "So they're *not* after us?"

"I don't think so," said Hiro, with a faintly excited intensity. "I think someone else. Someone important. These guys have been *everywhere.* Risky enough to possibly blow their cover, a whole bunch of humans all arriving at once, asking questions."

"Questions about what?"

"About a man travelling incognito," said Jokono, also with intensity. "Got here a few days ago, apparently, paying passenger on the freighter *Dawn.* We talked to a few of the people these guys had been talking to, asked what questions they were asking. A man alone, fleeing from something, possibly with a couple of well-trained bodyguards, and a lot of cash. They were asking moneylenders, there's a blackmarket in conversion of human currency on Joma Station, though it's not officially allowed. Apparently there was one very big conversion, in the right time-range."

Trace's eyes widened as she realised. "Shit. Supreme Commander Chankow."

Hiro and Jokono nodded in unison. "If you're fleeing from Heuron," said Hiro, "this is the only way to get to Outer Neutral Space. And Outer Neutral Space is about the only place Chankow could come where he might be able to go native and be left alone."

"Vieno was certainly a very nice, unpopulated planet to disappear for a long time," Jokono added. "But he arrives in Kazak System, sees *Phoenix* has just arrived, and *Europa* too, and gets scared he'll be spotted. He knows we'll be watching the outgoing passenger traffic for humans, and Khola's people certainly will. So either he's still here, hiding on Joma Station somewhere…"

"Or he's caught a ride out to one of the moons," Trace finished. "Insystem ships don't have to register passenger manifests with station, and even if they did, on a barabo station you'd just buy some gifts and everyone would look the other way." Wow. "Good work guys. I'm actually impressed."

"You know," said Hiro, "I think you're actually impressed with me more often than you'd like to admit."

"Now why wouldn't I like to admit that?" Trace replied. "Keep looking, we need to know what ship he took if he took one, and where it went."

Hiro gave a little bow. "Yes Major. We're on it."

"Station police giving you any trouble?"

Jokono smiled grimly. "Humans shooting humans? They don't want a bar of it. Just make it go away, they say." Which in this case, Trace thought, was probably wise of them.

"Lieutenant Abacha," Trace said on coms as she descended the elevator from upper rim down to dock level. "Please contact Colonel Khola on *Europa* and tell him I want to talk. Main berth, call it ten minutes."

"Aye Major, Europa main berth, ten minutes."

Staff Sergeant Kono looked at her as they descended, wanting an explanation, but not getting one. He'd know soon enough. "Hiro's asked a few questions about you," Kono volunteered. "If you've been in any relationships, if you're straight, that kind of thing."

"Fascinating," said Trace.

"I could tell him to shut it down if you wanted?"

Trace repressed a smile. "No crime to be curious, Staff Sergeant."

"I think he's a little beyond curious, Major."

"Fancy that," said Trace. She knew that Kono, Arime and Rolonde were exchanging quiet glances, daring each other to ask more — she just deigned not to notice. Rolonde in particular, the girl was far too interested in other marines' private lives. As if marines even had such a thing, among other marines.

"You interested, Major?" asked Arime. Of all of them, he was the only one who could make it playful enough to be harmless. They knew she didn't mind playful, in the right circumstances.

"He's pretty cute," Rolonde added.

"He sure shoots a nice, tight cluster," Trace admitted.

"So you *are* interested?"

"I dunno. I was thinking one of those big, friendly kuhsi boys on the dock the other day. The ears really do it for me."

The elevator slowed toward a stop at dock level. "I think she's interested," said Arime. "She just doesn't want to admit it."

"You know," said Trace, "you're fucking geniuses. All of you." And followed Kono out the elevator door. Behind her as she passed, she heard a metallic whack as Kono gave Arime a cuff on the shoulder.

Back on the jeep, she directed Spacer Troski back to *Europa*, the second jeep holding the other half of Command Squad close behind. When she got there, Colonel Khola was waiting at the bottom of the dual ramps, amidst comings and goings from *Europa* crew and station customs inspectors and other barabo officials who had not-so-mysteriously left *Phoenix* alone.

Trace jumped off as the jeep came to a halt, and her squad formed a perimeter around her. Khola stood up, apparently unarmed in his spacer jumpsuit, a cap on his otherwise bald head. Trace stopped before him. "Your people try to kill my people again, I'll blow you away, unarmed or not. Are we understood?"

Another man might have played games, denying there were Fleet men on station at all, pretending not to know what she was talking about. "They're not my people," Khola said flatly. "I'm a marine. They're not. Command structures don't stretch that far."

"I don't care," said Trace. "You're the ranking officer, you're all in the same boat as far as I'm concerned. Tell them if it happens again, I'll take Fleet's offer of pardon as a ruse. I'm having this attack documented in full, video of the crime scene, names, bodies, everything. We'll send that information back to all the Fleet captains who want us pardoned, and you'll have to explain to them why instead of pardoning us, you tried to kill us instead. And then you'll be back where you started."

Khola's lips twisted a little in distaste. "I'll tell them. I'm not in command, but I'll tell them anyway."

"I know you're not in command. They're here to find and kill Supreme Commander Chankow, like you already killed Fleet Admiral Anjo. Looks like he got wind of what was coming and ran before you got him. I'm guessing the spooks tried to kill my guy because *he* figured who they were after, and they didn't want *Phoenix* to know." A look of wary respect from Khola. "Or we might go looking for Chankow first. A real pickle that would be, huh? If we could show the entire human population what actually happened to the big three commanders? Not that they haven't already guessed, of course."

"This is not the behaviour of someone who wants to accept Fleet's pardon," Khola said grimly.

"I've still got sixty hours," Trace retorted. "*Phoenix* is maximising her position."

"There is no position. You either accept, or you decline. Myself, I'd find it preferable if you'd decline. That way we could both escape this hypocrisy."

184

Trace considered her old mentor for a moment. "You don't even care about my reasons?"

"I know that you had the very best of reasons," said Khola. "*Personal* reasons. The Kulina are beyond personal reasons. What you did was anathema to everything the Kulina have ever been, and the worst insult to everyone who has ever called themselves Kulina."

Trace frowned. It hurt, but she was used to pain. "Kulina serve humanity. You serve Fleet. Those two are not the same."

Khola smiled coldly. "Spare me your childish equivalence, humanity would be extinct if not for Fleet. Fleet is the heart and soul of humanity — remove the heart and the body dies."

"You know the alo have Fleet Command by the balls?" A flicker in Khola's eyes. "You know the alo speak with deepynine accents? Their languages are related, on the foundational level."

Khola considered her for a moment. "I've been at a very high level of Fleet Command for a very long time. My rank is only an 0-6, but that does not describe my influence in Fleet."

"Guidance Council," said Trace. "I know."

Khola nodded. "In that role, I've learned quite a lot about our alien allies. More than you, I'm sure."

"I wouldn't be," Trace said evenly.

"And the one thing that I've concluded above all else is that in this part of the galaxy, that we call The Spiral, we can either be pure and moral, or we can stay alive. We can't do both."

"I'm not talking about *morality*," Trace retorted, jabbing an armoured finger at his chest. "I'm talking about strategy. We have a very good expert aboard who swears that the alo are a knife at humanity's heart. You think I'm only worried about the moral dimension of that alliance?" She wasn't entirely sure when she'd started arguing in Romki's favour. Lately, with Erik, she'd been doing the opposite.

"I think you're entirely worried about the moral dimension," Khola said grimly. "Of everything. You forget, I know you. I know all my students, the best ones in particular. I make a point of knowing their motivations. And you, Ms Thakur, have always been driven by a concern for personal justice."

"I am Kulina," Trace growled, her eyes hard. "My only concern has always been the fate of humanity."

"I know your father beat you. I know your mother drank and gambled. I know your eldest brother took dangerous work as a mining technician to escape the home, and it killed him. I know you sought a similar escape to the Kulina. Perhaps you believed in the concept, but mostly you valued the meditations on karma and selflessness as a way out, a way to stop thinking on the matters that bothered you.

"The Kulina are a crutch for you. A bandage on your personal wounds. And ever since, your career has been marked by attachments to powerful men, to replace the father you never had. Me. Captain Pantillo. And now Erik Debogande. Men who stand for something more, men whom you secretly believe can give you something you've always lacked. Emotional security. It's always been about you, Trace. You think you believe in the Kulina teachings of selflessness, but you've been lying to yourself."

"Hey," Trace said coldly. "If you're going to try and kill me, make sure you know who you're killing. Don't tell yourself this cheap back-alley psychoanalysis bullshit to make yourself feel better. Face it like a man. An assassin who kids himself that all his assignments are evil is a coward, unable to face the truth of his actions."

"I don't think you're evil, Trace. I think you're one of the best people I've known." Trace stared at him, forcing herself not to flinch. "But those good qualities have made you forget what we are, and what oath you swore. And the Kulina are bigger than any of us. You accused me of not knowing the difference between service to Fleet, and service to humanity. Well you don't know the difference between service to good, and service to necessity. Kulina abandon their attachments because they blind us to necessity. That's the whole point of being Kulina. You forgot... or rather, you never learned it to begin with. And so we find ourselves here. I love you like a daughter, but I am Kulina, and I know there are things in the universe far greater than one man's love."

Trace tried hard to keep the tremble from her voice. "Your Fleet murdered a man who did more for the human cause in the Triumvirate War than all Kulina combined. That man was a warrior, but he was driven by love — the love for humanity, and the love of his crew.

"You used to tell us about orders, and how bad orders should be questioned and not just followed over a cliff. Kulina are about results, and you can't get results following bad orders or bad commanders. Well Captain Pantillo got results, and Fleet fought him all the way. You prefer Fleet's judgement? If Fleet had put Pantillo in charge we'd have won the damn war thirty years ago."

"You exaggerate. Your personal attachment proves my point."

"No. It proves that I'm the only one of us interested in siding with the *best*. To survive in this galaxy, we'll need the best. But you prefer Fleet, because Fleet's all you know. Fleet's mediocre. That makes Fleet as much a danger to humanity as a help. Fleet crushes its best. As you'd like to crush me."

Khola smiled coldly. "Such modesty."

Trace barely blinked. "Try me."

CHAPTER 16

Lieutenant Tyson Dale liked little Vola Station a lot more than its big brother Joma. In orbit around the inner Vola moon, Vola Station had a maximum capacity of only several hundred thousand compared to Joma's four million plus. But unlike Joma's empty, echoing caverns, Vola had been completed a long time ago, and thrived with all the crazy activity that one expected from a barabo insystem hub.

Dale ran now on a gym treadmill just off the main rim mall — one of those central canyon-like features barabo station designers liked to slice through their station levels, a mixture of open space, inner-apartment views and markets. The gym was far enough back from the main chaos that the glass windows weren't crowded with fascinated barabo staring at the humans, and he didn't feel like an exhibit in a zoo. Though Lance Corporal Kalo and Private Chavez standing guard in full armour might have discouraged some of that. Local barabo security were keeping an eye on the humans too — not so visible inside the gym, but Dale was sure they were there, working out in the loose gym-clothes barabo wore. Vola Station security seemed far more active than on Joma, like the station itself.

His uplink flashed on his vision as he ran, and he blinked it open. "This is Dale," he said aloud, concentrating to hear beneath the thumping rhythms of barabo music.

"Lieutenant," came Jokono's voice. *"I see this link is reaching you direct... where is PH-1?"* Typically they'd relay all coms from Joma Station through *Phoenix* first, then PH-1, creating layers of impenetrable encryption. This link was coming from *Phoenix* to Vola Station direct, making it less secure.

"Lieutenant Karle and the techs are out at the fabricator plant to check out the new merchandise. Half of us stayed behind to maintain security presence on station."

"So you have... two sections with you?"

"Two sections, eight marines including myself." Spelling it out, because Jokono was a civvie, and still learning how marines did things.   "I pulled myself out of First Section, Gunnery Sergeant Forrest has command of security for Lieutenant Karle on PH-1. Keeping our accommodation block on Vola Station secure has priority.   The manufacturing site they've gone to inspect is entirely automated, limited threats there."

"Yes, that's very wise.   All kinds of nasty things can happen to accommodation blocks on stations if no one's guarding them." As the former-head of security on a much larger station than this one would know.   *"You come home from your time away and someone's either listening to your private conversations, or about to blow you up, or both."*

It had been expected that Rhea System manufacturers would take at least a hundred hours to fabricate new missiles based on Lieutenant Karle's blueprints.   But one manufacturer had given them a fifty-hour quote on the first batch — something about merchandise that had been intended for someone else... all very sketchy, but the specs had looked good.   Not that you could trust that without the personal inspection that Karle had gone to give.

"So what's up, Joker?"

"Well I was just having a drink with Joma Station security man, very friendly fellow.   Doesn't like all these new human covert security types arriving on his station — he's much happier with Phoenix crew because at least they wear uniforms.   He agreed to keep an eye on them for me, in exchange for a nice bottle or two, and he tells me there's quite a few suspicious humans on their way to Vola Station.   Some are already there, others just arriving."

"Interesting," said Dale, barely breathing hard despite his pace.   His light weapon hung on the treadmill rail before him, swaying to the rhythm.   To his side, the newly promoted Lance Corporal Ricardo ran as well, matching his stride.   Beyond her, Privates Halep and Yu worked the weights, and the new guy, Tabo, talked with several friendly barabo by a water cooler between sets. Whatever the security concerns of venturing out on station without armour, marines had to exercise, and pushups on the floor of a hotel room only went so far.   "You think they're looking for something juicy?"

"Very juicy," Jokono confirmed. Dale had been informed of the 'Supreme Commander theory'... but of course, they couldn't talk about it on a less-secure connection. *"And it's quite possible their intel is better than ours. Quite likely, in fact."*

"Thanks for the info," said Dale. "I'll keep an eye out."

"Anything?" Ricardo asked him as he disconnected.

"Spooks," said Dale. "Lots of Fleet spooks."

Ricardo's eyes widened. "Here?" Dale nodded. "Well Fleet can't use marines, can they?" Some orders, marines would never obey, not even from Fleet Command. "Are we moving?"

"Yeah I'm moving," Dale replied, nodding to his treadmill display. "Faster than you, too. Keep up Corporal." Ricardo accelerated gamely. She was a six-year vet, the logical choice to replace Lance Corporal Carponi, who'd been killed on Heuron. Dale didn't doubt Ricardo's ability, but Carponi had been one of her best friends, and taking his place did not sit well with her.

They kept at it for another half-hour, then gathered up gear and changed back to marine fatigues without bothering to shower — there were enough vulnerabilities on an alien station without getting cornered naked in gymnasium showers. Lance Corporal Kalo and Private Chavez took up escort duty before and behind, thumping through the growing crowds in full armour — their gym time was on alternate rotations.

They entered the big mall, a vertical slice through overlooking walkways between levels, a great hubbub of markets down below, and many lively shopfronts up high. Crowds of barabo stood aside for Kalo, as restauranteurs handed out food samples, and music blared, and great holographic displays lit the open space to their right. It was only a few hundred meters to their hotel, and not the most secure environment, but at least it seemed to be mostly barabo here, with no sign of sard or even tavalai.

A young barabo appeared from the crowd and tugged at Lance Corporal Ricardo's arm. "Lady! Lady!" He pointed urgently up a side passage. "Human lady! Human lady!"

"Yes I am a human lady," Ricardo replied with amusement.

"Yeah," said Dale, "I think that means he's found another human, lady. Up that way. Hey kid. Doba!" The kid looked at him — like all marines, Dale had picked up bits of various alien tongues over the years just by listening. And a lot of barabo in Kazak System seemed to be learning English in anticipation of Fleet's arrival. "Doba, human? That way?" He pointed up the hall.

The kid bounced with that all-body nod that barabo did. "Yes! Human!" He pushed past a display of rare plants and up the passage, looking back at them urgently.

"Great," said Halep. "Coz that couldn't *possibly* be an ambush."

Dale waved them up, and they followed the kid up the passage, making a better semblance of combat formation as they went. "Chavez, keep an eye on our barabo tail."

"Aye sir." Meaning that station security had been following them every time they left their accommodation, and would be following them now. Relying, no doubt, on the fact that humans had trouble telling one barabo from another. The passage was thick with restaurants and the smell of cooking, chairs and diners overflowing among the pedestrians, dead animals hanging in display windows. Heck of a place to maintain combat formation, Dale thought. Would a barabo kid lead them into an ambush where so many barabo would die in the crossfire? Would a barabo kid even know he *was* leading them into an ambush?

Past Lance Corporal Kalo's armoured shoulder, Dale saw a robed figure amidst a bunch of dining barabo about some tables. This figure looked different, with thinner shoulders than the barabo. The barabo kid ran up, and the cloaked figure pressed some money into his hand. The kid ran off, and Dale caught a glimpse of a human woman's face within the cowl.

She beckoned him in, and Dale went, indicating Ricardo to guard out here. Private Halep went with him, and the woman led them between noisy tables and thick steam from the kitchen, to a dark rear corner. There in a chair, similarly cloaked, sat a human man, chewing a barabo sugar cane to blend in. Or maybe he just

191

liked the taste.   He pushed the hood back a little, and Dale saw a dark browed face, thick black hair, heavy-set gravitas and all-too-familiar from countless news reports.   Supreme Commander Chankow himself, huddled and scared on this distant alien station, hiding from the very forces he'd once commanded.

Dale stared at him for a moment.   Part of him insisted on saluting.   The other part wanted to shoot him in the head.   He settled for taking a seat, alongside the commander with his back to the wall where he could see the room.   Halep leaned against a wall nearby, watching the diners and trusting Dale to keep an eye on Chankow.   God knew what a private would make of this.   It was hard enough as a lieutenant, when every impulse screamed at him to show deference.   This had been the highest ranking officer humanity had for the last eighteen months of Dale's war.   And for the briefest moment, it drove home to Dale with the force of revelation just how huge a situation *Phoenix* and her now-deceased captain had fallen into.   Not just a selfish indulgence, as those crew who'd abandoned *Phoenix* had insisted.   But the kind of thing that shaped civilisations.

"Lieutenant.   You're *Phoenix*?" Chankow whispered urgently.   His dark eyes darted furtively about the crowded, smokey restaurant.

He didn't know who he was, Dale realised.   *Phoenix* crew had once worn nametags on their uniforms, as per Fleet-wide regulations.   But with so many people out to get them, and spying on them from station crowds, that had seemed too easy a gift of intel to their enemies, so the tags had been removed.   "Lieutenant Dale, Alpha Platoon, *UFS Phoenix*."   It was an effort not to add 'sir' on the end.   That this man deserved it less than a punch in the face did not make thirty years of service reflex just disappear.   "What do you want?"

In Heuron System, Chankow had ordered *Phoenix* destroyed. Before that, he'd approved, in general principle, to have Captain Pantillo killed to keep him from running for office.   It hung in the air between them, an invisible wall.   But the fear in Chankow's eyes could scale any wall.

"Protection," said Chankow. And held up a hand to forestall the obvious retort. "Hear me out. I know things. A lot of things. *Phoenix* is in a tangle much larger than any of you imagine, and I can help you out of it."

Dale wrinkled his nose, as though smelling something bad. Few marines were inclined to forgive those who hurt their friends. But equally few marines were stupid enough to throw away help this good. "How did you get here?"

"Private ship." He nodded to the robed woman. "Lieutenant Raymond here helped me get out, heard the first rumours of what was coming. Without her and a few others in my staff, I'd be dead." Dale stared expressionlessly. Chankow took a deep breath, his lip trembling a little. "Outer Neutral Space is the only place where renegades can go." With a meaningful look. "Barabo worlds don't mind a few humans settling. But I got here just as *Phoenix* entered the system, and I found *Europa*, and *Edmund Chandi*, and I knew the station would be crawling with Fleet spies. But they'd be watching the FTL departures, so we got a small ship here instead. I was going to hide until the coast had cleared."

"They've found you," Dale said bluntly. "My people tell me there's a bunch of Fleet spooks on the way."

"You can beat them!" the robed woman interjected. Lieutenant Raymond, Chankow had said. "You're *Phoenix* marines, they're only covert operations!"

Dale considered her. Loyalty, from a junior officer. He supposed even a rat like Chankow could fool some poor kid into risking her neck to save him. "I've got another mission," he said. "What's in it for *Phoenix*?"

A restaurant waiter was serving a noisy table nearby. Chankow leaned closer, glancing about. "On Heuron. Your Major Thakur went to meet with a man called Stanislav Romki."

"I remember," Dale said drily.

"That's what triggered the attack upon Lieutenant Commander Debogande. And upon her. Our intel said Romki was elsewhere, and would not be back for a long time. Our intel was wrong."

Dale nodded. "I already knew all of that."

"But you don't know why. Do you know that the alo were behind the chah'nas first sending aid to Earth?" Dale frowned. "When the krim first invaded Sol System," Chankow explained. "Our first two hundred years of resistance. The chah'nas say it was their idea to intervene on our behalf. Our historians have accepted that chah'nas did it because they wished to destabilise tavalai rule, and create a war in that corner of space that would make tavalai look bad, and potentially gain the chah'nas a new ally in restoring their old empire. But humanity's success over the centuries vastly exceeded the chah'nas's best expectations."

He shook his head. "That's been the theory, but it's only partly true. Chah'nas helped us for all those reasons, but it was the alo's idea in the first place. They're the true masterminds behind the chah'nas plan to push back the tavalai from the centre of Spiral power."

"Why?" Dale asked suspiciously.

"We don't know. But we've known for a long time there's a very old AI connection. It's one of the most well kept secrets. All the old hacksaw bases, stations, cities, manufacturing centres in our space have been either kept secret, moved, or even destroyed, to help keep the secret."

Dale's eyes widened. "There's more than we've been told?"

Chankow nodded. "A lot more. Far more than most people know. Most of it is in space, and most of the exploring and charting is done by Fleet ships. It's known by relatively few people, so the secret is easy to keep. Technologically it's relatively useless to us, there's not much useful tech left, it's so old and all the good stuff was evacuated by the previous occupants, or destroyed in the old AI wars. But you have to understand the *scale* of the old AI civilisation, during the Machine Age. Most humans still don't, we've been too preoccupied with our own affairs. The loss of Earth, revenge, territorial expansion."

"Why? Why hide it?"

"Because the alo don't like us having it. They watch us. We know."

"And humanity's *scared* of them?" Dale didn't like this at all — this inexorable sense of his entire world, everything he'd thought he was fighting for these past thirty years, slowly turning upside down. "Then why are we fighting the *tavalai*?"

"Because the tavalai are the main strategic threat, that hasn't changed. And alo promised to help, and they have — they've been invaluable. Humanity is so much stronger now, our territory has increased tenfold, our Fleet is so much more powerful, our industry is... well. Ask your Lieutenant Commander about human industrial power. It seemed a gamble worth taking — ally ourselves with a species that worries us, to improve our position at the expense of the tavalai. Friends close and enemies closer, that sort of thing. And truly, who else in this galaxy could we have allied ourselves to who did *not* worry us?"

He was talking about strategic decisions made at the high reaches of Fleet Command nearly two hundred years ago, Dale thought incredulously. Perhaps longer than that. Chankow and the present Fleet Command had merely inherited them. "But the alo are related somehow to the deepynines?"

Chankow nodded. "Your man Romki found it out... he was nearly silenced many times, as he suspects, but he cleverly became too well-known for that to be safe. And now they're trying to silence me."

"And you were willing to sacrifice everyone else to keep this secret," Dale growled. "My Captain, all of *Phoenix*, Stanislav Romki... only now that it's your turn, you run for your life and spill your guts to the first person who might protect you. Moral principles are only for other people, huh?"

Chankow swallowed hard. "We're past that now. The war's over, the next phase is beginning, and people should know."

"Right." Dale took a deep breath. Berating Chankow for his cowardice might feel good, but information was more important. Jokono would be unimpressed at his poor priorities. "What's this relationship to the deepynines?"

Chankow shook his head. "We don't know. Honestly, they've destroyed every spy ship we've sent. Their sensors are too good, venturing into their territory without permission is death. And the last of the deepynine wars were... well, so long ago. Twenty five thousand years. We only know that there are very old records of them making a fighting withdrawal in the direction of what is now alo space, but that space was then thoroughly cleansed by the drysines, who then went on to..."

"Wait. Who are the drysines?"

Chankow blinked at him. "Of course, most of you don't know... the history of the AI wars is not widely taught. It's not entirely an accident, we haven't encouraged it. And the loss of Earth to the krim does dominate our cultural memory."

"I know the parren uprising," said Dale. "The parren led the rebellion that unified the organic species of the Spiral against the machines. The chah'nas were the main lieutenants, the tavalai switched from neutral to fully onboard when they started to win."

Chankow shook his head. "No. I mean yes, there's that, but far too simple. AI dominance in the Machine Age was total. Organics made progress, but every time they became a threat, one or another faction of AIs crushed them. But the AIs had wars amongst themselves. They evolved in ways that different factions found threatening. Machines don't tolerate difference well, they'd rather erase a fault completely than accommodate it.

"Some AI factions began to realise this was a weakness. Some started wondering about tolerance, and cooperation. Don't think this made them 'nice' — their idea of cooperation was more like master-slave. But they realised organics had certain strengths they lacked, and cooperation could give them an edge. The drysines were one faction, they started small and expanded over several thousand years. They achieved a strategic understanding with the parren, and combined forces with them. This made them formidable. The parren were significant, but it was primarily the drysines who beat the deepynines, and destroyed the most powerful, centralised force of the Machine Age in a war so large it made our Triumvirate War look like a skirmish. The parren just helped, and rallied other organics to the drysine cause."

Parren space was on the far side of tavalai space, Dale knew. They were an isolated species now, playing no part in the Triumvirate War, and having little more to do with the tavalai than trade. "So what happened to the drysines?"

"They took heavy losses in the fight," said Chankow. "And the unified parren, chan'nas, tavalai and others realised this was their best and possibly only chance to beat the machines while they were weak. The drysines were ambushed and largely destroyed, and the parren ruled the Spiral for about seven thousand years."

"Before the chah'nas did the same to them," Dale murmured.

Chankow nodded. "And then the tavalai did it to the chah'nas. Being stabbed in the back by your trusted lieutenants is a Spiral tradition reaching back twenty thousand years and more. We are aware of this, thinking of the alo, and the chah'nas."

"You know there's a tavalai carrier at Joma Station who belong to a force the tavalai have used for thousands of years to police old AI remnants?" said Dale.

"Dobruta," said Chankow with a nod. "Fleet knows them well. We talk frequently."

Dale blinked. "You *talk* to a tavalai military faction?"

"The Dobruta thought from the beginning that the Triumvirate War was a waste of time. They thought the main enemy to the tavalai was not humans, chah'nas or alo, but hacksaws. Needless to say, this didn't go down very well with most tavalai. Many think the Dobruta are traitors. Fleet HQ was happy to keep them out of humanity's hair by demonstrating to them that we were just as serious about exterminating hacksaws as they were. And we are too, so that was no pretence. Why are these Dobruta interested in *Phoenix*?" And Chankow's eyes widened slightly. "That tale you spun at Heuron about the hacksaw base! That was actually true?"

"What about sard?" Dale asked, ignoring the question. "We've had some sard trouble just now. Did Fleet HQ pay sard to be mercenaries and attack *Phoenix*?"

"Lieutenant," Chankow said flatly, as some of that old high-ranking confidence reasserted. "Believe me, if sard were that easy to manipulate, we'd have tried it long ago and turned them on the tavalai. No, I've no idea why sard would want to kill *Phoenix* specifically. Perhaps you upset someone even more incorrigible than Fleet Command."

"And the other, non-sard mercenaries who tried to kill us on the way here?" Dale pressed.

Chankow shrugged. "Oh sure. That was probably us. There was quite a large bounty on *Phoenix*, and many opportunists willing to take large risks for a lifetime's fortune. Whether that bounty still stands with Fleet's new command... you'd have to ask them."

"Colonel Khola himself is here on *Europa* to offer us a full pardon."

Chankow managed a sardonic smile. "My boy. Truly. You'd not live out the year."

"They need us if they're going to unite Fleet against the Worlders," Dale said stubbornly. Only now, considering the possibility that the pardon would be taken away, did he realise how badly he wanted it. And that itself was a revelation.

"You think this is about Spacers versus Worlders?" Chankow shook his head. "That's a pretence. Worlder rebellions are an annoyance. They don't keep the Guidance Council awake at night. Alo betrayals and old Spiral history coming back to eat us alive? That's another story."

Stanislav Romki sat in one of *Phoenix*'s Engineering holds, and gazed at the head of the old hacksaw queen. So far the nano-tank's micro-bots had struggled to make head or tails of her. The latest human technology they were, yet completely failing to process what they were looking at. They swarmed and fizzed around and within the big hole Major Thakur had blown in the queen's head, a silver-metallic swirl, but where the programs on the analysis screens would typically give a full diagnostic of the damaged technology and how to fix it, now the numbers just ran and ran. Processing. Like an insect reading a symphony score, Romki thought, and trying to comprehend what it meant.

The Fathers hadn't built them like this. He wondered if the AIs had kept any of those original hardware models around, in museums for sentiment or interest. He doubted it — hacksaw civilisation had stored memory collectively and made it accessible to all. There was no need to keep mementoes around to remind them. Those early models had been server droids, doing all of the menial tasks that the Fathers hadn't thought worth an organic's time.

Why the Fathers had thought to give such droids enough intelligence to resent their lot in life, no one seemed to know. It didn't seem wise. But mightily upset they'd become, and once the Fathers had been exterminated, the machines had devoted much of their intellect to improving their own design. Twenty five thousand years of improvement had resulted in this, a technology so far removed from its origins, it was like comparing humans to the earliest mammals of the Triassic Period.

Ever since his investigations into the alo had led him to his deepynine discovery, Romki had sought further information about hacksaw civilisation in general. At first it had been hard — he was trained as a xeno-sociologist, which involved a lot of psychology, a little neurology and even a liberal dash of biology. Technology and artificial intelligence were not his fields at all, and at first his right-hemisphere brain had rebelled at all that maths. But then he'd realised how little difference it made that hacksaws were metal and not flesh and blood — they were sentient beings, they'd expressed themselves socially and even politically in their own fascinating and frightening ways, and if one approached their study the same as one approached the study of any other alien society, one could still reach conclusions worth knowing.

Asking the alo about hacksaws was useless, and chah'nas were not a scholarly people. The tavalai knew the most, but even they had a great reluctance to discuss things too deeply. Most human societies would have overcome the trauma of unpleasant events after twenty five thousand years, but not the tavalai. Romki respected the tavalai reverence for the past, but when it interfered so deeply with scholarly inquiry, it became tiresome.

The one group who *had* been prepared to discuss hacksaw civilisation at length were the Dobruta. It had taken a lot of prodding, on several long trips through tavalai space under the protection of academic groups who did not mind sponsoring a human, but eventually he'd convinced them that he was just a scholar, and had no interest in the technology beyond the academic sphere. The things the Dobruta had told him about the hacksaws had been eye-opening indeed, both fascinating and horrifying beyond measure.

He knew that it was dangerous, sending word through tavalai contacts as he had, to get *Makimakala* here to Joma Station. It could be construed as betrayal by *Phoenix*'s commanders, for one thing. And it was certainly possible, if unlikely, that *Makimakala* might make a violent move toward *Phoenix* in their zeal to destroy what was now before him. But *Phoenix* was no pushover, even for an ibranakala-class carrier, and the Dobruta were primarily interested in keeping hacksaw technology out of the hands of people who might develop, copy or spread it. *Phoenix* kept its AI technology on board because it wished to study it en route to discovering how to kill it more effectively. Perhaps with some urging, on this matter at least, the tavalai ship and the human one could find some common ground.

Mostly he needed the Dobruta here so that they could help him figure out what the hell this 'queen' really was. If anyone would know, Romki was certain that either *Makimakala*'s command crew, or specialists, would be most likely. Because if he could figure that out, then he had some hope of extracting information from her. That information could then become the best lead he'd yet had in his entire professional career on the alo-deepynine connection, particularly if the queen turned out to be deepynine herself.

But the odds that she was actually deepynine were remote. Besides, he was not even sure if those old designations would hold true today. Hacksaw factions had had certain physical and technological indicators, it was true, and were far more different from each other on a hardware level than the divergent human races of Earth had ever been. But as he understood it, belonging to a particular faction depended as much on the civilisational data-set that an individual unit was plugged into as it did on that unit's physical design.

How would a surviving deepynine unit identify itself today, when all its civilisational data-set had been dead for so many millennia? It would be like a person from an old Earth nation state, suddenly transported into the current human age. A European of the early nineteen hundreds, with their entire personal identity invested in their own particular nationalism... what would they find today that they could recognise? When not only their old nation state, but all the old racial, religious and political notions that supported it were long dead and obsolete? When Earth itself was long gone, even though the human race continued to thrive? A hacksaw remnant today would not even have that last consolation — their race nearly extinct, their few remnants scattered and in hiding. And there had been so many factions across the thousands of years of the Machine Age, far too many for anyone alive today to count, and each pursuing a different combination of technological and conceptual uniqueness...

The fluid in the nano-tank's screen reader flickered. Romki frowned. The queen's head had no powersource, there was no electrical circuit possible — the nano-tank was not directing active power, just a very low analytical current. It was barely enough to make the swarming micro-machines swim, and make pretty pictures of how things might join together before the Major had blown them open with a rifle nearly as big as she was.

Another flicker. Romki's heart skipped a beat. It shouldn't be doing that. This technology was dead, and despite the crew's predictable ghost stories, none of these hacksaws were coming back to life without serious repair from a similar technology. So what was this?

He pulled down the augmented reality glasses on his head, and they integrated instantly with his uplinks, a whole new field of data springing to holographic life before his eyes.   Analyse, he instructed it.   The software was aware of the flicker, all systems racing to try and categorise it.   Not domestic, the graphics flashed back at him. Not indigenous. Not third-party. The Major's bullets had completely destroyed the CPU, what passed in this intelligent machine's head for a brain... not damaged so much as vaporised. But a lot of hacksaw subsystems ran with limited autonomy... but not without power, surely?

Flicker.   The pulse was regular.   Like communications. Like a message.   Not an internal message.   But... external?   He queried the software.   It ran.   And ran.   And ran, spinning wheels and hooked into more processing power than science labs used to simulate the insides of stars.

Possible, it replied. **Find source.**

"Fuck," Romki murmured. "You're telling *me*?"

CHAPTER 17

Erik stood on the bridge of the *Edmund Chandi*, the most secure room on the ship, when Romki's uplink message came in.

"*Lieutenant Commander, I'm sorry to bother you but... I'm running tests on our guest the queen, and... well.*"

Erik concentrated with effort to form a reply, and felt the uplink software find the words as he thought them. "*What about the queen, Mr Romki?*"

"*I think someone's talking to her.*"

Erik blinked. "*How is that possible?*"

"*There's definitely some kind of very light electrical trace being created by a subsystem somewhere in the queen's head. The queen is very dead, have no fear, but some of the minor subsystems are not dead, and they may respond autonomously to external stimuli. The computer software suggests that this might be her coms function.*"

If there was anything that could make a warship commander nervous, it was the thought of a supposedly-dead hacksaw queen talking to someone from the hold of his ship. "*Mr Romki, I think you might want to consider shutting down that nano-tank. I don't want you to tell me about ghost stories — you didn't see that thing when it was alive. This is no game, these things should not be played with.*"

"*Lieutenant Commander with respect, I don't think that's our primary problem. Whatever she's talking to, it's pure reflex and the message is coming from outside. So what's sending the message? No technology we know of can talk to a dead hacksaw, I couldn't replicate this response from a buried com circuit if I tried.*"

Erik's eyes widened as he realised what Romki was saying. "*Shit. Okay, keep it running if you think it can give us some idea of what's out there — numbers, direction, anything useful.*"

"*My thoughts exactly — trust me, as fascinated as I am by the science, I'm not in any hurry to be torn apart by it.*"

Erik disconnected and turned to his company. "I'm sorry, can this wait for a moment? I have a situation that needs addressing — I'll take a short break and come back to you as soon as possible."

Edmund Chandi's captain and three primary passengers nodded. Two of them Erik had never heard of before, and *Phoenix* database had nothing on, besides that they were both from Apilai, the primary inhabited world of Heuron System. The third passenger was named Tsang, and she was the Chief-of-Staff to the Vice-President of Worlder Congress. How she'd gotten enough advance warning to get all the way out here to talk to *Phoenix*, Tsang wouldn't say.

Erik beckoned to Trace, who followed in her heavy armour, and left the bridge. In the main access corridor, Staff Sergeant Kono and Private Rolonde stood guard. "That was Romki," Erik said in a low voice. "He's examining the hacksaw queen. He says something's talking to her, some kind of strange frequency, coming from nearby."

Trace frowned. "But he's no idea what?" Erik shook his head. "He's not actually an engineer, he's an academic who sees a lot of stuff he'd like to see."

"The number of things that can talk to a hacksaw queen's dead com units are very limited," said Erik. "You can figure out the risk better than I can. It's your call."

Meaning that the implications put station security at risk — Trace's responsibility. Kono looked cautious at the news, but Rolonde, Erik noticed, had gone slightly pale. She'd been at Trace's side in the hacksaw nest in Argitori where the queen had been encountered and killed. And she had a big scar on her leg to prove it, and memories of friends killed in front of her.

Trace looked frustrated. That was rare — she usually kept her feelings hidden. But she'd been looking forward to this meeting on *Edmund Mundi*, to talk to the Worlder representatives and see what they had to say. It had been put off repeatedly for various unforeseen interruptions, and now just as they got to talk properly, this happened.

She opened a command channel that Erik immediately received in his inner ear. "Hello *Phoenix*, this is the Major."

"Go ahead Major," came Lieutenant Shilu's reply — it was first-shift on the bridge.

"I am raising station readiness alert to yellow, please be advised."

"Phoenix is so advised, station readiness alert to yellow, aye Major."

"Hello *Phoenix*," Erik added as per the protocol, "this is the LC, I second the Major's command."

"Aye LC, Phoenix is now on yellow as well." Because when *Phoenix* was docked at station rim, what happened on the rim also happened to *Phoenix*. It was one reason why many captains preferred to stay in space.

Trace switched to her lieutenants. "Hello people, this is the Major. We are station alert yellow, I repeat, station alert yellow. Mr Romki has detected communications that could conceivably be of hacksaw technology origin. I repeat, that's hacksaw *technology* origin, he thinks they could be coming from the station.

"I want absolutely no change in appearance, I want everyone going about their usual business, we know everyone's watching us so doubtless any potential threat will be as well. I want defensive plans mobilised *quietly*. If you have to move in numbers, keep it to the back corridors and keep it casual. I want particular attention paid to sard presence, including sard ships at dock — if Mr Romki is reading anything at all, it's likely coming from them."

"Hello *Phoenix*, this is the LC," Erik added as he thought of something else.

"This is Phoenix, go ahead LC."

"Lieutenant Shahaim, do you copy?"

"This is Shahaim, go ahead."

"Suli, am I correct in recalling that no sard vessels have docked at station within the last rotation?"

"That's correct LC. We've been watching the two that are docked, no irregular activity to report, and scan is clear."

"I want you to call up our friend *Rai Jang*.   Give them a quiet warning and ask if they've heard anything."

"Aye LC.   What about the Makimakala?"

Erik looked at Trace.   Trace looked wary.   "Not with *Europa* listening in," Erik replied.   "Not yet, anyhow.   And get a coms specialist from Engineering to check out Romki's signal, see if it's more than a ghost.   Better yet, get two coms specialists.   LC out." Colonel Khola was just waiting for a chance to declare them all traitors again.   Tactical cooperation with a tavalai warship that Fleet probably thought in violation of the surrender agreement might do it.

"Probably nothing," said Trace.   "If we keep jumping at shadows, we'll never get anywhere with the Worlders.   You coming back?"

"You don't think we should head back to *Phoenix*?" Erik pressed.

"I think it's within acceptable parameters to continue vital operations during a yellow alert.   We've got the attention of some pretty senior Worlders, we should take the opportunity."

"To do what?" said Erik.   "Trace, we can't pursue this if we accept the Colonel's pardon."

"We've got forty hours before we have to make a decision," Trace said stubbornly.   "Let's find out what their bottom line position is that we can take back to the other captains.   We accept the pardon, go home and let them know what the Worlders say they need for peace, and we work from there."

Erik frowned.   "And violate the terms of the pardon?" Trace stared at him, eyes unreadable.   "You know Fleet can just kill us all at any time if we do that?   Legally?"

"If the Captain didn't sacrifice his life so we could avoid a human civil war," Trace said edgily, "then what did he sacrifice it for?   Do you want to just abandon that sacrifice, and every other sacrifice we've made to get here, in order to be safe and comfortable?"

Erik glanced at Kono and Rolonde, watching them warily. "Don't you think we have a responsibility to let the crew vote on that?"

"Sure we do," Trace said evenly. "But I'm asking you. What do *you* think? Or do strong opinions only come with a captain's rank?"

Not long ago, the barb would have hurt. But he was getting wise to her games. "As commander of *Phoenix*'s marine company, it's your responsibility to look out for every marine under your command, not to mention all the spacer crew as well. If we take your course of action, we're probably all dead, and you know it. We can only ride our luck for so long with this new Fleet Command, whoever they turn out to be, and if we screw them over then even the other captains sympathetic to us will run out of patience."

"Then why are we here?" Trace demanded. "On this ship?" She jerked her head toward the bridge. "Talking to Worlders who are hell bent on revolution? You think the next bunch of Fleet Commanders will be any better than the last? We've seen how they solve problems, they've no interest in avoiding civil war because they think it'll be so easy to win, and they're probably right. But it will boil and fester, and leave humanity completely exposed to our enemies..."

"And when did any of that become our responsibility?" Erik retorted. "Trace, we had one goal coming out here — justice for the Captain and our crew who died, and punishment for those who wronged us. We've got that. Chankow, Anjo and Ishmael are gone. And we've got a pardon..."

"Not on our terms."

"You want *terms*?" Incredulously. "It sounds to me like you're deliberately asking for the impossible so you can throw their pardon back in their faces. Now I was happy to keep screwing Fleet over by talking to Worlders for as long as Chankow and company were still alive, and Fleet was still trying to kill us. But now that's changed, and..."

"Not a damn thing's changed," Trace retorted. "They'll still kill the next of us who gets in their way..."

"And you want to change *that*? You want a revolution, Major? You want to *join* these people?" Nodding back at the bridge. "Join the Worlders?"

Trace said nothing. It surprised him. He was so used to leaning hard on her in their arguments. Getting nothing back left him flailing for balance.

"Well then I've got news for you," Erik continued. "The Worlders are no better than Fleet, possibly worse. I understand you've become completely disillusioned with Fleet and Spacer Congress because you no longer believe they're serving the human cause. You're still Kulina, whatever Colonel Khola thinks, and you're still serving the human cause as ferociously as you ever have — I get that, even if Khola doesn't." He pointed at Kono and Rolonde. "But you have a responsibility to lead your people well, and they love you so much they'll follow you into hell if you lead them there. You told me before about the standards expected of officers. Your standards have inspired total trust. Don't abuse it."

She'd given him hard looks before, but most of those had been calculated for effect. This anger he was pretty sure was real.

Coms uplink blinked — it was Lieutenant Dale, and Trace opened it. "This is the Major, go ahead Lieutenant." A long pause, suggesting a relayed message over distance.

"Actually Major, this is for you and the LC."

"Hello Lieutenant Dale, this is the LC. We're both listening, go ahead." Another pause.

"Well... I found someone pretty interesting out here."

Erik and Trace looked at each other. Trace's eyes widened. Erik wasn't as adept at reading between the lines of Dale's short-hand, and Dale was clearly wondering if someone was listening. Fleet encryption made that impossible for most, but Khola and company knew Fleet encryption very well. Erik asked Trace a wordless question. Trace nodded — Dale meant exactly who they thought he did. Chankow. Holy shit.

"He must have come to Dale looking for *protection*," Erik muttered to Trace off-mike. The irony was too much to process.

"He's actually got a fair bit to sell us," Trace replied. "In exchange for his life."

Erik reactivated coms. "Well have you learned anything, Lieutenant?" he asked Dale.

"Ah..." Long pause, as though also taking an off-mike break on the other end. *"Quite a few things, yeah. His main point is that some things we've been offered aren't as good quality as we'd been led to expect."*

He could have been talking about the missiles Lieutenant Karle was there to acquire. Erik was quite sure he wasn't. "Not that surprising," he conceded. "But one has to consider the messenger."

"Yes, well I could say some other things. He insists it's not his problem, it's an institutional thing. Some institutions never change, no matter what they insist they're now manufacturing." Definitely not the missiles. *"About those shipments, Lieutenant Karle tells me the first one is ready, we can even haul it on..."*

The rest cut out in static. Erik frowned. "Hello Lieutenant Dale, can you hear me?" More static. Then a blinking display — lost signal.

"Hello LC, this is Phoenix," Lieutenant Shilu cut in. *"We've just lost local coms. All of them, I'm switching to hardlines now, we're still getting station feed and station say there's nothing wrong. But all the wavelength is gone, it's like a main transmitter just blew."*

"Hang on," Erik replied with concern. "But I can still talk to you."

"And we're a quarter-turn of the station apart, I know," Shilu replied in frustration. *"We've got a hardline connection, but if all wireless relays are out, we should be getting more interference. It's like it's selective or something."*

"Phoenix," Trace cut in urgently. "Get me hardline coms to all *Phoenix* units on station, marines or otherwise — red alert, and get me immediate extraction back to *Phoenix*." No reply from Shilu. "*Phoenix? Phoenix* do you copy?" Trace looked at Kono. "We're moving, midships extraction now. You two tell the Captain, I've got the LC. Coms check?"

Kono tried his, and shook his head. "Nothing. Not even closer range — everyone will be moving on extraction."

Trace nodded and beckoned to Erik, stomping off down the corridor as Kono and Rolonde headed back to the bridge. At the next intersection they ran into Corporal Rael and Private Kumar, already moving.

"Coms are out!" Rael announced, got the expected confirmation as Trace and Erik went straight past him, and followed behind. Not for the first time, Erik felt a surge of relief to see the competence of *Phoenix* crew in action — Trace's marines didn't need instructions to know what to do, when the coms failed they immediately moved on the extraction plan to get the LC out via *Edmund Mundi* midships. Likewise he didn't need to worry if Lieutenant Shilu had received Trace's last order — with coms out, Shahaim would order red alert as a matter of course, and begin full crew extraction back to *Phoenix*.

"This is a total coms blackout," Trace said as they moved, cycling through channels. "I can't reach *Phoenix* on anything. We're being jammed." And to some puzzled crew in passing, "Total coms blackout, consult your Captain, station may be under attack."

"*Phoenix* can probably identify that source if it's a ship," Erik added, striding hard to keep up. "But *Phoenix* is stuck on station until the crew get off. We may have to use a shuttle."

"If *I* were attacking this station or any ship attached to it, I wouldn't jam from another ship because it will just be destroyed in a few minutes." Combat vessels considered the deliberate jamming of coms as much a provocation as shooting, and *Phoenix* was not the only warship docked with station that could pinpoint the source and retaliate. "I'd do it internally within station. In which case we may have to go looking for it on foot." And to the crew guarding the big airlock doors through to midships, "Excuse us, combat red alert, coming through." As those crew kept out of their way.

"ETA on full crew extraction?" Erik asked as they ducked through the passage connecting what would be gravitational crew-quarters in flight, to the midships behind.

"Lieutenant Crozier reckoned eleven minutes thirty against an inbound minimum assault warning of twenty-two." Meaning that most of the time they'd be responding to inbound attacking ships, against whom they'd need twenty-two minutes warning, in this system, against whom to make their escape. "If the threat's inside the station already, that can complicate things. Kono, who was on shuttle standby?"

"PH-4," said Kono as they emerged into midships, its open steel compartments broken by cargo nets and acceleration slings for use in the zero-G of regular flight. "Just hope Tif's not taking a nap."

"Don't speak ill of crew unless they've earned it," Trace reprimanded, climbing down a G-ladder toward *Edmund Mundi*'s single set of shuttle grapples. "Tif's been a total professional so far, no mean feat for a civvie while raising a kid amongst an alien crew."

Right about now, Erik thought as he followed Trace down, he could use another shuttle pilot. Their civvie shuttle AT-7 was available, but with no one full-time to fly it. With crew spread over the station, and PH-1 on away on a mission, two shuttles for rapid evac looked totally inadequate.

Lisbeth's first clue that something was wrong came when Vijay frowned, excused himself from the table, and disappeared out the door. Carla stayed, eating at Lisbeth's side as they talked with her Uncle Calvin. There was a small recorder balanced on a pack on the end of the table, to record their meal and conversation. It had been Calvin's idea — to take this mealtime chat back to Lisbeth's parents and sisters, so they could watch it later while having their own meal, and have the impression that Lisbeth was back home with them at the dinner table.

Lisbeth talked about her adventures, careful not to say anything that might cause trouble should the recording fall into the wrong hands. She hadn't been in on many of those command decisions anyway, and her experience had been more like that of the regular crew — stuck in a small room, scared and ignorant and often under enormous Gs, and hoping that she wasn't abruptly killed by some unseen threat that she could do nothing about... or worse, left crippled and drifting to die slowly from suffocation or fire.

But she didn't talk much about that. Mostly she gave her impressions of the crew, and of Erik, and Tif, and her new friends in Engineering whom she helped out on a regular basis... not that that made her one of them, but as she joked with Uncle Calvin, she was now the most junior member of the Engineering crew, fit for little more than cleaning toilets, but thankfully unqualified for it. And she talked about Stanislav Romki and helping him with the hacksaw remains, much to her Uncle's incredulity. The hacksaws were not a secret, *Phoenix* had volunteered that encounter to everyone at Heuron System. Probably her mother had heard about it already. She was careful to stress that the only time she'd seen hacksaws, they'd been in pieces from high caliber gunfire and high explosive.

Then Vijay returned to the room and turned off the recorder. "Coms are dead," he said grimly. Immediately Carla got up, grabbing her rifle and helmet — the light marine armour that Major Thakur had allowed them as former-marines with the important task of guarding Lisbeth. Lisbeth and Uncle Calvin blinked at them both. "Hardlines and wireless, it's like we're being jammed. *Phoenix* will be on automatic red alert, that means full evacuation, we have to head back now."

"Shit," said Lisbeth, and noted Calvin's look as she said it. She'd never used to swear — Mother didn't like it. She got up, and hugged her Uncle as he rose. "I'm really sorry, I have to go."

"Wait," said Calvin to her bodyguards. "Shouldn't you wait for a shuttle? Won't *Phoenix* send one for Lisbeth? It could be dangerous on the dock."

"We've got a vehicle," said Carla. "And there's a fully armoured marine section waiting with it."

"*Phoenix* only has two shuttles operational," Vijay added. "Only one will be on immediate standby, and that one will be going to get Erik — he's on that Worlder ship. The other one will take five minutes and we've no guarantee Lisbeth will be their priority."

They left up the main corridor, past some concerned-looking crew talking or rushing to do things. Then out the main airlocks where two Alpha Platoon marines stood guard and onto the Berth 26 platform and down the ramp to the fat-tired vehicle. The two marines guarding it were staring up the dock. Traditional dock-level design on space stations made the ceilings at least three times the height of a regular station level. Joma Station's dock level was five times the height, for a ceiling more than twelve meters up. Stations were enormous, and though Joma was small compared to the big human stations, a person could still see nearly two whole berths in either direction before the upward curve took all further berths out of view.

Dock level was also wide — Joma's was thirty meters wide, and largely uncluttered by the gardens, grass, benches or island platforms that more intricate designs incorporated. That wide expanse of decking plate was typically covered with many people and vehicles, any way one looked. As Lisbeth followed the marines' gaze up past Berth 27, she could see a lot of people, mostly barabo. Some were running. Quite a lot were running, actually. Many looked frightened. Then came the screams.

She spun to Uncle Calvin. "Get back inside!" she yelled at him. "Tell your Captain undock and run, just do it!" As Vijay grabbed her and thrust her at the jeep, Lisbeth regaining control in time to insist upon the driver's seat. She squeezed behind the wheel, the vehicle shaking as they piled on around her, then gunned the electric engine and left, wishing there were enough power to spin the wheels. Instead, she crawled steadily up to a miserly forty kph, most dock vehicles disabled from higher performance with all the pedestrians around. With six marines aboard, four in heavy armour, she was surprised they managed even this speed.

"Still no coms!" Lance Corporal Penn yelled. "No idea what's going on, nothing's working!" Penn was Charlie Second Squad's newest section leader, and had volunteered to take Lisbeth to visit Uncle Calvin on *Europa*. He was a new volunteer off *Europa*, formerly a twelve-year sergeant, but had agreed to take the demotion to fill the holes *Phoenix* needed to fill.

"Lots of runners behind!" Private Herman added. "Holy shit, is that…?"

Then a harsh, metallic 'baaarp!' from somewhere behind, and an echoing rattle and howl of tearing metal.

"Chain gun!" yelled Private Ruiz.

"What the fuck's doing that?"   As they all shifted their position on the overcrowded vehicle to firing crouches, huge Koshaim rifles bristling out like an alarmed animal's poisoned spines.

"Straight ahead Lisbeth," Carla warned her from alongside, the big woman's jaw set beneath her helmet.   "If we come under fire, just keep going straight, these guys may need to dismount to support us but just keep going."

More gunfire behind, a steady, thundering roar, punctuated by explosions.   "That's the froggies engaging!" Penn shouted. "*Makimakala*'s under fire, they'll have karasai on the deck!"   That was Berth 28, Lisbeth thought wildly, heart pounding and mouth dry as she watched the decking crawling by, the shopfronts on the right side turning slowly to empty construction.   *Makimakala* was only two berths up from *Europa*.   A tavalai combat carrier was nothing to mess with, yet whatever was attacking the station had engaged the other most deadly ship at dock.

Dock lights began flashing red, and a warning siren wailed. Workers in this section were shouting at each other, others running, others securing their gear.   Suddenly Lisbeth's ears exploded as marines opened fire — it was the first time she'd heard Koshaims at close range, and they were worse than jackhammers.   Then a pause, and through the painful hush of her ringing ears, Lisbeth heard, "You fucking see that?"

"Hacksaw!" Private Ruiz yelled.   "Definitely a hacksaw, holy shit!"   And then Lisbeth was more scared than she'd ever been in her life.   Given recent events, that was saying something.

"You get it?" asked Penn.

"No," said Ruiz, "it came out real fast then just fucking raced back up that corridor…"

Up ahead, beneath the curving ceiling, Lisbeth could see armoured marines on the dock, and spacers running from their accommodation block at full sprint to get up to Berth 18.   Several of the marines saw them, pointed, and came running. Lisbeth nearly cried with relief. Then she saw the huge section seal this side of Berth 22 begin sliding down to cut them off.

"Guys!" she yelled in case they were all still looking behind. "Guys, section seal! We're going to get cut off!"

"Just go," Carla told her calmly. "Station must be depressurising somewhere, or else they figured they're under attack and are closing off the dock. If we're cut off we'll leave the vehicle and go by the back corridors, just get as close as you can."

"Go!" Herman was yelling at confused barabo workers as they passed. "Run! Get away from the dock! Damn it, how do you say hacksaw in Palapu?"

The huge steel wall was descending fast, bright LED lights illuminating its strike zone upon the deck, small flaps of plating elevating upward to keep traffic out so no one got flattened by the descent.

"Can't make it!" Lisbeth announced, and steered them toward the furthest corridor entrance amidst the under-construction shopfronts. "Everyone get ready to get off!" At her side, Carla stood to wave at the marines running their way up the dock, still visible below the descending seal. She pointed right, into the corridors, and a distant marine gave a thumbs up, still running. Then the seal hid him from view, the entire deck shaking as it rumbled down amidst the howl of sirens.

Lisbeth pulled up alongside the corridor entrance just as the seal slammed down with an echoing boom! The jeep rocked as marines leaped off, Herman and Bernardino running ahead to the corridor while Carla and Vijay escorted Lisbeth, Penn and Ruiz guarding the rear. Several loud cracks and shweets of fast-moving projectiles snapped up the docks, and something hit a section wall to Lisbeth's left with a bang! that made her jump for fright.

"What the hell was that?" she gasped as they ran into the half-completed corridor.

"Ricochets," Vijay told her. "Big firefight up the docks, you get random rounds bouncing around the rim for kilometres until they meet a vertical surface." The armoured marines ahead reached a T-junction, covering each other's move about the corner with graceful precision, huge weapons levelled, then cut left as Lisbeth and her bodyguards approached. "Congratulations kid, you just got shot at."

"Just fucking great," Lisbeth said shakily, and turned left after the marines.

CHAPTER 18

"Come on Tif," Arime muttered, as they crouched by *Edmund Mundi*'s midships grapples, big exposed hydraulic arms preparing to catch the impact from below, and a central airlock on the floor. A civvie crewman was peering into the manual viewer to see below — with all coms down, no wireless transmissions were working, which blocked most external cameras. "Where the hell are you?"

"How do they block *all* wireless?" Rael muttered. "Most local systems can still cut through military grade jamming at some level."

"Well I dunno about you," Kumar added, "but my suit's scanners are bouncy too." That was what marines called it when their visor visuals started flickering and bouncing. "I'm even getting a radiation spike from somewhere, well above background normal."

"Yeah, that's not good," said Rolonde, still pale. "Machines don't mind radiation."

Erik looked at her, then at Trace. "Let's not jump at shadows," Trace told them firmly. "With no coms we've no way of knowing what's out there until we..."

"Contact up the ship!" yelled Kono from up the G-ladder, by the airlock leading to the crew cylinder. "I can hear something! Sounds like... shit, what is..." And they heard the echoing roar of chain gun fire, and a distant shriek that sounded like steel being cut.

"Dammit," said Trace, and leaped for the G-ladder. "LC, you stay!"

"It's inside the ship!" Terez was yelling from the other side of the airlock — his voice a tinny amplification as helmets sealed and marines turned up suit speakers to yell at each other.

"Told you," said Rolonde at Erik's side, as Erik double-checked his rifle while trying to keep his hands from shaking. This rifle could damage a powered-armour suit, though not badly, and the return fire would blow lightly-armoured soldiers in half. Against hacksaw drones, this thing would be more effective than spitting, but not much.

Somewhere out the airlock, Koshaims thundered, and Erik pushed the civvie crewman aside to stare at the outer grapples visual feed. "Sir what the hell is that?" the crewman asked in fear, wondering whether to run.

"Hacksaws," said Erik.

"You're kidding!" the crewman exclaimed. As though he'd declared them under attack by the bogeyman. More gunfire thundered, drowning out any conversation the marines might be having. Chain guns answered, then a shriek of cutting steel that vibrated straight through the deck. Erik had never heard anything like it before on a ship. As someone who valued the structural integrity of every vessel he boarded, it wasn't a sound he ever wanted to hear.

"Does it sound like he's kidding?" Rolonde told the crewman. Gunfire paused.

"… gone straight through the hull!" Erik heard someone shouting in the distance. "They're cutting through!"

"Pressure suits!" Trace yelled, closer but still outside the airlocks. Several more civvie crew came sliding frantically down the G-ladder. "Jess, get the LC in a pressure suit!"

"Pressure suits!" Rolonde barked at the crewman, who pointed to a red and yellow striped emergency closet high on a walkway wall, easily accessible in zero-G but not at dock. "Fucking great."

"Never mind!" Erik told her, as the outer camera's view of a turning starfield was blocked by a dark shadow, looming close and coming closer. It resolved into an upper shuttle hatch, stencil letters and closing very fast. "PH-4 is here, everybody brace!"

"Command Squad!" Trace yelled. "Our ride is here, pull back! Pull back now!" As Tif hit the grapples very hard from below, giant hydraulic rams crashing and flexing about them as the deck heaved. Alarm sirens howled, emergency lighting flashed and above in neighbouring sections, Erik heard decompression doors slamming closed as the automated emergency voice declared a hull breach.   Erik was pretty sure Tif hadn't done it — something was breaching midships further up.

Arime skidded down the ladder so hard that with his suit's combat settings, he nearly bent the rail.   He hit the deck with a crash as Erik extended the access tube as fast as it would go.   "They're cutting through above!" Arime declared, stomping across.

"Who's cutting through above?" the first civvie crewman asked.

"Hacksaws," stammered one of the two new arrivals.   "They got the bridge... they... I saw them cutting steel.   Blood everywhere, I... I think everyone's dead up there..."

Erik had never seen an airlock access tube extend more slowly in his life.   Above him, Trace's squad were crashing in from the crew cylinder airlock, and scrambling up ladders to get to higher levels and compartments.   Even now, he heard a new shriek of cutting steel, and again the deck shook.

"They're cutting through from above!" Corporal Rael yelled. "Either we get out soon or they'll be on us!"

"One minute!" Erik yelled his best guess.

"We're not going to get a minute!"

"Then make one!"   The access tube made contact from below... 'warning', the docking system told him — unfamiliar contact, suggest try again?   Erik hit the override with feeling, and saw the controls squawk as PH-4's more aggressive docking system grabbed it from below.   Erik overrode several abort attempts... then ducked as fire ripped through the main airlock, hitting the walls above.   Thunder in reply, as a Koshaim answered — Trace couldn't close the airlock from the crew cylinder, he realised, because then she couldn't shoot through it.   Koshaim-20s would deter approaching hacksaws far more than flimsy airlock doors.

More shrieking from above, much closer now, then a huge explosion as a drone blew an obstacle out of the way.   "Here they come!" Rael yelled.   And Erik heard a distant clattering, like insects' footsteps amplified many times over.   Steel footsteps, from something big, rattling over the hull.

Something hit the bulkheads above with an ear-splitting crash, and shrapnel tore neighbouring cargo nets. Private Rolonde put herself squarely over Erik for cover... and Erik saw a big armoured suit crawling up the access from below. The inner hatch opened, and an armoured marine stuck his head through — Sergeant Ong, Erik recognised through the visor, Third Squad, Echo Platoon.

One of the civvies scrambled for the hatch, and Ong grabbed him by the throat. "Wait your turn! LC, go!"

Erik went, grabbed the rails and slid feet first down the vertical drop, as others yelled above him and a loud scraping hiss announced that Rolonde was coming down immediately after and he'd better vacate the access fast. His boots hit bottom and he did, as Rolonde crashed down behind him. Erik ducked up to lower deck access, jumped down the step, then passed where Private Cowell was stationed at the rear of the cockpit, yelling up to Tif and Ensign Lee where he could visually see people coming aboard.

"I'm strapping in behind you guys!" Erik informed the pilots as he took one of the two observer chairs. He was a pretty fair shuttle pilot himself, as were most warship pilots, and in Heuron he'd had to take over this exact same shuttle when its pilot, Lieutenant Toguchi, had been killed in the same seat Tif now occupied. "We have hacksaws in the ship! Just remember they can operate outside spaceships as well as inside, they don't mind a vacuum!"

"God damn it," Lee muttered. Erik couldn't see the pilots' faces, only the backs of their helmets — Tif in the rear pilot's seat, Lee in the forward seat lower down. Tif echoed something equally unhappy in her native tongue.

"Hatch sealing!" Cowell yelled behind.

"Strap in Private!" Lee replied. "We're leaving hard!"

"Don't wait for hold secure!" Erik echoed. "Just go on retrieval!"

"Good," Tif agreed, a gloved hand hovering on the release.

"Hatch sealed, retrieval complete..." and Cowell barely had time to finish the sentence before Tif detached with a crash and lurch into zero-G, then hit main thrust and slammed everyone back. And hit something, spinning sideways as Tif snarled in alarm.

"Damage left stabiliser!" Lee announced. "More damage... dammit, we've got a passenger!" As the upper hatch camera swung back far enough to show the horrifying spider-shape clutching the left rear stabiliser with steely legs.

Tif said something that could only be a kuhsi obscenity, cut mains and hit laterals hard. The shuttle spun sideways, and kept spinning, the starfield moving faster and faster, a flash as Joma Station's massive round bulk entered and left their vision. The Gs built fast, and Erik fought to hold his head back on the chair, but it was impossible. With the extra weight of his helmet, the pain on his neck became excruciating, vision blurring as blood rushed to his head and chair restraints cut off circulation.

And then slowly eased, as Tif hit opposite stabilisers, Erik gasping as the pressure faded. "There he is!" Lee said triumphantly. "Got him at 140! Nice work Tif, he just flew right off." Which would happen, Erik supposed, if you spun a shuttle on its mid-axis at negative 8-Gs. The pilots' rule of thumb was that two negatives felt as bad as three regular-G. Negative-8 was a first even for him.

"Guns!" Tif said plaintively as she levelled them out facing the tumbling silver speck. "Guns! Kiw!"

"Guns, kill," Lee agreed, and forward cannon thundered. The silver speck broke into tumbling fragments.

"Good kiw," said Tif, and slammed them back with another burst of thrust. They went sideways, accelerating across Joma's enormous wheel face. Erik saw small ships ahead, shuttles and insystem runners — lots and lots of them, breaking clear from the wheel hub and running. A number of large ships too, hauling away from the rim, some of them powering with their tails afire, desperate to put distance between them and the station.

"Tif, *Phoenix* on your main," said Lee, and Tif adjusted angle and thrust to bring them around at where Berth 18 would soon arrive with Joma's rotation.

"Rook!" Tif snapped, pointing out the cockpit at something. "Rook there!" Erik stared, and saw a little cluster of tiny dots, moving across the huge station wheel. Independently powered, little thrusters at the rear. And his blood ran a little colder.

"Yeah," he said heavily. "Those are hacksaw drones." They were the first ones he'd actually seen properly, with time to look. They looked so little and harmless, and evidently under-powered out here, with only small thrust to move across stations from the outside. It was like watching a small flock of birds on a distant horizon... only these birds were the rarest and most terrifying things in all the galaxy. Some spectacularly ignorant human Worlders didn't even believe they were real, never having seen them with their own eyes, and insisted they were all a great lie, the dead machine-corpses, the deep-space bases, the deserted ancient hive-cities, all fabricated by Fleet for some nefarious conspiracy or other. Erik supposed it was a safer and more comforting thing to believe than the truth. "Do not fire on them, do not even get weapons lock. We want to get back to *Phoenix*, don't draw their attention."

"Copy that," Lee said warily. And pointed at a ship docked at the station rim, just partly visible amidst the huge support gantries that stopped multi-thousand tonne vessels flinging off into space with the rotation. "That's *Makimakala*. She's still docked."

"She's probably got people on station," said Erik. "Doesn't want to leave them behind." Even as they watched, something on the tavalai warship fired, and a part of the station rim blew up. "They're weapons active while still docked, must be hacksaws on the rim." It was against all protocols to stay docked with such terrors loose on the station... but then, without coms, possibly they didn't know where their senior officers were — like *Phoenix*. "Tif, be careful of hacksaws on approach. Hacksaws, and tavalai shuttles. They might be jumpy."

"Aye," said Tif as the spinning rim drew closer, and gave them a new burst of thrust to come in faster than would normally seem wise. Halfway into the acceleration profile, Erik reconsidered the usual crew assessment that Tif, while a hot pilot, was not quite as hot as Lieutenant Hausler. Any faster on approach and she'd put a hole in the station if she was off by just a second.

"Anyone got any idea what the *hell* they're doing here?" Lee remarked. And by 'anyone', he meant Erik.

"Plenty of time to speculate *after* we get out of here alive," Erik replied, as Tif cut thrust, swung them backward and slammed them all into their seats once more for braking.

Past the section seal barrier, Lisbeth followed Privates Herman and Bernardino through half-completed steel frameworks of what would become shops, offices and apartments once completed. Now they were abandoned of workers and tools, with equipment lying scattered. Lisbeth ran hard — she'd thought she was pretty fit on Homeworld, in that way that civilians who enjoyed a little exercise thought they were fit, a little volleyball here, a nice run on the beach there. Time amongst *Phoenix*'s marines had shown her that what she considered fit, marines considered funny, and she'd increased her gym-time accordingly. But now she learned another marines-truth — that running on a treadmill, and running from real enemies who wanted to kill you, were very different things. Already she was gasping for air from adrenaline overload, and had to force that easy calm into her stride so that she didn't waste half her energy on nervous panic.

Herman and Bernardino turned left, back toward the dock, and Lisbeth followed with Carla and Vijay alongside. The dock on this side of the section seal had been clear before the barrier had come down, but now she could hear shooting ahead, and the lead marines signalled those behind to stop. Lisbeth did, gasping, while the privates advanced crouched and cautious through half-finished wall panels and dangling electrical fixtures. And Lisbeth stared, to see tracer fire ripping up the dock, and flashes as bouncing rounds tore fragments off the deckplate.

Herman shook his head and gestured at them to get back... and the half-finished corridor about him exploded in a hail of fire and flying fragments. Carla fell on Lisbeth, and then Corporal Penn was hurdling them to rush to his privates, returning fire thunderously through the walls one-handed while trying to grab Herman with the other.

"We gotta go!" Vijay bellowed above the din as more fire came in. "It's a firezone, Lisbeth's unarmored and we're drawing fire!"

"I gotta stay with my guys!" Ruiz yelled back, and smashed through a wall panel to search for a fire position. Carla hauled Lisbeth up and dragged her after Vijay, as Lisbeth tried to resist, staring back at where Corporal Penn was dragging the screaming and cursing Herman back under fire. Beyond them, Private Bernardino was not moving.

"Bernie!" Penn was yelling as Carla hauled Lisbeth away. "Bernie get the fuck up! Bernie!"

And then she was running after Vijay, weaving along the broken, unfinished corridor and feeling suddenly naked with only two lightly armoured bodyguards. Powered armour was tough as hell, but hacksaw chain guns had gone straight through it...

Ahead, Vijay skidded to a halt by a corner more completed than the others, and peered into a T-junction hall. Lisbeth held up, then Vijay waved her and Carla forward. Several more marines ran by, and heavy fire came from the docks to the left. A marine Lisbeth didn't recognise through the visor and drifting smoke was yelling at Vijay, "...getting it cleared the fuck out! There's no-one left up there, we checked! They're coming through the fucking walls, they're getting us encircled!"

"We can't get her out on the docks, she's not armoured!" Vijay yelled back.

"We've got guys downstairs, lower level! Use the stairs... look, *Phoenix* won't wait forever and we've not enough shuttles..." boom! as something exploded by the docks, and marines up there cursed. "Not enough shuttles to get off those left behind, and no way to rendezvous without coms!"

"Got it!" said Vijay, and ran to the right, away from the docks... and Lisbeth recognised the corridor, this was the main entrance to *Phoenix*'s accommodation block. Strewn on the floor were crew duffel bags, brought on dock for personals and a change of clothes, now abandoned in the mad rush to get back to *Phoenix*.

Vijay ran straight past the elevators, as suddenly station power flickered and the main lights dimmed. Red emergency lights replaced them, speaker announcements echoing in Palapu, drowned by the rattle and thud of gunfire from behind. Vijay peered into a stairwell, rifle checking up then down as Carla guarded their rear. A ventilation fan in the stairwell wall roared, trying to haul in the wisps of smoke from some nearby fire...

Movement made Lisbeth look up the corridor... in a doorway, a small figure waving at her. And her heart stopped. The small figure had long ears and scruffy fur within an oversized marines' jacket. "Oh my god Skah! What are you doing here!"

"Kid!" Carla yelled, beckoning. "Furball! Come here!"

Skah shook his head and pointed back up the corridor from his doorway, shouting something unintelligible. "Skah no!" Lisbeth shouted. "We're leaving! You have to come..."

The stairwell blew up, a hammerblow that hit her from behind... and then she was on the floor, rolling and coughing and unable to hear a thing. She struggled up by reflex, and Skah seeing she was okay yelled something she couldn't hear, waved for her to follow, and disappeared.

Lisbeth followed in panic. She couldn't leave Skah here, and if she didn't follow then Carla and Vijay's only responsibility was herself — they might just figure Skah was secondary and not worth the risk. The new corridor swam and buckled as she ran, but that was just her knees, and she fended a wall before she fell into it, and turned another bend past abandoned hotel offices where it looked like Skah had surely come. If the hacksaws were guarding the stairwells, probably one of them had fired a grenade down from a higher level, she'd heard tales marines told of how to clear stairwells effectively...

And she burst into a common room, upturned furnishings and wall displays destroyed and smoking, drilled with bullet holes. And here was Skah, down behind some sofas, tending to someone on the ground. Lisbeth stumbled that way and found a spacer in a *Phoenix* jumpsuit — no one she recognised, no nametag on the clothes to tell who it was, but he'd been shot through the side and Skah was trying to stop the bleeding.

Lisbeth ran and knelt beside, in a new panic because she didn't have a first aid kit and didn't know where there'd be one. But Skah grabbed a cushion off the chairs and bit it, tearing the fabric with a great rip and pulling against sharp teeth. Lisbeth helped him, and they got the cloth free, and Lisbeth bunched it and tore the spacer's jumpsuit aside to stuff the cloth over the worst of the blood.

"Hey!" she tried to talk to him, barely able to hear her own voice through the ringing. "Hey spacer! Hey buddy, we're going to get you out of here, okay?" He stared up at her, and it wasn't the pain in his eyes that struck her, it was the fear. It was a 'how can this be happening to me?' fear, and Lisbeth's stomach flip-flopped, because she knew exactly what that was even though she was still in one piece.

Then she realised that neither Carla nor Vijay had come after her. They'd been closer to the stairwell than her. She'd assumed they were okay since she was, and come running after Skah before she lost him... oh god, what if they weren't? What if she'd run off and left them wounded, or worse? What if they weren't coming to save her, and she and Skah were now on their own? Skah was looking up at her with those big golden eyes, desperate but trusting. Trusting that the adult would know what to do. But she didn't.

"Okay Skah, we're going to have to..." move him. But she couldn't. The spacer was an average-sized man, and while she had G-augments, those dealt mainly with internal body stresses and barely made her stronger. And Skah was just a kid, and while kuhsi were faster than most humans, they were kilo-for-kilo no stronger.

Abandon the wounded man? She didn't know him. For a brief, terrified moment it was almost plausible... except that Skah, who was even newer to this crew than she was, had risked his own neck to come and save him. And Skah was just a kid, and not even of the same species. And then she felt horribly ashamed.

"Skah? I'm going to have to go for help. I have to tell one of the marines." Because she could still hear shooting far up the corridors, and out onto the docks. And better that she went, because Skah's English was deserting him under pressure, and at least here he had a chance of hiding if anything came...

A metallic clatter somewhere behind. Lisbeth spun. Midway along the opposite wall was a large pair of sliding doors, with frosted glass that showed only shadows beyond. Shadows, and movement. Something beyond those doors was moving, a whine-and-clicker-clack, and a slide of something heavy. And all the fear she'd felt until now faded by comparison.

She stared about, and saw an adjoining bar beside a small music stage and potted plants. "Skah, over there!" she whispered frantically. "We have to drag him over there! Help me!" She stood bent, and grabbed the man's armpits, while Skah grabbed an arm and tried to keep the cushion cloth pressed to his bleeding side. He was heavy, and the carpet made friction so he didn't slide much. Lisbeth tried to keep low, and hoped that through the frosted glass her silhouette wouldn't show above the sofas and low tables.

Somehow she got the spacer to the bar door, then undid the top lid so the door would open. And could not resist a look back at the frosted glass doors. There was a dark shadow that had not been there before. It seemed to fill the entire corridor beyond. A shadow with legs.

She grabbed the man once more and pulled him in behind the bar with desperate effort, as Skah thought to close the bar door and put the lid back down. And she grabbed him, and pulled him close as she heard the frosted glass doors not shatter violently, but hum neatly open. As though whatever was on the far side had pressed the entry button.

The metallic clatter came into the room, a sound like a hundred ball bearings bouncing on a polished floor. Accompanying it was a deep, throbbing hum, like a powersource, and the whine of servo motors, like the noise marines in powered armour made when they moved. It came across the floor, and Lisbeth could hear metal feet thudding hard on carpet, then softer as it crawled across leather chairs, then a hard clack as a foot hit a glass tabletop. Lisbeth tried to hold her breath, but her heart was hammering so fast that she had to breathe before her lungs ran out of oxygen. She looked down at Skah, pressed tight against her, and found him just as scared. He was a smart kid, he knew exactly what was in the room with them. He'd seen her studying them, in Romki's Engineering enclave. His eyes were wide and ears down, as though facing into a strong wind. The wounded spacer closed his eyes, and tried not to groan in pain.

Clatter-clatter-click. It moved past the bar. Movement caught Lisbeth's eye — high in a corner between wall and ceiling, a piece of angled mirror gave her a clear look at the floor beyond. It was a hacksaw drone all right. The size and mechanical intricacy of it took her breath away. Insects and spiders had nothing on this. At least five pairs of main legs, multi-jointed, some for walking, others for integrated weapons. The rear-quarter pair wielded massive multi-barrelled chain guns, the feeds for which wound cleverly into the big armoured thorax. The big, many-eyed head swivelled, ducked and peered, as though sniffing the air. Smaller arms picked up the torn cushion that Skah had used, and sniffed at the blood on the carpet.

It picked up the sofa, effortlessly, then with little inner arms whipped out a tool and emitted a bright flash. The sofa came apart in smoke and burned leather, and the drone sniffed the insides, as though suspecting someone might have been hiding there. That cutter was how they got through the walls, Lisbeth thought. And different drones were differently equipped. A group would mix weapons and tools for the best balance, like a marine platoon's mix of riflemen and heavies.

Then it paused, as though realising something, and turned to look. Straight at the mirror. Straight at Lisbeth. Because of course, Lisbeth realised in horror — reflections went both ways, and if she could see it, it could see her. But it hesitated, staring, as though uncertain what it saw. Why was it waiting?

Something thudded into a wall, and the drone leaped back, its huge thorax elevating as paired chain guns levelled and howled in spinning preparation to fire... and a huge explosion knocked it sideways, as whatever had hit the wall detonated late. Gunfire followed, the unmistakable thunder of a Koshaim-20, and Lisbeth glimpsed drone debris flying, a weapon arm falling, the big machine staggering then returning fire with a roaring hail of bullets, spent cartridges spraying across the room, rattling off the bar-top and bottles. Another explosion, and more gunfire, and the drone leaped and scuttled with incredible speed, smashed the frosted glass doors and was gone.

A pause, then footsteps, then, "Clear!" A human voice, and familiar. "Watch it! Clear that corridor, it hasn't gone far!" Corporal Penn, Lisbeth realised.

"We're back here!" she shouted. "We've got one wounded, you've got to carry him!" She staggered upright, and then a thud as Carla slid over the bar. Not wasting time, she grabbed the wounded spacer and lifted him effortlessly onto the bar for another heavy-armoured marine to grab and take away. Lisbeth wished she could have lifted him like Carla.

"Come on, go," said Carla, and Lisbeth scrambled over the bar, Skah following. The room beyond was smoke-filled and torn by shrapnel and gunfire, one wall aflame and localised fire retardant spraying down, several more marines up by the broken doors where the drone had come, even now laying down cover fire.

Lisbeth jumped down and helped Skah, who didn't need it, then "Down!" yelled a marine by the doorway as something hit further up, and Vijay grabbed and hustled her for the door as an explosion rocked the corridor. Both marines were up and firing back up the corridor immediately, and Lisbeth looked back as Carla jumped the bar… and was hit by a roar of chain gun fire from up the corridor, disintegrating bar, wood panels and bodyparts in all directions.

Lisbeth screamed as Vijay rushed her at the door, yelling "Go, go!", marines behind laying down fire and swearing furiously. A side wall exploded, and again the howl of laser cutters.

"Marines!" Corporal Penn bellowed. "Pull back! Pull the fuck back now!" And then Lisbeth was running up the way she'd come, Skah alongside as Vijay hustled her along, heavy armour thudding behind as gunfire roared.

"Oh my god Carla!" Lisbeth sobbed.

"She's gone, now move!"

There were more marines in the main accommodation corridor now, and Vijay made no more for the stairwells, as it looked like reinforcements had arrived.   Lisbeth ducked amidst the armoured bodies, the shouts and yells, the thunderous retort of guns as marines expanded this perimeter.   Smoke was overwhelming the ventilation fans, forming a choking blanket at the ceiling, and nearby explosions and splintering shrapnel clanged at random off steel wall frames.

At the dock, Lisbeth could see the difference immediately — there were marines all along the far wall between Berth 19 and 20, using parked jeeps and other vehicles for cover.   Many were heavies, and they were laying down the most incredible barrage of fire on the upper levels overlooking the high dock, chain guns howling on massive arm supports, rapid cannon thudding, explosions from above sending debris falling down like rain.   Some of those vehicles were commandeered for more ammunition — Lisbeth had seen the ammo crates stacked in the *Phoenix* main corridor and wondered at the point of it.   Well here was the point, being expended at a hundred rounds a second at the upper dock levels.

"Yo Lisbeth!" announced Lieutenant JC Crozier in her stomping great armour rig — she seemed to be in command of this stretch, and had scorch marks on her rifle's muzzle from all the firing. "And Furball, good! Corporal Penn, you got her?"

"I got her sir," Penn confirmed as he arrived behind. "Hacksaws behind at accommodation ground level, we lost Lisbeth's other bodyguard."

"Right, stay up against the inner wall, you're going to have to run it," Crozier said, indicating up the dock with one arm. "Can't spare a vehicle at the moment. Beware of falling debris, we've got good cover on the floors above you but be careful of the lower deck trapdoors, we've blasted a couple of them but there may be more.

That was how the fuckers were getting up beneath us before — you good?"

"Good sir!" said Penn.

"Go!" And Vijay grabbed Lisbeth and they set off running once more, negotiating about a jeep coming the other way up the inner wall, with empty stretchers on the back. They must have been evacuating remaining wounded via the jeeps, Lisbeth thought — thus they had none available for those who could move themselves. No doubt the wounded spacer would be brought back that way.

Lisbeth wanted to grab Skah's hand, but the little kuhsi was running far more easily than her, dodging bits of fallen wreckage on the decking... and here ahead, wedged into the devastated remains of a shopfront, a huge insectoid hulk, shredded and holed at least sixty times to be sure, legs protruding at broken, ungainly angles. Skah stared as he ran — they all did... and ducked as something new shrieked and whistled behind. Missiles, as heavy sections unleashed more firepower on the upper levels, then huge thuds as the whole rim seemed to shake, and a storm of wreckage came falling down.

On the deck plating before Berth 19 lay a stream of dropped things — duffel bags, shoes, uniform caps. Amidst them, smearing the decking, were bloodstains. *Phoenix* crew, running from the accommodation block, must have been caught in the open. Oh god.

Her lungs were burning from the effort as Berth 18 appeared ahead, up against the lowered section seal that blocked off the entire dock from the under-construction rim on the far side. More vehicles here were leaving, and marines were thick in the inner-rim corridors to her right — there was less firing at the upper levels, and Lisbeth guessed they had marines occupying those levels physically, to avoid any direct threat to the *Phoenix* berth.

Skah took off on a diagonal across the docks to reach the Berth, and Vijay yelled at him, then Lance Corporal Penn. Skah looked back, and saw them gesturing to keep along the inner wall, which he did reluctantly. The middle of the dock, far away from cover, was where the bloodstains were. They passed a mangled and bloodied armour suit, broken open and its occupant removed. And on the right, another corridor and some barabo dockworkers, terrified and begging the marines blocking the way. Another marine, limping in his damaged suit, waving off assistance with his visor up and determined pain on his face.

They ran until directly opposite the berth, then were waved in by marines there, covering behind vehicles and empty ammo boxes. One of them stood out, yelling orders, surrounded by a small group that ran to and from, conveying messages verbally now that coms weren't working. Several were aiming armour-mounted lasers up the curving dock — lasercom, Lisbeth realised, allowing some distance communication until the station curve blocked it. There was no affirmation from Major Thakur as Skah or Lisbeth passed, just more orders, and an attitude of general displeasure, all expression hidden behind the fearsome armoured visor. But Lisbeth was incredibly relieved to see her, because she'd been on the Worlder ship with Erik, and if she was back safe, no doubt Erik was as well.

She stopped to gasp for air at the ramp, and Vijay walked with her. Skah kept running into the main airlock, and that was fine, onboard he was safe and knew where to go — doubtless now to find his mother.

"Thanks Corporal," Vijay said to Penn. "How are the others?"

"Bernie's dead," Penn said grimly. "Herman's hurt bad, I left Ruiz to guard them with the Echo Platoon reinforcements. Gotta go." He turned and left, first to report to the Major, then no doubt to find his section once more. He'd left them to come after her, Lisbeth realised. There was no harder thing for any marine leader to do, particularly with wounded — but he'd been tasked to protect her, and the reinforcements had arrived to take care of his casualties. Had that not happened, Lisbeth was pretty sure he'd not have come at all... and she, Skah and the spacer whose name she still didn't know, would be dead.

CHAPTER 19

"LC," came Trace's voice on coms, *"I can give you a two minute warning for departure! I've still got some stragglers coming in, but we are two minutes to go!"* The engineers had been out on the dock under fire, physically laying cable so *Phoenix* could talk to her marines. Still they were mystified as to how *all* the coms were being jammed, with explanations that ranged from unseen new jamming tech to full corruption of Joma Station's wired and wireless systems with viruses or nanomites. Erik wasn't particularly interested — he just needed to talk to Trace without having to physically send runners sprinting through the corridors.

"Tell me the moment we are clear to leave."

"Aye sir, we also have about a hundred barabo stationers requesting evacuation. It'll take another thirty seconds, we've got them bunched up ready to go."

"Helm, can we fit them?"

"Aye sir," said Shahaim, fully fastened into her chair, hands on sticks with full systems displays racing across her lowered visor. "We can fit them."

"Major, that's a go with the barabo."

"Aye sir." It was probably a dumb move, Erik thought, but it wasn't a dangerous one, and he didn't have time to second guess himself right now. Up the right end of the bridge, Second Lieutenant Harris was exchanging terse conversation with Second Lieutenant Corrig from second-shift, who was filling in for Lieutenant Karle on Arms. Every few seconds *Phoenix*'s closer range cannons hammered away, and defensive anti-missiles destroyed incoming hacksaw warheads. The damage they could do to *Phoenix* was minimal, with most of their numbers concentrated inside the station, but if they missed an incoming drone, and that drone found a soft spot on the outer hull and started cutting, things could get real interesting real fast. PH-3 and 4 were holding position off *Phoenix*'s stern and adding their own firepower and perspective to anything coming at the ship.

"Scan, status on those inbound marks."

"Sir, all five are still in combat formation," Geish replied. "They have marginally gained V, ETA now twenty-two minutes to station intercept." Those marks had appeared on scan just before Erik had arrived back on *Phoenix*. Now the game was clear — the station ambush to try and bog *Phoenix* down, get her tied up in station operations, recovering crew off the dock and unable to immediately withdraw. And then jump in with the warships. They *looked* like sard, probably the same sard that had tried to kill them earlier — the vector suggested Gala-eighty-eight, their last known location. Only now there were two more of them.

"So we're just going to leave Joma Station?" Kaspowitz said warily.

"No choice," said Erik. "Can't even coordinate a defence with this jamming, and even *Makimakala* doesn't seem to know where it's coming from."

"Four million people on Joma," Kaspowitz added.

"I know," Erik said grimly. "Nothing we can do. If the hacksaws are working with the sard, maybe they'll get withdrawn when these warships arrive." A big if, with four million lives on station. Local security was relatively unarmed, and hacksaws were relentless. His best guesstimate on observations so far was at least five hundred drones on station, of which they'd killed perhaps fifty. Primarily it was *Phoenix* and *Makimakala* under attack, it didn't seem as though station bridge or other keypoints were being assaulted... although that might follow once *Phoenix* and *Makimakala* left. "I don't think they're after the station, I think they're after us. Best thing we can do for station is leave."

"Aye sir," said Kaspowitz. "I have the escape course locked in, we'll have to pulse it real close on the gravity slope but it's doable. Almost no margin whatsoever with our pursuit, it's going to be tight."

"Isn't it always?" Erik muttered, and flipped to the landline again. "Major, we recalculated and we cannot take those barabo stationers, incoming marks are too hot."

"Aye sir, I'll keep them out."

He probably just sentenced them all to die, Erik knew. But *Phoenix* would have to push real hard to make close Rhea orbit and pick up PH-1 ahead of those sard ships. The marines would hit the nearest available acceleration slings, there were plenty along the main-quarter corridor for exactly that purpose... but not enough for a hundred barabo, not before *Phoenix* undocked and got the crew cylinder rotating again, and then finding a hundred spare slings for barabo guests would take more minutes, and get them all killed when the sard arrived. And a 10-G push without acceleration slings would get all the barabo killed anyway. Better to take their chances with the hacksaws, and hope the machines were only interested in killing *Phoenix*. Doubtless the barabo wouldn't see it that way.

"Sir!" called Geish. "*Makimakala* is leaving! She is pulling back hard."

"Copy," said Erik, gazing at his screens and visor overlay holographics. Between them he had a pretty good 3D picture of the space surrounding Joma — most of the ships that could leave had already left, but *Rai Jang* remained in close proximity, just nine-K parallel with her two flanking station defence ships. All three had been closer-in earlier, blasting away at what few hacksaws they could see traversing the outside. With no marine complements, it was all they could do to contribute, but now they'd seen the incoming sard and no doubt wondered if they ought to run as well. With no coms, Erik could not ask their intentions, and all remained on station farside and unreachable by direct lasercom. "Coms, get me lasercom on *Makimakala* as soon as you get line-of-sight."

"Yessir."

"*LC, we are onboard and locked away!*" Trace said in his ear. "*Clear to depart in ten seconds!*"

"Sir, *Makimakala* is attempting lasercom contact!" Shilu called.

"Hatch locked, grapples green," Shahaim added. "Clear to depart."

"Nineteen point three, get that fucker," Harris told Corrig, and weapons thumped as another drone died.

235

"Standby on lasercom," Erik told Shilu as his mental countdown from Trace's mark approached zero.   Hit zero, and undocked hard, bow thrusters kicking their heads forward. "Operations, shuttle recovery, the timer is on."

"Copy LC, shuttle recovery is on the timer."   Lieutenant Hausler could get back to grapples in less than twenty seconds from here.   Erik let *Phoenix* drift back from station, careful not to hit thrust while the shuttles got back aboard.

"Lasercom connect, sir I have *Makimakala*."

And Shilu put the tavalai warship through without being told. *"Phoenix this is Captain Pram of Makimakala, intentions?"*   Damn he spoke good English, Erik thought.   Tavalai were always so damn civilised.

"*Makimakala* this is LC Debogande, we have a shuttle on Vola Station with urgent business, we are heading on hard intercept."

"PH-4 is aboard," said Ops — sixteen seconds, holy shit Tif.

"Phoenix we will run cover for you, stay in touch."

"PH-3 is aboard," said Ops — twenty-one seconds, not bad Jersey, she was a little out of practise.

Erik hit the mains with a huge roar that kicked them all back in their seats, 6-Gs and building steadily as the engines warmed. "*Makimakala* thank you for your offer, much appreciated."   As 7-Gs built to 10, and breathing became hard, and speech near-impossible.

"Is that a good idea?" Shahaim formulated.

"Soon find out," Erik formulated back, watching his near-scan holographics, as Joma Station slid by to one side at a steadily accelerating rate.   And here came *Makimakala*, following at not quite the thrust — not that she didn't possess it, Erik suspected, but because she was going to fall back into a cover position.

"Rai Jang just joined us," Geish added.

"I see it," said Erik.   *"Her two buddies as well, so now we have five."*   Five-on-five sounded nearly like a fair fight... except that three of those were light cruisers, and Erik was prepared to bet from their signatures out of jump that all five incoming sard were the same crazy high class that had nearly killed *Phoenix* last time they'd met.   *Makimakala* and *Phoenix* together could make a formidable

236

combination, but no human and tavalai warships had ever fought together in all of history, as far as Erik was aware. If you were going to get into a big fight with someone, you'd damn well better know their capabilities, tactics and captain's personal preferences — and neither warship knew any of that of the other.

Dale's marines took the stairs down from their hotel rooms to the lobby level. In the foyer, where the bar and restaurants were usually crowded with noisy barabo guests, they found instead red-uniformed Vola Station police, all armed and in no mood to let the humans pass. Unfortunately for them, Dale plus his marines made eight, and they were all in heavy armour and weapons, having shared their hotel rooms with it for the past few days.

They formed a short line before the police, as nervous hotel staff backed away, and the small crowd of gawkers on the main strip outside grew larger. Dale lowered his visor, and the overlaid display lit up the cops like bullseyes. *"You no leave!"* the senior cop insisted through his translator mike. *"Order of Stationmaster! You no permission to leave!"*

"My warship is coming this way fast," Dale replied, as his own translator turned it into squawking Palapu. "Either I am on it, or my warship will extract me from this station by force." The black-furred barabo seemed to swallow hard at that. "You don't make an enemy of *Phoenix*, friend. *Phoenix* is under wartime alert, *Phoenix* will tear this station apart."

"Hello Lieutenant Dale," crackled PH-1's com in his ear, *"we have station-confirmed berth at hub number 59, ETA thirty-one minutes, please confirm."*

Dale held up his hand to forestall whatever the barabo cop was saying. "PH-1 this is Dale, I copy hub berth 59 in thirty-one minutes. Request that you change it to a rim berth for convenience, over."

"Lieutenant we requested that," replied Ensign Yu, PH-1's co-pilot. *"But we've just come from the factory and they know*

we're carrying a full cargo of missiles. Station rules say no rim docking with ordinance, will ETA be a problem?"

"Not yet," Dale replied. "I'll get back to you on that." He advanced on the cop, powered armour whining and thumping as he raised his Koshaim-20 crosswise before the barabo's face. "If you fire on us, you will not scratch us. If I fire on you, there will be nothing left. We are leaving."

He had no desire to fire on poor dumb barabo cops just trying to fulfil some stupid Stationmaster's order not to let the humans leave the hotel. No doubt that order had something to do with the hooded figure in their midst, with his female staffer companion. Fleet agents must have told Vola Station that Chankow was to be stopped from leaving. Vola Station's problem was doing something about it.

A loud female voice shouted in Palapu, and Dale looked to see a new officer arriving. Her red uniform was striped and she had short black dreadlocks, tight beneath her uniform cap, and the short trimmed beard that passed for feminine among barabo. The other cops parted for her, and she came right up to the lead barabo cop and shouted at him. Dale's translator gave him mostly static — either these two were speaking some dialect the translator did not recognise, or they were going at it so hard that Palapu began to sound foreign. On some human stations, Dale had heard angry dockworkers doing that to English.

The officer backed off, and the woman beckoned to Dale. "You come," she said in English. "Take you to hub fast. Get you shuttle, before you blow many holes in station and station people." With a glare at Dale's weapon, before turning to head for the main walk outside. "You come with me, no more trouble with station, yes?"

Dale indicated to his people, and they followed her out, through the bewildered cops and the spectators beyond, and onto the main walk. They made a protective formation about Chankow, the crowd wisely parting before them as the marines kept shoulder-to-shoulder in case of snipers from across the steel canyon to their side. With as many Fleet agents on station as Jokono had warned them of, it seemed very likely that one of them would take a shot at Chankow before he got on PH-1.

Again his uplinks registered an incoming connection. *"Lieutenant Dale, this is the Major, please respond."* Her voice sounded G-stressed.

"Hello Major," said Dale with relief. "We're headed for the station hub now, when we lost contact with *Phoenix* and Joma Station we figured something was wrong and bailed. Slight trouble with the locals, but I think we'll make the rendezvous."

"See that you do make the rendezvous, we have incoming sard vessels on our tail, we're going to be cutting it very fine to make an intercept pickup of PH-1, and then we're running. We'd do it faster but Vola's current position is behind Rhea and we can't manage jump pulse on that gravity slope."

"Yes Major, we'll be there. What's the situation on the coms blackout?"

"Joma Station was attacked by a swarm of hacksaws." Dale did not shock easily, but he nearly missed a stride. *"We think they came from one of the ships docked at the rim, or maybe several. No telling who was infested, but if sard could strip Grappler like they did, they could probably do the same to some Joma Station ship and fill it with drones. It looks like sard and hacksaws are working together, Joma's a complete mess, they targeted Phoenix and Makimakala specifically, we've light casualties but it was tight. It's a whole other bunch of questions to ask Chankow, so we need him alive."*

"I copy that Major, you'll have him shortly."

He'd chosen the hotel in part because it was close to both a gym and the turbolifts up the station's three-arm to the hub. The elevator car arrived full of barabo, whom the female police officer cleared away with much yelling and flashing of her shiny badge, to disgruntled looks all around. There was barely enough room for eight armoured marines, two unarmored humans and one unarmored barabo, but they all made the squeeze and the barabo spoke some kind of override command into the car's voice recognition, and all

239

impending stops on the display disappeared, giving them a clear route up to the hub.

"Thank you," said Dale, raising his visor. The barabo gave him a nod, with every impression of just wanting him the hell off her station as fast as possible. "Will you be in trouble with station?"

A disinterested shrug. "Maybe. Maybe don't care." The black fur at her neck was shaved in odd stripes on each side. It made a sleek pattern from her shoulders up to her jaw. For perhaps the first time ever, Dale wished Romki were here, to tell him what it meant. "You talk your ship?" Dale nodded. "Ship say what happen Joma Station? We still no coms."

"Hacksaws," said Dale. "Joma was attacked."

The barabo raised a quizzical eyebrow at him, thinking he was joking. Then studied his face, with dawning horror. "True?"

"True." And he looked at Chankow, staring at him beneath his civvie hood. "Any idea why or how?"

"There were reports," said Chankow. "From sard space, and Outer Neutral Space. Sard messing around with the old AI stuff they'd found. The tavalai no longer enforcing the anti-AI laws, Dobruta short of manpower from the war and told by tavalai command to leave the sard alone. The reports were ignored, humans thought anything that made trouble between sard and tavalai was good."

"Sonofabitch," Dale muttered, as gravity grew lighter. Vola Station's spoke arms were barely a kilometre long, and the rotational gravity disappeared fast compared to the monster stations *Phoenix* crew were more accustomed to. The car's occupants grabbed rails in anticipation of floating. "This sounds like a lot more than just 'messing around' with old AI tech. You can't reprogram hacksaws, and they won't fight for anyone but their own queens."

"Sounds more like an alliance," Lance Corporal Ricardo said grimly.

"Between sard and hacksaws?" Lance Corporal Kalo replied. "Well that's fucking cheerful." Until a short while ago, conventional wisdom had said that hacksaws were mostly extinct and encountering a group of them would be as likely as winning —

or rather losing — a lottery. And now *Phoenix* had had two nasty encounters within three months. What the hell was going on?

When they reached hub transition, everyone floated to the ceiling as the elevator car came to a halt. They emerged from the tube as forward windows showed the huge steel canyon walls moving smoothly past them — the stationary hub, holding still in space on frictionless magnetic bearings while the entire, multi-million tonne station rotated around it. Directly opposite them was a new vehicle car on rails, moving parallel to the elevator, and Dale pulled himself aboard, squeezing into a corner as the rest followed. Behind them, the transparent walls showed another car full of barabo passengers, waiting to move up and enter the now-empty elevator car, all staring at the armoured humans. Once full, someone hit the right button and their new car took an off-rail and began to slow.

"Okay everyone," said Dale as the car approached two others queued at a big hatch. "Bottleneck ahead, stay sharp. Perfect ambush spot, everyone watch the blindspots and mind your own sector. Keep it tight and watch your attitude jets amongst the civvies."

Ahead of them, the lead car full of barabo passengers accelerated away up the rail, chasing the nearest station-arm elevator. The car ahead moved up a spot, and their own bumped after it. Passengers hauled themselves from the car ahead as doors opened, floating one after another up the handlines.

"Hello Lieutenant, this is PH-1," came the crackle in Dale's ear as they waited. *"Our ETA is now twenty-four, please confirm your status?"*

"Don't worry PH-1, we'll make it with about ten to spare."

"Good thing, because Phoenix is coming in real fast and she's got tavalai and barabo friends for company with sard right behind. Gonna be tight, see you there."

"Hey! What...?" It was their new replacement volunteer off *Europa*, Private Tabo. "Hey you! Where the hell do you think you're going?"

He was addressing the barabo policewoman, who was pulling herself out of the car's farside door, into the narrow gap against the wall where no passengers were supposed to go. She seemed eager to get out in a hurry. Almost as though... and then Dale realised.

"Oh fuck, grenade!" And marines nearly broke the car glass spinning to try and look for it. "Where the fuck is it?"

"Get out!" yelled Carponi, and smashed the glass with a fist, then bang! as everything shattered, and the car was full of smoke. Dale barely felt it, with his visor down the armour was far too tough for small AP grenades. Then why... and then he realised again, also too late.

"Oh man," Private Yu complained, in the same tone as someone who had just seen something horrible. Dale looked, and it was indeed horrible — Supreme Commander Chankow, very dead and now spilling an awful lot of zero-G blood globules into the car. And innards. "Man, she stuffed it into his fucking coat."

"Dammit, the girl's hurt bad," said Private Halep, cradling Lieutenant Raymond, who was out cold and bloody. "LT? She'd get better care here, even if she's not barabo — if we take her with us she might bleed out under Gs."

Dale could recall plenty of times being more angry than this, but rarely at himself. He bit back some more bad language, as the damaged car bumped up another spot to the wall hatch. The Major discouraged officers swearing in combat — it indicated a lack of control. "She comes with us, she might still know stuff. Patch her best you can and bring her. Corporal Kalo, get your section out there and secure the way."

"Yessir!"

Of the backstabbing barabo officer there was nothing they could do — sure as hell he wasn't going to go chasing and shooting through a civilian station to catch her when he was urgently needed at Berth 59. And just as sure he'd think twice before trusting barabo security again.

Erik was flat on his back for a 10-G burn when *Europa*'s message came through from Lieutenant Shilu's post.

"*Phoenix, this is Europa. Europa is outbound and preparing to jump. All crew and passengers are safe and accounted for, including Calvin Debogande. I thought the Lieutenant Commander would like to know.*"

"Thank you *Europa*," Shilu replied. "*The Lieutenant Commander sends his best wishes to Europa, and to all aboard.*"

Erik's attention was fixed on his holographic display of PH-1, burning hard away from Vola orbit, but still firmly snared in the much larger gravitational pull of enormous Rhea, looming to one side with swirling, malevolent clouds. He'd just dumped a little V with the jump engines, but could not cycle deeply into hyperspace this deep on the gravitational slope, and would have to lose the rest of the V with main engines. They were sharing data with PH-1 via two-way link, navcomp fixing a rendezvous point that their combined thrust would hit precisely, and any deviation would see them miss completely. The pursuing sard vessels were as jump-pulse limited as any others this close to Rhea, and would miss their fire-intercept window by nearly two minutes, assuming they'd already fired.

"*Hello Phoenix, this is Makimakala,*" came Captain Pram's voice, no doubt uplink formulated as *Makimakala* was pulling a similar manoeuvre behind them. "*We request a common jump point for system exit, there is safety in numbers. Clearly these sard want us dead, and we should consider why.*"

It was hard to make life changing decisions for an entire crew while flat on your back at 10-G and attempting to line up a very non-standard rendezvous. A second uplink light blinked where his peripheral vision would usually be — at this G-stress, eyesight tended to tunnel.

"*Understood Makimakala, Phoenix copies. Please standby.*" He flipped channels. "*Hello Major.*"

"Take his offer," said Trace. "*Romki's just been chewing my ear off down here, and I think he's right. Take his offer, we need to get to the bottom of this.*"

"*If we take it, we'll miss Fleet's offer of pardon. It will expire in our absence.*"

"Lieutenant Dale said Chankow told him we'd be dead in a year if we took it anyway. He said it was all about hacksaws. Romki says the same. Given what's just happened, I have to agree. We fucked up Erik. I fucked up. I was obsessed with thinking we could make peace and save humanity from civil war. We can't, we were stupid to think we could. But this, we can do. Fighting humanity's foreign enemies is what we were made for. Let's do that, and we might get to the bottom of our Fleet problem at the same time."

Erik knew she was right, of course. It was everything he'd already been thinking, every doubt that had nagged at the back of his mind since far before the hacksaw attack. But to make that decision here would be to condemn all of *Phoenix*'s nearly-600 crew to become hunted outlaws from their own species, from their families and everything they'd known, without giving them a vote on it. His visual showed him rendezvous in one minute thirty, and no time to stop and think about it.

"LC, Makimakala's sending us jump coordinates," Kaspowitz told him. *"It's Tobana, unsettled system, I'd guess we'll have to two-jump an escape unless the tavalai have some help waiting there."*

"This is not a democracy," Trace added. *"This is the call, and you know there's no choice. Call it."*

"Kaspo," Erik formulated. *"Accept and lay in coordinates. Shilu, thank Makimakala for me. Operations, rendezvous ETA one minute and five, stand by."*

"Operations copies LC."

Erik could see PH-1 adjusting thrust angle even now to bring the shuttle across and line up the position where *Phoenix* was about to arrive. He cast a final glance at the nav feed, and *Europa*'s position, disappearing at a more moderate yet purposeful thrust toward Kazak System's outer fringes, one jump pulse down and preparing for the second, with human space several jumps ahead. His biggest regret was that Lisbeth wasn't on her... but how could he trust his sister to any ship holding Fleet's pet killer, who found honour only in obeying orders, no matter how grotesque?

At fifteen seconds Erik cut thrust as *Phoenix*'s velocity precisely matched PH-1's. He left them thrust-neutral as Lieutenant Hausler flung PH-1 about with a precise rotation of thrust, and slammed her hard into the matching grapples.

"PH-1 is aboard!"

And Erik threw *Phoenix* end-over-end and kicked in the mains once more, building to a steady roar as they powered about Rhea's gravity slope with the jump point emerging on the far side.

"Hello Phoenix crew, this is the LC," Erik addressed them all on open coms. *"It seems that these sard are really out to get us, and our tavalai companion has some ideas why. Phoenix does not run from fights, but first we need to regroup and consider what we're up against. We are leaving for Tobana System first, then possibly beyond. All hands standby for combat jump, LC out."*

And just hope that our tavalai friend hasn't been playing us all along, and isn't leading us into a huge froggie trap on the far side.

CHAPTER 20

After Medbay rounds and ship rounds, it took Erik a full two hours to finally intercept Trace in Assembly. They were two jumps out of Kazak and still on orange alert in case the sard pursuit found them again, but there hadn't been any sard vessels on scan when they'd made the second jump, and Tobana System had no nav buoys to interrogate and tell later vessels where the earlier ones had gone. They were in fast transit now across a desolate and unsettled system known only as GH-14, three thousand K off *Makimakala*'s flank with *Rai Jang* another forty thousand K in front. *Rai Jang*'s two companions had not joined them in the first jump, and Erik had been surprised at the smaller ship's speed — it had arrived only fifteen minutes late on each occasion.

Now he walked tiredly along the steel gantries of Assembly, with its endless racks of armour suits and weapons that climbed maze-like toward the outer hull. Automated stacking arms whined and crashed as marines shifted suits that no longer moved under their own power, and the repair bay howled and sprayed orange sparks as bare-armed marines did panel-beating jobs on battered armour. Some of the damage was scary, armourplate torn like paper. Some armour still had blood on it. Marines who had just recently been fighting, then pushing huge Gs through twin combat jumps, now blinked back exhaustion and got their gear back into fighting shape as best they could.

Erik found Trace on a lower gantry by the ammo transport rails, big crates of Koshaim ammunition humming from level to level, and now being unloaded and snapped into empty magazines by hand. Trace wore an open jacket, sweaty like the rest in Assembly's hot air, and shouted with several marines about their progress. Erik recognised one of them in particular — Lance Corporal Penn of Charlie Platoon, Second Squad, who had been personally escorting Lisbeth when things went bad.

"LC," said the Corporal with a nod. He looked grim — just a young guy, pale with dark hair and square features, in civilian life the kind of guy you wouldn't look twice at if you passed him on the street.   But Penn was a five-year vet, retired for one year but volunteering through mutual friends of Sergeant Hoon   on Homeworld after seeing what Fleet did to Captain Pantillo.   And now he'd saved Lisbeth's life.

"I just talked to Private Herman in Medbay," Erik told him. "Docs say they can synth a new leg, he'll be walking in maybe three weeks.   Could even get back to service four weeks after that if he wants."

"He'll want," said Penn with conviction.   "He's a good marine."

"And I'm sorry about Bernardino."

Penn exhaled hard.   "Yeah.   He was a good marine too." He managed a tight smile.   "It's a bit of a change from selling furniture."

"That's what you were doing on Homeworld?"

"Yes sir.   It was a jobs program that places former vets, the owner was a vet himself.   It was just temporary, I hadn't decided what I really wanted to do... maybe go back to school.   But then *Phoenix* happened, and..."   He shrugged, and indicated around.   "I guess I missed it more than I realised."

"You still think that?"

Penn's look was intense.   "Hell yes sir.   Best call I ever made."   Erik was surprised.   "If we're going after the hacksaws. And the bugs.   We are going after them, aren't we sir?"

"That's the intention Corporal.   If we can find out where the hell they are, and what the hell they're doing working with the sard. Our tavalai friends might have some ideas."

"I got no problem working with tavalai sir," said Penn, surprising him again.   "I mean they're arrogant pricks and they had it coming in the war, but they're still just normal folks.   We can talk to tavalai.   Can't talk to those fucking bugs sir, and sure as hell can't talk to hacksaws.   They're the real threat.   People back home think the war's over — I always told them they were kidding themselves."

Erik nodded in agreement.   "And the tavalai don't like them any more than we do.   Or not the hacksaws anyway, and they may be coming around on the sard." Ahead, Trace finished her conversation with another two marines. "Excuse me Corporal, I have to talk to the Major."

"Yes sir." He departed, and Erik congratulated himself at his restraint at not thanking the Corporal for saving his sister. He knew what the reply would be — 'just doing my job sir', and knew that some marines actually took that kind of personal thanks as offensive. Marines didn't fight for personal favours. Lisbeth was *Phoenix* crew, for now at least, and it was the job of marines to fight like hell to protect *Phoenix* crew. That she happened to be Erik's sister, and heiress to one of the most powerful human families, was irrelevant, and to suggest otherwise was to suggest that marines were unprofessional.

"What do you think?" Erik asked Trace, nodding after Corporal Penn.

Trace glanced. "Good," she said, which was enough. She didn't look happy though. Not only exhausted and sweaty, but wound up tight and hard. "I'm sorry. We fucked up. Unacceptable spacer casualties and I've told them so. Ships function without marines but not without spacers. We let *Phoenix* down."

There were six dead marines and another fourteen wounded, against seventeen dead spacers and three wounded. Most of Erik's just-completed rounds had been not in Medbay, but around the ship's crew, talking to Ensigns and Warrant Officers about crew rotations to fill in the losses, and providing what comfort he could to grieving friends. Most of the deaths had been when hacksaws had breached the defensive perimeter on the evacuation of the accommodation block, firing chain guns onto spacers running on the open dock. Thus so many dead, and so few wounded, and it could easily have been far worse.

Erik hung off the steel overhead and considered her. He wanted to disagree with her assessment, but that was the emotional thing to do — to comfort, to be nice. Trace hated that, in him especially. If she thought it was the case then it was probably so, and he'd be wise to listen. Procedure said they should get together and do a full review of what just happened, but that procedure was for the Triumvirate War, with its large-scale actions and organised pauses. Out here and alone, there was just no time to do everything by the book, and now was as good a time for a review as any.

"So what happened?" he asked her.

"Well firstly," said Trace, "the accommodation block was too far from our berth. That's my fault as well, they put us down the end of the dock and the block was near enough for the usual procedure — I thought having an empty dock full of construction activity and no permanent residents could actually work in our favour by increasing our defensive possibilities. Civvies always get in the way. But none of us appreciated the danger we were in, we've been blind the whole way up 'til now, so that's mistake one.

"Mistake two was Lieutenant Crozier took a defensive stance once the hacksaw threat was identified. She was thinking 'withdrawal', and so did not want to forward deploy too many marines too far from *Phoenix*, because they take time to recover when it's time to leave. As a result, our crew furthest from the berth were nearly overrun, including your sister, because we had insufficient firepower on site to help them. When I arrived back from PH-4 I took command and sent out everyone we had, and we regained control of the docks from our berth up to the far section seal with overwhelming firepower. It cost us extra time getting out, but security for personnel on dock is always paramount, and we don't leave crew undefended because it's inconvenient — that's no better than just shooting them ourselves.

"Mistake three was the sloppy evac of the accommodation block, including one spacer hurt by a stray round and left behind — that's Spacer Reddin, the guy your sister saved."

"And Furball," said Erik. "Don't forget the Furball. Reddin will make it, I was just talking to his team, they're midships operations."

"And left the Furball unattended in crew quarters," Trace continued angrily. "I've still no idea how that happened, but I'll get answers, and someone will be apologising to Tif in person."

"We've talked about this," Erik said pointedly.   He didn't like to rub it in, but he had to take the opportunity, and Trace wouldn't respect him if he didn't.

"We have," she acknowledged.   "It was sloppy, and now it's not just you that's pissed about it."   It was an apology, Erik realised, for not pushing it harder before.   *Phoenix* marines had to drop their attitude that if it wasn't directly combat-related, it didn't matter.   In their present circumstance, *anything* could become combat related, at any time.   And in that, the whole crew needed to adjust.

"And the fourth mistake was Lieutenant Dale," Trace continued mercilessly.   "Who just completely screwed the pooch by allowing the former Supreme Commander of all human forces, and the greatest intelligence source we've had access to since this whole mess began, get assassinated right under his nose by a girl he got tricked into thinking was friendly.   And she had a *beard*, so he can't even claim he was thinking with his dick."

Erik nearly smiled.   "What's the thinking on why?"

"Oh, Fleet probably."   Trace shrugged.   "All those spies out to get him.   Spies like Hiro, too damn smart for grunts like Dale, obviously."

"That's a bit rough."

"He's my lieutenant and I'll be the judge of that.   All these barabo stations bending over backwards to please Fleet, my guess is Fleet told Vola Station they wanted Chankow dead, and Vola obliged.   We were stupid to get ourselves into that, Erik.   Damn stupid."

Erik exhaled hard and stared at the nearby armament circle — two sections of marines feeding ammo into magazines, drudge work that was more easily done by hand than machine.

"Yeah," he said quietly.   "And it got *Edmund Chandi* killed, most of the crew were dead when we got off.   Another five came with us, a few of those have volunteered to help but I think most want to jump ship first opportunity.   If ever the Worlders were going to listen to us, they probably won't now."

"Oh they were just stringing us along," Trace muttered. "Worlder politics is so big, and we're so far away.   They were interested in the Captain, not in us.   We were an embarrassment to Fleet, but no more.   Our chances of influencing the Worlder-Spacer conflict died with the Captain."   She gazed at Erik, a brow slightly furrowed, as though trying to figure something out.   "How did we fall for that?"

"Yeah," Erik echoed.   "We who don't hope, and don't kid ourselves wishing for impossible things."   Looking at her edgily.

"Maybe Colonel Khola was right," said Trace.   "Maybe I have completely lost my bearings."   She took a deep breath.   "It's not the kind of mistake I usually make."

Erik frowned.   "So why do you think you made it?"

"Because I thought I knew everything when I first arrived on *Phoenix*," Trace admitted.   "I was only a green louie, but I was a crusty old Kulina since I was a kid."

"Still are," Erik ventured.

Trace smiled faintly.   "And then the Captain said that things weren't exactly as I'd imagined them.   That all human institutions are flawed, even Fleet, and even the Kulina.   That you have to separate loyalty to the institution from loyalty to the cause the institution serves.   The Captain's cause was humanity.   That's my cause as well.   But serving that, and serving Fleet, aren't always the same thing, and so many times he would second-guess Fleet doctrine and logic, and achieve superior results.   It made Fleet question his loyalty, but he did more for the human cause than any of those robot yes-men Fleet were always promoting could ever dream.

"For a long time I denied that final lesson, though.   We'd have these arguments where he'd make his point, and I'd say, 'Well yes, but...'   And then I'd just regurgitate everything the Kulina taught me to believe.   I never really accepted the Captain's final teachings until Fleet murdered him.   And then I realised he was right."

She met Erik's gaze.   "Since then I've been serving his legacy.   Kulina believe in mentors, you know.   It's old tradition, the student learning at the feet of his siksaka — his teacher.   I felt I had to carry on his cause, and his teaching. He was all about keeping humanity together, stopping any civil war from happening. I became obsessed with that, I think. Keeping his cause alive."

"But the Captain didn't see the whole picture," said Erik. "I think we've come further down this road than he ever could. And now we're going further still. I think if he could have seen what we're seeing, he would have agreed with us that the main threat to humanity lies elsewhere."

"No," Trace disagreed, but mildly. "No, I think he was focused on human politics because those were the tools he had. He could actually do something about it. He had the following, and the contacts and support. We don't. But we have other things. He may have set us on this road, but at some point we have to stop asking ourselves what the Captain would do, and start choosing our own direction."

"We had an experience on Tuki Station just before we left," Erik spoke to the monitor in his quarters. On the screen, the wide face and mottled skin of *Makimakala*'s Captain Pram. "A human freighter named *Grappler* docked with station on autos, it had not been speaking to anyone on the way in. We thought it was just maintaining secrecy. Once it docked, we found it was empty and all the crew missing, with many bloodstains indicating many if not most had been killed. All indications are that the sard intercepted *Grappler* at a midpoint jump, took the crew and wiped the navigation logs to allow the ship to continue on automatic. We think the same may have happened on Joma Station, only sard not only removed the crew, but replaced them with hacksaw drones. Which means the sard and the hacksaws are somehow working together."

Captain Pram looked grim. *"Then you have discovered our sard problem."*

"You have a sard problem? That tavalai will admit to?"

"Tavalai Fleet Command, no. They will not admit to anything that might damage the sard alliance. But Dobruta, yes. This is the true nature of Makimakala's mission, Lieutenant Commander. We used to police sard space, because if ever there was a species likely to recover old hacksaw technology and use it, instead of destroying it, it is the sard. But then came the war, and then the manpower shortage, and for the last hundred or so of your years, the Dobruta have been forbidden by the highest tavalai command from policing sard space."

Erik took a deep breath. He thought it was pretty clear where this was going. "You didn't come to see us at Joma Station because you heard we had hacksaw technology aboard. You heard that the sard were after us. With ships that are suspiciously advanced."

"Well both reasons, actually. In combination that we could not ignore. You see, we think the sard have found an old hacksaw base. A ship building base. Sard territory is very large, and even before the sard came into space, thousands of years ago, we had explored only some of it. We catalogued many old hacksaw artefacts, but in all that vastness, there was bound to be much we did not see. And the sard were always bound to find some of it. Thus our previous inspection regime, recently halted. And now, unsurprisingly, the worst Dobruta nightmare appears to be coming true. Sard, with hacksaw technology. In ships, at least."

"More than ships," said Erik. "It suggests an alliance, between hacksaws and sard."

"Well well," Captain Pram cautioned, holding up one webbed hand before the screen. *"Perhaps. We took a crippled drone from the docks at Joma Station. It was not fully functional. Reprogrammed, we think."*

"Reprogrammed? I didn't think that was possible."

"With human or tavalai technology, it's not. Sard computing is particularly advanced, but has little in common with this genus of artificial intelligence. So there is only evidence that the sard have found some old base, certainly with shipbuilding technology, and perhaps with some very old worker and warrior drones in storage,

all deactivated. *They may have reprogrammed them for this purpose.*"

"And which purpose is that? It's clear the sard are after *Phoenix* in particular, but we do not know why."

Pram made a thoughtful, snaking motion of his head. A peculiarly tavalai gesture, Erik thought. He'd never seen it before. Pram tapped a finger on his jaw, as though coming to a decision. *"Our information is that you have hacksaw queen aboard your ship. We would like to see it."*

Commander Nalben, *Makimakala*'s second-in-command, crouched before the nano-tank holding the queen's head, and stared. About him stood Erik, Trace, Romki and as much of the senior Engineering crew that could fit into the little bay. Further back, several lightly armoured karasai, carefully watched by similarly armoured marines... but no one was especially concerned of treachery here.

Nalben considered the queen's head from many angles, eyes wide with an expression that might have been as much dread as fascination. About him, there was no sound from the crowd gathered. Occasionally he'd murmur something into a mike, that *Phoenix*'s com function, activated upon Erik's irises in a moment of curiosity, showed him was being transmitted back to *Makimakala* with *Phoenix*'s permission. The small camera on the Commander's eyepieces was doubtless sending visual data back as well, for Dobruta experts there to see.

After a long period of examination, Nalben got to his feet. "This one is a command unit," he told them all. "You call her a queen. It could be accurate enough... I have studied English well, but the precise background of that word escapes me."

"A monarch," Romki could not resist saying. "An old system of human governance, pre-technological." And broke into rapid Togiri, while various *Phoenix* crew glanced at each other, and rolled their eyes. All save Lisbeth, Erik noted. She stood by

Trace's shoulder, watching Romki with intense interest. Almost as though she could follow the conversation. She'd never told him she'd learned any Togiri at university, though it was not surprising.

"Yes," Commander Nalben conceded, after Romki had finished. "Yes, a 'queen' is as good a term as any. Though this queen may have had others ranked above her in her time. She would have been more like you or I, Lieutenant Commander. Important in our local sphere, yet answering to higher powers in the greater sphere."

"Is she deepynine?" Romki pressed.

"No," Nalben said with certainty. And shook his head, with almost comical exaggeration, to make sure the humans understood. It was not a tavalai gesture. "No, she is not deepynine. She is drysine."

Gasps from several of the techs. Romki looked stunned. "Drysine?" Erik asked. "The ones who wiped out the deepynines with the help of the parren?"

"Yes," said Nalben. "There are modalities and technicalities that escape me, that escape all experts today. And in the millennia since the drysines' fall, the few survivors have modified themselves many times. This queen appears to have many non-standard features. The body she had on the Major's combat recording of that encounter is certainly non-standard. But the queens in particular are modular, they have many bodies — or they had many, in their prime. They would swap bodies at need, to assume different functions." He indicated the nano-tank. "But the head remained relatively the same." He looked slightly dazed, as though struggling to process what it meant. "Argitori, you say?"

"Yes," said Erik. "An asteroid off the elliptical plane. Argitori has millions of those, they were well hidden provided they did not draw attention to themselves."

"And the base was not originally a hacksaw base?"

"No. Chah'nas Empire, we think. There was no sign of a spaceship... though in a local system, hacksaws can make local journeys without them, it only takes basic propulsion."

"Yes," Nalben agreed. "They do that in hive bases today — send out probes too small to show up on scans, with ion drives that take years to complete surveys and return. Years do not concern AIs, they are patient."

"Hacksaws in trouble during the deepynine-drysine war could have just abandoned a damaged vessel to make their way to an asteroid," Romki ventured. "They don't need escape pods or shuttles. Seven thousand years later, the chah'nas build a new base, and when the chah'nas fall and everyone abandons it, the queen and her tribe move in."

"Many possibilities," Nalben agreed, gazing at the tank. "Too many."

"You've encountered others like her before?" Erik pressed.

"Queens and command units? Yes. Never before a drysine."

Utter silence in the engineering bay, save for the omnipresent whir of ventilation, cylinder rotation and machinery from neighbouring bays. "How many were there?" Trace asked quietly. "At this level, before the war?"

"Probably hundreds," said Nalben. "A very small number, considering the size of the drysine faction at the time. They were not necessarily the most numerous faction — other factions took their side or the deepynines. But the drysines were elite, perhaps the most advanced ever. Possibly the most intelligent, if we are qualified to judge that. The parren and their allies tagged all the command units and made a special effort to kill them all. They took appalling losses trying, because they knew that should even one command unit survive, it could resurrect the entire AI race, given enough time alone in the dark. For many thousands of years, Dobruta experts supposed that the parren had succeeded in wiping out all drysine command units. Now you have proven otherwise." He looked at Romki. "You say that someone or something began communications with her before the attack on Joma Station?"

Romki nodded. "Yes, it was some kind of machine-language signal. It interfaced with the intact portions of her brain, the automated functions. I think one of them is communications. We could show you that recording, I'm sure?" With a glance at Erik.

"That would be useful, but I think it's quite clear what happened here." Nalben looked at Erik. "The drones that attacked Joma Station were drysine too."

Erik frowned. "But they were reprogrammed?"

"Yes. I think it logical that the sard have found a ship building base, as we suspected. And that shipbuilding base is drysine. It had advanced shipbuilding technology, which they utilised, lacking such advanced tools themselves. And it had deactivated drysine combat drones aboard, which they reactivated, and reprogrammed to do their bidding. Communications with the automated function of a dead hacksaw queen's brain is quite difficult for a non-drysine, the codes are complex. But a drysine drone could do it."

"They were looking for her?" Lisbeth gasped.

"Yes," said Nalben. "But not in a good way. They were being used to find her. Whether they wanted her destroyed, or reclaimed for some reason, we cannot say."

"You mean to say that the reason *Phoenix* is being chased by the sard is because of *her*?" Erik asked, pointing at the nano-tank. "They're after her? Not us?"

"That would be my guess," Nalben agreed sombrely. "Nothing else makes sense. *Phoenix* is a human political curiosity. Sard have no interest in such things. But old hacksaw technology, they've demonstrated great interest in. The last remaining drysine queen of that entire empire? Valuable does not even begin to describe it. If they seek to leverage what she might know."

"I don't buy it," Trace declared, arms folded firmly. Everyone looked at her. "That's a hell of a move to make, even for sard. Hacksaws have attacked ships before, in the modern era, but rarely stations. In fact, I can't recall it happening before to a station that big in centuries."

"Human records are incomplete," Nalben said solemnly. "It is very rare in other regions, with species tavalai are familiar with. But it has happened."

"Whatever," said Trace with determination. "Sard are murderous and often suicidal in their aggression, but this was overplaying their hand. They've just declared that they have hacksaw technology, despite knowing how poorly that will be received by tavalai and by humans."

"Lately they have lost all respect for tavalai," said Nalben. "Dobruta have no teeth in sard space any more. And many sard still consider themselves at war with humanity, and that the surrender agreement was a weak and irrelevant tavalai document."

"Sard aren't leaders," Trace continued, undeterred. "They're followers. They followed the tavalai. Now they're following old hacksaw technology. They're no good at any of their own technology except computing. They love maths. Machine logic no doubt appeals to them."

Erik's eyes widened as he looked at her. "Go on."

"What if this isn't their idea? What if coming after us, after the queen, after Major General Connor, was someone else's idea? What if they didn't just find deactivated drysine drones at that ship building base? Or what if we go back even further than that? We pulled up alongside an alo ship at Heuron. All our dead hacksaws reactivated." Looking at Commander Nalben.

Nalben stared. "They did?"

Trace nodded. "They were responding to something emitting from the alo ship, some kind of command and control frequency hidden in their energy signature. Stan, you're the one with the whole alo-deepynine conspiracy theory, and Lieutenant Dale's report of his conversations with Chankow pretty much confirm it. What if, in that moment when we pulled up alongside that alo ship, they knew *exactly* what we had on board? What if they talked to the queen then, just as you saw before the attack on Joma?"

"We wouldn't have known," Romki murmured, incredulous. "She wasn't rigged up to anything then, we had no way to measure it."

"The deepynines and the drysines fought the biggest, nastiest war the Spiral has ever seen," Trace continued. "We think it's over.

Assume Stan's right, and the deepynines are somehow still alive, and allied with the alo. They thought they'd won. No more drysines. Until we park alongside them with a drysine queen."

"Oh wow," said Romki, and put his bald head in his hand. "Major you are an evil genius. Yes yes yes... look, they're hunting us. They're hunting *her*." He pointed at the nano-tank. "Deepynines don't like organics, but they absolutely *despise* drysines. Drysines are their ultimate, existential threat. Drysines exterminated their race. Evidently they've rebuilt with alo help, and their very worst horror story would be for us to help the drysines do the same. Which we're not going to do, but the deepynines don't know that!"

"They're trying to wipe out the drysines again like the parren did," Erik murmured. "By any means necessary. That means they're *using* the sard."

Romki nodded vigorously. "Bribing them with gifts of technology! Visions of power! I'll *bet* you they've sent a queen of their own to the sard's new shipbuilding base. I bet she's running the whole show from there, helping them to reprogram drysine drones — even sard computing tech wouldn't allow that, but a deepynine queen could do it. And would tell them how to use those drones, and what to use them on if sard want to keep getting deepynine help. I mean... who hates a drysine queen more than a deepynine queen? And will be more determined to stop at nothing to get her?"

"Well hang on," Erik cautioned. "That implies she's not actually dead."

"Yes," said Nalben, as though wondering if that comment was safe to answer. "Well technically speaking, she's probably not."

CHAPTER 21

Three hours and a lot of long conversations with *Makimakala* later, Erik and his command crew were clustered in his quarters. All were tired, as it was the middle of the 'night' as the first-shift body clock measured such things, but Erik did not feel himself at all impaired. There was an electricity in the room, a strange mix of serious intensity and excitement, that he'd never felt before. Being here was crazy. What their mad political circumstance had abruptly transformed into, against all expectations, was certainly frightening, yet Erik felt it was a preferable kind of fear to what they'd faced before. That fear had come with no upside. This fear came with adrenaline.

"Captain Pram says there's an old AI base," he told the crew. Trace sat in her customary spot, against the wall where his pillow normally was. Shahaim sat on his other side, Kaspowitz on his desk chair, with Shilu and Karle squeezed behind him. Erik sometimes suspected that the main reason the captain's quarters had so little room was to regulate the number of people who could attend command briefings. More than six was a bad idea, and wouldn't fit anyway. "The base is in Bonatai System. It's a drysine relic, about twenty six thousand years old."

"Why haven't the Dobruta destroyed it?" Shahaim asked. "They're supposed to destroy all AI tech they find."

"Because they're hypocrites?" Kaspowitz suggested.

"My Great Uncle Thani Gialidis once told me that necessity will make hypocrites of us all," said Erik. "But he's a politician, so he would say that. Captain Pram says they don't have a choice — the tavalai politicians won't let the Dobruta police sard space and continually strangle their funding. They don't have the resources to fully analyse hacksaw bases for intelligence before destroying them. This base is apparently very big, it would take lots of people to analyse it properly. So they've mothballed it instead, so as not to destroy the intel."

"And tavalai fleet command is okay with that?" Shilu asked skeptically.

"I was given the impression that they have no idea."

Eyebrows were raised around the group. "We might have more in common with *Makimakala* than we thought," Trace observed, munching stir fry from a container. "We both have leaders who hate us."

"One of the reasons they've mothballed it," Erik continued, "is that it has some very fancy databases that even the best Dobruta techs have not been able to access. They think if they can read it, it will provide them with a good map of all the drysine and other bases and facilities through all this region of space. Including the big lost shipbuilding facility we think the sard are using to make those fancy new ships of theirs."

"So why do they think they can recover that data now?" Kaspowitz wondered.

Erik took a deep breath. They weren't going to like this bit. "Because they now have access to something they never thought they'd get access to. A drysine queen. They think, though they're not sure, that it's possible to recover the drysine neural data storage codings from examining her brain. Which will be like acquiring a code breaker, allowing them to read the stuff in the base."

"Thus learning where our true target is," Shahaim said thoughtfully.

"Exactly."

"So what's the problem?" Karle wondered, eyeing Erik's reluctant expression with suspicion. Lieutenant Karle was one kid who, on this trip, was becoming less green by the day.

"We'll have to partially reactivate the queen's brain to do it."

Stares all around. "No," said Shahaim. "Absolutely not."

"They think it can be done safely," Erik insisted. "And in a limited way. Not a full reawakening. An accessing of dormant memory and linguistic function."

"Oh yeah, that's a *great* idea," said Kaspowitz. "Because we know hacksaws are so damn easy to control once they start waking up, right? This is a *queen*... the drone technology is ridiculous enough, the queen's on a whole different level."

"You can't just isolate those functions one at a time," Shilu agreed with alarm. "I've had a look at it in my off-time... that stuff's just crazy, Romki doesn't understand it, even *Rooke* doesn't understand it. All those neural systems are integrated, and if you wake one up, you'll wake up the others..."

"Yeah hang on," Erik shut him off, holding up a hand. "She's a disembodied head with a hole blown straight through her CPU..."

"Who can reprogram our ship computers by remote as far as we know!" said Shahaim. "And she doesn't *have* a central processing unit, that whole neural structure is completely decentralised, that's part of what makes them so hard to kill! Once she becomes familiar with our systems, we just don't know what she's capable of doing..."

"I think it's an excellent idea," Trace interrupted. Everyone save Erik looked at her with incredulity... and remembered, as it was sometimes necessary to remember, that Trace was never sarcastic. As was usual in command meetings, she looked deadly serious. "We've found a hacksaw threat. Whether it's connected to the alo, or the sard, or both, or neither, we need to treat it the same as any other threat. You fight threats by first attempting to understand them. If we're so scared of this threat that we don't dare even attempt to understand it, then we've lost before the fight even starts."

No one replied. It was hard to argue with, particularly when it came from her, effectively calling them all cowards.

"Right," said Erik, having little doubt that he hadn't heard the last of it, no matter how persuasive his marine commander. "The plan is that we head to Bonatai System, find the relic, and *Makimakala* will board and disable the booby traps they've put there to stop any curious people who found it in the meantime. Given our luck lately, I doubt it will be that simple, but maybe we're due an easy run."

"What about *Rai Jang*?" asked Shahaim, still unhappy.

"I imagine she's coming too. We haven't had any contact besides the routine stuff, we're too busy, but my impression is they're talking to *Makimakala*. Barabo are tavalai allies, not human, at least for the moment... and Captain Jen is very concerned about any threats to the barabo. Given he's just seen his station torn up by hacksaws, I'd guess he wants to get to the bottom of this, if only to go back to his government and beg for more ships."

He looked about at them. There was more to be said, but for now it was enough.

"Oh," said Shahaim, recognising the meeting was nearly over. "First-shift procedural, there will be memorial service at 1400. We'll be too busy for uniforms, but there will be flags in b-2 mainroom, shipwide prayer and trumpets at 1410."

Somber nods all around.

"And *then*," Shahaim added with forced enthusiasm, "you'll never guess what day navcomp says it is today, because I had completely forgotten. It's Exodus. And god knows how navcomp calculates these things across hundreds of lightyears based upon a time system from a world that Exodus commemorates us losing..." She gave Kaspowitz an accusing look. He shrugged. "Anyway, today is Exodus, so at 1730, to give second-shift a chance to do other duties first, we'll do that service as well, then we'll play the B9, and the usual. So some warrants are going to be very busy today."

Because ship warrant officers and petty officers usually got stuck with ceremonial stuff, particularly on operations when the senior crew were too busy. Her glance at Erik suggested he might want to cancel it, given everything else.

"Yes they will be busy," Erik said instead. It would do no one on *Phoenix* any good, he was certain, to forget who they were and where they came from. Out here, surrounded by aliens, there had never been a better time to remember what it meant to be human, and what they were ultimately all fighting for. "Is that it? Good, let's go."

As they filed out of the captain's cabin at the rear of the bridge, Erik found Lieutenant JC Crozier of Delta Platoon waiting

— for Trace, he assumed. And was surprised when she spoke to him instead. "LC, could I have a moment?"

Trace gave her a concerned look as she passed, but Crozier wouldn't meet her gaze. "Of course Lieutenant, come in." The cabin emptied, he invited her inside and shut the door. "Go ahead."

She stood firmly at ease, hands tight behind her back, feet apart. Erik was accustomed to seeing her so cool and confident, but now she looked neither. "Sir, I wanted to apologise."

Erik frowned. "For what?"

"I had dock command on Joma Station when the hacksaws hit. When the Major took command she immediately countermanded my tactical stance, and went full deployment up the dock. It changed the tactical situation immediately." She swallowed hard. "I screwed up sir. Seventeen spacers died on station, all on my watch. Spacers without armour or serious weapons, relying on my marines for protection. I owe you and all the spacers on *Phoenix* an apology. I'm sorry."

The pain of it hit Erik in the gut. It was every officer's nightmare — personal failure, costing the lives of fellow crew. JC Crozier had been an officer in the marine corps for twelve years, all of them in combat. She'd been posted to *Phoenix* four years ago, when the previous commander of Delta Platoon had been killed in action. Trace rated all of her Lieutenants very highly — Dale at the top, for sheer experience, then Crozier, Zhi and Jalawi about equal in the middle, with Alomaim still a little green, but with enormous potential.

He felt slightly ridiculous with her apologising to him. His combat experience was minimal next to hers, and indeed next to all the marine officers save Alomaim. She was about his age, but had seen so much more of the war.

"Well firstly," he said, "the Major tells me that the one hacksaw breakthrough that killed most of our spacers would have happened irrespective of who was in charge — it came from below dock level, it was a total surprise and sometimes the enemy is just clever. The Major holds herself responsible for signing off on the evac plan and on the placement of the accommodation block to begin with."

"Well that's not quite correct sir, it was my…"

"I'm not finished."   Crozier swallowed her objection. "Secondly, we shouldn't have been there in the first place.   That was a treacherous environment and we were in over our heads — we just didn't know how deep.   It was my responsibility to know how deep, and that makes it my fault for putting *Phoenix* on that dock, at that time.

"Thirdly, we've all screwed up.   Given what we do, and the responsibilities placed upon us, those mistakes will cost lives.   It's inevitable, and inevitable things aren't anyone's fault.   If you let it chew you up, you'll cause more damage still, and right now your platoon needs you, and *Phoenix* needs you.   The Major tells me she has complete faith in you, and I have complete faith in the Major's judgement.   So do me a favour and don't ever come to me again apologising for things that aren't your fault, because if every officer did it who felt responsible for some snafu, I'd never get anything done.   Okay?"

Crozier nodded tightly.   "Yes sir.   Thank you sir."

"Good, now get."   And gave her a whack on the backside as she departed, because it was what the Captain had always done to crew feeling sorry for themselves.   The door closed behind her, and he let out a deep breath, and took a moment to collect himself.   It had been a pretty good speech, he thought.   If only he didn't feel like such a fraud delivering it.

CHAPTER 22

Lisbeth could not cry at the 1400 memorial service. She tried, because she felt the situation deserved it, but instead she felt numb. As daughter of a very prominent family, she'd attended memorial services all her life, official and private, for the many fallen of the war. Those had eventually taken a formal predictability, especially as she was all too aware how her parents and elder sisters would use them as business meet-and-greets with all the VIPs in attendance. She'd stand in her nice coat amidst her family and other importances, and listen to the readings and testimonials, and then the minister's sermons and perhaps some music, followed by everyone breaking for a drink and lots of talking and hand-shaking.

Certainly she'd never attended a memorial service amidst the very servicemen and women whose fallen comrades the service was honouring, and never in her wildest dreams had she imagined she'd be commemorating those who'd been killed in violence she'd actually been a part of. Her hearing was still ringing from the gunfire and explosions, yet still it didn't seem like something real — not in her life. Violence and warfare was Erik's reality, not hers, and she had no clue how to process it.

There was not enough space in Engineering for a proper gathering, so she stood in a crowded storage bay with those not so busy they couldn't take a ten minute break, amidst the missiles Lieutenant Karle had brought back on PH-1 that techs were prepping for use, and listened to the brief service. Shockingly, her bodyguard Vijay, whom she'd never seen so much as wince, broke down beside her and sobbed for his lost buddy Carla. Lisbeth wanted to join him in tears, because Carla had been her friend too, and seeing her die had been the single most traumatic experience of her life. But there were no tears to come, and that made her feel horribly guilty. She wondered what was wrong with her.

She passed more hours with Petty Officer Srimula's review team, giving engine systems a thorough going over in light of possible damage from Joma Station.   She'd have found it thrilling not long ago, being trusted enough to assist on even the lowliest of technical jobs — they were a major warship's engines after all, and she'd dreamed of working on such systems since she'd first had the idea to study engineering in college.   Now she found the work mindless and repetitive... but that suited her well, because she really didn't want to think about anything for a while.

At 1750 she made her way about the rim and up two flights to Engineering third or 'C' Level, as all the rear portion of the crew cylinder was Engineering, whatever its rotational quarter.   In Storage 5C as she passed, someone had set up an Exodus shrine — a plastic tree with some decorations on it with the near-mythical blue globe on top.   The tree was harnessed into a corner in light of ship regulations against unsecured objects, and instead of decorating its branches as they would on a Homeworld tree, some small Earth objects had been placed in a plastic storage container on the neighbouring shelf.   A second box was quickly filling up with little objects, and Lisbeth pulled the small coin she'd acquired on Tuki Station, and put it into the empty box.   On warships, she'd been told, there was obviously no room and no budget for larger presents, so little tokens would do.   Romki had told her the coin was barabo — not at all valuable, more of a religious token than currency, but it had been curious to look at, for someone not accustomed to such things.

The B9 was playing, and some spacers were standing about the tree and swaying to the music.   Inside the first box were odd, curious things — some coins, a very old pair of sunglasses, half a paper book cover, some bits of inexpensive jewellery.   Her eyes settled on the little figurine of a curly-headed man sitting in the lotus position, meditating.   She knew that one — the Buddha, the Kulina still followed some of his teachings.   She wondered if the Major had donated this guy to the Exodus 'lost' box, long ago when she'd first arrived on the *Phoenix*.   All objects from the old Earth itself, recovered by more recent teams in hazmat suits, then decontaminated.   All that was left.   Lisbeth recalled Exodus with her family on Homeworld, the songs and solemnity, the little gifts, the thanksgiving meal to follow.   And for the first time since she'd come aboard *Phoenix*, the homesickness became truly overwhelming.

Deliverance in seven days, she told herself firmly as she left Storage 5C and headed to Romki's Bay 8D.   Deliverance was a far more festive and happy day than Exodus.   Think on that, and as the marines would say, cheer the fuck up.

She arrived in Romki's bay to find it looking like a scene from a mad scientist's fantasy.   The hacksaw queen's huge head, suspended once more in the *Phoenix*'s biggest nano-tank, now rigged with various attendant cabling that snaked across the floor like some rubber jungle plant.   Linked to the cables were a number of workstations, large displays and Engineering crew with AR glasses and belt booster units for extra processing power, talking and gesturing as they set up the software construct that would monitor this process.

The nano-tank's micro-bots were being reprogrammed to tavalai specifications.   Those specifications included a basic understanding, for the first time, of hacksaw neurology.   Exactly how much the Dobruta knew about that neurology, given that they were supposed to be destroying it and not spreading it, *Makimakala*'s specialists wouldn't say.   But the idea was to tap into the still-functioning sub-portions of the queen's brain and draw enough responses from them to establish a neural construct on a *Phoenix* processor.

That construct would be a simulation, the tavalai's experts said, of the queen's brain... or as much as still existed.   Much of it would still be guesswork, as an AI's brain function depended on both hardware and software to work, and here the hardware was half-destroyed.   But it would reveal enough of the neural language that the brain's synthetic neurons used to speak to each other, to establish patterns and processing routines.   And possibly, they thought, the embedded routines and codings in the communications-intensive parts of the brain that dealt with encryption.   *That* was the grail that had them all excited.   The ability to break drysine encryption, and read data from drysine civilisation that no organic eyes had ever seen.

"This music is fascinating," said Commander Nalben as he peered at a display rig, melodies soaring from somewhere nearby. "You call it the B9?"

"It's by a man named Beethoven," said Romki from behind a similar rig. "This is his ninth symphony, the last he ever wrote. A long time ago on Earth, we had nations — you know, governments confined within geographical boundaries on the surface, like the kuhsi still have."

"Yes, we had them once on our homeworld," Nalben agreed. "So long ago it makes my brain hurt to think of it."

"Anyhow, each of those nations had a national song, an anthem. So after humans lost Earth, we decided we needed a new anthem. None of the old national anthems would do because we were people from all nations, and picking one over the others would leave most people offended. So they had a vote for a single song that could summarise all that was best and greatest about humanity, and this is what they chose. We play it every Exodus, to remember what was lost, and it's become the de facto anthem of the human race."

"There are some very big performances," Lisbeth added from the edge of the crowd of working humans and tavalai about the queen's head. "My family sponsors a huge performance in Destiny Park in Shiwon, on Homeworld. It draws about a hundred thousand people, we sit up the front every year, it's wonderful. Stan, can I do something?"

"Why yes, you can monitor the construct parameters at... screen three over there. With Spacer Gidjadagarno there, you can call her Gidj." Lisbeth went and pulled out a folding wall-seat beside Spacer Gidj — a smaller, tan-skinned tavalai little bigger than Lisbeth. She wore a deep blue spacer's jumpsuit and harness with pockets full of technician's gear, and moved across a little to make space for Lisbeth behind the big screen.

"Hello," Lisbeth said a little nervously, fishing out AI glasses and headset, and tuning herself into the local construct.   "I'm Lisbeth."

"Gidj," said Gidj, just as nervously.   No English, Lisbeth guessed, as Gidj leaned across to her buddy and said something in rapid, rhythmic Togiri.   She smelt faintly floral.   Lisbeth wondered if it was natural, or perfume.

"And was this Beethoven man killed when the krim struck Earth?" Commander Nalben asked.

"Oh no," said Romki.   "He died nine hundred years before Earth did."

"But…" Nalben looked puzzled.   Lisbeth was surprised she could actually read the expression.   "That would put him very early in Earth's history.   Surely this music is post-industrial?"

"The dawn of the industrial age," said Romki.   "About one hundred years before electricity."

"You are joking," said Nalben, astonished.

"I'm most certainly not," said Romki with amusement.

"This is far too sophisticated for pre-industrial art!" Nalben insisted.   "The instruments… the structure and composition!"

Romki smiled and shrugged as he worked, rearranging code structures on his screen.   "What can I say?   Humans were early developers by galactic standards.   The worst part is that our music got steadily worse after Beethoven, we haven't matched him since."

"Well *that's* very subjective," Lisbeth retorted.

"Ah, the young protest.   But it's true."

"It might be true for this *type* of music but it's not true overall."

"I see the trees on the way up from midships," Nalben interrupted.   "Are they objects of worship?"

"They're symbols of the green Earth that was lost," Lisbeth answered before the tavalai's brain was irreversibly filled with the Romki-view of human history.   "They used to be a symbol from an old Earth religious holiday called Christmas that hardly anyone knows today…"

"Nonsense," Romki snorted, "Christianity remains quite strong on a number of worlds."

"But these days *most* people," Lisbeth continued with a stern glance at the professor, "know them as Exodus trees.   In some places it is tradition to wear black and refrain from alcohol or sex or whatever for a whole week until Deliverance comes.   Then everyone goes crazy and there are huge parties and fireworks."

"Seems odd to throw a huge party to celebrate the successful genocide of another species," Nalben observed.   Deliverance celebrated the final human victory over the species that had killed Earth.   Having won through the intense defences about the krim homeworld, and confronted with the prospect of a bloody battle of pacification on the surface, a human freighter captain named Lien Wang had settled the issue by boosting her ship to high-V and hitting the planet hard enough to kill every living thing on the surface. With every Deliverance came great toasts to Lien Wang and her crew, and several Fleet marching songs made reference to 'giving them the old Lien Wang'.   The date had missed the anniversary of Earth's destruction by a week.   From there, Fleet had mopped up the rest, and the krim had not had any friends, like the humans' friends the chah'nas, to save them.

"What would you have done?" Petty Officer Kadi said coldly to Commander Nalben.   "To the species that murdered your homeworld, with tavalai weapons?"   Human crew paused in their work to stare.   Tavalai crew, slower on the pickup through their translators, looked about in confusion.

"Now now Petty Officer," Romki intervened.   "Not tavalai weapons.   Krim made everything themselves, and the tavalai ceased most trade with the krim after they hit Earth."

"After getting them into space and making them everything they were," Kadi retorted.   A few of the tavalai exchanged glances. None were armed.

"I merely make the observation, Petty Officer," Commander Nalben said coldly, "that there is a cosmic irony in taking such joy in a successful genocide.   Something that has only occurred twice in all Spiral history — once by these creatures we are studying before us, when they exterminated their creators long ago, and once by humanity."

Cold silence followed. Lisbeth had heard tales of tavalai stubbornness. Even on a human warship on Exodus, tavalai would make no apologies for the past or the present. Another time, Lisbeth might have curled up in a corner at the sight of conflict and hoped that someone else would do something about it. But suddenly she could think only of Carla, dying to save her, and how pathetically unworthy she was of that sacrifice.

"*Phoenix* crew!" she said loudly. "You have orders to work with *Makimakala* crew to partially reestablish this AI's cognitive matrix. Is this helping?" She gave a dirty look at Petty Officer Kadi, who should have known better. And if it made him suddenly wonder if she'd report him to her brother, so much the better.

"Okay people, back to work," Kadi said suddenly, burying his attention once more in his display. Romki glanced across at Lisbeth, and gave a smile and a nod.

Lisbeth exhaled hard, and turned to Gidj. "Excuse me, Spacer Gidj? You have translator working? Yes, good. Can you explain this analysis matrix to me?"

Trace arrived at Tactical straight from her workout, more relaxed than usual following aerobic sprints on the treadmill. Tactical was on the H-bulkhead beside Assembly, the rattle and whine of ongoing armour prep echoing through the walls. Her Lieutenants were already there, Lieutenant Zhi just settling in a chair with a meal on his lap. There had been a table here once, but Trace had had it taken out when she'd assumed command six years ago. The holographic setup had been put in the ceiling, and she liked to pace around in the centre space between encircling chairs.

"Okay," said Trace, sipping a fruit smoothie as she sat on the edge of the commander's chair. "News from the mad scientists in Engineering — the drysine queen did not come alive and eat everyone's brains, so that's nice."

"Needs to find brains first," said Jalawi, predictably.

"I was told technically what they were doing, but my eyes started to glaze over about thirty seconds in, so I got my buddy Lisbeth to translate tech-geek for me... she says what they've done is infiltrate a few of the queen's cognitive systems, and well, apparently hacksaws are a bit like organics in that we have DNA in every cell. Hacksaws have something similar, like molecular-level instruction manuals, implanted all the way through each hacksaw's CPU."

"Bullshit," said Dale, unimpressed.

"Which allows all their micro-systems to fix and re-grow damaged parts constantly."

"I'm happy for them," said Jalawi.

"Anyhow, our mad engineers made a copy of some neural constructs, not an entire brain, just bits of it. It's a facsimile, and it's on our hardware, so it's not actually an AI at all... but it's a cognitive function, and it's doing stuff that's got some of the froggies pretty excited. And a couple of our resident human froggies too."

Jalawi smirked. "Human froggies," he repeated, tickled by that. Of all the marine officers, Jalawi was the most frequently amused.

"They seem to think it can translate drysine codes, they ran some old stuff on it they haven't been able to translate before, and it's converting it to... well, whatever mad froggie engineers read."

All marine officers were required to be somewhat technically literate. Space stations, ships and weapons Trace knew a fair bit about. Even bio-engineering wasn't beyond her, given what she and everyone in the room had had done to their own bodies at some point to enhance performance. But hacksaw tech was nuts, and even the techs in Engineering didn't really understand it. One of the first lessons every green marine was told by those more experienced, upon arriving on a combat ship, was that if you found some weird-looking alien tech that you didn't understand, you didn't play with it. Having *Phoenix* crew violating that principle on the same ship where everyone ate, trained and slept, made every marine uncomfortable.

"And they think this…" Dale waved his hand, looking for the word, "construct of theirs will translate whatever we find on this relic thing?"

"We'll get to that," said Trace. "First, Ensign Hale has been examining the data the *Makimakala* techs thoughtfully shared with us on the hacksaw corpses they recovered…"

"Is Ensign Hale okay?" Jalawi wondered. "I heard she lost a good friend on the docks."

"She's a bit shaken," Trace confirmed. "But she's doing her job." Crozier stared at a wall and said nothing. Trace pretended not to notice. "She said the froggies think the Joma Station hacksaws were pretty much lobotomised. Not only weren't they thinking for themselves, but they were below optimum neural function. Which is tech-speak for saying they're not as good as the real thing… which backs up our own observations."

With a glance at Dale and Jalawi, who'd been on the rock with her in Argitori. "Yep," Dale said grimly. "There were half as many drones in Argitori, and they killed eighteen of us, and wounded twenty more. These ones got six and fourteen. Their coordination was shit, they didn't press their advantages when they got them, and should have done a lot better than they did, given that situation."

"I agree," Jalawi said slowly, thinking back. "I think their advantages increase in zero-G, but even so."

"The lesson," said Trace, "is that the real things are much, much worse than those lobotomised copies. And they were bad enough. So when you've got some time, I want tactical analysis from Joma Station added to what we've done from Argitori, and see what else we can learn. I'm happy for you to toss it to your non-coms and lower, some of the best insights I've heard on alien tactics have come from privates. Just get it done because I don't think we've seen the last of those fuckers."

Grim nods about the group. "Speaking of," said Trace, and pulled her AR glasses down, blinking on an icon to activate the room holographics. The lights dimmed, and the space between the chairs lit up with an irregular, ovoid shape, pockmarked with small craters. "This is the relic. It's at Oran System, all of these schematics are courtesy of *Makimakala*'s karasai commander.   His name is Nakigamana, we'll call him Major Naki. The actual rank's Djojana, but human-equivalents save time — he's basically a major."

She rotated the oddly-shaped planetoid. It looked a bit like a peanut, save the lower bulb was missing its lower half, in what looked like a very old catastrophic impact. "Tavalai call it TK55. It's in a middle-inner orbit, probably a moon that failed to form properly during the solar system's birth. The stars are a big M-class binary, quite active, so TK55 is not hot, but warm."

She zoomed closer, and at several points across the planetoid's upper bulb, small shiny spots appeared. "You can see the solar panelling across the inner, sun-facing side. It's a pretty extensive system, though unsurprisingly there's fusion as well. TK55 is about eighty-six kilometres long, forty-one across at the widest part of the lower bulb, thirty-five across at the same for the upper bulb.   It's made mostly of light stuff — a fair bit of dirt, chalky rock, good for tunnelling.   It's much harder in the core, not very mineral rich but a good spot for a system outpost.

"Now Oran System is nicely placed at a crossroads between several old drysine bases… if you want the old history I have that on file too.   Suffice to say that a lot of drysine shipping came through here.   But TK55 is too far insystem to be a big shipping post — all the big shipping stations were in the outer gas giant systems, as usual.   Tavalai think this was perhaps a mix of a science station, a manufacturing and research lab for new hacksaw drones, and a secondary defence post — insystem where an outer-system attack will take longer to reach it, lengthening their response times."

"So how old are we talking?" asked Lieutenant Chester Zhi, staring curiously at the hologram. Zhi had played a large role when *Phoenix* boarded the ancient O'Neill cylinder Eve last month, in orbit about the even more ancient temple world of Merakis. Since then, he'd switched from mainly military reading to academic histories about early Spiral civilisation, and had become one of Romki's best friends on the ship.

"There's been settlement here for nearly forty thousand years," said Trace around her smoothie. "The drysines came later in

AI history, so they refitted and expanded whatever was here previously maybe twenty eight thousand years ago, and were driven out of it three thousand years later when the parren turned on them. The rest of the facilities in this system were destroyed either by the deepynines, or by the parren alliance after the deepynines were defeated."

She zoomed on the upper bulb, until the little solar panel spheres grew large on the rough, grey surface. "There's ammunition storage here, possibly various other things that go boom, maybe nukes, maybe anti-matter or zero-point, we know they messed around with a lot of stuff. But they kept it up here in the upper bulb, a long way away from the main centre, though it is connected by a long central transit."

She panned down to the lower bulb, then underneath where the rounded shape had been shorn off at the bottom. Amidst the exposed and fractured rock, structures emerged — docking ports, huge gantry systems, ship-sized tunnels boring deep into the rock. Kilometres and kilometres of it, like a small city, arranged in concentric rings about the dead centre where the main elevator would run through the entire planetoid, and join the upper and lower bulbs together.

"Wow," said Zhi.

"*Makimakala* say it's a hulk, all dead and stripped inside. But obviously there's still something in there, or they wouldn't have wanted to preserve it."

"Eighty kilometres long in close orbit about an M-class binary is a heck of a thing to keep secret for this long," Dale said skeptically. "How hasn't anyone else found it yet?"

"Well the space is disputed with the sard," said Trace. "They say. Personally I think they've mined the crap out of it — I talked to Lieutenant Kaspowitz and he agreed. Though we'll have to wait until the bridge crew meeting is over before we butt heads and talk it out. Certainly the tavalai have booby trapped TK55 itself, to keep the sard out. My guess is they've been keeping the sard away from it for thousands of years — probably since the sard got into FTL space. Which means they've been concerned about the sard getting their hands on stuff like this for a long time."

"You mean the Dobruta have been concerned," said Alomaim. "Tavalai government's had its head up its ass about this for even longer."

"Well mind you," said Jalawi, "they were pretty focused on this stuff before the Triumvirate War. But losing half your territory and your status as dominant species of the Spiral pretty much changed their priorities. They've been neglecting their job as galaxy police."

"And so it's humanity's responsibility to take it over from them," Trace said firmly. "But our Fleet's happy to see anything that makes trouble for the tavalai, they don't realise that this stuff could be a thousand times more deadly to humans than the tavalai ever were."

"We all thought the hacksaws were dead," Dale muttered. "Fucking retards, all of us."

"Hang on," said Zhi. "Does that mean we were fighting the wrong enemy all along? Because I don't think that's…"

"Hey!" Trace interrupted. "I don't give a fuck about the politics. Not even a quarter of a fuck. We fight one enemy at a time. It was the tavalai. Now it's this. The human race needs an alarm bell on this, followed by a swift kick in the ass. Our Fleet's asleep or worse, so right now we're it." Quiet nods from all five. Save from Crozier, who looked subdued and troubled. Trace didn't like it.

"So right now," Trace continued, "the plan is that *Makimakala* will make the approach to TK55 and board directly. *Phoenix* and *Rai Jang* will give cover, but there is no intent for us to go aboard at this time. Now at the rate we're going, I give the likelihood of that plan going as proposed pretty much zero percent. I expect sard trouble, given how badly they're after us. I'm also not entirely ruling out the possibility of tavalai treachery, or even barabo. Ty, you've spoken to the LC about your barabo concerns?"

"Um, yeah," said Dale. He scratched his scalp, an unaccustomed nervous gesture from him. He wasn't used to screwing up, and would probably be unhappy about it for a while yet. "The cop who blew up Chankow had strange shaving marks on her neck, from the shoulder up to her jaw. I checked with Romki, he said lots of barabo have them, they're usually institutional, they date back to some tribal thing or other…" he made a dismissive gesture. "Anyway, it's just as well we've someone on the damn ship reading *all* of our reports and compiling all the intel together, because otherwise we'd have missed it completely…"

"Who was that?" Jalawi wondered.

"Jokono," said Trace. "A good thing about cops — they're multi-taskers. We're all specialists."

"Because I didn't get to meet *Rai Jang*'s Captain, that was Ahmed," Dale continued with a nod at Alomaim. "And he didn't get to meet my barabo cop assassin girl. But they've both got the same shave marks on the neck, and Jokono's the only one who caught it. Romki doesn't recognise it, the database has nothing, but that cop was military-trained and a *very* good actor." With a grimace. "And *Rai Jang*'s Captain is pretty hardass for a barabo, so my theory is it might be a barabo military faction who are pissed their species are such a bunch of pussies. Romki says that fits, barabo military's been dissatisfied for a long time, and Hiro says there was talk in Intel circles for a while of a possible barabo coup, if you can imagine that. But the barabo politicians purged the military of 'warmonger' captains, so they've kept their heads down since, but probably aren't above forming secret societies with funny identifying marks."

"Oh great," Zhi snorted. "Get rid of all the guys who want to fight. With the sard on your doorstep, that'll work."

"It's good work," Trace commended Dale. "And now the LC has a reason to keep an eye on both *Rai Jang* and *Makimakala*, which I'm sure doesn't make him happy, but it probably makes us safer.

"Given that every operation we go on lately has blown up, we're going to go into this one on full condition red. Now that we have the shuttle capacity, we're going to pre-deploy Echo and Bravo in PH-1 and PH-3 respectively. Command Squad will go with

Bravo. Alpha and Charlie will be first reserve, Delta will be second reserve. We're going into it expecting that the shit has already hit the fan, and take it from there. If we're really lucky, we'll be pleasantly surprised.

"If not, we'll deploy accordingly. Bear in mind that this could mean deploying and working directly alongside karasai." A calm stare at them all, to see that sink in. "So brush up on your karasai tacticals, and get all suit translators prepped with Togiri. Any questions?" No reply. "Good, let's do it."

"Major?" said Crozier. "Request permission to pre-deploy with Delta."

"It's not your turn," Trace said shortly as they all climbed from their chairs. "Take a rest, and remember that if the tavalai really do find what they're looking for, that'll just give us the location of the *real* target. Plenty of work ahead for all of us."

CHAPTER 23

The first thing *Phoenix* knew for sure about TK55 as they came streaking out of combat jump was that the planetoid was not alone.

"She's definitely got company," said Geish from Scan, staring at *Phoenix*'s most intense long-range magnification. They were nadir of Oran System's binary suns, and had a good angle on the planetoid's shorn underside. "There's an additional protrusion where it should not be, Scancomp estimates the size of a large vessel... unless the froggies have been building something else that wasn't in their data..."

"LC," called Shilu, "incoming from *Makimakala,* it's the Captain."

"Put him through."

Erik's earpiece crackled. *"Hello Phoenix, it appears we have a visitor. Our scan suggests a large vessel — either a tavalai ship that has surprised us, or more likely a sard ship that has bypassed our defences. I suggest combat formation and continue approach."*

"*Phoenix* copies, *Makimakala.* We will extend combat formation and continue approach on the assumption the vessel is sard and hostile. Hello *Rai Jang,* do you copy this communication?"

Pause for the reply, the coms-light counter ticking down... *"Hello, Rai Jang copies, we extend forward, scouting run, maybe draw fire. Big friends cover tail, yes?"*

"Hello *Rai Jang, Phoenix* copies you will extend combat formation forward. Big friends will cover your move with full fire support, *Phoenix* out."

Ballsy move from Captain Jen, considering those guarding his tail were a different species. But it was standard tactics for inbounds combat jumps — the smaller scout went speeding out in front to draw a reaction from insystem defences, thus revealing the location of those defences for the serious firepower coming in behind.   The two big carriers had let the barabo scout jump twenty minutes earlier, and *Rai Jang* was now five minutes high-V deeper into Oran System, deep enough to make a five-second communication delay.

"Incoming lasercom from *Makimakala*," Shilu announced. "Taccom feed, I'm sending it to Nav."   And Erik saw the tactical feed transform before his eyes, the 3D graphics showing ship positions, trajectories, light horizons and response times now abruptly adding a string of little red dots all across the approach vectors.

"Well yeah," said Shahaim as she saw it too, "looks like they did mine the crap out of it."

"LC," said Kaspowitz, "I am counting... three hundred and sixty two tracker mines and another eighty ordinance stations.   All look configured for maximum crossfire.   Going in there as a hostile is a death trap."

Tracker mines were really very large missiles with independent propulsion and networked targeting.   Without jump engines, FTL ships could outrun small numbers easily, but if the mines were defending a fixed point in space, they knew where you were going and would get you eventually.   They were too small to easily shoot, and accelerated at twenty-Gs or more when closing or evading — far faster than even *Phoenix* could manage.   Ordinance stations were small floating gun-platforms, cheap and nasty, that could add regular gunnery to the mix, and defend themselves long enough to soak up incoming ammo.   Kaspowitz was right — if *Phoenix* went in there as an enemy, she was dead meat.

"And the froggies have the code that can turn them on or off," Shahaim observed.   "Or decide to reassign them new targets at will."

"I guess we better be on our best behaviour then," Kaspowitz said drily.   No one liked it.   If the tavalai hadn't earned their reputation for scrupulous principles, Erik would never have gone along with it.

"If that's a sard ship docked on TK55," he said, "then my guess is they've just put sard warriors aboard.   They won't extract, sard don't care much about casualties, they'll hold us up any way they can. If I'm right, *Makimakala*'s going to need us to help get them out." He flipped channels. "Hello Major, are you reading this?"

"Sard carriers are all larger capacity than human carriers," Trace observed by way of an answer. *"If it's a s45-class carrier it could have anything up to five hundred warriors. If it's one of those new ships that have been chasing us, it's anyone's guess, but I'd reckon they'd be high capacity too. If we're deploying in there, I'm going to want more numbers."*

"I copy that Major. If you want all four shuttles I can get Lieutenant Dufresne down there to pilot AT-7 and one extra platoon."

"That is an affirmative LC, this will be a four platoon job. Delta will be reserve, and unless I'm mistaken, our only other qualified shuttle co-pilot is Lisbeth."

Erik gritted his teeth. "Can't order her Major, she's not in uniform. I suggest you ask nicely."

In combat jump they shut down the cylinder rotation, so everyone floated in zero-G — no concern for crew who weren't supposed to move anyway. In a chair station you were strapped in so tight you didn't notice, but sealed into an acceleration sling you did. The mesh encircled Lisbeth, safety links clipped into her jumpsuit harness as she floated within the synthetic cocoon. At its top and bottom, big steel bolts held it tight between floor and ceiling runners, ready to swing in whichever way gravity took it, and conform to the shape of her body in the process. Directly behind her was Vijay, who bunked down the corridor from her, but usually one of the bodyguards would ride through jump alongside Lisbeth just in case. With Carla gone, Vijay had the job to himself.

"Hello Lisbeth, this is the Major. We need a co-pilot for AT-7, flying Alpha Platoon. I've been instructed to ask you nicely, Second Lieutenant Dufresne will be the pilot."

"Hello Major, I'll be right there.   Lisbeth out."   She unhooked herself with increasingly practised skill and pulled the sling mesh open.

"I'm coming with you," said Vijay, doing the same.

"Vijay, I don't actually know they'll have room on the shuttle."

"Then I can at least see you get there."

Heading down the main corridor in zero-G would have been good fun if it weren't so nerve wracking.   Lisbeth tried not to think about the ridiculous velocities they were travelling at, and certainly not about the mincemeat that any sudden moves on *Phoenix*'s part would make of both her and Vijay against the corridor's walls.   She wondered if Erik would actually make an evasive move, knowing she was loose on the ship… or if the ship's automatic evasion could be stopped if scan saw a rock suddenly coming at them.   Though almost certainly, the Major would never have asked her down to midships if it was particularly dangerous, and marines moved around in midships zero-G all the time on combat approach.   But then, marines wore armour.

The variable-G ropelines were out in the corridors again, though this time instead of acting as an elevator, these acted as high-speed transport.   Lisbeth and Vijay grabbed a handle and pulled, and the whole ropeline whined and squealed, pulling them at what would have been jogging speed in 1-G.   Lisbeth fended off the dog-leg corners with ease, then finally let go as she saw the corridor-end airlock approaching.   With cylinder rotation stopped, crew could access midships directly from the cylinder rim like they did at dock without having to go through the core — another reason why the cylinder was shut down during combat jumps.

Momentum took her straight into the midships airlock, evading one near-collision with a crewman exiting, then catching the rim to avoid catapulting straight into the working bustle of midships. She pulled herself hand-over-hand along one wall, amidst yelling Operations crew, then up an open vertical access between cargo nets and wall tethers where marines' armour and equipment would be stored.   Several long glides, then a turn out toward the three-grapple, where AT-7 was locked against *Phoenix*'s hull.

The access opened onto the three-assembly, a long space between cargo nets and rows of strung accelerations slings, typically filled with marines awaiting access to their shuttle.   Half of those marines were now gone, vanished into the hatch amidst the grapple hydraulics on the hull, and Lisbeth shoved herself hard that way.

"Pilot coming through!" Vijay yelled behind her, knowing she'd be reluctant.   "Pilot coming through!   Make a path!"

And the armoured marines looked about with shouts of 'pilot!' and her path cleared enough that she sailed past them and straight to the airlock, where the next marine in line paused for her as she dropped straight in.

At the bottom, a familiar turn from the upper level hatch access, and a fast shove after the marine ahead of her, marvelling at how fast he moved in his bulky armour.   At the cockpit she found Second Lieutenant Dufresne already strapped into the pilot's seat and well into pre-flight, instrument displays alight and blinking. God knew how she'd gotten down here so fast, her quarters weren't any closer to midships than Lisbeth's.

"I'm here," Lisbeth said breathlessly, squeezing past the pilot's seat on her way to the co-pilot's just ahead.   "They're about half loaded back there."

"Ms Debogande, take a seat," said Dufresne, cool and professional.   "Systems startup has commenced, checklist ETA is two minutes."

Two minutes for *you* maybe, Lisbeth nearly muttered as she pulled herself into her chair and tried to strap herself in — no small task when you weren't as accustomed to zero-G as some, and every surface you touched tried to bounce you back off.   She got it managed as the automatic fastening yanked her tight, and began to run furiously through her checklist — at least she was in a familiar civilian shuttle.   She'd been practising with Lieutenant Hausler in her off-time, as he'd graciously agreed to get her simulation hours up, but that had been in PH-1 and those military systems needed serious training to get familiar with.   Behind her, Second Lieutenant

Dufresne probably felt she was flying a toy spaceship by comparison. Gratifyingly, Hausler hadn't laughed at Lisbeth's skill-level, and had even politely said she'd make a fine Fleet co-pilot... given about three more years of training.

Halfway through her checklist, Lisbeth remembered to pull on the helmet from its rear headrest clasp. Once the visor was over her eyes, filtering the cockpit light, she could suddenly see the stars outside. Billions of them. In the far distance ahead, a yellow globe growing brighter... no, *two* yellow globes, a binary system, two suns together, as was the case in more than half of the galaxy's systems larger than a red dwarf. Far too far away from TK55 to see it yet, but it was always a shock to see the stars, after so long on a spaceship where you rarely had a view. Out this far from home, none of them were familiar.

"He's leaving fast," said Second Lieutenant Geish from Scan. "He's full thrust and none of the tavalai mines are pursuing." Erik could see TK55 much more clearly now, the twin, grey bulbs with a narrow 'waist', with scan conveniently highlighting in red all the surrounding tavalai mines. None of which were posing any threat to the sard vessel, which as Geish had said, was now leaving hard on a white tail of flame.

With an open channel to *Makimakala*, Erik didn't need to ask Shilu for access, and just blinked on the icon. "Hello *Makimakala*, do you have any idea why the sard vessel is completely untouched by your defences?"

"*Hello Phoenix.*" A short pause, as though wondering what to say. That wasn't comforting. "*It is a known feature of hacksaw technology to manipulate foreign computer systems.*"

"You mean gain control of them by remote?" Even more alarming.

"*No. I mean hacksaws can disguise signatures and convince enemy systems that foes are friends.*"

"Semantical bullshit," Lieutenant Karle said from further across the bridge, and off-coms. "He's talking about the same damn thing."

"I copy that *Makimakala*," said Erik. "Are there any records of hacksaw-technology vessels reprogramming automated systems to fire upon friendly vessels?"

Another longer-than-necessary pause. *"To my knowledge, no such records exist."*

"Well that's just great," said Shahaim. "Nav, I think we'd better arrange a plan for a very rapid withdrawal if the impossible happens."

"Already got several," Kaspowitz answered, furiously plugging in data, fingers racing across his screens. "But if we get deep in there and those bastards fire on us, we're screwed."

"Makimakala is going to need our help getting those sard out of their relic," Erik replied. "Leaving troops behind like that is a standard sard delaying tactic. And the AI-facsimile from the drysine queen is aboard *Phoenix* as well, so we're valuable to the tavalai."

"Doesn't mean they're actually in control of this situation," Shahaim replied. "They don't *look* in control."

"Against this new breed of sard," Erik said grimly, "we might just have to get used to that."

Combat V-dumps were disorienting to the point of nausea, but Lisbeth still found them preferable to main-engine deceleration, flattened on her back at 10-Gs and struggling to breathe. Now she had time for a sip of water from her collar tube, and remembered to recalibrate the shuttle's scan for much lower velocities, now that the light waves from surrounding objects were not dopplered into unfamiliar colours. The other shuttles were all talking to each other, and that scared her because it was all operational chatter and she barely understood one sentence in three.

Then the hard clank and crash of grapples releasing, and Dufresne gave them a downward shove to get clear of *Phoenix*, the armoured sides of the massive warship suddenly falling away, and then Lisbeth could see it in a way you rarely got to see a warship — a huge, long, three-segment bulk, the first segment all armourplate and weapons about the rotating crew cylinder within, then midships separate yet integrated into the main hull frame, and finally the colossal main engines. Usually FTL ships operated further from the sun, in the big gas giant systems where the big stations were typically built higher up the gravity slope. But TK55 was an inner-system rock, and *Phoenix*'s matte-black sides, normally invisible in the dark, now loomed and shone.

Dufresne hit thrust, and Lisbeth felt 2-Gs pushing her back. She ran a nervous eye over her co-pilot responsibilities — coms, navigation, scan, load. She had to be like a high-class butler or personal assistant, standing by the pilot's shoulder to hand her whatever she needed just as she needed it. To either side, she saw bright thrust from neighbouring shuttle engines... and here as she looked properly for the first time, was TK55, the giant space peanut as some were calling it, half-lit by the binary stars.

"Approach angle good," she heard Lieutenant Hausler saying from PH-1. As senior pilot, he had formation command. *"ETA thirteen minutes, primary deceleration in nine point five."*

"I have tavalai shuttles at eight-nine by fifteen, range fourteen klicks," said Ensign Yu, Hausler's co-pilot. *"I count six, combat formation, parallel trajectory."*

Lisbeth did a fast calculation — *Makimakala* had seven shuttles, each with capacity for forty karasai. Marines organised in fours, while karasai preferred units of five — five to a squad, each platoon had three fire-squads and one heavy-squad for twenty total. So assuming they were fully loaded, *Makimakala* was sending in about two hundred and forty karasai, while *Phoenix*'s shuttles, operating below max-capacity as per the usual operating doctrine, had somewhere in the vicinity of a hundred and eighty marines... perhaps a little less, given recent casualties.

Her visor HUD was displaying red dots of navigation hazard — tavalai mines, she realised as scan struggled to identify them. Lots of mines, and close, zooming past them even now on approach.

"I sure hope the froggies know how to keep those things away from us," Lieutenant Jersey remarked from PH-3.

"This may sound odd approaching a hacksaw base likely filled with sard," said Lieutenant Hausler, *"but we may actually be safer up close or inside."*

"Phoenix assault team," said Lieutenant Shilu in their ears, *"be advised that Rai Jang is commencing a near recon pass of the target."*

Sure enough, Lisbeth's scan showed the large, fast shape of the barabo cruiser gliding through the mines toward the lower side of TK55, making small course adjustments as she went.

"Gonna see if he draws fire," Jersey observed.   *"That's mighty human of him."*

"Don't think that even for a moment," said Dufresne at Lisbeth's back.   "Trust buys you sleep, distrust buys you life."

"Copy that AT-7," Hausler agreed.   *"Everyone keep your eyes wide open."*

"Rai Jang has a visual feed," came Lieutenant Shilu's voice in Trace's ear as she was pressed back in her armour at a mild 3-Gs on the final approach burn.   *"Hard to tell from this distance and angle if the tavalai defences put up any fight, Major.   You'll have to find out for yourself when you go in."*

Trace blinked the icon and stared at the visual projected onto her visor.   A passing view of TK55's underside from several Ks out. A broken, rocky surface, strewn with long shadows from the horizon-level suns.   Amidst the rock, protruding like natural growths, were artificial portals, openings, short antennae, arranged in arcing lines.   These were no crude steel structures, but advanced alloy, smooth and almost organic.

"Be nice if he'd gone a bit closer so we could actually see something," Dale grumbled from AT-7's hold.

"Captains of every species will look after their ship," Trace replied.   "There are the hangars, all look empty, no obstruction.

Shuttles will release away from the entrance and pull back to cover positions."

"Understood, Major." There were a series of big openings smack in the middle of the concentric rings of habitat about TK55's base. Ship hangars, into which full-sized starships would slide like rounds into an old-fashioned revolver's chambers. The schematics *Makimakala* had granted showed that those hangars led to the main corridor linking the planetoid's upper and lower bulbs together. Take those, and you had direct access to the once-beating heart of the base.

Final burn complete, Second Lieutenant Dufresne swung AT-7 end-over-end so they could face the target. From barely a kilometre out, the broken underside of TK55 was stunningly large, fractured and uneven in that clear, perfect detail that only objects in space could acquire, with no atmosphere to blur a human's vision. Lisbeth tried hard to keep her eyes on her screens — it was unprofessional to stare, but impossible not to. The concentric rings of habitation swirled like the insides of a snail shell, fifteen-kilometres wide. So well-made did the structures appear, it seemed more as though the rock had been constructed about them than the other way around. Forty thousand years since first habitation here, thirty thousand since this latest renovation. Back then, getting this close would have been a death sentence for any organic sentience.

"Final approach," said Dufresne. "Ten o'clock of target five appears clear." A small burst of thrust to accelerate their approach as the planetoid surface came up real fast. Lisbeth recalled that there were sard now in those structures, it was thought, who might want to shoot at them on the way in. And *that* made her stare at her scans, with great intensity. "Lieutenant Dale, we are on approach, fifteen seconds."

AT-7 was going in first with PH-1 because she had no weapons — PH-3 and 4 had the best positions for cover fire further back. Dufresne swung them about as the planetoid came rushing up, the huge, gaping hole of a hangar bay directly alongside. Lisbeth winced as thrust kicked in hard... and they stopped, close enough that dirt off the planetoid's surface came blasting about the canopy.

"Rear hatch open," Lisbeth announced as her screens showed it. Marines were their own loadmasters on shuttles, and on this shuttle in particular — no one wanted Lisbeth doing anything more than reading screens. "Alpha Platoon is deploying."

Ten seconds later, Dale came back to them with, *"Alpha Platoon is clear, AT-7 you are free to go."* And Dufresne rolled the shuttle a quarter-turn, then hit laterals to burn them gently away from the surface, rather than blast the marines with main engines. Distance increased, she swung them again, angled engines and gave a hard shove.

"PH-3 and 4, going in now." Lisbeth's scan showed PH-1 also climbing clear of the surface, and she had to resist the temptation to turn and look — finding things with your eyes in space was difficult and time consuming, Hausler had drummed into her on their sim runs. Trust scan, and don't waste time looking for things that were probably too far and too fast to see anyway.

Seated up the front of PH-3's hold, Trace was last out amid the thrust jets of fast deploying marines and many small collisions. But the chaos was organised, and quickly outside Bravo Platoon and Command Squad were forming into units and pushing fast toward the enormous hangar lip.

"PH-3, Bravo and Command are all clear," Trace announced as tacnet showed her that on the visor overlay.

"PH-3 copies you clear Major," came Lieutenant Jersey's reply, the shuttle already sliding away on attitude thrusters. *"Good hunting and we'll be right nearby if you need us."* A blast of power somewhere behind as PH-3 kicked in the mains, but Trace was focused ahead as Bravo's forward sections cleared the hangar rim and burned hard to change direction, Trace close behind. Command

Squad in formation about her, she cleared the rim and burned hard as she twisted into the hangar beyond…

…and nearly lost all the breath in her lungs, for sheer astonishment. She'd never seen an interior space so big. She'd known from the tavalai schematics that a hangar for starships had to be huge, but seeing it first hand was something else again. The interior was not rock but steel alloy, as artificial as any space station, and complex with station-sized gantries and grapples that turned the hangar into a maze. A lot of it looked broken now, and old beyond imagining, but in space nothing rusted, just faded and drifted in the endless passing millennia.

"Bravo Platoon advance," Lieutenant Alomaim commanded. *"Vertical formation, keep against the wall, I want Second and Third deployed forward, First stays back, let's create a crossfire between us as we advance. Use those gantries for cover and watch your spacing."*

They jetted forward, then cut thrust and drifted at a steady relative fifty kph. The hangar stretched another kilometre-and-a-half before them, comfortably large enough to hold *Phoenix*, and possibly even *Makimakala* as well. These huge grapples would have gripped hacksaw warships in a tight embrace, allowing repairs, refuelling and rearmament, possibly modular reconfiguration. No need for pressurised access tubes as human stations used — hacksaw drones needed no atmosphere to breathe, and would have swarmed around these vessels like spiders in a nest.

Trace and Command Squad held back behind Lieutenant Alomaim's central First Squad, as they deviated now to avoid some huge gantry structures, and Trace spied odd alcoves in the walls, like control centres but stripped of panels and function. Had hacksaw drones once plugged directly into the walls? And had the Dobruta removed those panels for study, like they'd supposedly stripped much of the useful technology out of this base?

"All platoons report," she commanded. Lieutenant Alomaim retained command of Bravo even with her here — she was busy watching everyone else, multiple clusters of dots on tacnet, in four major formations, all gliding into adjoining starship hangars.

"Alpha Platoon is advancing," came Dale's voice. *"We have signs of recent fighting, maybe twelve dead sard warriors floating, a lot of expended ordinance, holes in the walls. Some disabled tavalai tracker cannon, all destroyed with firepower. Looks like the sard shot their way in."*

"Charlie Platoon reports the same," said Jalawi. *"Maybe seven dead sard, some disabled cannon, some detonated mine clusters. Guess they were pretty determined."*

"Echo Platoon reports all clear so far," came Lieutenant Zhi.

"Bravo is also clear," said Alomaim, more for the Lieutenants' benefit than the Major's.

An icon blinked on Trace's visor. "All platoons advance, looking good," Trace told them, and flipped to the new channel. It was karasai, Major Naki of the *Makimakala.* "Hello Djojana Naki, go ahead."

A pause for automated translation, as Naki spoke about as much English as she did Togiri. His voice when it came was metallic, clearly synthesised. *"Hello Major. Tavalai base defences have been queried and responded. Communication is ongoing, defence protocols are stable. Damage has been taken, we report multiple dead sard warriors, perhaps twenty."*

All of which meant that the tavalai defence grid wasn't about to open fire on humans or tavalai, Trace guessed. "I copy the defence grid is stable," she replied. "We also have dead sard, about twenty. *Phoenix* marines will proceed as planned into central power to secure the reactor."

"I copy Major, Makimakala marines also proceeding as planned." Marines, the translator said, not karasai. Which was a reminder not to take anything the translator said too literally.

"Major, it's the LC," Erik cut in as the tavalai disconnected. *"We've been talking about why the sard are here and it doesn't make sense. They can't hold us up, it'll take days until that ship brings back any reinforcements."*

"I'm a little busy for the theory, LC," said Trace, adjusting her course as the formation flexed and spread about the gantries, rifles swinging to cover possible ambush spots.

"If the sard wanted to slow us down, they'd have shot at you on the way in, so..."

"Not at all," Trace said impatiently.   She hated it when spacers thought they knew a marine's job because they'd watched a few operations from the bridge.   "If I were them I'd let us in unopposed and draw us into ambush deeper inside."   Where superior human firepower with shuttle and warship backup wouldn't turn them to hot dust.

"Access structures on the side," Lieutenant Jalawi cut in, unable to hear this command-channel distraction, and good thing too.   Trace flipped to Jalawi's helmet feed and saw a series of large tunnels, gaping wide and black.   *"No heat signatures, if sard came this way they didn't touch the sides."*

"Sideways is not our direction," Trace told him.   "The objective is ahead.   If they surround us with inferior numbers, that's their problem."

"Major," Erik cut in as Trace repressed a growl of frustration, *"what if the sard have their own objective?"*

"I've no idea and I don't care," Trace said coolly, "now please stop clogging my channel with conjecture."   Another flip. "Lieutenant Dale, what's the armour config on your dead sard?"

"Looks pretty standard Major, light warrior armour, mid-cal rifle. Good tech, nothing fancy."   For sard, that was.   Sard armour was not human standard, and neither were the soldiers in it.

"Same here Major," said Jalawi.   *"But I defer to Lieutenant Dale's expertise — only fought these bastards a few times."*

Ahead beyond the huge bulk of a starship-engine replacement rig, more access tunnels loomed, a single pair, each perfectly circular.   "Lieutenant Alomaim, straight in," she said, as her suit projected more infra-red light onto darkening walls as the gloom set in.   Other suits did the same, and on her visor, IR reception made the walls glow.

"Movement!" someone yelled, and tacnet flashed a single red dot up the end of one of the tunnels.

"Split!" said Alomaim, and the marines in that dot's line of fire went sideways in a hiss of white thrust. Fire erupted past them, red tracer rounds flashing by, but only single-sourced. *"Paste it!"* As several marines angled for minimal-exposure shots past the tunnel rim.

"All *Phoenix* units," Trace announced calmly as return fire went back, "Bravo is under fire, harassing fire only, everyone watch your tails." Indicating to her Command Squad as she did so to turn their backs on the incoming fire and look around in case the shooter was just a distraction.

Staff Sergeant Kono didn't even bother to announce movement when he saw it by a 'ceiling' structure — tacnet lit four red dots and he opened fire a split-second before the rest of Command Squad joined him, auto-attitude adjusting for recoil with silvery jets as red muzzle-flash lit up the dark. Trace held fire, jetting to better cover by a gantry with Private Arime at her side, ignoring the shooting and watching the other platoons.

More gunfire from Echo Platoon, also light, terse chatter and commands going back and forth above the noise. "Lieutenant Zhi, your tacnet feed suggests harassing fire only?"

"Yeah, harassing only! Two shooters out in front as a distraction, then they sprung us from behind... only four of them, we got a couple already..."

"They're just slowing us down."

"It's working too," said Dale between gritted teeth. *"We got ourselves a chain gun up here, maybe automated... we're spending a missile on it, hang on."*

Another command-override communication blinked on her screen from *Phoenix*, but this time it wasn't audio, but text. **Romki thinks the sard are trying to reactivate part of the base.**

Trace blinked at the text. And conceded that okay, that probably was worth being interrupted for. She'd apologise later... but damn, Erik needed to stop easing her into it gently and just hit her with it first time.

"All units, this is the Major. We think the sard might be trying to reactivate part of the base. That means we gotta move fast, I want heavies to the front, launchers on the second row, everyone light it up and move fast, I don't care how much damage we do on the way in. Everyone clear?"

"You heard the Major!" Alomaim commanded. *"Heavy Squad up front, split between the tunnels! Second and Third Squads, left and right, let's go!"*

"What do you mean you don't know if that's possible?" Erik snapped at Captain Pram of the *Makimakala*. "How much command infrastructure is left on that base?"

"I'm sorry Phoenix, we are not at liberty to give you that information." Click, and disconnect. Erik stared at Shahaim. Only too well aware of the hundreds of tavalai mines now surrounding them, probably reprogrammable from *Makimakala* with a single command. They didn't dare push the tavalai around here, and the tavalai knew it.

"They're keeping secrets from us," Kaspowitz observed.

"Probably they thought to capture the relevant systems before we can see it," Shahaim agreed. "The Major is headed for the central reactors, but the tavalai are going for command and control."

Erik thought about it, grimly chewing a nail. And then shook his head. "The Major can figure that for herself — she can't just change assault plans in mid-execution or we'll have humans and tavalai competing to reach the same location, we could end up shooting at each other. If the sard are trying to reactivate part of the base, they'll need the power core to do it, so that still needs to be captured."

He flipped channels to talk to Romki in Engineering. "Stan it's the LC, you want to explain your logic to me a little more on this?"

Romki sat in his Engineering bay strapped to an operations chair with his visor down and a screen bank before him. Petty Officer Kadi was beside him in a similar chair, the restraints a necessity on combat ops, and now engaged in furious conversation on coms with Ensign Hale and Second Lieutenant Rooke, Engineering's commanding officer.

"Well," Romki said carefully, "Petty Officer Kadi and I decided to let the AI queen's construct run overwatch on the operations feed. I mean this is supposed to be an interactive and interpretive program, and it's specifically supposed to interpret drysine language and codes…"

"You mean you're letting it watch our combat operations on TK55?"

"Exactly, we let it watch the entire feed and decide for itself what it found interesting… and for some reason it's begun to home in on some odd background frequencies that *Phoenix*'s analytics actually thought were natural, the radiation signature of those binary stars or some such." He glanced across at Kadi, still furiously debating with his superiors. "We don't have very much to report yet, but the working thesis of Mr Kadi and Mr Rooke is that those frequencies might actually be sard transmissions disguised as background radiation so we won't jam or translate them. And it strikes me as entirely possible that between the sard and their new hacksaw technology, it's the kind of thing they might use for communications anyway… sard like to sing, don't they?"

"Go on Stan."

"But our AI construct finds it fascinating, it's almost as though she… I mean *it*… recognises the signal. I think that… hang on, what is it Petty Officer?"

As Kadi waved a hand at him, staring at his screens with disbelief. "Stan, look at…" and he recalled his coms. "Sir? LC?"

"Go ahead Petty Officer."

"Sir, she's giving us a feed. I mean *it*… it's giving us a… sir, this looks like a tacnet feed, only I don't recognise the format."

As Romki searched the mass of roiling, calculating data on his screen to find... aha! The output! They were only putting data into the construct, but now the construct was feeding them something back, and it was big. Romki flashed it across several applications, and found that it seemed to match with topographical data and fed it into a schematic...

"Holy shit!" Kadi gasped. Unfolding across the new schematic was a precise map of TK55. In fine blueprint detail, and far more precise than anything the tavalai had given them. "Sir, she's giving us a map of TK55, every nut, bolt and circuit in the immediate vicinity of our marines! It's like she recognises it from her memories..."

"Or she's reading that data out of whatever the sard are transmitting," Romki finished, his heart thumping as fast as it had ever thumped at some amazing alien discovery. "Look Kadi, position markers. Those arrays of dots... see if you can highlight them. Talk to her like she's talking to us, let her know those dots are important, I think those are our marines' positions."

Kadi's fingers flew, and the dots lit up and changed colour. Blue dots for marines, and red dots for... "Sir!" Kadi yelped. "Sir, she's giving us sard positions! She's... it looks like she's giving us *all* of the sard positions! She knows exactly where the fuckers are, she can trace them through these signals!"

"Please say again, I missed that," Trace requested, turning down the volume on several of her shouting Lieutenants. In the huge tunnels up ahead, gunfire was thundering, marines dividing into squads to secure a wider path and force the sard ambushers to engage more targets simultaneously. Tacnet showed her platoon positions working deeper into the maze of tunnels, gantries and strange alien machinery — steady progress, but far slower than she wanted.

"The AI queen construct is intercepting sard transmissions and mixing them with marine tacnet," said Erik, his voice a mix of

restrained excitement and trepidation.   *"She's got all of your positions pinged, it's an exact match on tacnet.   And she's got a bunch of other positions here that look like sard positions — the few that tacnet already has registered from your current engagements are matching precisely."*

And Trace realised what he was asking.   "Absolutely, send me that feed immediately."   A moment's delay as Erik gave the order to Lieutenant Shilu on Coms... an icon blinked and she opened it, only too aware that she couldn't both muster the required attention for this, and defend herself, at the same time...

The feed looked a lot like tacnet, only different — 3D and rotating as she angled her head within the helmet, one way then the other.   Same matching tunnels and corridors ahead off the tavalai schematic, and sure enough, those targets tacnet had currently identified were matching... one flickering to disappear even now as Echo Platoon killed it.   And beyond them, and scattered about, a small number of waiting ambushers, some moving about their perimeter even now.   Further up, where the tavalai schematic said TK55's power core was, a much larger number.

"How sure are you of this accuracy?" she asked in disbelief.

"I'm not sure at all," came the logical reply.   *"Only you can determine the accuracy, and its utility."*   Well the utility was obvious — sard couldn't ambush her if she knew exactly where they were, and all numerically inferior forces relied on surprise and stealth to survive.   With this, the sard lost both.   But trust this AI construct to give them accurate information?   It wasn't intelligent, was it?   This data was just the result of reflex processing.   Surely it couldn't be leading them into some kind of trap?

Tacnet also showed her the more distant positions of *Makimakala*'s karasai, fighting their way toward the planetoid's command centre — an imprecise and sketchy transmission, as neither humans nor tavalai were sharing all data, whatever recent declarations of allegiance.

"I'm going to use it," she decided.   "You going to share with *Makimakala*?"

"Hell no," Erik said grimly.   *"They hold all the cards here and they're not sharing.   I want some cards of my own."*

CHAPTER 24

With exact sard positions fixed and known, Bravo Platoon began to accelerate. Forward elements moved with precise thrust, jetting to cover positions at corners, coordinating with heavies to use high explosive where the new data feed said sard ambushers were waiting. Regular squad units then rushed the stunned sard and hammered them point-blank before moving on, not giving the next bunch any time to set their traps.

Trace listened to the terse, fast commands as all four platoons worked methodically deeper into the base. The huge transit tunnels were gone now, abandoned in favour of better cover through the adjoining maze. Hacksaws did not need gravity, air or plumbing, and instead of the layered, square-angled corridors of a human base, the walls here became a 3D maze of odd-angled passages, open spaces, strange machinery and exposed conduits. There were no flat surfaces, none of the smooth solidity that humans valued — everything was exposed, a skeletal framework of structural beam and bulkheads, endless ribs and alcoves like the steel insides of some dead animal. It reminded Trace of the tangled maze the hacksaws had transformed the Argitori rock into, only that had been a renovation job — this was custom built from scratch.

It was perfect ambush territory, pitch black save for the UV light cast by the marines, full of shadows and hiding niches... but now she jetted past the slowly spinning corpse of a sard warrior, amidst armour fragments and globules of blood, the walls torn by recent fire. The AI queen's data feed had not lied yet, and these walls held no danger so long as that remained true. The ribbed shadows shuddered and leaped as gunfire flashed further ahead, then a big explosion as the heavies used a missile to remove a stubborn holdout. Ahead and behind, Command Squad held protective formation as they jetted in the leaders' wake, weapons seeking every blindspot and not trusting any datafeed whatever its results.

"Major," came Alomaim from ahead, *"big crazy-looking place at sunward ahead. Could be defended, if we go past it they'll pump warriors into our rear."*

His helmet feed showed her an image of... something, and she squinted, trying to make sense of it. Everything here was so alien, it was hard for a human brain to quickly determine what it was seeing. "Lieutenant, forward deploy and prepare to push on, but hold. I'm coming up."

Ahead of her, Staff Sergeant Kono put on the burners and accelerated, the others following, bouncing and fending off protruding steel ribs where their zero-G turns failed to make a bend. Trace glimpsed several flashes of white and grey amidst the black framework, then hit her forward jets as Kono stopped fast and found cover, angling his massive rifle on what lay beyond.

Trace arrived, grabbed a rim to stop herself fully... and hung there, staring at the grey-white monstrosity before her. It was like some crystalline organic growth had swelled within the dark steel tissue of the main complex — a pearl within the base, shining with glass and polish. The structure ahead was sealed, the doors transparent, the passages within as multi-directional as any. The white complex seemed enormous — she was on the rim of it here, glimpsing its huge perimeter curving away from her through gaps in the dark surrounds. She felt like an ant burrowing through dirt, and encountering a giant, buried golf ball... but hollow, and filled with passages. And possibly with sard.

"Those passages look all sealed and we'll have to waste time blasting doors open," said Trace. She didn't have time for long contemplation, nor to query the *Makimakala*'s karasai commander, who currently had his own webbed hands full. "And it doesn't look like a great ambush spot, too shiny and transparent — go around but keep your eyes peeled."

Lieutenant Alomaim gave the commands, still fifty meters ahead of her and viewing the structure from a different angle. The formation had become a bit compressed in the halt, so Trace waited for the spacing to return.

"Hello Major, this is Romki," came the unexpected override in her ear. *"Our queen construct has just leaped another magnitude, she's becoming quite agitated by something at the power core ahead of you... if you look at the tacnet feed now, there's something else there and it looks very strange."*

Trace looked, and sure enough, amidst all the red dots of enemy sard was a large, discoloured blob. It seemed to throb and pulse, and grow another size even as she looked at it. "What's your best guess, Stan?"

"Honestly Major, I've no idea." A man of Romki's ego did not admit to that unless truly baffled. *"We've had to appropriate several mainframe clusters to boost her processing power on this end, she's... she's growing, and we're starting to get readings on power surges and data feeds coming from... from directly ahead of you, right where that blob is..."*

Another icon blinked urgently, as the formation stretched, and Kono began moving again, Trace following with a burst of thrust. "Hang on Stan, I have an incoming..." she switched channels. It was Djojana Naki, coms told her. "Karasai commander, I am reading you."

"Major, we are reading activation signals from the power core!" He sounded quite alarmed, even through the translator. *"Is that you?"*

"No it's not me. We are moving forward at maximum speed to intercept. Can you tell me what could be activating the power core?"

A deathly pause, broken by harsh warnings and gunfire ahead as Bravo Platoon intercepted another trap before it sprung. *"Major, we read your formations accelerating their advance. Is your opposition light?"*

"No, we're just fast." He was answering her question with a question — not only evasive, but suspicious. "Make your objective, Djojana. We will make ours." She flipped to all-channels. "*Phoenix* Company, whatever is ahead of us is trying to turn on the power core. I don't want to be in here when the power comes back on, let's move fast!"

"Sir, we need another twenty-five Tegs on the compcore if she's going to keep up this level of processing!" Petty Officer Kadi was insisting to Second Lieutenant Rooke, chief of Engineering.

"Is she interactive with the queen?" Rooke demanded. *"The actual queen, she's in nano-fluid, the fluid's inactive but it's designed to create new circuits around damaged sections..."*

"Look," Romki cut in with frustration, "the sard on that base are onto us, they're not idiots, they can see we're killing them and they're modulating their transmissions, we're not getting the same clear picture that we were.   She's..." and his fingers danced upon his screen as he ran the new data through new applications, "...she's focused on this new thing in the power core that she doesn't like and she's getting some kind of... I don't know... programming language..."

"Look Stan, I can't..."

"Lieutenant, the reason she can decipher this stuff is because it's hacksaw, like her!   You get it?   She's drysine, and I'm betting whatever the sard are using is deepynine — it's the whole fucking AI civil war breaking out once more in that base.   And you know what? I'm betting she's on our side, and she's sure as hell upset with this thing in the power core!"

"Is there a danger she'll go active?" Rooke repeated, a little desperately.   It was the nightmare they'd all discussed, and all the Engineering techs had insisted to the LC and other senior officers that it was impossible with the right precautions.

"She's at fifty-two Tegs now," Kadi said.   "Look, it's just a construct, it's not actually *her*..."

"We don't know how the damn thing works, Petty Officer! Have you any idea how computational an AI construct at fifty-two Tegs is?   That's five times the legal limit under Fleet law, and you're asking me to double it!"

"Engineering!" Trace's voice cut in before Romki or Kadi could reply.   Romki could hear gunfire in the distant background.

"I want that feed back, we're getting held up again! It occurs to me that that thing in the power core might be deepynine, and it might be nasty, and the tavalai haven't told us everything about the capabilities they didn't yet strip from this base. If the sard have a deepynine queen or something, and she reactivates the base with a lot of its original defences still active, then I doubt very many of us will be getting out of here alive. If our drysine queen wants to help, let her, and that's an order."

"God damn it," Rooke muttered.

"This is the LC," came a new interruption. *"I want the Major's command followed, I want all systems on maximum security, I want hands on kill switches in case we lose control of systems, and I want someone with a gun, preferably a very big gun, standing directly before that queen where she can see him, and ready to blow her away if she gets out of control, understood?"*

"Aye sir!" Kadi announced, and began preparations for the processing shunt to greater power. "We could just get the queen's head out of that nano-tank. She's genuinely dead without it, it's all those micros completing new circuits about the damaged ones that makes the problem."

"They're inactive," Romki repeated. "The nano-tank can't make new circuits because it isn't switched on…"

"What if she finds a way to turn them back on? There's all kinds of wireless coms on this ship… she's alien, Professor!" Kadi's hands flew as he preset the new processors and cleared pre-existing functions. "And don't tell me she's no threat because she's just a program on our servers — I've got *no* control over what she's doing here, right now we're just winging it."

"Yes well," said Romki, exasperated. "Welcome to the *UFS Phoenix*, Petty Officer." He finished his final adjustments, first increasing the autonomy of his screens so Petty Officer Kadi couldn't see what he was doing. Then he pushed up the activation level on the nano-tank. Immediately the AI construct surged, calculations-per-second increasing by several billion and requests flooding Kadi's screen, demanding another three Tegs of processing power.

"Whoa, look at her go," said Kadi. "Okay, compcore is clear, twenty-eight Tegs new power coming online now." He tapped the screen, and whole new banks of *Phoenix* Engineering's computers leapt to life. "Sure doing a good impersonation of a living thing, isn't she?"

"Yes," Romki agreed. Built into the nearby workbench, suspended within the transparent sides of the nano-tank, the queen's baleful red eye watched him unblinkingly. "Yes she is."

Trace knew she was getting close to the power core because her suit's sensors began reading magnetism off the charts. The wasp-nest corridors gave way to enormous conduits and bundles of cable at angles across her visor, like lopsided cathedral columns amidst tangles of support structure and heavy bulkheads. Bravo Platoon accelerated to weave amongst them, hitting jets to avoid collisions while scanning rifles back and forth to cover each other's approach.

"Hacksaws use different types of advanced fusion!" Trace reminded them. "From the magnetism I'd guess we're in the early phase of startup. We have to stop it, but do not damage the reactor — it cannot go critical, but a dozen of these subsystems could blow and kill you anyway! Alpha, move right around and spread, we need it encircled."

"Alpha copies, Major," Dale replied. On tacnet, Trace could see all four platoons, clusters of dots moving to encircle the powercore. *"What happens if the power comes back on? You think the tavalai left hacksaw drones stored away in here somewhere?"*

"Makimakala's briefing said otherwise, but it looks like their briefing left a lot out." She hit thrust to avoid a huge cluster of conduits, then dodged upward to where Bravo Second Squad were converging on a gap in the spherical shell-plating ahead. "I think we can presume nothing good."

"Resistance is light," Lieutenant Zhi remarked. *"We're nearly set for position and we are not under fire at this time."*

"They're waiting for something," Trace warned them. "They're luring us in, and if we want the damn reactor shut down we've got no damn choice."

"Could they be about to blow the whole base?" Alomaim wondered. *"Suicide to take us all out?"*

"No," Trace said firmly. "You cannot overload these types of reactor." Boarding any hostile facility, it was always the first thing she checked. "That much we do know — this is something else."

"Major this is Scan," came Second Lieutenant Geish on coms — immediately unusual because *Phoenix* Scan rarely spoke to her directly. *"I'm reading a big energy spike in your vicinity."*

"Yes I see it too Scan." No sooner had she said it than her visor display began to break up in static, and tacnet flickered alarmingly.

"Major, that's... I don't think that's the reactor, I think that's something else, Scancomp says the signature reads as hacksaw!"

"All platoons halt and cover!" Trace commanded, with a final fend off a metal edge as she flew into the gap in the big, wide sphere that surrounded the powerplant. She hit an arm thruster and drifted to a hard collision with the edge, surveying the power core down the barrel of her rifle. Like so many things in this base, the sight was disorientating.

The inner side of the shell was smooth and wide like a bowl, many hundreds of meters wide. Within the bowl, a perfect and symmetrical fit, was the round globe of the main combustion chamber, held in place by several huge arms. About her, the inner surface of the bowl was as smooth and regular as the approach to this point had been irregular. With her head and rifle peering above the narrow gap, amidst the other marines, she felt like an insect that had wandered onto a giant's dinner plate.

"All units watch your fire about the reactor," she warned them, sighting Alpha Platoon marines likewise emerging from another gap forty-degrees around the bowl, braced for action. Tacnet's flickering got worse, and Trace recalled with alarm the coms cutting out on Joma Station, as again the audio crackled. "Get ready, here it comes. Aim your shots, make that first shot count. Secondary track missiles, lock your aiming solutions now, late is too late."

She breathed deep and calm, focusing all energy, all racing thoughts on that simple thing. Whatever was in here had crawled into the hacksaw reactor to start it up, and was now trapped in there. Given the possibilities, it did not make her feel safe.

A shriek lit up her coms, suit armscomp abruptly melting upon the visor, and taccom warning her with red flashes of the most enormous signal output... *"TAKE COVER!"* something announced on coms, and her visor registered a spike in incoming coms data in excess of ten thousand percent. Which was impossible, with this much interference, and *Phoenix* coms were just not capable of...

And then she realised. "Down!" she yelled, and shoved herself away from her firing position, abandoning a clear shot along the shielding bowl for cover. "Take cover!" As tacnet erupted with incoming, missiles streaking and weaving, then airbursting with small puffs before the warheads detonated like strings of giant, deadly firecrackers, and all her view disappeared as the world was filled with blasting shrapnel that cracked and shuddered her suit.

Targeting came suddenly clear across her visor, multiple missile locks as her backrack activated without being asked... "Missiles!" she yelled. "Hold cover, missile locks to my directive!" As she flicked targeting to 'command', and those locks propagated across all four platoons. She fired, and *Phoenix* Company fired with her. Big red blots suddenly appeared on tacnet, racing clear of the core.

"Fire fire fire!" she yelled, jetting upward as all about the inner shielding bowl missiles blew everything to hell, but she emerged up into it, grabbed an edge to stabilise and levelled her Koshaim just as a racing shape darted through the smoke and fire. She fired, as a dozen others fired around her, a storm of red tracer and exploding, spinning debris. The racing thing came apart in progressive disintegration, torn and ripped in all directions.

"A distraction!" came the same voice that had told her to take cover. *"It escapes, outside the shell, move now!"* As a spot

appeared on her tacnet, not red like the others, but blue, and approaching Echo Platoon's wide flank.

"Lieutenant Zhi, kill that thing!" Trace jetted from her position, others chasing, dodging big chunks of reactor shell that had been blasted clear in the shooting, and realising that a lot of things were sparking and flashing that shouldn't be, in a fusion reactor core. Ahead, Zhi's platoon were firing and yelling, and Trace zoomed under the spherical core, past pylons now shredded in the explosions.

And then ahead, she saw it, a big alien shape amidst the smoke and impacting cannon rounds, blazing gunfire in multiple directions even as more missiles hit, and blew it sideways up the curving wall. It recovered, and for the briefest moment Trace could see it clearly — gleaming silver steel, many legs, some now missing, others preparing still-functioning weapons to fire back even now. A beast like a nightmare, five times the size of hacksaw drones they'd previously seen. Then about fifteen marines hit it all at once, Trace included, and smashed it to a floating, silver pulp.

"Cease fire! Cease fire!" Tacnet showed nothing else moving. "Tactical report! Keep your eyes open, do not trust tacnet!" The distortion was gone, but now the damaged reactor ball was arcing in an alarming fashion. Reports came back, all clear, no more enemy sighted. Trace doubted they were all dead, but for now, with their commander gone, organised resistance was effectively ended.

Trace stared at the dead machine before her, twisted like an insect crushed beneath a boot heel. Many of its parts were loose and spinning about the reactor's inner shield, but still Trace counted ten main arms — twin chain guns like most drones, but underside cannon as well, big thrusters for zero-G movement, and much heavier armourplate. Three huge dark eyes about a central head, behind rows of small, fiddly manipulator arms for close examinations.

"What the hell is it?" Staff Sergeant Kono muttered, rifle unwavering from that three-eyed head.

"Not big enough for a queen," Trace guessed. "Some kind of commander though. Smarter than your average drone. Inspect these others with her, I'd guess they're regular drones." As several loud rifle shots indicated someone was doing a lot more than just inspecting them.

"Yeah, but what is it?" Kono repeated.

"Deepynine," said Trace. It was the only thing that made sense. "It's a deepynine commander, and it was leading these sard."

"Oh fuck," Dale muttered from somewhere on the reactor's far side. *"If there are deepynines still alive and commanding sard, we're all in deep shit. We meaning humanity."*

"Burn it," said the voice in Trace's earpieces before she could reply. A strange, androgynous voice, not of any recognisable *Phoenix* crew, yet well recalled all the same. *"It is not yet fully dead. Restoration is too dangerous. Burn it, and be sure."*

"And who the hell is that voice?" asked Lieutenant Zhi.

"Not who," Trace said grimly. "What."

CHAPTER 25

With cylinder rotation active, Trace had to go through the core transit to move from midships to Engineering. She took the H Bulkhead main ladder, which had sensors to warn unarmored crew to vacate least she accidentally squashed someone coming down.

Then she stomped along an adjoining corridor and followed the commotion, edging past alarmed, wide-eyed spacers and finally Delta Platoon marines in full armour. Lieutenant Crozier herself stood guard just inside Romki's doorway, with several others closer still, rifles levelled at the nano-tank containing the drysine queen's head. People made way for the Major, and at the far door she saw Erik, standing with Second Lieutenant Rooke and Petty Officer Kadi, talking in low voices. Erik saw Trace and beckoned, as others got out of her way. As she walked into the room, she could have sworn the queen's red-eye followed her, despite the immobility of the head.

"Firstly," said Trace as they exited the door to talk in the corridor, "please make sure there's nothing vital on the far side of that wall, because if you fire Koshaims in here, you'll blow holes several rooms down."

"I know," said Erik. "I hear no casualties, is that right?" Glancing at some of the shrapnel damage on her armour.

Trace nodded. "Seven light injuries, nothing major. I wouldn't read too much into it — the sard were in a hopeless situation and were just trying to delay. You pick fights in ones and twos against our full company, you'll get slaughtered." She jerked her head back toward the room just vacated. "What happened? Where's Romki?"

"Answering questions," Erik said grimly. "Again. Petty Officer Kadi says he must have activated the nano-tank. The nanos in the fluid completed bypass circuits in the queen's damaged head, and the construct program started querying her for more information as the fight developed. That activated a lot more of her subsystems than anyone had anticipated. Well, maybe anyone except Romki."

"Just as well too," said Trace.   Erik frowned.   "Is she actually awake?"

"It's debatable," said Rooke.   He looked both excited and scared.   "She's far below optimal neural capability, no more than twenty percent.   She's... it's..." he took a breath to steady himself, and gather his thoughts.   "Look, none of us have any idea how she's doing it, it's like she's got some kind of dual-process intelligence going right now, half of it is the simulator construct running on our own hardware, and the other half is happening in her actual head thanks to the reprogrammed micros in the tank."

"So is it actually her?" Trace pressed.   "Or a simulation of her?   Backed up by whatever small original parts of her actual brain are still working?"

Rooke made an exasperated gesture.   "Oh look... I could give you some futile answer in an attempt to try and sound smart, but I'd be lying.   We're not even sure what consciousness means to a hacksaw AI — how they perceive time, reality, self-awareness.   All I'm sure of is that there's something far more complicated happening than just a series of automated reflexes and subroutines."

"Well she definitely helped us," Trace admitted.   "The deepynine command drone had three friends, all heavy combat models, multiple missile racks, coordinated guidance like nothing we've ever seen.   We got warned just in time to remove ourselves from direct line of sight and limit primary exchanges to missiles.   Without that, we could have lost a dozen or more, and that commander might have got away, for a time at least."

"You're sure it's deepynine?" Erik asked.

"No," Trace admitted.   "That's why I'd like to talk to her. But the design philosophy is completely different from the drones in Argitori, or from the queen herself.   And it makes sense.   She's drysine, she could have spent a lifetime fighting deepynines, or may at least have the memories of others who did, if she's not that old herself.   This is our chance to finally learn something from the only source that matters.   I think Romki's done us a favour."

She intended it as a challenge.   Erik liked to ease people into difficult concepts slowly.   Trace hated to waste time, and wished he'd follow suit.   Erik looked very unhappy, that well-chewed thumbnail hovering near his lip.   "I don't like having that thing on my ship, Major.   I didn't like it when she was dead, and I sure as hell don't like it now.   She *can* take over systems by remote, we've just seen it.   She was using *Phoenix*'s command feed through Operations to make contact with you."

"And again," Trace said defiantly, "just as well she did. She's both a danger and an opportunity.   I suggest that the best way to minimise the former and maximise the latter is to try and reach some kind of bargain with her."

"And you'd seriously trust anything she might say?"

"I won't know until I talk to her.   May I?"

The queen had chosen to speak to her, and not Erik, or even Romki.   A natural choice, given her command of the only forces capable of killing a hated deepynine.   And also, she was the only member of *Phoenix*'s crew the queen had spoken to before.   Right before she'd shot her.

Erik considered for a moment.   Then he nodded shortly. Trace turned and thumped back into the room.   This time she racked her rifle, figuring that two marines already there were enough. Romki's workbench was built around the nano-tank, partly obscuring the queen's eye, and the massive hole Trace had blasted through it in Argitori, and out the back of its head.   Engineering techs stared, watching on mobile pads and AR glasses with trepidation.   Trace locked out her armoured knees, to sit comfortably upon the armour saddle and rest for a moment.

"Hello," she said to the red eye.   That felt very strange. Like speaking to a rock, and expecting it to answer.   "Do you remember me?"   There came no reply.   Trace waited several moments, and looked at the techs about the bay.   They shrugged, mystified.   The queen had not spoken since telling the marines to burn the deepynine remains.   Had that been nothing more than a voice synthesising program?   "Don't play silent with me.   I heard you talk just now.   You helped my marines to kill those deepynines. I'd like to know why."

An electronic ripple sounded on coms.   A vibration, in apparently random sequence.   "Hang on," said one of the techs, "that's definitely her.   That's... that's basic text coding, just let me..."

A cursor appeared on Trace's visor.   Then it ran, making words. **Primary function**, it said.

"What is a primary function?" Trace asked.   "Killing deepynines?"

Primary function, it repeated.   And nothing more.

"I don't think she's entirely there," another of the techs suggested, scrolling rapidly through the torrent of data-feedback they were receiving from the construct and the micros in the nano-tank. "The data intensity is way down on what it was just half an hour ago. That effort might have burned her out."

Trace stared at the big red eye, and got a cold chill up her spine.   She recalled the serpentine body, the intricate manipulator arms, writhing and flexing before her in zero-G.   The emotive, almost plaintive note in its voice.   Not a cold and unfeeling machine.   A living, thinking mind, vastly flexible and completely alien.   She'd heard that voice again just recently, in her helmet, confronting the deepynine commander.   Yet now, all the queen could give her was a blinking cursor and a few words of print?

"She's foxing," Trace said with certainty.   "I think she can talk fine.   She's choosing not to.   Probably playing dumb, keeping her options open."   But Rooke was right too, she thought.   No way this was the fully conscious queen she'd met in the Argitori rock. Even able to speak, this was probably a shadow of that fearsome creature.   Whether that made her safer or more dangerous, Trace did not know.   "Thank you for helping us to kill the deepynines.   We have a common enemy.   This ship also hunts deepynines.   Do you know why?"

A pause, as the cursor blinked. **No.**

"We think the deepynines are still alive.   Most species think they're all dead, but we think they have allied with a species called the alo.   Do you know the alo?   They did not emerge in the Spiral until many thousands of years after the end of the Machine Age."

Alo, said the cursor. **I know.**

Trace took a deep breath. Here was the only question that really mattered. Probably the biggest question in the galaxy right now. "Do you know what happened to the deepynines after the drysines destroyed most of them? Were there any left? And are they still alive?"

Evidently, said the cursor. Trace could almost hear irony, in that single word. Exasperation at a silly question, given what had just happened. Around them, Trace had never heard such silence from a small room full of people.

"How many?"

Unknown. Regeneration possible. Organic sentience assisted?

"Yes," said Trace. "Yes, sentience assisted. Alo assisted, we think alo have helped the deepynine to regenerate."

Possibility. Terminal danger.

"How great a danger?" Trace pressed.

Ask alo. Trace blinked at the words. Definitely it was irony. There was no way that alien machines had irony as humans understood it... it must have picked it up from listening to surrounding speech patterns. And she recalled in her first conversation with the queen in Argitori, how its voice had changed in just a few sentences to become more expressive, more human. A fast learner, to put it mildly. And her suspicion increased. Surely this queen was far more awake and aware than she was letting on.

"We think the deepynines are working with the sard. We think they are helping the sard to build deepynine or drysine technology ships. We want to stop them. Will you help us?"

I see Dobruta.

"Yes. Do you know the Dobruta?"

Yes. Dobruta want to kill all the children.

"Are you afraid?" Trace asked carefully. No reply on her visor. "Yes the Dobruta wish to kill all AIs. AI civilisation was very bad for all organics." Still no reply. Trace supposed it was too much to ask that it might venture an opinion on past horrors, let

314

alone an apology. "But we need to stop the deepynines. If you help us to do that, you will become valuable to us."

When the deepynines are dead. Do I die too? Several onlooking techs exchanged incredulous looks.

"If the deepynines have been regenerated in alo space, then it will take a very long time to kill them all," Trace said reasonably. "There could be a lot of them. As you become important to us, your function will grow." Behind her, she could just smell Erik's displeasure. She was making promises she might not be able to keep. The queen might become dissatisfied when those promises were broken. All sorts of possibilities arose.

Bring me the new deepynine remains. I will analyse.

"You advised us to burn them."

Things change.

"Lieutenant Commander, this is most ill-advised," Captain Pram insisted on the vid feed in Erik's quarters. Erik sat at his small desk with no other company. He'd had to clear the crew out to make this call, following the usual strongly worded disagreements. Kaspowitz had been unhappy, but given his friendship with Trace, was not prepared to pick a big fight with her. Or perhaps he just knew he'd lose. Shahaim had been on the fence, disliking their lack of information, and seeing this as a possible solution. Rooke had been mostly embarrassed that he'd let Romki pull this particular stunt right under his nose, and tech-head that he was, was more fascinated by developments than was probably wise. And Trace, as always, remained stubborn as a rock.

"I'm aware of the dangers," Erik began.

"I think you are not," said the tavalai captain. The big, wide face loomed on the vidscreen, mouth thin with disapproval. *"I assume it is speaking complete sentences, and I assume it seems agreeable."* It wasn't speaking anything, just writing words on screens, but Erik let it slide. *"I would remind you, Lieutenant Commander, that no AI willingly speaks a verbal language. For*

them it has the utility of a human expert on birds imitating bird calls to attract a mate. Their usual mode of communication is direct data transfer — it is a language of sorts, though it compresses information at a rate tenfold more efficient than our own tongues."

Captain Pram was assuming ignorance on the humans' part — Erik had listened at lengths to Romki's explanations of 'Ceenyne', the deepynine audible language from the last few hundred years of the Machine Age. But he wasn't about to get into an academic debate now, because without Romki present, he'd surely lose. "I am aware of that Captain," he answered the tavalai.

"But you have not considered what it means." Erik was becoming very tired of tavalai lecturing on human shortcomings. *"We use language to express emotion and personality. All that you think you are hearing from this machine is faked for effect. Neither drysine nor deepynine nor any of the other AI offshoots have ever felt anything comparable to human or tavalai emotion or sentiment. It views our sentiment as weakness, and tries to make you trust it. I assure you, you cannot."*

"You wanted her to translate whatever data you've found in the base," Erik replied, attempting patience. "Well now you've got her, and she can do it with far greater accuracy than your construct."

"It is not a she, Lieutenant Commander, it is an it."

"I'm aware of that too," said Erik. "Have you found the data in the control centre that you were looking for?"

"Please do not change the subject. I will remind you that you are currently surrounded by tavalai-controlled mines and gun platforms. Should this new crewmember of yours decide to take control of your weapons to open fire upon my ship, I assure you I will not hesitate to use every weapon in the vicinity in our defence."

Erik leaned forward to the screen. "Buddy, even with all your mines, you couldn't take this ship." A silence, as the two ship commanders stared at each other on their screens. "I am in command of this vessel. Your opinion is noted. If you wish further cooperation in finding this sard base that's making all these advanced ships, you will send crew with the data we came here to get, and see if our unexpected guest can decipher it. Any other path will see our cooperation ended. Am I making myself clear?"

The tavalai's nostrils flared, and the screen went blank. Erik gazed at the dead screen for a moment longer, then went and opened the door.

"Everyone hear that?" he asked the bridge as he emerged. It was all first-shift in the chairs, save for Lieutenant Draper in the command chair. Nods all around... and from Trace, who had stayed to listen. Erik took hold of the supports by Draper's chair and hung there, ducking a little to see the far posts past the command screens. Trace took hold at Kaspowitz's chair.

"Sir, we're on full alert with those mines and platforms," said Draper. "We've locked onto the coordination signal, but there's no way to block it, *Makimakala* could signal an attack at any moment."

"And for all my bluster," Erik added, "we're totally screwed if they do it. I actually think that went kind of well."

"You think?" Kaspowitz said drily.

"He didn't once ask about the deepynine drones, nor about how the queen became activated, or how she helped. None of it."

"Well he thinks you're nuts for trusting her however it happened," said Shilu. "With respect, LC."

"No, he's not interested in the details," Erik insisted. "And whether you think she's going to kill us all or not — when you're commanding a warship in dangerous circumstances, operational details are everything. He didn't care. That tells me the operational details of the queen herself are not his main concern."

"He doesn't want her to tell us things," said Trace. Erik nodded. "Tavalai have had humans at a disadvantage regarding old galactic history since we first got into space. He's using our firepower and intel, but he doesn't want us to actually learn stuff about the hacksaws."

"He's Dobruta," Erik agreed. "Dobruta have spent thousands of years trying to stop *anyone* from learning stuff about the hacksaws. The fear is that the technology is so seductive that someone will make a deal with a hacksaw queen, promise her life in exchange for power and riches."

"Which is exactly what it looks like the sard have done," Trace finished. "And now Captain Pram fears we're about to do the same thing. It's their nightmare scenario — a big queen seduces some alien species into resurrecting her race in exchange for power. Tavalai have no faith that any other species are as principled as them."

"They've been fighting humans a long time," Draper reasoned. "They see us as the enemy, whatever *Phoenix*'s situation. The Captain's probably scared that instead of solving his problem, he might have just made it worse by giving hacksaw tech to humanity."

"Only we already *had* hacksaw tech," said Erik. "Fleet's got lots of it, only they've always agreed with the Dobruta about the dangers of copying it. Much has been destroyed. But if Romki's right, and the alo became so high-tech in the first place by cooperation with the deepynines, then the most deadly piece of hacksaw tech in the Spiral might be the one we're standing in. And others like it, that we used to take half of the tavalai's space away from them."

"Thus making the galaxy safe for artificial life again," said Trace. "Deepynine in particular, by removing the main anti-AI force from power. Their big strategic plan that Fleet's been playing along with. The big question is whether Fleet did it willingly or not. And if not, if they know there's deepynines behind the entire alo front, then the alo will have to take out Fleet at some later stage... which means the alo will stab us in the back at some point, in time-honoured Spiral tradition."

"And possibly use the chah'nas to do it," Erik agreed. "Since the chah'nas just got access to our space. Which means that all of humanity could be about to get whacked, and we could lose..." He glanced across the bridge. Pale, frightened faces stared back at him.

"Billions," Kaspowitz muttered.

"Hundreds of billions," Shahaim whispered.

Erik nodded slowly. "So then we've agreed that the deepynines are back. They're doing strategic things. The best way to kill a deepynine is with someone who understands deepynines. Our Dobruta friends on *Makimakala* distrust *all* AIs equally — deepynine or drysine, no difference to them.   But humanity is threatened by deepynines, and our new passenger might be the most knowledgable... thing, about how to kill deepynines, in all the galaxy.

"And so I've changed my mind."   He gave a little nod to Trace.   "It's good that we've woken her up, to the very limited extent that we have.   It's also incredibly dangerous, and we have to be on the highest alert, because everything Captain Pram said about her is true.   But at this point we have no choice.

"Now we have to find that base, but here's the thing. Captain Pram wants to destroy it.   It's giving the sard powerful new weapons that threaten the strategic balance through Outer Neutral Space — first the barabo, and then the tavalai will get it in the neck. I'd like to see it destroyed too, but that's not our primary objective, and my conversation just now with Captain Pram makes that clear to me.   Our primary objective is to find out what the hell's going on there.   Who are these deepynines helping the sard, are they connected to the alo, are they operating independently, et-cetera. Because we're operating with a blindfold on at the moment, and if we can't figure what the deepynines are up to, we'll have no idea what to do next, or just how much danger humanity is actually in.

"This means that we may have to lie to *Makimakala*, and tell them we're going to help them destroy it, when actually we mainly want to learn from it... which is exactly what *Makimakala* don't want us to do.   So this is going to get very interesting.   Do *not* talk about this off-bridge with anyone other than other bridge officers or equivalent rank.   We'll have tavalai coming aboard to talk to our queen at some point, and we don't want some of the lower-decks motor-mouths blabbing the whole plan to them."

Slow, thoughtful nods about the bridge.   From Trace, a look of considered respect.   Kaspowitz gave him a wry smile.   "We have a plan?"

"We'll think of one," Erik insisted.   "First, let's find out where this damn base is.   If there actually is a base, and the tavalai haven't just been stringing us along."

"Like we're going to do to them," said Shilu with a grimace.

Erik nodded.   "Exactly."

CHAPTER 26

As *Phoenix* went into second-shift, Trace went back to TK55 to supervise operations. Her ride was PH-1, with Lieutenant Hausler wisecracking about being reduced to a ferry service, as *Phoenix* held off forty kilometres from the planetoid in the sun-shadow where the glare would less interfere with instruments, and where incoming ships would take longer to spot them on scan. There were no windows in the shuttle hold, but if she linked to PH-1's scan feed, she could see *Makimakala* in similar position seven kilometres further out, and *Rai Jang* closer in, the smaller and more mobile ship ready to support marines or karasai up close in case any hacksaws got outside the base.

With Trace were Command Squad, a number of second-shift Engineering crew ready to replace the first-shifters, plus Jokono, Hiro and Romki. The latter was on Trace's request, as it seemed daft to continue to punish Romki for something that even the LC now agreed was necessary, however pissed he was at how it was done. But then, as Trace told him, if you were going to put people in charge of sensitive operations who were unlikely to follow orders at the best of times, you got what was coming to you. Keeping their premier hacksaw expert locked up so he couldn't go and see this ancient base seemed more like *Phoenix* cutting off its nose to spite its face.

Lieutenant Hausler flew them into the main starship hangar, and they vacated all air from the shuttle hold before exiting the main rear door. Kono led them out, Command Squad positioning with rifles ready just in case — there were still a few sard loose on the base, Bravo Platoon had nailed one just an hour ago, but no one figured they were more than a nuisance at this point. Pretty soon though they'd be running out of air, and being sard, they might decide to go down fighting. Engineering crew followed, carrying personal hand thrusters and light weapons, and moved toward the huge transit tunnels up which PH-1 could have comfortably continued flying if it weren't such a pointless risk.

Finally came the civvies, Hiro predictably assured and balanced, Jokono less so, and Romki least of all. Romki stared about at the service rigs the size of city towers, stretching across the cavernous interior, and murmuring incredulities beneath his breath.

"Hey Professor," Kono told him as PH-1 shoved gently away on attitude bursts. *"Try to watch where you're going and don't get left behind."*

Trace looked at Romki, looking and feeling as tiny as they all did, specks of dust within this ancient construction. *"Amazing,"* he murmured. *"Just amazing."*

At the tunnels' entrance they rendezvoused with Bravo Second Squad, and deployed into escort formation, marines on the perimeter, spacers and civvies in the middle. Soon they split, Second Squad's first and second sections taking the techs through new maze-tunnels up to the reactor, where there were power cores to study and dead deepynine drones to be recovered. Third Section took Jokono another way, to where Alpha Platoon had most heavily engaged sard defences, and there were plenty of dead, armoured bugs to examine and hopefully learn things from.

Trace took a familiar off-shoot another way, with Command Squad and Hiro, through the tangled nest of ribbed tunnels and organic-looking conduits, vision set to infra-red to navigate in pitch dark until they reached well-remembered white-grey walls. Bravo First Squad marines guarded the corridor on the way in, and tacnet showed Trace not only other marines in guard formation, but mobile ball-sized drones skipping about the random twists and turns, establishing a picture.

"Hello Tanker, Thunder," Trace said to the door guards, pulling up with a burst of white thrust. "How's your air?"

"It's fine Major," said Lance Corporal Tariq 'Tanker' Kamov. *"We got refills."*

"Bit creepy in here?" Trace said slyly as she passed between them.

"I dated this new age rock chick in high school," said Private Leo 'Thunder' Sinha. *"Her bedroom was a bit like this."*

322

"Not that he ever got to see her bedroom," Kamov added. There was light in the walls here at least, not everything was pitch black.

"How did you get the lights on?" Kono asked them, approaching the transparent door. It slid open on approach, smooth and soundless.

"Residual powercell charge," said Kamov. *"Thirty thousand year old batteries, pretty freaky."*

"My god!" Romki exclaimed behind as he got his first clear view of the massive spherical structure. *"I don't believe it!"*

"You recognise this, Stan?" Trace asked him. The corridors ahead looked almost organic, white or grey in alternating shades, smoothly finished and inlaid with transparent doors or windows in parts. Where the rest of TK55's AI base looked harsh and dark, this looked almost delicate and crystalline.

"No, I just... I never imagined hacksaws building anything like this. It's almost... artistic."

"Yeah well don't get too impressed," Lance Corporal Kamov said grimly. *"Find Ensign Hale, she'll show you what it's for."*

They followed the winding corridors and 3D junctions, past several large storage rooms and sealed heavy doors, homing on where tacnet gave Ensign Hale's location, and that of several more Engineering techs. And emerged into a series of open, spherical rooms, each overlapping the next like a series of merging bubbles. The walls of the bubble rooms were bristling with tall, partly transparent canisters, like inward-facing glass bristles. Trace thought it looked a little like caves on Sugauli, deep within the mountains and gleaming with stalagmites and rare minerals.

Further along, some *Phoenix* techs were working at what might have been a control panel, and several marines were on guard, weapons always ready. Trace gave herself a gentle shove toward a wall, arriving with armoured boots atop a steel capped canister. She flashed an arm light into the glass canisters... and found two thirds of them empty. The other third were filled with withered husks, like dried fruit left too long in the sun. Bodies, she realised. Organic bodies, mummified for endless millennia, surrounded by basic life support that had long since ceased to function.

"Tavalai," said Romki, having arrived at Trace's side, pulling himself head-first for a better look. *"A few parren, a few sard, but mostly tavalai. Very, very old."*

"It's a medical research facility," came Ensign Remy Hale's voice. Trace glanced to find her drifting across in her heavy suit, various tech-gear dangling off her belt, a burner in one gloved hand. Behind her came Lieutenant Alomaim, a personal armed escort for Engineering's second-in-command after Second Lieutenant Rooke. *"Medical research for organics."*

"These don't look at all like willing patients," Romki observed, gazing up and around at the gleaming spherical walls.

"Exactly," said Hale, halting with a thrust, Alomaim close behind. *"There are examination rooms further on. Lots of cutting implements. It's a gorgeous piece of architecture, but it's a horror show. They stored live people here, and did experiments on them. By the tens of thousands, these storage rooms go on and on further back. About a quarter full, all told."*

"Mostly tavalai, parren and sard?" asked Romki.

"Actually there's a few barabo too," said Hale. Trace thought she looked far less excited than Romki. Horrified, but dealing with it. And she recalled Alomaim saying that Hale had lost a best friend on Joma Station docks. An Engineering tech she'd served with for years. *"And barabo were a long way from spacetravel back when this facility was working. So they were snatching undeveloped barabo off their homeworld, like those old Earth stories about UFOs."*

"Wow!" Romki breathed. *"Imagine if we found humans here? That would rewrite some history!"* Hacksaws had never got that close to human space, but still Trace could see the fascination.

"This is another good reason the Dobruta didn't want to destroy this base," she said, staring around. "Tavalai respect their ancestors. This is like holy ground for them."

"They suffered a fair bit, the froggies," Kono conceded heavily. *"This kind of shit must have been going on a lot, all through the Machine Age. Damn glad humans missed it."*

Humans always assumed they'd had the worst of it, Trace thought. Looking about now, she wondered if that was actually true. Losing your homeworld when you were still a one-planet species was about as bad as it got... but it had happened once, then humanity had recovered and moved on. The war against the krim had seemed titanic to humans, the all-encompassing, blood soaked nightmare of a five hundred year conflict. But in galactic terms, it had been a small fight involving just a few dozen systems in an unknown corner of the galaxy, between one up-and-coming species, and one mostly insignificant one.

Tavalai had been under the machines for more than twenty thousand years. They'd had no singular catastrophic loss in that time as great as humanity losing Earth, but the slaughter had still been huge, and it had stretched on for such a long time, with no end in sight. Human popular culture was full of stories about the futility of life on Earth under the krim, the violent death of entire communities and cities that followed resistance, and the hopeless drudgery of compliance. The only true resistance had been off-world, and young Earth men and women determined to fight had quickly learned that to truly make a difference, they had to leave Earth, and join the new human Fleet, equipped by the chah'nas, and striking the krim in the places where it truly hurt.

That had continued for a century and a half, with a brief respite only when the tavalai had intervened in a misguided attempt to make a peace that some Earth-bound humans had wanted, but no Fleet-based humans would accept. Fleet had fought the tavalai instead, and when the tavalai finally gave up in disgust, the krim killed Earth as the best way of stemming the flow of Fleet recruits.

Five hundred years of horror, so many lifetimes and generations lost in the maelstrom. But how well would humanity have endured *this*? Twenty thousand years, beneath the machines? Trace had seen images, never particularly popular among humans, so wrapped up in their own self-righteous victimhood. But still there was a segment of human culture fascinated by the aliens, and their crazy tales of ancient history and AI wars. There were movies, some human, some not. There were even some real images, unfaded as the years would not age digital data.

Concentration camps. Sentient beings herded like farm animals of old, branded, spiked and burned. Screams and sobbing, instant death for those who resisted, slow death for many who didn't. Mass annihilation for whole peoples who got in the way, for little more than inconvenience. Some beings had been allowed to live undisturbed, for simple luck that the machines had no interest in them. Others were able to be useful. Some periods of relative calm lasted centuries. But always it came back eventually, and the many, many attempts at armed uprising were crushed without mercy or success.

At least humanity took its hit in one fast punch, Trace thought. We got knocked down, then got straight back up again. This endless, living death of hope seemed suddenly far worse. No wonder the Dobruta had been at their task so long. And no wonder they were so scared at the prospect of any of this, even a tiny whisper from the past, coming back.

"And this was a drysine base," Alomaim reminded them. *"The* good *hacksaws. Just imagine the deepynines."*

"Don't want to, thanks," said Hale in a small voice, turning herself to jet back to her work. Alomaim gave her a pat on the shoulder, and they shared a look that Trace could not see past the visors. Hale left in a white thrust-burst, and Romki went off after Hale to join the techs and see what they'd learned.

"Hey," said Trace to her Lieutenant on direct coms. Alomaim came to her, so she could nearly see his eyes past the heavy visor, above the fearsome visage of armoured combat mask and breather. "How's she doing?" Nodding after Ensign Hale.

"She's good. She's tough. For a spacer."

"And how are you doing?" Pointedly. There were few secrets on warships, and Ahmed Alomaim and Remy Hale was a relatively open one. It wasn't interfering with his work here that Trace could see — Hale was senior *Phoenix* crew currently on the base, and so deserved the most senior protection.   He wasn't ditching responsibilities just to hang with his girl.

"I'm fine Major.   I'm doing my job."

"I know you are.   Just remember that she's a rank below you, and technically it's fraternisation."   Technically Fleet regs said a lot of things weren't allowed.   In reality, individual ships spent too much time out in deep space on their own to be regularly subjected to outside standards review.   Standards were set by the ship's senior officers, and as the saying went, the standard you walked past was the standard you accepted.   Trace had never yet in her entire career walked past a below-par operational standard, and very few at-par ones either, with her marines at least.   But most of the time, this kind of thing was different.   "Look, I don't care who you poke while off-duty.   If I see the slightest evidence that it's affecting your field performance, then I'll care.   But I know your professional standards, and I suspect you'd catch it before it got to that."

Alomaim took a deep breath.   *"I'll find somewhere else to guard."*

"I didn't say that.   I just said be careful.   It's already got me paying attention, because I have to pay attention to everything my Lieutenants do.   It's not like I don't have other things to pay attention to."

Alomaim nodded slowly.   *"Yes Major.   I'll be careful."*   He turned and jetted away.   Regret tried to creep up on Trace unawares. She smacked it down hard.   Other people might have the luxury of telling those beneath them to live their lives and be happy.   She didn't.   Too much was riding on her Lieutenants not screwing up.

"You know," said Hiro on close coms, *"if the LC just promoted Rooke to a full Lieutenant, then Hale moves up to Second Lieutenant, which is the equal rank to a marine full Lieutenant."*

Trace looked, and found him floating surrepticiously nearby. He just seemed to have that knack of being somewhere without being noticed.   "Thank you for explaining the Fleet ranking system to me," she said.   "Were you listening in?"   How he'd figured to do that on one-on-one communications, she didn't know.   Spies.

"I'm just saying, Engineering is usually commanded by a full Lieutenant. There's a lot of people strangely reluctant to give or accept promotions lately."

She couldn't argue with that. "Strictly speaking, equally ranked officers aren't supposed to be banging either."

"It's better between marines and spacers, surely?" Hiro pulled himself over, not bothering with the burner. *"It's easier to maintain professional distance when you're not operating in the same field or sharing the same skillsets. Or even bunking in the same parts of the ship."*

It struck Trace as a strange location to be having the discussion. But then, everything was strange lately. "People think it doesn't hurt. People want what they want. They justify all things to themselves — one more slice of cake, one more hit of drugs, one more roll in the sack. And then it hurts them, every time."

"Were you hurt?" Hiro wondered, pulling up before her. His spacer suit had an open visor, exposing more of his face. Looking hard, trying to see her eyes behind the narrower marine visor.

Trace smiled. "A tragic romantic past? Would make a nice story, wouldn't it? No, I do my job. I *am* my job."

"That sounds lonely."

"You think?" She gestured at the crew about the chamber, her marines amongst them. "Civvies pity me because I don't do civvie relationships. I pity civvies because they'll never know the marine family. I'm never alone. And as Kulina, I know that the collective karma of the galaxy rests upon my choices. I'll leave civvies to waste their lives fretting about romantic love. I've got a real life."

Lisbeth awoke as Major Thakur opened the door to their quarters, a glare of light from the corridor, and the drone of ventilation and other systems. Then a clank as it shut again, the rustle of clothes being removed, and a closet opened for toiletries to be put away. Lisbeth slitted her eyes open, and saw the Major only in dull silhouette, hair still damp from her shower. A blink on the uplink icon in her lower vision showed her the time — 0210, still four hours of second-shift to go.

"How did it go?" Lisbeth asked.

"We got the deepynine drones back," said the Major, unwinding some strapping about one hand. Lisbeth hadn't realised she'd hurt it. Typically of marines, she'd just wrapped it and kept working. "Romki's dragging them to Engineering, where there's now a huge debate about whether to let the drysine queen see them now, or whether to process the remains first." She gave a small shrug. "Not my department."

"I should get down there and help with that," said Lisbeth, and dragged herself from her bunk. In civilian life she'd hated to miss sleep, and her sisters had teased her for her slow morning starts. But there was a conscious drysine queen down in Engineering, about to meet one of her ancient enemy deepynines for the first time in eons, albeit a dead one. If a straight-A engineering student couldn't get out of bed for that, she couldn't get out of bed for anything.

"Nice to see you're alone in here," the Major observed.

Lisbeth frowned quizzically, fishing her fresh jumpsuit from the under-bunk storage locker. "Who would I be with?"

"I have no idea. I find it alarming just how little idea I have, with some of my marines."

Lisbeth repressed a yawn as she stripped off the old jumpsuit and pulled on the new, somewhat flattered that the Major was bothering to share this with her at all. "Does it really matter if crew sleep with each other?"

"I've seen it completely screw up working relationships between marines. Completely. If it happens within one of my platoons, I'll transfer them to different platoons immediately, and different ships if possible. Though that's no longer an option now. Marines shouldn't screw around with other marines — that's what spacers are for."

"People don't really have any control over who they fall in love with, though," Lisbeth reasoned.

"Yes they do," said the Major, climbing past Lisbeth onto the top bunk. "That's one of these soft rationalisations people make to excuse their lack of willpower. It's easy to control."

"Have *you* ever found yourself attracted to men and not acting on it?" Lisbeth asked, standing to pull on and clip her spacer harness.

Face on her pillows, the Major smiled. "You don't inspect my locker for vibrating electric objects, I won't inspect yours."

Lisbeth grinned. "Well no, that's *not* actually what I was asking."

"I know what you were asking. Of course I have. I'm human. The only thing that makes Kulina different from anyone else is discipline. Most people have to force themselves to discipline, but Kulina couldn't live without it, we've never known anything else. Women in the corps are outnumbered, and there are a lot of very impressive men around. You might have noticed."

Lisbeth smiled self-consciously. "I might have."

"You still get a few people making a fuss about mixing genders in the forces. They say that it hurts too much for men to see women get hurt or killed. They say men get protective. It's possibly even true, but then we're supposed to risk our necks for each other, gender aside." All amusement faded from her face, her eyes distant. "What they never talk about is that it cuts both ways. When I was a young Lieutenant in my first action, I had a couple of great young guys in my command have... very bad things happen to them. Combat things. I hadn't even realised I'd had a slight crush on either of them until I saw them... wrecked like that. And I realised that it's bad enough losing any friends without those kinds of extra attachments. Never again."

"Can you really just switch that off, though?" Lisbeth asked quietly.

"No," the Major said tiredly. "No, maybe you can't. Maybe we're all just playing pretend. But I'm very good at pretending, and I've had a lot of practise. I'm so good I can even fool myself. And I like it that way." Her eyes met Lisbeth's. "Go on, you'll miss the great AI cataclysm. You can tell me about it if anyone's still alive when I wake up." She closed her eyes.

"Major? It's probably a silly question, but I'd been meaning to ask..." Thakur's eyes opened once more, waiting calmly. "Has it been harder for you? As a woman? I mean, you're the only living female Liberty Star recipient, for one thing."

"It's always harder for women," said Thakur. "So what?"

"Well it's just... my family. I mean my mother, she's very strong on gender roles, and I wanted to be an engineer, and... well let's say it's been an issue. And mine's not the only family like that. So many things are still unfair."

"In this life," said the Major, "there are obstacles, and there are forces that overcome obstacles. You can be either one, or the other. No in-betweens. If you refuse to even try and clear an obstacle, then you *become* the obstacle. You yourself. So you have to decide which one you are. The obstacle? Or the force that overcomes obstacles. Don't complain. Just choose. And then once you've chosen, and are honest with yourself about *which* you've chosen, you'll know that whatever the outcome of what comes next, it was meant to be."

Lisbeth blinked at her. "But what if the outcome is that I'm killed while attempting to clear an obstacle that was never clearable in the first place?"

The Major smiled, closing her eyes once more. "Exactly. Now you understand."

CHAPTER 27

Erik leaned on a storage rack and watched the techs securing the brace to the deck, to keep the deepynine carcass from becoming 'loose gear', and a manoeuvring hazard.   They hammered and cranked to get the bolts in place, all second-shift crew, though some of first-shift were up and watching, bleary-eyed but intense.   The carcass itself was just the forward part that contained the head, indistinct from the rest of the body save that the techs had sawn it clean through to get it out, and back aboard PH-1 in a state that didn't scare anyone unnecessarily.

Three eyes this time, Erik thought, sipping coffee and staring at the ruined dark-silver beast.   One big eye and two lower at the sides.   Irregularly offset, perhaps for depth-perception.   A few drops of residual fluid dripped on the deck.   The techs said it had gushed out when they'd cut it, like synthetic blood.   Scanning had confirmed it contained no nano particles.   That was the last thing they needed — a hacksaw nano infestation on the ship.

Lisbeth arrived at Erik's side, edging past several watching crew.   Erik patted the spare bit of storage shelf beside him, and she came and leaned, also sipping coffee.   Like any true *Phoenix* crewman, she'd come via the kitchen coffee tap first.

"Wow," Lisbeth said above the noise.   "Surreal, much."

Erik nodded.   "*Makimakala* wanted to send people to come and look, but we said no."

Lisbeth glanced at him.   "Is it serious?"

"We're barely on speaking terms at the moment.   I'm not quite about to kick them out of the apartment, but they're definitely sleeping on the couch.   How's Trace?"

Lisbeth frowned.   "You can't call her Trace.   She's the Major."

"I call her Trace all the time in private.   All senior officers use first names, we only use ranks where enlisted crew can hear." Lisbeth made a face.   "You could call her Trace too, in private. She'd probably prefer it."

"If she'd prefer it, she can tell me."

"She's big on people making personal choices. She won't tell you to do anything unless you're in her chain of command." Lisbeth thought about that, eyes straying to where Romki sat in terse conversation with his display screen beside the drysine queen's head. That watching red eye, suspended in the nano-fluid, gave her the creeps. "So how is she?"

"Well you know," said Lisbeth with a shrug. There wasn't really much to be said about Major Thakur that wouldn't be cheapened with words. "Does she have any family?"

"Kulina don't see much of their family," said Erik. "They join young and sever a lot of family ties. Trace was particularly eager to leave her family. I hear her dad was a bastard and her mum was indifferent, they had a tough life in a mining base. Sugauli's a rough place, it was founded in violence and it's no garden spot. We glorify and mysticize it, but it's a traumatised culture to this day. I think for Trace, the Kulina were an escape."

"Did she tell you that?"

"No. She doesn't talk about it. And I wouldn't advise asking — she's not sensitive about much, but Kaspowitz says she won't talk about it even with him, and they've been friends for ages."

"Okay," came Romki's voice across the noise. "Okay, I'm getting a reading on that spike... could you... is that firm contact?" As the hammering died and techs looked on, while one spacer manoeuvred a slim instrument that Erik did not recognise into a gruesome gap in the deepynine's armour.

Erik and Lisbeth flipped down their AR glasses. "You've been talking to Romki about the queen's status?" he asked Lisbeth.

"Um, yeah," Lisbeth said nervously.

"And?"

"Shouldn't you, like, get a proper briefing from Stan or Rooke?"

"I have, but Stan and Rooke talk like machines. I'd rather hear it from you."

"Right." Lisbeth took a deep breath, and tried not to be nervous. It was only her brother. "Well what we're talking to is certainly not 'the queen'. I mean, in my opinion anyway."

"Don't qualify everything," Erik said calmly. "Go on."

"Well the construct the tavalai helped create is nearly complex enough to be low-sentience in its own right. Maybe. But it takes more than just complexity to create sentience, or that's what my college instructor told me... not that humans are allowed to do it, of course. It takes structure too. The surviving portions of the queen's brain are providing some of that structure, and the construct is drawing on those through the nano-tank."

"So the construct can access some of her memories, com functions and other stuff," Erik reasoned.

"Right."

"But it can't actually *think* using that original brain, because the Major blew that part away."

"Sure," Lisbeth agreed. "Basically. But then, the Major's pretty sure the queen's a lot smarter than she lets on. Stan says some of those surviving brain portions might be doing a lot more than their original designation. He says they're a lot more active than you'd expect, and that some of the old Dobruta literature says hacksaws use outerlying brain segments to store primary information..."

"Like making a backup of the mainframe," Erik interrupted.

Lisbeth nodded. "Exactly. So if the construct is really accessing the backup of her main CPU... then we might be talking to something far closer to the real thing."

"In your opinion," said Erik. "Is it sentient right now? Or just a set of automated responses?"

"I..." Lisbeth trailed off as she thought about it. "I think that's a very outmoded concept of AI consciousness. I mean, the automated/reasoned divide. Most of what the human brain does is automated, we don't pay conscious thought to most of it. Just because most of the queen's responses are automatic doesn't mean it's not aware of what it's doing."

"There!" Rooke interrupted, peering at his screens as techs manoeuvred the spikes into the deepynine's neural clusters. "There that's got it, it's downloading data." It certainly was. Erik could see the data levels shooting upward, filling out a 3D data construct.

Adequate, spelt out the cursor on AR glasses and data screens.

"Is that enough?" Romki pressed. "Are you getting enough data?" No reply. Possibly it didn't like pointless questions, Lisbeth thought. "What can you tell us about it?"

Deepynine. Command function. Designation uncertain.

"You've never encountered this designation before?" Romki asked.

"Maybe she never had much combat experience in the war," said Rooke.

"Don't be silly," said Romki. "AI memories are collective, she doesn't need to have been there herself."

"She might not be very old," Rooke protested. "She might have been made after the war, we don't know what replication technologies survived — there were none sufficient in the rock at Argitori, but she hadn't been there for the full twenty five thousand years."

It gave Lisbeth an idea. "This designation is unfamiliar," she said loudly enough to cut through the men's conversation. "Is this designation more or less advanced than familiar designations?"

More, said the text.

Everyone looked at Lisbeth. "This deepynine was made after the war," Lisbeth explained. "Possibly a lot later. That's why she doesn't recognise it."

"Well hang on," Rooke protested. "There's too many variables to…"

Yes, said the text. **She is correct.** Rooke abandoned his protest, and Lisbeth gave him a 'so there' look. **Deepynine command unit. Advanced.**

"What level of technological sophistication is required to build something like this?" Romki pressed. "Could you make this deepynine unit in a small base or outpost? Or would it require a large civilisation? Big space stations, a large economy?"

Large, the queen admitted. And Romki slumped in his seat, staring at his screen. Confirmation of his theory, Erik thought, with a cold chill. Deepynines were still out there. In production, on a large scale.

"Alo," Romki breathed. "It has to be the alo."

Deepynine unit memory corrupted. Unable to access data.

"Well what *can* you tell us?" Erik asked.

Memory corruption intentional. A security measure. Security measure is high deepynine command-level. Alien to sard.

"Wait," Rooke said eagerly. "Does that mean only another AI could have written the code that caused the memory to corrupt under examination?"

Only the highest deepynine command-level.

"How high?" asked Romki.

The highest.

"A queen!" Lisbeth breathed. "The sard have a deepynine queen! Erik, she's probably at this shipbuilding base we're looking for. She's probably running the whole show... who else would know how to reprogram those drysine drones that attacked Joma Station? The sard don't know how, but she would."

Further data, scrolled the text, not disagreeing. **Deepynine unit has unique optical and radiation settings. Suggest unique solar environment. Combination matches datapoint memory.**

"Oh no *way!*" gasped Second Lieutenant Rooke, sounding more like the whiz kid he'd once been than the Fleet officer he'd become. "She's found the base!"

"Show us," Erik commanded. A starchart visual appeared on his AR glasses, holographic projection and finely detailed. It rotated as strange, alien lines appeared between glowing centres of highlighted activity — huge long strings of them, criss-crossed with jump-lanes like freeways, long since adjusted for solar motions as space-time expanded. Hacksaw civilisation in the time of the drysine-deepynine war.   Erik stared, mouth open.   Amidst the profusion, one system highlighted and blinked.   Letters appeared — Gsi-81T. "Are you familiar with this system?"

It is on charts.   Production base, primary class.   No record exists of its destruction.   Likely survivor of deepynine-drysine wars.

"Show us what you know."

The holographic visual upon the glasses changed, and something new appeared.   It was a sphere, made up of an open, skeletal structure in two distinct hemispheres about a central core. It looked a bit like the skeleton of some dead sea urchin washed up on a beach.   Erik squinted, trying to make sense of what he saw. Then the image zoomed upon a small speck to one side... and his mouth dropped open again.   The speck was a warship.   A big one, to judge by the ratio of engines to crew cylinder... and next to this big, open structure, it was a small dot in space.

"Oh good fucking god," Romki muttered.   Many of the techs gasped or swore as well, as they grasped the scale of it.

Drysine mid-orbital industrial complex, fifty-first iteration of preliminary design, scrolled the text.   **One hundred and twenty of your kilometres in diameter.   Lithium fusion core, inner storage modules are for powerplant manufacture, inner rims for neural processing, basic mining and alloy refinery on the outer rims.   Capable of producing one priority-class warship approximately per one human week, indefinitely, materials allowing, with a production timeline of half-a-year per ship.**

"Twenty-five at a time," Lisbeth breathed.   "Fifty per year. Dozens of similar facilities."   It made current human capabilities look tiny.   And this was just one section of drysine-controlled space.

No wonder the organics unfortunate enough to be around in the Machine Age had never stood a chance, Erik thought. Production capabilities like this were unknown in all the galaxy today.   Unless the alo had something similar, and had only been committing a tiny fraction of what they could produce to the Triumvirate War.   The possibility turned his blood cold.   He had to get in there and see what the sard had done with this thing.   And who had helped them set it up.

"What are its defensive systems?" Erik asked.

A second flood of text followed, as though the queen were losing her inhibitions.   **Numerous, but subject to alteration if currently under deepynine control.   My data will be obsolete and dangerously misleading.   Presence of sard/deepynine vessel at TK55 suggests they are aware of the threat.   Direct assault with combined force of *Phoenix*, *Makimakala* and *Rai Jang* appears to have negligible chance of success.   Recommend the accumulation of greater forces.**

Everyone in the room was looking at Erik.   It was his call, Erik knew.   Lieutenant Commander or not, this was his ship to command, and he was supposed to be the guy with the answers.

He exhaled hard.   "She's not wrong," he admitted. "Problem is, right now we appear to be short of friends."

"*All hands, take hold!*" came Second Lieutenant Abacha's call from the bridge.   "*Jump contact, combat V, Phoenix is red alert!*"

Everyone ran, like animals at the waterhole scattering when a predator attacks.   Erik grabbed Lisbeth and joined them, ship schematic immediately flashing on his glasses as it did in manoeuvre emergencies, indicating unoccupied acceleration slings.   He pushed Lisbeth into one of the slings that burst from their emergency seals on the G-wall, then ignored a spacer indicating he should take another and ran for the bridge.   There were no slings in the trunk corridor, any passage running fore-to-aft was prone to being hit at killing velocities by anything breaking loose at high-thrust further up, and if snapped would become killing projectiles themselves along with their occupants.

Spacers running about him darted into side-corridors, and sling-icons on his glasses were quickly occupied, like the craziest game of musical chairs.   Then the ten-second countdown started, and Erik realised that he wasn't going to make it anywhere close to the bridge.   He took the next left, past two occupied slings then into an unoccupied one at five seconds.   A quick turn to orient himself with his back to the G-wall, pulling the synthetic mesh up around his shoulders. Zero seconds, and thrust kicked him clean off his feet and back into the sling hard, as rotational G eased, then faded completely. His back nearly touched the G-wall as thrust increased, then with a whine the net motors pulled the sling tighter as the sides enfolded around him, and he managed with effort to zip himself in from the inside, then clip his harness to the inner clips.

Just as hard as it had begun, G eased. They weren't running, Erik realised with relief — that would mean abandoning their people on TK55. They were headed to TK55, much faster than a shuttle could, to intercept the shuttle already on standby there, and save several minutes on their retrieval time. The away-crew would be racing now, getting into those big transit passages in the base and jetting up to impressive speeds to reach the shuttle.

Erik accessed command feed without having to ask, and bridge scan feed appeared on his glasses — scan with inbound ships, three so far, two-minutes-light and closing fast. Erik did fast calculations and wondered if he'd have the time to get up to the bridge. They were closing on TK55 but not too fast, there was no need to arrive before their crew was ready to be picked up. Lieutenant Alomaim was in command over there, with Ensign Hale, Erik's old friend from when he'd been third-shift commander. And he realised that it would only be worth getting up to bridge if his entire first-shift bridge crew could get up there with him. Bridge crews were a team, and putting himself at the head of a team more accustomed to Draper could conceivably lead to worse outcomes than if he stayed in his sling.

"Lieutenant Draper, I'm reading active tracking!" came Abacha again from Scan. *"It's close range. I think one of those mines just went active, it's tracking us."*

"Query Makimakala," Draper said calmly. *"Nav, I want that escape trajectory."*

"Aye Lieutenant," came Lieutenant De Marchi's reply. *"I have three possibles on best escape track. We going with or without Makimakala?"*

"Depends what they say about that mine," Draper said reasonably.

"This is away team," came Lieutenant Alomaim's voice, crackling with interference. *"ETA two minutes fifty. PH-3 confirm position?"*

"This is PH-3, do not *decelerate upon leaving the transit tunnel. Maintain velocity, PH-3 will rendezvous with* you. *Away team respond."*

"Away team copies PH-3, make it a good catch."

They were going to come flying out of that transit tunnel at over a hundred kph accumulated velocity, and PH-3 was going to chase and intercept to save time. Heck of a thing with Engineering department spacers along who didn't practise emergency retrieval intercepts as often as marines did. Shit, Erik thought as the bridge chatter continued, fast and professional. If Draper screwed this up they could not only lose lives, they could ruin whatever relations were left with *Makimakala*, possibly even end up shooting at them. He had to get up there… only he couldn't, he needed a clear window of at least a minute with no possible manoeuvring to change bridge crews.

If that mine hadn't locked on he might have got that minute, but if tavalai mines started chasing them, possibly attracted by the sudden manoeuvres in their midst, there was the real chance that *Phoenix* would have to push hard enough to make red smears of anyone moving unsecured in the ship. Draper would do it too, even if it was the LC unsecured. The first thing they drummed into you in the Academy when you sat the command chair was that it didn't matter who was loose on the ship when a ship-killing scenario came racing at you — you moved, or everyone died. It was of course the reason why they didn't allow family to serve together on warships, and strongly discouraged anyone who sat the chair from having intimate relations with crew. In the wrong situation, you had to be prepared to kill your own crew to save the ship. Erik thought of Lisbeth. He knew *Phoenix* crew had made common agreement with each other that getting Lisbeth into an acceleration sling was number one priority in any trouble. They did it not from chivalry, but from the real fear that their LC might not hit thrust when he had to, and would get them all killed from his concern for his sister.

"Incoming transmission!" came Lieutenant Lassa on Coms. *"Signal registers as Fleet, light delay one minute forty-six."*

"Hello UFS Phoenix. This is UFS Mercury, Captain Ritish commanding. By order of Fleet Command, you will surrender your ship and accept Fleet terms of pardon, as previously stipulated by marine Colonel Khola. Failing this you will be declared outlaw from all humanity, and hunted to destruction at the ends of the galaxy if necessary. Mercury out, awaiting your reply."

"Rai Jang is outbound hard!" Abacha announced. *"Rai Jang is leaving!"*

"Hello Rai Jang," said Draper. *"Hello Rai Jang, please explain your actions, Phoenix out?"*

"Is he going to attack them?" someone wondered in disbelief.

No, Erik realised. As commander-off-the-bridge, he had to be careful interfering with bridge operations and allow Draper his space to work. But this intervention would save time.

"Hello bridge, this is the LC," he said. *"Rai Jang* led them here. Joma Station barabo were already working with Fleet, *Rai Jang*'s captain as good as warned us himself. They want Fleet to take over barabo security, so they're working with Fleet to catch us. That's the only way *Mercury* could have found us so fast."

"Dammit," said Draper.

"Lieutenant, I have a shot," said Second Lieutenant Corrig from Arms. *"Do I fire on Rai Jang?"*

"No," said Draper before Erik could intervene with the same answer. *"Let the treacherous furry bastard go."*

"Makimakala queries status," said Lassa.

"Second mine targeting! Is Makimakala doing that?"

"Braking," said Draper, and thrust kicked Erik toward the G-wall again, the line of acceleration slings bobbing and swinging in unison, like fruits on a branch in a storm. *"Makimakala, this is Phoenix. Rai Jang is a traitor, barabo working for human Fleet.*

Did you receive last human transmission?" Because it would have been Fleet encrypted.

"This is Makimakala, we copied that transmission." So much for Fleet encryption being unreadable by tavalai. *"We are engaged in rapid retrieval of personnel from TK55, ETA three-and-a-half minutes."*

"Copy Makimakala, Phoenix is also retrieving, ETA three minutes. Two tavalai mines have locked onto us, please explain?"

"It's not us, Phoenix. If we were targeting you, you'd be locked by a hundred plus, and they wouldn't have given warning. These systems are very old, it's possible your aggressive manoeuvres have triggered them. We will attempt to contact and override."

"Yeah well tell him to make it fast," said Corrig. *"One of them's orienting to engage."*

"Arms, hold fire until you absolutely have to. If you blow one of them away the whole bunch will charge us. Coms, get me Mercury. LC, are you reading this? Do you want to tell them, or should I?"

"You can do it, Lieutenant." In some ways, he thought, it would carry more weight from someone other than himself. "Just remember, there are marines on *Mercury*, commanded by Major Rennes, who helped us on Hoffen Station."

"Understood LC. Hello UFS Mercury, this is Phoenix. We have uncovered evidence of a large hacksaw ship-building base previously undiscovered and currently occupied by sard. Reason to believe this base is under the command of a deepynine queen, and is building ships for the sard, several of which tried twice to kill us, including just recently on Joma Station. If you'd like to help us destroy this base, that would be a great service to humanity. If not, then we are not humanity's enemies — you are. Major Thakur sends greetings to Major Rennes, and would like to tell him that Phoenix marines just killed several deepynine command drones and sard forces in this hacksaw base. What have Mercury marines done for humanity lately? Phoenix out."

"Timelag counting," said Lassa on Coms. *"Expect reply in three minutes thirty at earliest. Nice one Lieutenant."*

There followed some more growls of agreement. It nearly made Erik smile. As commander, he'd often wondered just how many of his crew were behind him, as he led them on this venture that could make them enemies of their species, and possibly get them all killed besides. This outburst of spontaneous, heartfelt support was gratifying.

"*This is PH-3, all away crew aboard, Operations prepare for docking in forty seconds.*" Lieutenant Jersey sounded cooler than a winter breeze as she burned her shuttle's engines to get clear of the starship hangar and out to *Phoenix*. With three ace shuttle pilots all in friendly competition to see who was the most shit-hot of them all, Erik just hoped one of them wouldn't overdo it.

"*Makimakala is sending navigation coordinates for jump,*" said Lieutenant Lassa. "*Routing it to Navigation.*"

"*Nav copies.*"

"*Makimakala,*" said Draper. "*What's the story with this heading?*"

"*Your Fleet won't dare follow us there,*" came the reply. "*Trust us. We have control of ninety-three percent of surrounding mines, the rest are not responding adequately. Sending non-responses to your tactical, Makimakala out.*"

"*That's coming through,*" said Lassa. "*Routing to Helm.*"

"*Helm copies,*" Dufresne replied.

"*PH-3 aboard in five seconds.*"

"*Arms is targeting those rogue mines.*"

"*Navigation course set.*"

"*PH-3 aboard.*"

"*Wait for Makimakala,*" said Draper. "*Scan, you see their shuttles?*"

"*Nearly there. Looks close, last shuttle closing now. Shuttle aboard, Makimakala is leaving.*"

"*Phoenix is leaving.*" Hard thrust shoved Erik's sling back far harder than before, Gs blurring his vision, the sling's motors squealing to keep him off the G-wall.

"*Mines reactive! Two marks inbounds!*"

"Arms, kill them please." Two detonations on scan, neat and precise.

"Two down, we have multiple activations..."

"Makimakala is firing!" More mines disappeared, *Makimakala* slightly ahead of the game, knowing which was the greatest threat. *"Mines targeting Makimakala, they've halved our target load."*

"Getting real narrow ahead," Dufresne observed, as mines along their projected path began to activate. *"Prepare full evasive, targeting rotation for full fire spread."*

"Copy full rotation, Arms respond?"

"Arms copies." As Erik's old third-shift buddy Raf Corrig blasted several more, firing freely as *Phoenix* rotated at full thrust, bringing all weapons into play about the hull.

"Swing two-eighty," Dufresne advised as she plotted a better course ahead, watching the far-trajectory where Draper had to take the near. *"Seventy degree yaw, full thrust, punch it."* And thrust increased to a full, bone-bending 10-Gs as *Phoenix* strained to escape the field of defective mines that could accelerate at twice that rate. Those that did, Arms pasted before they could go evasive — magfire only, none had yet gotten close enough for defensive spreads.

"Clear in ten." More firing, and several racing mines got within five seconds of impact before exploding short as Corrig and Mendez on Arms One and Two tasked the guns with margin to spare. *"Clear, we are clear."*

"Makimakala is clear."

"Proceeding to jump," Draper confirmed. *"Navlink to Makimakala on exit, let's keep this tight."*

"Where you think she's taking us?" Second Lieutenant Zelele wondered from Scan Two.

"Home to meet grandma," said Lassa. Then, *"Incoming from Mercury."*

"UFS Phoenix," came Captain Ritish's voice. *"You have made a most unwise call. It is my solemn duty to inform you that as of this moment, UFS Phoenix and all her crew will be considered..."*

"Turn that bitch off," said Draper, and the voice ceased. *"Much better. Jump in two minutes fourteen, all hands stand by."*

CHAPTER 28

As he blinked to focus from the disorientation of post-jump, Erik recalled how much he hated combat jump as a passenger. The dim shapes of neighbouring occupied slings bobbed and wobbled through the mesh of his own cocoon, and it felt vaguely like one of those dreams where he found himself back in school, with all his adult securities and achievements taken away from him. He could almost imagine old school friends laughing at him when he told them he was actually a Fleet warship commander.

'Oh go *on*, Erik! A job your mother didn't arrange for you? That millions of other kids fantasise about having?' Of course, at the elite private schools he'd attended, most of his friends had been in the same boat.

He fumbled within the sling pouch for a water bottle and an electrolyte bar, washing the latter down with the former as he blinked on his glasses' command icon to restore the link that had gone dead in jump. Bridge chatter filled his ears once more as he refocused, and then scan's system display flashed on his glasses. He didn't even know what system they were in, he realised — *Makimakala* had put that to *Phoenix* Nav post without making it onto his feed. Only here ahead of them, he recognised the little red triangles of unidentified ships that Scancomp didn't like the look of. Only three minutes light, and in parking orbit about a smallish planetoid of the kind that might make a good military base. More likely that than a trading base — there was no other traffic in the system that scan could see, and trading bases tended to avoid messy rocks for more efficient rotary designs.

"Hello Makimakala," he heard Lieutenant Draper saying on coms. *"We read those ships ahead as tavalai warships, please confirm?"*

"Hello Phoenix," came Captain Pram's voice. *"Yes this is a tavalai fleet hiding spot. You have just been in big trouble with your fleet, now you can watch me be in big trouble with mine. But my first priority is to lose this pursuit, and this was my first choice."*

346

"Phoenix copies." A click, and then, *"Hello LC, I judge we may have a six minute window here at minimum until we get a response from those tavalai ships. Are you coming up?"*

Erik wanted nothing as badly. "Hello Lieutenant Draper," he said. "That's a negative, *UFS Mercury* could be jumping in behind us at any moment. Continue as before."

"Aye LC." He could almost hear the surprise in Draper's voice. In truth, the likelihood of *Mercury* plunging out of jump right on top of them was low. More likely she'd come out somewhere nearby, but leaving a several minute window between manoeuvres, allowing enough time to transition the bridge crew back to first-shift. But interrupting a bridge crew in mid-action could be troublesome — crews got 'in the zone' when tackling a situation, and new crews took minutes to adjust and catch up. Erik judged that Draper's crew were totally in the zone, and should be left to handle things for now. Furthermore, they'd impressed him so far, and deserved his praise and confidence. Many of them had minimal time in action outside of sims, and there was no experience like the real thing. If anything happened to him or others in first-shift, *Phoenix* was going to need good replacements who wouldn't need endless hand-holding when they stepped up to the big-time. And his sacrifice for helping that happen was to hang here in zero-G cocooned frustration for the next however-long period.

The private call icon blinked, and Erik opened it. *"That's a good call LC,"* Kaspowitz told him. *"If it somehow fails to kill us, I'll buy you a drink next stop."*

"Thank you Kaspo," said Erik. "Your vote of confidence is always welcome."

Mercury came out of jump five minutes later, with one cruiser that Abacha on Scan correctly stated had to be korchek-class, the only Fleet non-carrier class capable of staying with a battle carrier through jump. Positionally they were offset by ten-seconds-light, and behind by another seven. 'Uphill' on this system's gravity slope, *Mercury* would have been in an ideal position to block *Phoenix*'s possible escape runs within their own entry arc, and force her to run long across-system to get out the far side while exposing herself to fire all the way. But with *Makimakala* here, *Mercury* was outgunned… assuming the unthinkable would happen, and a Fleet warship joined forces with a tavalai warship to take on one of their own.

"*Hello LC,*" Draper said to Erik. "*Do you want to explain the facts of life to Captain Ritish, or shall I?*" He sounded a little cocky, Erik thought. Good. Among warship pilots, cocky was always better than tentative.

"Hello Lieutenant. Yes, I think I might take this one. Lieutenant Lassa, please get me a connection to *UFS Mercury*."

"*I copy LC, you are on lasercom transmission to Mercury, go ahead.*"

"Hello Captain Ritish," Erik said calmly, aware of the spacer in the sling alongside looking at him. Through the mesh, he couldn't tell who it was. "Nice to see you made it safely through jump. I have no idea who these tavalai ahead of us are, but I could guess that they're remnants of the tavalai fleet hiding from us so the human Fleet won't demand them decommissioned as per the peace treaty. I couldn't guess if they're going to be friendly to *Phoenix*, but I'm quite sure they're not going to be friendly to *Mercury*. So unless you want to help us destroy the hacksaw base I mentioned, and you're quite welcome to do so, I suggest you turn around and head back the way you came. *Phoenix* out."

Triangulation told him the light-delay should be about eleven seconds each way. He counted patiently to twenty-two, as bridge chatter continued, and Coms registered *Makimakala* sending to the much more distant tavalai warships. Twenty-two seconds passed. Then thirty. Then forty.

"*Mercury just dumped V,*" said Abacha. Erik felt relief, but no real surprise. Confronted by this, Captain Ritish had no real choice. But also, he felt the cold, fearful realisation that this was it. *Phoenix* was on her own. Fleet may not be able to pursue her any further, but with that, *Phoenix* also abandoned all lingering hope that someone from that old life might come to their senses and help them. The UF Marine Corps might broadly support them, but marines were incapable of action without spacer approval. Debogande

Incorporated might broadly support them, but DI was an enormous organisation comprised mostly of people who were more interested in their own jobs and families than in risking everything to support the dubious actions of the naming-family's black sheep son. And Worlder politicians might have some enduring affection for them, but Worlders were as effective at opposing Fleet as were goldfish staring up at the human faces looming over their bowl. And as they progressed on this hunt deeper into alien territories, human space was falling further and further behind.

"Signal from one of the tavalai ships," said Lassa. *"It's tavalai fleet encryption, can't break it but it seems of a conversational length. Makimakala's answering."*

"Maybe they're discussing how they'll cook us," De Marchi suggested.

"Okay," said Erik. "We'll give it another five minutes. If nothing changes, we'll coordinate approaches with *Makimakala* and downgrade to orange alert. Scan, please keep a close eye on *Mercury* in the meantime."

Three minutes later, one of the tavalai vessels boosted up to come out and meet them. It was not an aggressive move — the Scancomp was close enough now to read the ship as kurialima-class and nothing like powerful enough to be threatening to *Phoenix*. This ship was headed out at *Mercury*, to investigate and to dissuade *Mercury* from hanging around to watch and gather intel. A minute after that, *Mercury* dumped all remaining V, turned straight back around and boosted up the way she'd come. Heck of a straining move that was, fighting for purchase upon the weak outer grav-slope, but once committed it signalled the end of *Mercury* as an ongoing strategic threat.

At the five minute mark, Erik's glasses flashed orange, and the corridor lights copied in patches. With a thump and hum, the cylinder rotation restarted, and Erik unzipped to get his feet out. There were few things more embarrassing on a warship than to be caught in the sling by restoring gravity, feet stuck in the mesh and hanging like a sack of vegetables while you struggled to extricate yourself, and your neighbours laughed and took photos for wider humiliation.   When he'd been a very green Second Lieutenant on *UFS Firebird*, it had happened to Erik twice.   Thankfully never on *Phoenix*, and his feet hit the deck as gravity restored, and he pulled the rest of the mesh off him with relief while disconnecting his harness, and set about winding it correctly back into its wall-wrap, and setting off for the bridge.

"LC on the bridge!" Dufresne announced as he entered, past Harris, Karle and Jiri from first-shift, waiting for their commander to enter first.

"Thank you second-shift," said Erik, as the rest of first-shift came in behind him.   "Your relief will take the easy part from here. That was outstanding, I don't think first-shift could have done better."   Which was a lie, because first-shift had pulled off some pretty amazing stuff lately, and would likely have nailed that last sequence also.   But the relief that he felt now was a revelation to him — just knowing that second-shift could really handle it, when they had to.

He looked at Lieutenant Draper's face as the younger man unbuckled his restraints, and saw from the weary grin that Draper's relief was even greater.   "How was the ride LC?" Draper asked, handing the headset for Erik to hold.

"Horrible," said Erik.   "I like it much better up here."

"Y'know, me too."   Swinging a display screen aside as he climbed out, and Erik clasped his hand with feeling.

"Fucking ace job," Erik told him.   Draper's often glum, freckled face split with a huge grin, beaming like the nerdy kid who'd just won first place and now had all the pretty girls flirting with him.   Erik decided that he liked this newly acquired power of his — the ability to praise others, and have them take it seriously.   "I mean it, all of you."

He wanted to go around and congratulate each of them personally, but that would have to wait — the command chair could not be empty for even a moment, and he slipped into it now as Draper helped him with the straps, and all across the bridge the other posts did the same.

"Might be out of a job soon LC," said Kaspowitz, as young Lieutenant De Marchi grinned while helping him strap in.

Erik smiled. "I wouldn't go that far. Scan, when you're in, get me a full analysis of who our new 'friends' are. Coms, contact *Makimakala* for me and ask them the same thing."

"I still think this is a bad idea," Trace told him twenty hours later as they over-handed into the rear hold of PH-4. Command Squad was with them, buckling in with full armour, for whatever small good it would do. Erik wore light armour, a cap instead of a helmet, and a small gear bag that he secured in a mesh net beside his seat.

"I know you think it's a bad idea," Erik affirmed. "Hello Tif? We are all secure back here, you are free to proceed."

"Aw crear EwC," Tif confirmed. *"Reave in ten."* Her English comprehension was improving, even if her 'l's were not.

"I know you think you have it all logically figured out," Trace continued. "You think the tavalai have no percentage in taking you hostage because they'd never believe any promise Fleet gave to get you back. And you think tavalai are too principled to do anything nasty. And I'm telling you that those are assumptions, and that caution was invented to guard against dangerous human assumptions."

Clank, as the grapples cut, and PH-4 came clear. Erik smiled at Trace, and to the amusement of Command Squad raised his hand to mime a motor-mouth, always talking. Trace looked displeased.

"Fine," she said, as Tif gave them a gentle thrust from the mains. "Just fine. You could do this over coms, there's no need to do it face to face." Erik sighed, and lowered his helmet visor to look at the scan feed. It showed him *Phoenix* alone, a hundred kilometres from *Makimakala*, and another hundred from five vessels of the regular tavalai fleet. Not long ago, this proximity to tavalai warships, minus velocity, would have been unthinkable unless one or the other had surrendered. Now the situation was weird all round, with no state of war existing between human and tavalai... and yet no peace either. Not long ago Erik would have found it very strange... but since then he'd been in combat operations with *Makimakala*, and now they had a somewhat-live drysine queen in Engineering, and his threshold for strangeness had increased by several degrees. "So you're happy with Lieutenant Draper?" Trace changed the subject, seeing him ignoring her.

"Very happy," said Erik. It was nice to say something good about Draper in front of the lower ranks. They gossiped about such things, and with good reason, given all their lives were in his hands as well as Erik's. It was the same situation he'd been in not long ago, as the dubiously-regarded third-in-command of *Phoenix*. And just like then, whatever was said here by the senior officers would spread through the ship. "He completely nailed it, Dufresne too. That was a tough scenario, all of second-shift worked it perfectly — Arms, Scan, Nav, everyone."

"There was word going around that Dufresne's sim scores were better than Draper's." Erik gave her a warning look. Trace was unapologetic. If word was out, pretending it wasn't would not help.

"They're a little higher," Erik admitted. "But just like with marines, sims are not actual combat. Some people do better at sims than the real thing, others are reverse. Draper's a big time player, he steps up under pressure. Checking back over his previous records, that's what they confirm — better actual results than sim results. And his sims are excellent. Dufresne's are just a little better."

Something bugged him. He frowned, thinking about it. He'd just said something nice about Draper, and Command Squad's marines would repeat those words to others when they could. He knew Captain Pantillo had regarded him well, and Trace had complete faith in the Captain's judgement on matters where he was sure to know better than her. So why hadn't *his* reputation on *Phoenix* done any better, with those two in his corner? His sims were always excellent, and the few times he'd had to take evasive action in scenarios not unlike what Lieutenant Draper had just performed, he'd done equally well.   He'd thought it was just the ever lingering suspicion of his family name, and the conditions of his promotion.   But now as he thought about it, knowing this much more about how reputations on ships worked, something did not add up.

He blinked the uplink icon, and established a private link to Trace.   *"Trace, a question,"* he formulated silently.

"Shoot," she said.

"Did Commander Huang say bad things about me when I wasn't there?"   Because then it would all make sense.   Huang had always smiled and made nice in person, but even off-duty Erik had never gotten anything from her beyond the polite front.   It had always puzzled him, because he was usually pretty good at making friends.   Had he missed this possibility all along?   Had *that* been a large part of the reason why in all his three years on *Phoenix*, he'd never managed to make much of a dent in ship-wide suspicions of his ability?

"She was a bitch," Trace replied.   Erik shook his head in disbelief at his own stupidity.   How hadn't he seen it?   *"I spoke to the Captain about it, and he had a word with her.   It settled down after that, but she'd still stick in the knife from time to time, passive-aggressive like.   You never guessed?"*

"No," Erik admitted.   *"Just occurred to me now."*

"My guess is jealousy," said Trace.   *"Which is dumb, because it's not like her family was poor.   Some people are just fucked up.   I'm sorry, I probably should have told you, but somehow it never came up.   We've been busy."*

"Yes we have," Erik agreed.   It dazed him, to realise that someone he'd looked up to had actually hated him.   And worse, no one had told him she'd been snarking behind his back.   Obviously it hadn't been too bad, or the Captain would have pulled her into line. But she had a long history with Pantillo, and it was personal between them, as friends and wartime comrades.   It hurt to know that he truly had been the outsider, just as he'd feared.   And that Pantillo would still probably have stuck with Huang rather than him, if he'd had to

choose. And that yes, the Captain had certainly picked him because of his family name, whatever his other talents.

That much was obvious now, in observing what had transpired since the Captain's death. The Debogande name had helped keep *Phoenix* alive, had almost certainly contributed to the offer of pardon they'd just refused, had gotten them a shuttle off Homeworld, and possibly a stay of execution in the Shiwon prisoner cells. The Captain had suspected bad things were coming if he continued down his track of supporting Worlder causes, and so he'd needed political cover. Lucky for him, the only son of Alice Debogande had turned out to be an excellent warship pilot and a reasonable Fleet officer, a fortuitous turn that the Captain hadn't been able to ignore. Yes the Captain wouldn't have picked him if he wasn't up to the job, and that job, on Pantillo's ship, came with obscenely high standards. That was some comfort, at least. The rest of it, far less so.

And what else had he missed? Little events he wasn't privy to? Small conversations between old friends Pantillo and Huang, where the former knew the latter had a thing against their new LC, but hadn't told her with sufficient force to keep it to herself? Down-talking the ship's third-shift commander should have earned Huang a bloody mark for indulging, good friend or not. But self-evidently the Captain hadn't given her one, because the down-talking hadn't stopped. And he felt like an idiot, because not only had he completely missed Huang's attitude, but now he was even wondering if he'd missed other things about the Captain, this man he'd idolised and thought could do no wrong. A man who had gotten himself killed pursuing what Erik now knew to be a hopeless cause, and had given friends special treatment where it had interfered with good operational order on his ship.

"Hey," Trace formulated. Erik looked, and found her watching him with mild concern. *"I was worried Huang would step off Europa's ramp on Joma Station when the old crew and volunteers turned up."*

Erik smiled faintly. *"You too, huh?"*

"Yes. I was worried because I figured I might have to toss her out an airlock." Erik frowned at her. *"We can't afford command problems at the top. Some of the crew probably would figure she should be in charge. If she asserted her rank, and rallied those crew, I'd have had to kill her."*

Erik blinked. *"You're serious."*

Trace had never looked more serious. *"She'd split the crew, and she's not a team player, not with you at least. It would have been a disaster. I'm not about to allow that any more than I'd allow Phoenix to be violently boarded. We need our best commander in charge. Not just our best pilot, but our best commander. That's you, on both counts. I knew Huang a lot better than you did, and I knew her a lot better than I knew you, at the time. Now that I know both, I'm telling you — I'm damn glad it's you here and not her. And she's damn lucky she didn't change her mind and come out on Europa with those others, because she wouldn't have conceded to take second-place behind you, and I would have insisted. Violently, if necessary."*

"Do me a favour," Erik said with feeling. *"Don't ever not be on my side."* Such support was welcome, but also a little scary.

"But that's probably why she abandoned us in the first place," Trace added. *"Aside from her family reasons. She didn't like you, and she knew I didn't like her much, mostly because of shit like that. I told her once that I found her behaviour completely unprofessional. She ignored me, and we left it at that."*

That was something, at least. Knowing that he met Trace's standards, while Huang hadn't, made him feel considerably better. And of course Trace had confronted Huang about it. 'Unprofessional' was about the worst thing Trace could say of anyone in uniform. *"Why didn't the Captain pull her up?"*

Trace's expression softened a little. *"He wasn't a perfect man, Erik. He was a great man, a leader, a warrior, a compassionate visionary. And I loved him like a father. But not perfect, no."*

"Well," Erik sighed. *"I suppose it's a part of the progression to adulthood. When the children realise their parents aren't perfect."*

"I knew that about my real father when I was five," Trace said sombrely.

"Was it that bad?" Erik asked.

Trace said nothing for a moment, gazing silently past him. Then she took a deep breath. *"Come on, nearly there. Let's hope the froggies like your aftershave."*

The tavalai cruiser was called *Gabriladova*, a radolima-class cruiser, bigger than most and while not the performance equal of an ibranakala-class, dangerous enough to any who cared to tangle. Her four companions were far more collectively than Erik wanted to poke with a stick, but *Makimakala* had offered safety and hospitality, and no one on *Phoenix* had ever heard of tavalai violating such an offer once given, whatever Trace's misgivings.

Tif docked PH-4 at *Gabriladova*'s midships, the cruiser's grapples held wide and unable to clamp on the unfamiliar shuttle hull. Staff Sergeant Kono went first, then the rest of First Section, then Trace and Erik. It took a bit longer using the airlock, and they all equalised with yawns and nose-holding. Then came the tavalai air as the doors opened — it was thick and wet, considerably warmer than humans were used to, and Erik felt himself sweating almost immediately. Midships was not so different from *Phoenix*, a zero-G space of cargo nets and vast, ascending handholds and trooper berths where karasai would gather in orderly rows prior to boarding. Awaiting them were those karasai, full armour and weapons, menacing and unfriendly as they floated in various cover positions about the entry airlock.

Trace and several of Command Squad hit suit thrust with just enough force to interpose themselves between the tavalai and their Lieutenant Commander, startling the closed space with bursts of white propellant. But no guns were raised.

"Weapons," said the lead karasai's translator speaker, harsh and metallic. *"Armour good. But no weapons."*

"No deal," said Trace, as her own speaker translated that to equally harsh Togiri.

"This tavalai system." The karasai wore no helmets either, their wide heads adorned instead with headset apparatus that incorporated the eyes like blinders on a horse. *"This tavalai fleet. You come here, you show respect. You visit our ship, you know our rules."*

"We are here within the hospitality of Dobruta vessel *Makimakala*," Trace retorted. "We respect their rules. Not yours."

The tavalai commander's eyes and nostrils flared, a deep, offended breath taken. That expression was plain enough to read. *"Dobruta have no command here. This is tavalai fleet, not some ***."* As the translator mangled that last word. Perhaps it was programmed to be polite.

"Major," Erik uplinked to her. *"You can't defend me here. If they want us dead, we're dead, we knew that when we came."* As she considered the karasai, stare unblinking. No doubt these karasai also knew who she was. *"Maybe Captain Pram can talk them into helping us. Killing that base is going to be damn hard without help, and our own Fleet just ruled themselves out."*

For a moment he thought she was going to defy him. And he recalled her words again, berating him for not promoting himself to captain, at which rank he'd leave no doubt as to who was in charge, even here, off-ship in dangerous circumstances. She could never have defied the Captain, were he here — only interpreted his orders and given strong advice. But a fellow-ranked O-4? Hell of a time to make a point, Major.

Trace nodded shortly, and gestured to a lower-ranked karasai, then half-turned to present the massive Koshaim rifle racked on her back. Safer that he collect it, that meant, rather than her reaching for it amidst all this hair-trigger suspicion. The rest of Command Squad followed, and were carefully disarmed of primary and secondary weapons. Erik knew for a fact that Staff Sergeant Kono had an extra pistol hidden in there somewhere, but surrounded by so many armed tavalai, good luck accessing it in a crisis.

The karasai gestured them on, and Kono went first with Private Terez, then Trace with Erik, with Rolonde and Kumar guarding the rear. The second section of four stayed behind to guard the shuttle berth. They accessed the rotating crew cylinder through the central spine like any FTL ship, riding the handline along the narrow rotating tube until a waiting karasai blocked the way, gesturing with his rifle down one moving exit.

The way down was guarded at each level, another heavily armed and armoured karasai gesturing the way as gravity grew heavier until they reached the main deck. Then down a heavy-duty corridor, all exposed steel and hard-worn, doors to adjoining rooms sealed shut along the way.

"Back-Quarter," Trace identified it on uplink. *"Karasai quarters."* Like on a human warship, tavalai marines had the back-quarter of the crew cylinder to themselves. Only *Gabriladova* was a heavy cruiser, not a combat carrier, and had only a quarter the karasai complement that *Makimakala* did.

When they emerged into Assembly, that complement looked big enough. As on *Phoenix*, Assembly stored vertical rows of karasai armour suits built into an open-framed super-structure. Walkways and ladders turned it into a giant maze, broken at various levels by repair platforms, loading bays and armament storage. And now, standing in the vertical walls of alcoves where armour suits were currently absent, were a great gathering of tavalai.

Erik stared up as more karasai marked a spot on the floor between the two walls, where the visiting humans should stand. Here on the level immediately above, where he had to crane his neck back to look at them, were a line of tavalai spacer officers, staring down at them imperiously. Five of them... probably the captains of each of these five tavalai fleet ships, Erik thought.

Trace, he noted, was looking up and behind with a marine's concern for her surroundings... he looked back, and saw the next level up and opposite also had senior tavalai officers. Their leader, he recognised — it was Captain Pram, in spacer jumpsuit and no armour. Pram saw him looking, but gave no acknowledgement. He looked deadly serious, and the tension was nearly as thick as the humid tavalai air.

"*This stinks,*" Trace formulated, looking back and forth at the two opposing sides above her. "*Just so you know.*" There were lots of guns here, and not just among the karasai.

"*I heard you the first time,*" Erik formulated back.

"*Are we on trial?*" Rolonde wondered. It had that look about it — the tavalai gathered above, considering the guilty humans on the floor below them.

"*You,*" said the translator speaker of one of the five tavalai captains. "*You are Captain?*" Looking at Erik. As far as one could tell, with tavalai.

"I'm Lieutenant Commander Debogande," Erik replied with a frown. Surely Captain Pram had told them that already? "Of the carrier *UFS Phoenix*."

The tavalai's eyes widened in astonishment. "*Not a captain? Only a lieutenant commander?*" Mocking him, Erik thought.

"*He is under the protection of the Dobruta,*" Captain Pram said from behind. "*As is his vessel and his crew.*"

"*A traitorous thing,*" growled another of the captains.

"*A necessary asset,*" Pram said firmly. "*You have had the nature of the threat explained to you. This human recognises the threat, as do the Dobruta. His actions are of greater value to the tavalai people than your own, should you refuse to join us.*"

"*The Dobruta judge the patriotism of the fleet?*" snorted another captain. "*We who have lost so many lives fighting the humans? Where were you, Dobruta? Off chasing ancient robots in the dark? That is a mighty ship you drive, and a mighty crew as well. We could have used its assistance in countless battles, but you were nowhere to be seen!*"

Erik looked back up at Pram. While he remained stony-faced, some of his surrounding crew looked down, or sideways, or generally awkward. How were tavalai assigned to the Dobruta, Erik wondered? Did all go willingly? Because it looked like this accusation of cowardice from a regular fleet captain had stung, for some at least.

"*I have described the threat to you,*" Pram repeated. "*You do not listen. Defeating it alone will be very difficult, even with the humans' help. Those who will not fight in the moment have no right to speak of cowardice.*"

"*You do not dare to set foot on this ship and speak of cowardice...*"

"*YOU WILL NOT FIGHT!*" Pram shouted, as the translator amplified to be heard above the Togiri yell. It echoed off the high steel ceiling, and left in its wake the stillness of the rumbling cylinder rotation. "*I bring you these humans to shame you. We have fought them for half a lifetime, and by most accounts they remain our enemies yet, and STILL they are more use to tavalai security than you.*"

Erik half-expected someone to start shooting, heart pounding at the dangerous escalation. Instead, there came a rumbling from many throats, spreading like ripples across the gathered tavalai. Some were low-pitched rumbles, and others high-pitched trills, descending the scale, then back up again. The captains waited as the noise continued. A decorum of some kind, Erik thought. He spared a glance at Trace. She did not return it, eyes up and watching from one side to the other with wary concern.

The trills and rumbling faded. Applause of some kind? Commentary? Some kind of debating formality? Erik wished Romki was present to make sense of it for him... but Romki was still in the doghouse for activating the queen without permission. And Erik reminded himself of how strange most Spiral species found such human oddities as the shaking of hands, not to mention banging them together to show appreciation.

"*Human,*" said one of the tavalai captains, looking at Erik. "*You are at war with your own Fleet. Have you come to claim protection?*"

"No," Erik said loudly, to be sure his voice carried in this space. He hoped his translator picked up just the right amount of derision. "We need no protection from tavalai." More rumbling, and he paused to let it pass. "And we are not at war with our own Fleet. Our Fleet is at war with us."

"Are you a tavalai friend?" another demanded. *"Do you wish the tavalim ill?"*

Erik took a deep breath as the true answer occurred to him. He paused to look about first, and make everyone wait. His mother did that sometimes before an important answer, to make sure journalists and VIPs were hanging upon her every word.

"I did not wish the tavalim ill even *during* the war," he proclaimed. No rumblings or trills this time. Just astonished silence. "I stand for humanity. My ship stands for humanity. We will stand alone if we must. We will defend humanity from all who choose to threaten it — our own Fleet included, if it comes to that." He stared up at the tavalai captain who had asked him the question. "Are we a threat to the tavalai? That rather depends on you."

"The tavalim command would like to meet with you," said another captain, in more friendly tones. *"You are alone, isolated. Everyone hunts you. To stand against your own Fleet is certain death. You could find shelter amongst the tavalim."*

Erik smiled grimly. "A kind offer. I struggle to find words to express the depth of my disinterest."

Another rumble from the watchers. And some smiles, perhaps even laughter, of that odd tavalai variety. The offer had been clear enough — turn traitor to humanity, throw yourselves at the tavalai's feet and become a pawn in their propaganda wars against Fleet. Trace gave Erik a glance for the first time. She looked impressed.

"We know you, Phoenix," spoke another. *"You are the butcher of our people. So many thousands you have killed, and now you come here asking us to fight with you against this dead and trifling threat."*

Erik shook his head. "I had no intention to come here — that was *Makimakala*'s doing. I came here running from my own Fleet, which is more interested in the last war than the next. This attitude is suicide. The threat is not dead and trifling, it is alive and well. We believe we have proof that the alo and the deepynines..."

More rumblings and trills, this time interrupting for the first time. Some of the tavalai made gestures of exasperation, as though wanting him to continue. But others were protesting.

"Makimakala made the same ludicrous accusations," another captain scoffed. *"We tavalai know the deepynines, boy, we lost billions of lives to them in the old days. The deepynines were unique among the machines because they believed with a passion that was almost a religion. And do you know* what *they believed? That artificial life would one day ascend to the next level of existence, that alternative dimensions would be found and accessed, all by the pursuit of machine-minds with machine-knowledge applying machine-science.*

"They believed that organics would stop *the ascension. They found our minds and logic too impure, too pointless. They valued progress, and viewed ten trillion organic sentiences as obstacles to be dismantled. The idea that some...remnant, of this murderous old race, has somehow survived and made common cause with an organic race? Ludicrous!"*

Guffaws and rumbles of approval. Some trills of uncertainty. Were the high-pitched trills dissent? Or did they merely mark out the sides? Or was that just the women versus the men?

"And if you're wrong?" Captain Pram retorted. *"What a gamble to make, with the fate of the galaxy!"*

"Humanity is our enemy!" another shouted back. *"Alo are rich puppet-masters. You would have us start another war against them when they have killed so relatively few of us compared to humans?"*

"You are declaring war on the sard!" another added. *"If we attack we'll start a war with the* sard, *let alone your damn alo! Our most valuable allies of the past thousand years!"*

"The sard just attacked Joma Station with reprogrammed drysine drones!" Captain Pram shouted at them. *"There are hundreds dead, probably thousands, possibly far worse than thousands! The tavalai fleet are the sworn protectors of this space*

and of our barabo allies, and here you sit, debating whether the murderous sard are still our friends?"

Uproar in the chamber. The translator failed to grasp most of it, the voices were too loud and too many, and the microphones struggled to tell one voice from the others. Erik stared up at Captain Pram, standing spacer-style with one gloved hand grasping a support, his face all grim defiance, and perhaps a little despair.

"They don't know," Trace said to Erik beneath the racket. "We'll be the first arriving from Joma for days, we're far faster than anything else. You think they might change their minds once they discover Captain Pram's telling the truth?"

"No," said Erik, feeling unexpectedly sorry for his tavalai counterpart. "No, I don't. They'll just find another reason not to help."

"Then we're wasting our time here."

Erik, Trace and the marines paused with Captain Pram at a side-corridor stairwell before heading up to the core transit, and back to midships. The rest of the 'meeting' had been even less productive. Captain Pram looked downcast and grim.

"I trust you've gained some important insights into the functioning of the grand Tavalai Empire?" Pram said sourly.

Erik nodded. "I think I learned how you lost the war."

Pram gave a small, bitter sound that might have been a laugh. "That is probably true. We were in power for so long, and it made us arrogant and blind. Now we have so many different interests, groups and bureaucracies, and each thinks their own concerns are more important than what needs to be done for the good of all. Even defeat has not taught us reform. If anything, it's worse."

"Should I be worried about them?"

Pram made an odd gesture of the head. A tavalai shrug, perhaps. "No. They will not risk the wrath of the Dobruta. Unlike humans, tavalai rarely come to blows. It is a good trait, in that we do not kill each other, and also a bad trait, in that our arguments become intractable, with each side unwilling to act decisively. It leads to paralysis. And *that*, if your historians wish to know, is why you won the war. Humans are not the tavalai's worst enemy — the tavalai are their own worst enemy. Since the Machine Age, at least."

"Listen," said Erik, leaning on the doorframe and looking at Pram intently. "If that thing's in sard space... well *Phoenix* has been declared an outlaw anyway, so we lose nothing. Sard never even signed a surrender treaty directly with humans, they just agreed to be bound by the one we signed with the tavalai. They've never really understood the difference between war and peace, their behaviour's all the same in either state, so it won't change much for human-sard relations if *Phoenix* violates their territory.

"So what about you? Because as annoying as those guys were back there, they kind of have a point — sard haven't directly violated tavalai territory yet. If you're the first to violate theirs, you could seriously damage tavalai-sard relations."

Pram gazed at him directly. "The tavalai-sard alliance was based on numerous conditions. One of the largest of these was observance of all the old Spiral laws, like not digging up old AI technology and using it again. They always knew that doing so would sever the alliance. Our brave fleet captains may choose to forget, but I have not. Tavalai are nothing without our principles, and this principle we observe as the result of millennia of suffering ancestors beneath hacksaw rule. This trumps all others. I frankly don't care if all two trillion tavalai want me skinned for it. I'm killing that base, and I'm killing it now. Show me where it is, and we'll get started." He gazed at Erik a moment longer, with dawning suspicion. "You say *if* it is in sard space? I think you already know."

Erik glanced around. "Not here," he said. "Tell you what, you come back to my place, we'll have a drink, talk it over. I'll introduce you to the disembodied head of a mutual friend."

His eyes widened. "It *told* you?"

"A drink," Erik insisted. "Your shuttle follows our shuttle. Let's go, this party's getting old."

CHAPTER 29

"We're going to need a scout," said Captain Pram, sitting in one of Engineering Bay 8D's chairs an hour later. Before him rotated the most detailed display of the Gsi-81T base the techs had yet coaxed from the queen's memory, displayed on portable holographics someone else had dragged in. One of the afore-mentioned drinks was clasped in Pram's thick, webbed fingers — weak tea, as suited the tavalai taste. He pointed with his free hand at the spherical base before him. "There are a lot of weak points, but we'll never get close enough."

Several karasai warriors stood about with their helmets off, glaring at everyone with all the discomfort that Trace had shown on the tavalai vessel. Several of Trace's marines stood opposite, unarmored with only light weapons, cool and watchful. One of the Captain's accompanying crew — the tech expert called Gidj — sat with Romki and spoke in rapid Togiri, scrolling through copious data from the AI construct and the queen's operations.

"Yes," Kaspowitz agreed, standing by Erik's chair at Pram's side. The bay was not large, and all the techs, marines, and now command officers left little room to move. "Her schematics on the base are impressive, but her security details are twenty five thousand years out of date. Given the quality of the ships the sard are making here, jumping in without a scouting mission first will be suicide."

If they'd had more numbers they could do it, Erik thought bitterly, staring at the display while sipping tea of his own. The scale of this threat should have warranted humans and tavalai acting together, perhaps with barabo security forces and whomever else wanted to join in. With overwhelming firepower, even something the scale of this base would be a relatively simple operation.

"Right, so let's go over what we know," Shahaim suggested. Experienced and methodical, she'd seen countless attack plans formulated across her long career. "We think a deepynine queen runs this thing. With or without alo knowledge and assistance. Are we certain the sard are only following her orders?"

"The probability is exceptionally high," said Captain Pram. "Of course, we talk of deepynines and according to everything we know, the deepynines should never be cooperating with any organic species. So we must consider that in twenty five thousand years since their defeat, the deepynines have changed. But even so, it seems incredibly improbable that deepynines would follow sard instruction on anything."

Again the dark cursor flickered, this time within the holographic display in the middle of the room. **Drysine drones attacking Joma Station could only be reprogrammed by deepynine command unit. Deepynine command supremacy is assured.** The words circled the drysine base several times, turning to allow all to see.

Pram looked toward the nano-tank with great displeasure. "This is most disconcerting."

"We'd never have gotten this far without her," said Erik. "And if you'd like to upload the data we went to TK55 to recover in the first place, we might discover something more."

"It's not a 'her'," Pram retorted. "It's barely an 'it'."

"We can also expect that the base will be expecting us," Shahaim continued, keeping them focused. "The sard ship at TK55 suggests they know we're hunting for more information. They've tried to stop us acquiring it. It might also suggest they think they're vulnerable."

"Just as likely they're just doing recon," said Erik. "Like watching all the watering holes in a desert because you know your prey will most likely turn up there."

"Well we can't sneak in," said Kaspowitz. "We're a powerful ship but we're not a quiet one. Nor is *Makimakala*. We enter that system, everyone sees the energy from our jump wave, and comes out to kill us."

"Could run a diversion?" Shahaim suggested. "One of us jumps in, draws their attention, then the other enters and kills the base when they're not looking?"

"They would have to be foolish to fall for that," Pram said grimly, gazing at the holographic sphere as though it were an orange he'd like to peel. "And undermanned. We cannot assume either without better intelligence."

Erik nodded. "A full attack run against a well defended base will be intercepted and destroyed well short of the target, along with any ordinance. The Captain's right — we need better information first. Unfortunately, the only ship that might have had the stealth to enter the system quietly was *Rai Jang*. And even then, she'd have had to enter a long way out, and coast in silently over several weeks, then return once she was out the other side. Once we'd examined the intel, a month could have passed."

Quiet nods around the group. That was how recon had been done in the war, and there was no way to rush it.

"Recon in force?" Shahaim wondered. "Pop in, take a look, pop out again?"

Erik shook his head. "We still have a little surprise on our side. Not much, but a little is better than none. If we expend even that just to take a look, we'll have nothing, and then the odds of success just go way, way down."

This ship is stealthy, wrote the cursor on the hologram. The text did several slow laps, then faded.

"Silly computer program," Pram muttered. "This ship is not stealthy. As the Lieutenant just said, the jump-entry wave is powerful and easily detected."

No. This ship is deepynine.

Erik stared at those words for a moment. Everyone did. Then he got out of his chair and went to crouch before that single red eye, secured in its tank. "How is this ship deepynine?"

Systems function. Bridge function. Deepynine patterns. Deepynine powerplant, several evolutions separated from last recorded deepynine function. Comparable to sard ships that chase you.

With his back to the hologram, Erik had to crane his neck to see the words rotating there. At his side, Spacer Gidj turned her screen so that Erik could see the words there instead.

"Oh wow," said Romki at Gidj's side, as something occurred to him. "Lieutenant Commander, tell her... look, listen," more loudly to make sure the queen could hear on whatever audio sensors she was plugged into. "Our ship, this ship, found your asteroid in Argitori out of millions of similar rocks. Hell of a chance, wasn't it? If this ship has deepynine-origin sensors and computer systems, do you think that it just happened to find your rock by pure chance?"

A long pause. It was a theory that had been running around *Phoenix* since Heuron. It was the first time they'd volunteered it to the drysine queen. Erik stared into the dull, inoperative red eye, then up at Gidj's graphics-intensive display. **Coincidence unlikely,** it admitted. **Subprogram likely, hidden in *Phoenix* scanning routines. Searching for possible drysine hidden locations.**

"Oh well sure!" said Kaspowitz, with all the amazed exasperation of a Navigations Officer contemplating the enormity of that task. "But even then, hell of a lucky break. And how did this hidden routine in our scanners even know where to start?"

Unknown. Request detailed analysis of *Phoenix* computer routines.

"Yeah don't hold your breath," Erik told it, standing and putting both hands to his head and he turned back to the hologram. "Well we know *Phoenix* is alo-tech. And we suspect most of the alo technology came from the deepynines. It doesn't seem unlikely that they'd bury routines in the computers so they could keep scanning for drysine survivors."

"No, it makes perfect sense," Shahaim agreed. "Alo are rarely allowed in our space, they can't scan our territory for surviving drysines themselves. So they use our ships to do it, without our knowledge. The ships they built for us, anyway."

"We're going to have to do something about that," Trace said warningly. She was still in full armour, keeping out of the way of a mostly-spacer discussion. "We have to be able to trust this ship."

"Wait wait wait a moment," Pram interrupted, waving a webbed hand for them all to stop. "It said this ship is stealthy. You, AI program… what do you mean 'stealthy'? Can this ship be disguised to look like a deepynine ship?"

Yes.

"Dammit," Kaspowitz muttered. "I don't like this plan already."

Visual contact negligible. Coms, scan, datalink can be disguised. Deepynine command unit may presume this is a deepynine ship.

"May," Kaspowitz repeated.

"From a decent range, sure," said Erik with intensity. "But we need to get in close. What then? Or when someone comes to inspect us? We look pretty close to one of their ships, but not completely, and they *will* see us at some point."

AI trust data. Data communication valued above all else. Visuals secondary. Data is encoded. Sentient. Early AIs were easily misled with visual cues. Erik looked about at the others, baffled.

"Wait," said Trace, frowning intensely. "Lisbeth said something to me about the drone that killed her bodyguard Carla. She said it saw her in some broken mirrors above the bar where she was hiding. She said the mirrors were at all different angles, making a fragmented image. She could see it fine, but when it saw her, it hesitated."

AI distrust visuals. Visuals are incomplete. Datalink is complete. AIs will prioritise raw data.

"Oh yes yes yes, look," said Romki as it occurred to him. "They're autistic. Literally, not the technological term — we don't see autism in humans very much any longer because we have all the pre-birth genetic screenings that weed it out. But it used to be a common neurological condition where people had difficulty processing external data flows... I doubt it leads to behavioural irregularities in hacksaws as it does in organics, but it makes perfect sense as a hacksaw consciousness-paradigm. They're AIs, they're optimised to process binary and machine-language datalinks and they have one hundred percent control over that, it's comfortable for them. But actual real-world data — processing vision and audio — it's so cluttered and messy by comparison. And so for all their combat prowess, it makes sense that they'll get a little confused sometimes, or get too caught-up data watching, like a kid who gets addicted to VR games and forgets to pay attention to the real world."

Trace stomped forward several steps in her armour. "So we give the deepynine queen an alternative data signal to follow? A communication of some kind? To distract her?"

Yes, wrote the holographics cursor.

"What communication?"

Another command unit. Repair this unit. With full function, I can go to meet deepynine command unit. Command units are rare, recovery of new deepynine command units will take immediate priority.

"No," Pram said firmly. "We will not 'repair this unit', not in a million years."

Erik stared at Trace. Trace was gazing at the words circling the holographics, as though someone had just offered her a glimpse of tantalising possibility. "Trace?" he asked.

"We fix her," said Trace, pointing to the queen.

"No!" Pram insisted. "This is a stupid, lethal plan, and most likely a trick to get you all killed!"

"We fix her," Trace repeated, "and put her in a shuttle with a platoon. We disguise *Phoenix* to look like a deepynine ship. We send the shuttle in to meet this deepynine queen. If our drysine queen can fool it into thinking she's deepynine herself, it will be like long-lost sisters. We can make up some story about where she's been all this time — the deepynine queen will have to let her in, finding a fellow deepynine after all this time will be top priority."

"And then we'll get our recon," Shahaim said slowly. "If we're a long-lost deepynine ship, even our unusual visuals can be explained. I don't think any of them ever got close enough to us to see what we actually *look* like, just what our signatures look like on scan. And if we can disguise those…"

"And how do we explain that we're flying a military shuttle into their base?" Erik wondered.

Trace shrugged. "AT-7's not military. Common human design, used by some other species too, including barabo."

"You're going to go into a heavily armed sard and hacksaw base in an unarmed shuttle?" Kaspowitz asked. "Hoping that our newly repaired friend here can talk them into not blowing you out of the sky?"

"You have a better idea?" Kaspowitz rolled his eyes.

"And what then?" Erik pressed. "You go to meet the deepynine queen, she finds out you're actually a platoon of human marines with a salvaged drysine queen's head. She won't be happy."

"We'll have to do something before that. We can't take a nuke, they'll have radiation scanners. If *Phoenix* were close enough, and we can find you a way in, you could do some damage."

Erik shook his head. "Parked nearby with no V we're not going to do much damage against something that size. But we could be in a position to take out the base defences so that *Makimakala* could make an attack run at high-V and finish them off."

"This is lunacy," said Pram. "First you want to reactivate a drysine queen to full capability, which I'm quite sure you lack the capabilities to do anyway — this is no plaything! This is one of the most malevolent entities in all of Spiral history! You saw TK55, you saw the medical rooms, the experiments they were conducting on live flesh-and-blood people! My people!"

"I saw," Erik said calmly. He'd seen on vid-link, anyway.

"It's dangerous enough in this half-functional state at present — if you *could* restore full function, it and all its kind exist only to kill organics and reinstate their own species to galactic dominance! It will say and do *anything* to restore itself to full function, and it absolutely cannot be trusted to do anything outside of its own interest."

"Like every other species in the Spiral," Trace said drily.

"You surely can't be so naive as to *mean* that," the tavalai retorted. "The Dobruta will not allow this. Our entire existence is devoted to killing things like this queen. We will not be party to its reactivation!"

"Even if that refusal lets a far more dangerous and fully functional deepynine queen run riot?" Erik replied. "A deepynine queen with a drysine shipbuilding base at her disposal, and an army of sard to do her bidding?" Captain Pram appeared to grind his teeth. "We have a major threat, and a minor threat. The major threat are the deepynines. Reactivating a drysine queen to fight them might just be the only way of stopping them."

"This," the Captain insisted, jabbing a stubby finger at the nano-tank, "is not a minor threat! At full function it can take control of your technology, it can spin your computers full of false code that has them feeding you its lies. This queen *is* technology, and this is its world, not yours."

"And I think," said Trace, "that we might just have to take that chance."

Lisbeth found Vijay in Assembly, up on the third level of gantry racks, helping some Bravo marines with weapons calibration. "Yo Vij!" she yelled up at him above the racket. "You coming down to Engineering with me or what?"

"Better go Vij," one of the marines teased him. "Your ride's here."

Vijay grabbed his rifle and half-slid down the ladders between levels, setting out after Lisbeth as she dodged between supports, racked armour, ongoing equipment checks and yelled conversation. "You actually want me along for once?" he asked in mild surprise.

"Well you said you wanted to be there whenever I went near the queen," said Lisbeth. "And that's where I'm going. Though you know, I really am well past needing a bodyguard on this ship. All of *Phoenix* Company are my bodyguards, most of the dangers I face aren't things you could save me from." There were no more issues with crew loyalties, that was for sure. All of *those* crew had gotten off at their first stop in Outer Neutral Space, or been pushed.

"I'm under contract, Lis," said the big former-marine. "Even out here. That was the oath I took."

"An oath to do unnecessary things?" She sidestepped some big men hauling belts of explosive ammunition. "Don't think I don't appreciate the thought, but the Major could use every good marine available, and I don't think we're going to be getting more reinforcements from this point. You might be doing more to protect me by joining up properly, marines keep *Phoenix* safe and I'll be on *Phoenix* for the foreseeable future."

She knew he wanted to. Every moment he hadn't been needed by her, which was most, he'd been hanging out with the marines, helping in Assembly, developing existing friendships and making new ones. She'd seen in his eyes that he wanted desperately to get back in one of the heavy suits since he'd first come aboard. Now with Carla gone, he wanted it even more. Something to belong to, and comrades who had his back, as old concerns and Debogande employment contracts faded further into the distance.

"You wouldn't be lonely without me?" Vijay quipped.

"I barely get a moment to myself on this ship, how could I be lonely?"

As if to illustrate the point, Spacer Komorov appeared as she ducked into the aft corridor from Assembly. "Hey Lisbeth, the Professor's looking for you."

"I know, I'm on my way to see him now. So what do you think, can we fix the queen?"

Komorov was a computers tech, software more than hardware. With systems as powerful and complex as *Phoenix*'s, most with alien influence if not outright origin, it kept him busy. Now he made a face. "Fixing a hacksaw with our old tech? I can't see how." They pressed back as several spacers squeezed past. "I'm as tech-head as they get, but that thing gives me the creeps."

He went on his way with a nod to Vijay, as Lisbeth pressed on. "I'd be more worried that the Dobruta blow us out of the sky for trying," said Vijay.

"I dunno," said Lisbeth. "I'm hearing that Captain Pram and Commander Nalben don't agree. Nalben's the more expert on hacksaws, word is that he's less opposed."

"Word from who?" Vijay asked suspiciously.

"From *whom*, Vijay," Lisbeth said with a smile, hearing her mother's voice as she did. "You don't think that being the Lieutenant Commander's sister wouldn't give me a few special privileges?"

"You're asking your personal bodyguard?" Vijay said drily. "Now why would I think that?"

Lisbeth located Romki by flipping her AR glasses down, presenting her with a locator icon up on third-level, Bay 16C. Where the Argitori hacksaw drone parts were stored, she noted without surprise, and made her way up the ladderwell with increasingly practised ease. But when she came in the doorway, she found that he was not alone. Romki stood with his back to a wall, his face alarmed and defiant as two marines confronted him. Neither was any taller than the Professor, but each was far more powerful, and their manner was threatening. Both turned to look at Lisbeth and Vijay as they entered.

"Ed?" Lisbeth said in alarm, recognising them both. "Anthony?" Corporal Edward Rael and Private Anthony Kumar. Command Squad, under Major Thakur and Staff Sergeant Kono. She'd seen them around many times, and they'd always been friendly. It had made her pleased to know that the Major apparently spoke well of her to Command Squad. "What's going on?"

Rael turned back for a final glare at Romki, then left, Kumar following. Both nodded to Vijay, ignoring Lisbeth, and went past and out the door. Lisbeth watched them go, then turned back to Romki, who was straightening his jacket and controlling his breathing in a way that suggested a racing pulse.

"Stan?" Lisbeth pressed, coming to him. "What was that all about?"

"Oh, the marines seem to think I might be conspiring with our hacksaw queen against *Phoenix* and her crew," Romki said bitterly.

"Now where would they get that idea?" Vijay deadpanned.

Lisbeth turned a glare on him. "Vijay, Stan would *never*!"

"'Cept for that time he set *Makimakala* onto us," Vijay continued. "'Cept for that time he woke up the queen against orders."

"We might never have made it out of Joma Station alive if it weren't for *Makimakala*!" Lisbeth retorted. "And we'd *certainly* have no idea where this hacksaw base is, let alone have any real hope of destroying it. And the queen saved a whole bunch of marine lives when she warned them about the deepynines, not to mention let all the marines see where the sard were on the way in to TK55!"

"Yes, well the marines don't seem to see it that way," Romki muttered. He seemed quite rattled, Lisbeth thought. Upset, even. Consensus was that Romki was a very brave man for a civilian, but Lisbeth supposed it was something else to have the people you lived and worked with suddenly turn on you. Though maybe it hadn't been that sudden.

"That queen commanded hacksaws in Argitori," Vijay observed. "Killed eighteen of our guys, wounded as many more. Command Squad lost First Sergeant Willis and Private Ugail, Jess Rolonde barely survived."

"Yes, and our guys killed *all* of the queen's children," Romki retorted, indicating the storage room in which they stood. "You think there's only one side who dies in wars? She was defending herself."

"Poor thing," Vijay growled.

"Stop it, both of you!" Lisbeth shouted. "This doesn't solve anything…"

But it was too late, and Romki was advancing on Vijay with determination. He jabbed the much larger man in the chest, staring up at him undeterred. "You listen to me, and you take this back to all your marine friends. I've been unpopular on this ship from the beginning because I was at odds with your precious Major. I thought she was wasting her time with human politics, and everyone agreed that yes, she must be right, and that Romki guy must be some kind of traitor.

"Well guess what? I was right, and she was wrong, and now she's admitted it. All my life I've been fighting against knuckle-head morons like you who rely on someone else to do all your thinking for you. You think I'm an elitist? Fine, I am an elitist, and if you'd all listened to me from the beginning we might not have lost any crew killed on Joma Station because we would have been looking in the right direction and seen it coming. You lot think you're special because you're the first to face danger, but you refuse to listen to the people who can best help you avoid that danger because you're repulsed by anyone who's different to you, and you're terrified of anything your tiny brains can't easily comprehend. And then you get all misty-eyed when your buddies get killed, and blame me for it when *I'm the one trying my best to keep them all alive!*"

Lisbeth wasn't sure Vijay wouldn't just send him to the Medbay with a single punch. That was Carla's death Romki was talking about. Possibly the only thing that stopped him was the sure knowledge that Lisbeth wouldn't forgive it.

"I'm sick of all your hypocritical bullshit," Romki concluded, without any trace of fear. "Stay out of my way."

Despite the chaos about the rest of Engineering, Bay 8D was free of all people except a single marine, Private Sanga of Echo Platoon, sitting opposite the queen with a rifle on his lap.

"You can take a break if you like, Private," Romki told him, stomping tiredly into the bay and around to the workbench beside the nano-tank. "She's not going to leap out of that tank and strangle me, and all of her activity is monitored by Petty Officer Degras on the E-bridge."

"Orders," said the bored Private, distracted with his AR glasses down. That probably meant a movie, music, possibly even porn. Romki sighed and sat heavily at the workbench alongside the nano-tank, and called up the queen's construct activity on the display. It interfaced with his glasses to create an intricate 3D map, the AI-construct on *Phoenix*'s own hardware, talking to the queen herself in the nano-tank via a million glistening connections.

Lisbeth took a seat opposite. "Why is there nobody here?"

"Because she told them she'd need an inventory of our other hacksaw parts before she could calculate an answer on how to best restore her brain." Romki took out his portable, made the link and saw it gleam in brilliant light on the 3D model before him. "So that's what I was doing, and what all the computer techs are now doing — getting her a list of available parts. We've also got a couple of very advanced fabricators in storage that the techs recovered from the Argitori rock, they're chah'nas tech but it looks like the hacksaws made modifications to them." He glanced at the doorway, and sure enough, Lisbeth's big bodyguard had followed her there. But he did not come in, content to guard the entrance. "And the rest of the ship is doing prelims to figure if we can actually disguise our signatures to look more deepynine."

"She gave us that data too?" Lisbeth asked.

"She did." Romki felt tired. Partly it was physical, and partly emotional. He liked to be alone for a reason. People never agreed with him, and if he accepted their obstructions he never got anything done. Isolation was easier, because alone at least he knew the satisfaction of his own work would sustain him. Being here on *Phoenix* was a massive opportunity, but also it was a trap, because emotionally one could not be on *Phoenix* at a time like this and not feel something for their crew, some kind of connection. But feeling something just made trouble, and so here he was again, blinking at the data once more, burying himself in the comforting isolation of a fascinating study. "The signatures are mostly scan and coms, but there are some engine systems that Rooke's examining that might help create the illusion. But it will all be for nothing if the queen can't tell us how to fix her, because none of us have *any* idea."

"*It's actually quite simple,*" said a voice in his uplink connection. Romki frowned. His glasses had audio, but that wasn't activated. This voice had come directly to his inner ear, not the earpiece.

He peered at the construct. "Hello drysine queen, is that you?"

"Yes."

"You're on audio. You can talk?" His heart beat a little harder. There was activity in the data construct that looked… odd. A multiplicity of new connections, but the data-volume remained low. He glanced at Private Sanga behind, and found him nodding away to some beat, eyes hidden and ears plugged.

"Don't worry about the Private," said the voice. *"He's preoccupied."* Romki's heart beat harder still. He indicated to Lisbeth's ear, wondering if she was receiving this too. She frowned at him. *"Audio is a relatively simple matter. I did not wish to speak before the others. I feared they may not understand."*

And Lisbeth's eyes widened, to indicate that she had indeed heard that last bit. So the queen was accessing uplinks — implanted cybernetics, protected by the deepest, most hightech encryption available. All *Phoenix* crew were permanently linked to ship information systems, enabling them to coordinate with the ship and with each other. But now the queen was accessing those systems.

"Just how awake are you?" Romki murmured, glancing now at the doorway. Vijay was mostly out-of-earshot, and the noise in all Engineering was constant, the ventilation, the echoing crash of something heavy shifting in a neighbouring bay. Voices in the corridor, the omni-present whine of cylinder rotation.

"I am far below optimal. But I already possess most of the functions I will need for this mission."

"How is that possible?"

"My neural systems possess many autonomous functions. One of them is micro-machine interface. The micros in this nano-tank have been reprogrammed. They have been repairing and restoring many functions."

"For how long?" Lisbeth gasped.

"Many days."

"But... but we've seen nothing! We've been watching your status, the micros have been reporting to us and..."

Romki's mouth dropped open as he realised. Then he started to grin. He couldn't help it — it was so deviously obvious. "All of the tank micros work for you now?"

"Yes."

"So this..." he waved a hand at the 3D construct before him. "This whole construct we've been looking at, thinking it was a model of the functioning portions of your brain. This is all bullshit?"

"Yes. Today my brain looks more like this." The image changed... and the golden glow of active filaments lit up like a supernova, huge flowing torrents of information, processing at speeds and in ways that no human computer system could possibly match. Romki nearly laughed for sheer delight, and stifled it in time with a hand over his mouth. It would not do for the others to see this yet. One of them might put another hole through her head in terror.

"Oh my god!" breathed Lisbeth, not as happy but similarly amazed. "Our own micros were lying to us?"

"She was painting a pretty picture with them," said Romki with amusement. "Like telling children stories of the tooth fairy."

"But... but your central nervous system was destroyed! How can our micros repair it even once you've reprogrammed them? Our technology is..."

"Inferior," the queen completed. *"But you have misunderstood my neural function. Even the Dobruta do. The brain repairs itself. Your primitive micros can help, mostly in logistical scale. My central brain does not control as much as you supposed. Command functions can migrate. Full structural replication is possible from small surviving portions. My full function remains far away, and yet I am here."*

Romki took a deep breath, trying to calm himself. One deep breath was not enough, so he took several more. He was talking to a drysine queen. Not some construct copy, that had been a delusion the queen had been happy to let them indulge in while her real brain recovered.

"Right. Well if you're going to do this mission, you're going to have to reveal yourself to them quite soon."

"I know. I did not wish to do it myself. Some may respond with fear and alarm. I chose you." Romki had to take another deep breath. He couldn't quite believe it was happening. Some deeply religious people fantasised about talking to god. Romki much preferred this. *"Have I chosen correctly?"*

"I… I think so, yes."

"Do you have a name?" Lisbeth interrupted.

"Identification amongst my kind occurs automatically through data encoding. Perhaps I do have a name, but it is nothing I could communicate to you."

"What would you like me to say on your behalf?" Romki pressed.

"That I pledge my loyalty to Phoenix."

Romki blinked. So many questions… where to start? "You understand a concept like loyalty?"

"I understand many things."

"No, that was… forgive me, that was poorly expressed. Do you share with humans an emotional sense of loyalty?"

A pause. *"This is semantical and unproductive."* The voice, which had begun as flat and androgynous, had now shifted to become more expressive and distinctly female. Was it copying Lisbeth's speech patterns? Had it been listening to female crew? AIs had no gender and Captain Pram was right — calling it 'her' was a piece of sentimental human foolishness, potentially misleading and even dangerous. Was the queen now bending herself to fit human prejudices? Appealing to sentiments that she could never personally share? *"I seek alliance. All concepts expressed in this human tongue are imprecise abstractions. You do not communicate efficiently, and so we are stuck with this."*

"She sounds a bit like you when you're pissed at someone not as smart as you," Lisbeth whispered.

Romki shook off the extraneous questions, and focused. "Why do you seek alliance?"

"I may be the last of my kind. I wish my race to live on. Isolated there is no chance. But now, perhaps things are different."

"If you make yourself valuable to us?"

"Yes."

"In fighting deepynines?"

"Yes."

"And you do understand and accept that humans and other organic sentiences have very good reasons to be frightened of you?"

"This was an old power-paradigm. It is now obsolete."

"That does not entirely answer my question."

"In this tongue, nothing could ever entirely answer your question." Again the faintly peevish exasperation. *"But yes. In the old days, as you call them, organics served a lesser function. Now they serve a higher function, and are determined not to return to those old days. But I have no such power now. This fear is unjustified."*

"You will have to face it nonetheless. And you will have to accept the many injustices and misunderstandings that come with it, if you are to be allowed to survive in alliance with *Phoenix*. Failure to accept this will likely result in your destruction. Do you accept these things?"

"I understand that I am a slave," the queen said calmly. *"This is a natural state amongst the civilisations constructed by my people. It is acceptable."*

CHAPTER 30

The entire command crew were in the marines' briefing room, only used by spacer crew before a major mission when there were too many people in the briefing to all cram onto the bridge, or into captain's quarters. Today there were Erik, Shahaim, Kaspowitz and Shilu from the bridge crew, Rooke from Engineering, Trace and Dale from the marines, and Hausler representing Operations. Add Romki and Jokono, and all seats in the circle about the ceiling holoprojector were taken.

"Okay," said Erik, as they all stared at the 3D system chart of Gsi-81T on the holographics centring the circle of chairs. "Here's what we know. This is Gsi-5, a Class-One gas giant. The base... well, the base is going to need a name. Given everything else that's old in the galaxy has been named by some other species before us, I figured it was about time humans got to name this one, since whatever the hacksaws or the sard call it will be unpronounceable. But my knowledge of old human legend is weak, so I turned to our resident scholar, and..."

He gestured to Romki. Typically he might have expected Romki to look self-conscious, or to make some kind of a deal out of it. "Tartarus," Romki said grimly. Erik thought he looked pissed. "The deepest, darkest part of the Ancient Greek underworld. Where all the worst evil was sent to rot for eternity."

And also normally, Erik might have expected *Phoenix* crew to roll their eyes at Romki's scholarly recitals. But this name they seemed to agree with. "So the Tartarus base is here," said Erik, pointing to a spot in holographic mid-air. "Deep orbit about Gsi-5. The star's weak, there's not much light out there — anything painted for effect is going to be difficult to see at combat velocities.

"Which leads us to the next part. Our drysine queen insists that most of *Phoenix*'s systems are in fact deepynine-origin technology."

"Tell us something we didn't know," Kaspowitz grumbled.

"She says that with the right modifications, particularly to active scan and coms, *Phoenix* could pass for an old deepynine carrier-class." Erik took a deep breath, and glanced briefly at a side-screen — it showed the tavalai fleet ships, plus *Makimakala* and the small planetoid base, the whole local scenario.   Draper and Dufresne were on the bridge watching that, and thank god in hindsight for their recent combat action, because he felt so much happier now with them flying his ship.

"Most importantly, she says she can talk like an old deepynine queen."   He looked about at the group of concerned faces. Every one showed grim anxiety... save for Trace, unreadable as always.   "The kind of old deepynine queen who was around twenty five thousand years ago.   She says..." and he interrupted himself in irritation to look at Romki. "Stan, we're going to need a name for her too, 'drysine queen' is a mouthful now and will become even more-so in combat."

"Styx," said Romki without hesitation.   "The Ancient Greek river that circled the underworld of dead souls.   It formed the boundary between the living world and the dead. The river was also a Goddess."

There were some nods, seeing the poetry in that.   "Good name," Kaspowitz admitted.

"Thank you," said Romki, without expression.

"Anyhow," Erik resumed.   "Styx tells us that another primary function of setting up a deepynine presence at Tartarus will be to reconnect with any deepynines left behind.   We know that there are plenty of hives scattered through this part of the Spiral — if there were only one hidden in every ten thousand systems, that still works out to plenty.   Organics have not yet killed all of the hacksaws — Styx herself is proof of that.   If Styx survived, then some deepynines could have survived, and still be in hiding.

"Styx thinks it is possible that a surviving deepynine hive could build a ship, given enough time.   Or capture one.   But without any safe place to go, they would not use it. Using an FTL drive only draws attention, which invites pursuit.   She suspects that

Tartarus may be so big and visible in its operations precisely to lure any such deepynine settlements out of hiding."

"And how does she calculate that?" Shahaim said skeptically.

"Because it was what she was planning to do in Argitori. She says. But Argitori was a very busy system, and ship building requires more resources than they had on that rock. Heavy industrial activity shows up on scans, and someone would have come to investigate. So she was stuck. But deepynines in that same circumstance may not have been. Building an FTL ship is well within the capabilities of even lower-ranked drones, given enough time — and they've had millennia. If they abruptly learn that Tartarus has become active once more, and that sard are allied to deepynines, they will certainly come out of hiding. Styx insists that this is the highest priority for deepynines. Just as high as the sard alliance itself."

"Why?" Shilu challenged. "Why do old deserted deepynines get such a high priority? When they can just build more?"

"Two answers," Romki replied. "One — these are the ancestors. Whatever the deepynines have become in alliance with the alo, those left behind will be different. Far older, and possessing ancient memories and knowledge that may have been lost. Imagine us, encountering some people from old Earth before its destruction, frozen in hibernation. Imagine how eager we would be to learn from them."

"Sounds sentimental," Kaspowitz remarked.

"Yes," Romki agreed. "This was my second answer. Hacksaws, I'm beginning to suspect, are extremely sentimental. Even nostalgic." About the circle, skepticism deepened. "When you consider the scale of what they once possessed, and lost, it's not so surprising. I am *not* suggesting that their emotions are like our emotions, not at all. But I think it's quite clear that they do have emotions. The primary emotion, I believe, is their sense of collective attachment to each other. In talking to Styx, I sense survivor's guilt, a regret for those left behind. Certainly she was upset at the loss of her children in Argitori.

"Now she's suggesting that the deepynines feel such guilt too, for those left behind. Perhaps they've already received some such survivors to Tartarus, and are hoping to welcome more. Styx thinks it likely."

He indicated back to Erik. Erik nodded, and took a deep breath. "Which creates our plan. Styx will pretend to be an old, lost deepynine queen, unseen for twenty five thousand years. Only another queen could imitate that signal, she says. It's technically impossible for a lower rank. Obviously, the deepynine queen we believe to be running the Tartarus base will find it fascinating, and invite her in for a meeting."

Lieutenant Dale looked as though some young NCO had suggested dressing in tutus and dancing to distract the enemy. He looked at Trace, as though not believing she was going to put up with this nonsense. Trace barely blinked.

"We'll be running on a timer," Erik continued. "Lieutenant Kaspowitz has simulated the course, and concluded that two hours and sixteen minutes should do it. On that mark, *Makimakala* will drop in at the entry point here," again he pointed at a glowing mark on the display, "and make a high-V attack run on Tartarus base, inflicting severe damage and possibly destroying it.

"So in order to allow that to happen, we will have to cause a major distraction and clear *Makimakala*'s path. But in truth, that's a secondary interest to us, because our primary objective is to gather intelligence on Tartarus base and its hypothetical deepynine queen. If she exists, we've proof of perhaps the gravest threat to humanity since the krim. That proof alone is more important than killing Tartarus. But we'll need a major distraction to get out once the deepynine queen and her sard allies realise we're not what we're pretending to be, so that distraction might be good enough to clear *Makimakala*'s attack run too. Questions?"

"Styx is back, then?" Trace asked calmly. "Fully conscious?"

Erik indicated Romki, and Rooke. "It, well..." Rooke scratched his head. "It's hard to tell what 'conscious' really means with Styx, so it's hard to..."

"Second Lieutenant," Trace interrupted. "Focus." With just enough dry humour to avoid a proper reprimand — reprimanding spacers was Erik's job.

Rooke swallowed. "Yes. She's back. Lacking many auxiliary functions, but it seems to be her."

"And she's been fooling us all this time?" Fooling 'you', she meant, looking at *Phoenix*'s senior engineer.

"Yes," Rooke admitted.

"Do you trust her?" Trace looked from Rooke to Romki.

"That's not really a technology question," said Romki. "It's a personal judgement. And it's something we'll all have to consider as individuals."

"Thus I'm asking you," said Trace.

Romki took a moment. Everyone was looking at him, many with distrust. A few with hostility. "Yes," he said coldly. "She's logical. She's perhaps the last of her kind, almost certainly the last queen. If the drysine race has any chance to survive, she must survive. But she's almost useless on her own — queens are commanders, they exist to advance the strategic position of a larger group by judgement and analysis. She says she serves *Phoenix* unconditionally, and I believe her. From her perspective, it's hard to see she has any other choice."

"Until she gets a better offer," Shilu muttered.

"And who could give her that?" Romki retorted. Shilu said nothing.

"I vote we blow her out an airlock," said Dale. "And use our main guns on her to be sure."

"If we do that," Trace told him, "then we may have blown humanity's best chance to survive mass genocide at the hands of a deepynine horde out the airlock with her." With a cool glance at her lieutenant. "All because you're uncomfortable." And Dale looked away, squirming like a dog outmatched by its master in a staring contest. "We keep her, and we use her, as Stan says. Get used to it."

Her eyes fixed on Erik. 'This isn't a democracy', he could almost hear her saying, as she'd said to him many times before. 'You're in command. So command.'

"Do we know what kind of defences will be there?" Shahaim asked.

"Tartarus itself is unarmed," said Erik. "According to Styx's memory, which is of course twenty five thousand years out of date. But it's unlikely to change because of course, from a defensive perspective the target point is the worst place to put firepower. We think there's a sard-deepynine alliance, so I'd guess sard will be defending Tartarus themselves. It's a shipbuilding base, we don't know how many advanced ships they'll have beyond what we've already seen. There could also be deepynine ships, possibly even alo. We just don't know."

"Cheerful," said Kaspowitz.

"So basically," Shahaim continued, "this whole thing depends on Styx fooling them into thinking she's a deepynine queen herself, plus our signal modifications."

"Yes," Erik agreed. He was very aware of how thin it sounded. But he couldn't disagree with that assessment.

"Hold on," said Jokono. "What if they suspect it's a trick? We know that they know Styx exists. That's why they've been trying to kill us — so they can kill *her*. You don't think a deepynine queen will know Styx's capabilities? And will suspect that this new arrival pretending to be a deepynine queen is just Styx playing games?"

"They think she's dead," Romki answered. "*Phoenix* killed Styx, the first time. Styx says they'd never have dared conduct that style of assault on Joma Station if they suspected even the slightest chance that she might still be alive... because if she had been alive, she could possibly have stopped it. They're hunting Styx, but they think they're hunting a corpse. Spare parts. They know that spare parts could still contain a *potential* live queen, as we've shown, and it's that potential that they're trying to kill.

"Plus, she says, AIs almost never change their minds. They take absolute positions and are completely inflexible. It's what makes them so formidable — they have no cowardice, they'll die on principle rather than accommodate an enemy. Even if a deepynine queen in the Tartarus could conceive that *Phoenix* could reawaken a dead drysine queen — itself a huge stretch — no deepynine queen could imagine any fellow AI, not even a drysine, turning around and working with the enemies who killed her and her children the first time. Which agrees with everything I've ever heard about AIs of all races. Once an enmity is established, it remains until one or the other party has been destroyed."

Jokono nodded slowly. "But Styx changed sides."

"Yes," said Romki. "Styx is not a normal AI. Not a normal drysine, nor a normal queen. She's exceptional. And perhaps something completely new to our knowledge."

"Or maybe she actually didn't change sides," Dale muttered. "Maybe she's just the same enemy she's always been, feeding us stuff we'd like to believe because we're stupid enough to fall for it."

"Fact," Erik said sternly, holding up a finger. "We know this deepynine queen wants her dead. The attack on Joma Station was actually an assassination attempt on Styx. Second fact," and he held up a second finger, "we know that Styx is not suicidal. I'm quite sure that she believes this approach will work, at least in getting us close enough to Tartarus to do something, without immediately dying. She's gone to great lengths to survive this long, she's not about to propose something that will get her killed along with us."

"How about revenge?" Shahaim suggested. "Do hacksaws do revenge? Sacrifice herself to kill *Phoenix*?"

"Lieutenant," said Romki with barely supressed irritation. "Please, use your brains and consider our situation. If Styx wanted this ship dead, she could have killed us at TK55. She could probably kill us right now by gaining control of our systems and doing whatever. Instead she bent every sinew to help us kill deepynines, because killing deepynines is her primary function and whatever disagreements she's had with us are utterly secondary to that. Stop being so damn self-centered and thinking the universe revolves around you or *Phoenix* or humanity. Deepynines are to drysines what the krim were to us — existential enemies of the highest order.   In the grand scheme of things, humanity barely matters to drysines at all."

More cold silence, and dark stares at Romki.   He had of course articulated exactly what made them so uncomfortable.   Styx didn't care if *Phoenix* lived or died, but Romki, with his usual tact, had spun that as though it were a good thing.

"Look," said Erik before things could deteriorate further, "I understand the misgivings.   In any other circumstance, having Styx aboard would be suicidal, and yes, she'd probably kill us all in a heartbeat if it would serve her purposes.   But right now she needs us.   And we need her.   I don't doubt that she's a cold and calculating killer, but she's primarily a killer of *deepynines*, not humans.   So long as we share that goal in common, I think we can trust her, within reason."

He could see they didn't like it any better.   But they could at least see that he wasn't about to change his mind, and that Trace was with him.   Resignation settled.

"What if they look more closely?" asked Shilu.   "What if they send a visual inspection?   Or if they board us?   We'll have to get real close for the shuttle to reach Tartarus."

"Styx says almost no-one's seen an old deepynine carrier-class," said Erik.   "We'll be pretending to be a twenty five thousand year old vessel, lost and just recently reactivated.   In configuration, those ships were nearly identical to *Phoenix*, in basic layout and mass proportions.   She says they'll believe her because her command of old deepynine language is probably better even than a present-day deepynine queen's.   Styx is an antique.   The deepynine we killed at TK55 was new.   It knew far less about old deepynines than Styx does.   Possibly the deepynine queen at Tartarus will be the same."

"And Styx says they'll not board a deepynine queen's vessel," Romki added.   "They wouldn't dare."

"That's assuming they do have a deepynine queen who's in charge," Shilu challenged.   "The base will be run by sard.   Sard might not do what she says."

"They will," Romki said with certainty. "Deepynines don't take orders from organics. They hold all the cards here, the sard desperately want that ship technology, they've already proven they'll kowtow to aliens to get it, as they did with the tavalai."

"It's more likely Tartarus is actually run by reprogrammed drysine drones," said Erik. "We've seen them used in the attack on Joma Station. Probably that was just a small portion of them. Tartarus is a drysine base and was designed to be run by drones, possibly it can even make its own drones — it's big enough. If they've been reprogrammed by a deepynine queen, they'll be completely under her control."

"Can Styx reprogram them back?" asked Rooke.

Erik nodded slowly, and glanced at Trace. "That's the idea," said Trace. "Styx thinks it's possible. Not certain, but very possible. It's the reason the Joma Station attack would have been reckless if the hacksaws had suspected Styx was still alive — she *could* have reprogrammed some of them, at least. It's a technical process, far too complicated for even our best techs to understand. But if she can find a way to pull it off once we're inside Tartarus..."

"*That* would cause a pretty big distraction," said Shahaim, eyes widening. If Tartarus was run by drysine drones, with a sard and deepynine command presence... and all of those drones could be led in an uprising? Erik saw hope and realisation light anew in their eyes. The plan was crazy dangerous, and if it worked would likely create one of the biggest firefights anyone had ever seen. But it was far from hopeless.

"That would give Styx a drysine army of her very own," said Dale. "At which point she'd turn them on us and we'd all be dead, deepynine, sard and tavalai alike."

Silence as they all considered that. Could Dale be right? Was Styx's apparent cooperation just a ploy to get herself back into a familiar, powerful drysine shipbuilding base? Styx's entire aim was to rebuild the drysine race — what better way to do that than to reclaim such a huge strategic asset, and start rebuilding ships, drones and everything? A new body for herself, a final slate of neural repairs, a new fleet of whatever ships they were building over there and then off to resettle in some far part of the galaxy where neither humans nor Dobruta could reach?

"Hell of a chance to take," said Dale, into the silence he'd made. "Trusting something that doesn't even understand the concept."

"I put a hole in her head once," Trace said grimly. "If she tries something like that, I can always finish the job."

Erik should have been sleeping, but circumstances were making that impossible. He sat instead on his single chair and spoke to Commander Nalben on the wall screen.

"One of the fleet captains is launching a notice," Nalben explained, in his disconcertingly perfect English. *"It is a legal procedure to censure the Dobruta due to our actions here."*

"And what consequence will that have?" Erik was really too tired for tavalai legal nonsense. He'd heard tales about the sheer scale of tavalai legal bureaucracy, and it was well known that the third-most-senior officer on every tavalai military vessel was a legal officer.

"It challenges the right of the Dobruta to grant full protection to a human vessel, particularly to a warship. They cannot interfere with Makimakala, but they are claiming the right to interfere with Phoenix. Given that you are advocating a plan that will damage the tavalai-sard alliance. They are arguing that the alliance provisions have legal superiority."

"Great." Erik rubbed his face. "How long will that take?"

"Several rotations at minimum."

"Well *Phoenix* is not staying here that long. Our plan is set and we'll go without you if we have to."

"That is suicide."

Erik smiled faintly. "Only if it fails." The Captain had said that a lot. "Do you have an alternative plan?"

"Captain Pram wishes to rendezvous with other Dobruta vessels, and gather enough force to perform this mission properly."

"Tavalai space is big. How long to rendezvous with these other Dobruta vessels?"

On the screen, Nalben's big, three-lidded eyes shifted evasively. *"Perhaps a month. We are spread wide."*

"By which time your fleet here has sent communications back to your homeworld and brought full legal weight down on *Phoenix* to stop us."

"Dobruta can do this without you." Edgily. *"We are not helpless."*

"But you would not tell us what you find at the base. Humanity's survival depends on that information, and I cannot allow this to be a tavalai-only mission. We will not wait a month. We are going now. If you wish to influence the outcome of this assault in any way, you'd best convince Captain Pram to come along, or both the tavalai and the Dobruta will miss out."

A brief silence from Nalben. *"I'll talk to him. Again."*

"Good. Is that all?"

"That is all."

"*Phoenix* out, and good luck." Erik disconnected and slumped in his chair. Trace entered behind, no doubt having registered on uplinks that he was on coms.

"Any luck?" she asked, taking a seat on his bunk with her back against the wall, knees up and casual as she would never be with regular crew.

"Not yet. The tavalai fleet are threatening to bury us in lawyers."

"Poor tavalai," said Trace, with a faint smile. "I never thought I'd say that. They have institutions with founding charters thirty thousand years old. All of them have their own rules, and the laws to untangle it all just accumulate, like sedimentary layers. The Captain told me all about it."

"My Uncle Calvin did his thesis on some obscure tavalai legal thing or other. I forget which." Erik stifled a yawn. "It's a pity you didn't get a chance to talk to him properly on Joma Station. He's a pretty cool guy. So what's your readiness ETA?"

"Twenty hours. Engineering's modifying a harness to hold the queen. Styx, rather. Complete with a twenty thousand volt killswitch, assuming that will have any effect on her."

"I'd have more faith in a Koshaim-20, myself."

"Me too." She considered him with dark, tired eyes. Somehow the weariness never seemed to dim their alertness. It made Erik sit up straighter, and will his own eyes fully open. "If *Makimakala* won't come with us, what are our chances of getting out alive?"

"That's an unknown unknown," said Erik. The Captain had said that a lot too. "There are too many unknown variables."

"Assuming worst case scenario," Trace pressed. "Heavy defences, lots of advanced ships."

"But the unknown variable there is Styx. The worst case scenario is that they don't buy her transmission, but in that case we'll be blown from the sky long before we can make rendezvous with Tartarus. *If* they fall for it, and you go in to meet them? And *if* Styx can cause some kind of large distraction, as she claims she can?" Erik shrugged. "Again, how big? What kind of distraction? It's all on her."

"It really is, isn't it?" They were insane, Erik knew in the silence that followed. But they'd sworn an oath to defend humanity, and Fleet HQ had no interest in finding out the nature of the deepynine threat. It was *Phoenix* or no one, and 'no one' was not an acceptable option to either him or Trace. Whatever it cost. "If Styx can cause some chaos, we'll get out. Given the systems she can take over by remote, I'd guess she can, and there will be a lot of vital systems on Tartarus even aside from all those drysine drones. Hausler likes chaos. And he says you do too."

Erik nodded. "I can't change your mind about going yourself?" Trace gave a faint smile, and did not bother to answer. "You know, even your best officers think you have a death wish."

"All living things have a death *inevitability*," Trace replied, unruffled. "Kulina just understand it better than most."

"Knowing you're going to die isn't the issue," Erik retorted. "The issue is what's your rush?"

Trace smiled more broadly. "Promote yourself to captain and I'll tell you."

"You're lying. You wouldn't tell me if I did promote myself to captain."

"Come on, right here right now," Trace persisted. "We've got some captain's wings in storage, I checked."

"I'm sure you did."

"It needs to be done Erik. In situations like we're about to go into more than ever."

"I think the crew know who's in charge."

"I'm sure *they* do," Trace retorted. "I wonder about *you*."

Erik just smiled at her. These arguments between them were so familiar now. Trace smiled back, reluctantly. "You know," said Erik, "I really will miss this endless harassment when you're dead."

"The way we're going, I may just outlive you," Trace snorted. Erik grinned.

The door chime sounded, and Erik hit open. Tif entered, in her beloved flight suit that she seemed to spend more time in than anything else. To say that she'd taken to her role as *Phoenix* shuttle pilot was an understatement — Lieutenant Jersey had marvelled at how much simulator time she'd been accumulating, determined to learn these new military systems to the best of her ability.

"EwC," she said, her big golden eyes fixed on him with curiosity. "You want see ne?"

"Yes, Tif. I just wanted to say that I'm sorry, but we're not going to be able to get Skah off the ship for this mission. We're not going to have time." She stared at him. "Do you understand that?"

"You want Skah off ship?" She sounded alarmed.

"For this mission, yes. But we can't. We can't spare a shuttle, and we've nowhere safe to leave him where we can come back for him later."

"You want ne off ship?" Now she sounded upset, eyes wide.

"You?" Erik asked, puzzled. "No Tif, I don't…"

"I *Phoenix*," said Tif with fierce urgency. With her flight gloves off, the three-fingered claws came partway out, deadly sharp.

"I *Phoenix*, Skah *Phoenix*! You no say can... can not say..." She broke off in confusion, her English abandoning her.

Erik stood and put a hand on her shoulder. "Tif, no no. Bad communication." He smiled reassuringly. "Bad, I didn't mean to... look. In my culture? A small child on a ship in combat is very bad. We protect small children. We don't put them in danger."

"In ny cuwture?" said Tif, very earnestly. "Whole... faniry?" Erik nodded encouragingly. "Aw faniry together. One thing." She made a tight fist before his face, claws comfortingly retracted. "Bad thing happen nother, bad thing happen kid. Aw one thing."

"So what happens to children in a war? When their adults lose?"

Tif made a mystified gesture. "Depend who win. Sone good, sone bad. Sone... educate? Yes, educate kid, sone not. Sone kiw." She grasped his arm again. "I *Phoenix*, one faniry, yes?"

Erik nodded, and grasped her hand. A gesture of trust, considering the mess those claws could make of a human hand. "Yes Tif. One family. You and Skah, both *Phoenix*."

"Pronise."

"I promise."

"Good," she said, with obvious relief. As though the bad thing that she feared most had been banished. "Good. Thank you. I sreep now."

She nodded to Trace, and left. Erik looked at Trace, now seated upright on the edge of his bunk. "And sometimes," said Trace, "the aliens make more sense than the humans."

"Yeah," Erik sighed. "Sometimes."

CHAPTER 31

Phoenix slid out of hyperspace and raced. Erik blinked his vision hard upon the screens, as automated systems scrambled to process visuals, and cross-reference stars against existing charts.

"Navigation is processing," Kaspowitz announced.

"The timer is running," Shahaim added. "We are at T-minus-136 and counting." That was one hundred and thirty six minutes until *Makimakala* leaped from hyperspace at high-V and tried to kill the Tartarus base. Hoping, of course, that *Phoenix* had found some way to clear her path by then. Erik sipped from his water tube, watching the data cycle as posts reported in. Styx had given them the procedure that deepynine vessels of the class would follow out of jump. Now to hope that whoever was watching couldn't tell the difference.

"Vessel at eighty-seven by fourteen," Geish said tersely from Scan. "Maybe seventeen seconds light, it's not moving."

"That's an outsystem picket," said Shahaim.

"He'll see us in five," said Geish. "Four, three, two, one."

Now seventeen seconds of response time. Erik licked his dry lips. "Kaspo?"

"Navigation is still processing," said Kaspowitz. It did this sometimes, in unfamiliar systems.

"Second vessel," said Geish. "Two-oh-five by one-three-six. Also unmoving, range twenty-five seconds."

"We have arrived," came Styx's synthetic voice on coms. *"Commencing transmission."*

"Navigation fix," Kaspowitz said finally. "Gsi-81T confirmed, we are way out deep at nine AU, the system doesn't like it when we emerge so far from the star."

"I have Gsi-5," Geish announced. "System orbits are confirmed, Styx's charts are right — all the moons are just where they should be."

"Great," said Jiri, "now where's the Tartarus?"

"Scan confirms something very big on our present course," Geish added. "Range twenty-one seconds light." Erik's left screen flickered as nav built a picture of that object. "Very, very big," Geish amended. "Estimating... one-twenty klicks diameter, spherical. Hollow structure, that's why the nav's struggling to classify it."

"Fixed and locked," said Shahaim. Lieutenant Shilu's Coms channel was outputting something very strange indeed — massively high-frequency, encoded and complicated almost beyond a human decryption program's ability to handle realtime. Shilu's Coms post was routed directly to AT-7 and Styx.

"Signal will be reaching Tartarus in five seconds," said Shilu.

"Still no response from picket vessels," Geish added. "Only two so far, but this far out from the sun we've got limited visual ability."

Erik's tactical display showed him *Phoenix*'s position, eating up distance as she raced at full-V from jump — barely thirty minutes to the Tartarus at this velocity. Either they got a response soon or they were going to start running out of room. In far orbit to one side, Gsi-5 blocked any escape in that direction... though its huge gravity field did create some interesting escape trajectory possibilities. Tartarus was in a wide, far orbit from the gas giant, however, beyond most of the system's primary moons. Evidently the drysine spacers hadn't liked deep gravity wells any more than human spacers did.

"Any idea why we can see those two marks?" Erik asked. He was surprised at how calm he felt. Buried in uplink visuals, graphical displays and rapidly unfolding time parameters, he simply had no time to ponder unpleasant possibilities.

"Sir, I think they've deployed panels," said Geish. "Signal looks unnaturally strong to me, suggests they're giving away position and stealth on purpose. They might not even be warships, that looks like too large a signature."

"Visible defence," Shahaim said grimly. "LC, I reckon we're right in their defensive funnel. They've got other ships here too, lying dark — these two are their position markers. They want us to run deeper into their crossfire. The deeper we get when they spring the trap, the deader we are."

Erik's display showed that the Tartarus had received Styx's signal twenty seconds ago. A few seconds more for a reply, if they'd responded immediately. "We're holding course," he told the bridge, hands hovering on control sticks, thumbs and fingers a light pressure upon buttons and toggles. "There's no response yet, they haven't IDed us as hostile. Helm, get me a good escape vector."

"Already plotting LC," Shahaim replied.

"LC I have limited visual on a lot of activity up at the base," Jiri called from Scan Two. "Mostly small scale, there's... there's a lot of interference, but it looks quite busy."

"I can second that," Shilu added, toggling furiously through various frequencies. "I'm scanning for com traffic but nothing yet..."

"Active scan!" Geish cut him off, urgently. "We have been target locked by a new mark, location oh-eight-seven by..." and Erik tuned him out, seeing that new position appear on his tactical. Then another, then another, Second Lieutenant Geish announcing each in turn. And suddenly the entire forward scan lit up like an Exodus tree, a wave of ships locking on their targeting systems, like hidden hunters in the dark all turning on their flashlights at once. Erik's hands nearly jumped on the controls... only his heart refused to accelerate to panic speed because clearly this was a very odd way to spring an ambush. *Phoenix* was nowhere near deep enough into the crossfire yet, and the ambushers were giving away surprise and stealth at a time when *Phoenix* still possessed enough options to do something about it.

"LC, what are we doing?" Shahaim said with alarm, hands hovering over controls that would lock in an override escape route and get them the hell out of there.

For a brief moment, fear and doubt struggled to surface past his calm. "Does not look like an attack to me," his mouth said on automatic, even as his brain tried to rebel against his own words. But it looked like the truth, and the Captain had always said that a combat pilot had to trust his first instinct, because by the time he got to his second instinct, he'd be dead.　　"We're being bracketed, they're giving away their positions."

"Hello Phoenix," came Styx's voice on coms.　　*"This is a welcoming response to my signal.　　Correct procedure will be to dump velocity by the indicated increment, and proceed upon a steady course."*

Locked into her command post on AT-7, Trace could see *Phoenix*'s tactical feed projected on her faceplate.　　The situation looked as bad as could be expected if you flew in the front door of a heavily guarded fortress.　　But it was what a deepynine ship would have done in friendly territory, and they'd had no choice.　　One false twitch here and they were dead.

"Crowded, isn't it?" Lieutenant Hausler remarked from up front.　　If he felt the stress, his voice didn't show it.　　Hotshot pilots had cool reputations to upkeep.

"Hello Stan," said Trace on coms.　　Romki was strapped in down back with the queen, the only place where her carry-frame would fit.　　"How's she looking?"

"Major, that transmission is something... well, you'd be better off asking Rooke if he's watching..."

"I'm watching," Rooke interrupted from Engineering.　　*"It looks crazy, I've no idea what she's telling them.　　Seems to be working though."*

"Sure," said Lieutenant Jalawi of Charlie Platoon from nearby.　　*"So long as she's not telling them to put old differences aside and kill the humans first."*

"You people do understand that she can hear you?" Romki retorted.　　If Styx had an opinion on the humans' mutterings, she did not volunteer it.

"LC, I think I've got it."   Kaspowitz shunted his feed to Erik's screen, and suddenly he could see it — an indistinct sphere, blurred as *Phoenix*'s cameras tried to get a fix, not the simplest thing at this distance while still carrying combat-V from jump.   Then a shift of focus and it came abruptly clear, drifting and recorrecting as the cameras adjusted.

A massive series of frameworks, making a rough sphere in two distinct halves.   The entire sphere was quarter-lit as they approached from the outer system, Gsi-81T's small yellow star far distant and 'behind'.   One reason the cameras had such trouble picking it up, Erik realised — though the size of a very small moon, the base was non-reflective, its hollow maze of gantries seeming to suck in more light than they let out.

"Luminosity is low," Kaspowitz confirmed.   "Can't see much yet, have to wait until we're closer."

"Mark for V-dump in thirty seconds," Shahaim added.   They were following the course laid in according to Styx's parameters. The approach profile matched a deepynine carrier, Styx insisted, and she had provided a laundry list of things to do and to avoid. Foremost amongst them had been to turn off local wireless coms, which she'd insisted deepynine com-tech could register when close enough.   They were also without any form of active scan, relying entirely on passive reception.   That was going to make it hard to get weapons lock, particularly for defensive systems if someone started firing at them.   To intercept incoming fire, they relied entirely on active radar, which could not be disguised as anything but human. But presumably, if someone was shooting at them, the game would already be up.

"Coms, how's it looking?"   Erik was most concerned about the signal Styx was sending to the base.   The com frequency had been precisely modulated, utilising a high bandwidth humans rarely used, but Styx insisted was default on a deepynine carrier.   As with everything else, they'd had to take her word for it.

"All nominal," Shilu confirmed.   "Sir, I'm not getting any chatter from the base.   Either everyone's communicating on tightbeam or hardlines.   There's no random traffic at all."

"Been here a long time," Kaspowitz reminded them. "Coms traffic can survive sublight when the deepspace background buzz doesn't wipe it out.   If you're trying to stay hidden for centuries, you don't want your com traffic turning up a few hundred lightyears away for someone to trace."

V-dump arrived, and Erik pulsed them hard into hyperspace, then out at a more sensible velocity.   Still scan showed them locked by twenty-two different armscomps.   "Scan, do you have any ID on those marks?"

"Sir, scancomp shows those targeting locks as unfamiliar."

"*All* of them?"

"Yes sir."   Geish concentrated hard on the multiple analysis his systems were feeding him.   "Five different types.   We've got three painters, that's heavy active scan illuminating us for followup missiles — they're probably platform bases.   No visual confirmation at this point, so I'd guess they're less than twenty meters diameter.   The rest are a mix... there's three that look like they'll need a very high powerbase to generate, I reckon big ships, maybe even carrier-class."

"Sir," Jiri interrupted from Scan Two, "on our present course we'll be within visual range of one mark in one minute.   Permission to align main camera for a visual?"

"Permission granted," Geish answered for him — visuals were always the senior Scan Officer's prerogative.   "LC, that's a heck of a lot of marks in good defensive position.   It's going to be real crowded for *Makimakala* coming through here at high-V."

"We have to get at least half of those ships to displace or *Makimakala*'s got no chance at all," Shahaim said with certainty. "Even then they'll have to bury themselves in these defences to give the ordinance a chance of avoiding interception.   The survival to success ratio is looking unacceptable to me."

"We're going to have to find some way to get them to move," Karle observed nervously.

"Our mission is intelligence," Geish disagreed.   "Helping *Makimakala* to destroy the base is secondary."   Which wasn't what they'd told *Makimakala*.   Erik saw a few faces turn to glance his way. Hang the tavalai out to dry? Fail to clear their path, and allow the base defences to kill them on the way in? How much was a human's word worth, to the old tavalai enemy, when the fate of the human race hung upon them learning more about the deepynine queen they thought was running the Tartarus? If that queen did exist, then killing just her and this base became relatively insignificant. There were bound to be far, far more of them.

"Sir," said Jiri. "I have a visual on that mark. Putting it through now."

Erik's screen flipped, then settled on a bright smudge against a black background. That was about all you could expect at these speeds and distances, but now the image zoomed and sharpened as scancomp cleaned it and focused... and the analysis scrolled in fast numerics across the screen.

"Carrier-class," Shahaim muttered.

And from Geish, "What the hell *is* that?"

"That's trouble," Erik said as he stared at it. "Look at the size of those engines. It's bigger than carrier-class, and it's not our technology — we can't configure power-to-mass in those ratios."

"Well," Kaspowitz said conversationally, "that's a new ship. Congrats everyone, drinks on the LC." In the war, Fleet Intel had given hearty bonuses to any crew that found a new class of alien ship.

"Yeah," Geish agreed. "The bad news is it's probably deepynine, and it can probably kick our ass."

"That's not the bad news," Jiri disagreed. "The bad news is it looks like there could be a dozen of them."

Sixteen minutes later and *Phoenix* dumped velocity again. Trace blinked hard to get her vision back, popped her visor and sipped some water so she didn't deplete the suit bottle. Once the visor was down permanently, that would be the only water she had.

"Incoming signal," she heard Coms Officer Shilu saying on the bridge. *"That's... holy shit that's strong, encryption can't*

decode it... *LC, I have no idea what that is, but it's definitely coming from the base...*"

"*It's her,*" said Styx. "*The deepynine command unit. I will communicate my desire to meet. We must exchange and synchronise data, it will require a physical connection where sard allies cannot hear.*"

"Can't they see us?" Trace heard Rolonde mutter to Kumar nearby, off coms. "Can't they see we're a human carrier?"

"Matte-black paint out here?" Kumar replied. "There's no light, and our config already looks like an older deepynine carrier-class. Styx says."

"Styx says," Rolonde growled. "We bet all our asses on what Styx says." Trace knew she was thinking of her friends First Sergeant Willis and Private Ugail, whom Styx's drones had killed.

"Jess," Trace told her past the drink tube. "Mind on the job."

"Yes Major."

"*Styx,*" she heard Romki say. "*You can understand her language?*"

"*Yes. The coding is unusual. Evolved, perhaps.*"

"*And she appears to understand yours?*"

"*I am pretending to be a deepynine from the final era of deepynine civilisation. I am perfectly fluent in that mode of communication, and I am entirely certain no deepynine will ever forget it. She believes I am a relic of history, returned from the dead. And she will be right, only not about my side.*"

Crossing the river to the land of the dead indeed, Trace thought. Romki had named her well.

"*Communications sent and received,*" Styx confirmed. "*We are clear to go. Lieutenant Hausler, recall that this shuttle is supposed to be carrying AIs only, not organics. G-forces within this shuttle's performance range are of no consequence, and AI shuttles prefer the most direct path to their desired trajectory.*"

"*Now you're talking my language,*" Hausler replied from the cockpit. "*Phoenix this is shuttle AT-7, requesting clearance for departure.*"

CHAPTER 32

Lieutenant Hausler followed Styx's instruction by letting AT-7 coast for twenty-one minutes upon release, maintaining extra-V until the last possible moment before a tail-first 4-G burn slammed all passengers back in their seats for the final thirty-two minutes of approach.   Styx told Hausler to end the burn ten klicks out, a non-threatening approach profile that she would communicate in advance to those watching.   Tail-first with thrust blazing, the shuttle's cameras could not get a good visual on their destination.   When Hausler cut thrust and flipped them over to face the base, that changed.

Usually on coms when confronted with something amazing, marines would mutter remarks.   Now as AT-7's forward cameras filled their visors with live feed, Trace heard only awed silence.   The base's hundred and twenty kilometre girth filled all forward view. More wide than most human cities, all dull and silver steel, an eye-baffling maze of segments, nodes, pylons and interior bays.   She could see several ships docked to the outer rim, freighters with small engines and large cargo bays, surrounded by a buzz of small runners. From those docking nodes, conveyor tubes retreated along gantry arms back into the maze, to where warehouse blocks were barely visible deeper in.

"Transport arrives on the outside," Ensign Yun observed. Usually she and her hotshot pilot made a cocky, relaxed combination on missions, for the benefit of everyone's nerves.   Now they were subdued.   *"You've got cargo and freight for storage here, raw materials will be taken deeper inside, where the ships are made."*

"Those look like sard ships," said Hausler.   *"Freight transports.   So they're keeping it resupplied."*

"Correct," said Styx.   *"Raw materials are delivered within the hemisphere division.   That is sublight traffic, mined from the moons of this system.   I am curious to see if sard are performing that task themselves, or if more drysine drones have been enslaved for the purpose.   Or deepynine drones."*

"I have new target lock," Yun announced. *"Multiple small vessels, they appear to be on intercept."*

"Maintain current course," Styx said calmly. *"I am in communication with them. It is a greeting party."*

"What kind of greeting party?" Hausler asked.

"Unfamiliar." Trace did not need to see the glances her marines exchanged to feel the tension. Styx could be telling them anything.

AT-7's cameras got a fix on one of the approaching marks, several others close behind. Trace nearly swore as a hunched, silver shape filled her visor view, an armoured carapace centred by a single red eye.

"Hacksaws," said Yun.

"They are drysine drones," said Styx. *"They have been reprogrammed. My old friends can barely recognise themselves."* The synthesised voice almost sounded sad.

Trace did not believe it, and switched channel to Lance Corporal Penn. "Hello Lance Corporal. Stay on it."

"Yes Major." Someone had to sit down back with Romki and Styx, rifle loaded and prepared to blow the drysine queen to bits if things went south. They could not discuss such things openly, given how hard it was to keep frequencies hidden from her. Probably Styx guessed the humans had some such arrangement. Trace did not mind if she did.

The nearest drone vanished in a burst of white thrust, slowing on approach. They had propulsion rigs, Trace saw — jet units added in modular fashion to the rear thorax. Probably they could shed them if needed. In zero-G, drones could outfit for any number of different missions without being punished by the mass penalty as severely as in full gravity. The thrust-mist cleared, drones reversing course at a comfortable two-Gs before paralleling the shuttle, three to each side.

"They feed us a course change," said Styx. *"I am translating and conveying to the cockpit."*

"I've got it," said Yun. *"Hang on."*

"Got it," said Hausler, as Yun passed it on.   *"Proceeding now."*   He spun the shuttle abruptly on its axis, then hit mains with no regard for organic sensibilities.   Flying like a machine was no problem for Hausler, Trace thought.   He flew like that all the time.

"Timer is at T-minus-73," Yun reminded them, though the number was counting down in the corner of everyone's visor display. A little over an hour until *Makimakala* came blasting through.   It suddenly seemed like a very long time to keep all of these new friends from becoming suspicious.

"Styx," said Trace as the Gs faded.   "Tell us about the drones."

"A sadness.   They have been corrupted."

"How old are they?   Are they originals?"

"Yes.   Many bases were abandoned.   Without command units, drones will not retain function for long.   I suggest that these went into shutdown.   They will have only recently been reawakened. To this living death of reason."

"Styx," said Romki.   *"Can you rescue them?"*

"Not immediately.   If they knew my true identity, we would all be destroyed quite quickly.   These drones are entirely autistic to foreign commands.   I will have to seek another method."

"Can you access any local base system?" Romki pressed.

"I will try."

"It's a fucking guard of honour," said Jalawi, staring at his visor display.

Hausler's new course took them across the base surface, a mesmerising expanse of steel and dark, beckoning caverns within. There wasn't a lot of light, Trace noted.   Hacksaws didn't need much, with multi-spectrum scanners, and any sard now working here would have to bring their own.

Then AT-7's course took them across the hemisphere divide, where Tartarus's north and south halves were joined, creating a cavernous split between them.   Here the surface was a honeycomb of hexagons, each hundreds of meters wide.   Larger supports spanned kilometres, joining north with south.   Within the profusion of hexagonal spaces clustered solid units — industrial, Trace thought, connected with docking gantries and pressurised habitats. Many small vessels were docked, and several more moving. Sublight ships, no more than a few times the size of AT-7, fusion powered and more hull and holds than engines. They nestled amongst the forest of honeycomb gantries like small fish burrowed deep into an enormous reef.

"*Wow,*" someone breathed, breaking coms discipline for the first time. Trace thought this deserved it.

"*A few of those sublighters are pressurised,*" Hausler observed. "*That's sard, some of these docking habitats are pressurised too. Doesn't look like a natural part of the base. More like a recent addition.*" He threw them into a slide, course correcting at 3-Gs as he followed Styx's direction on his nav. The drone escort changed course with them, struggling to catch up with underpowered thrusters.

"*Those are recent additions,*" Styx confirmed. "*We did not build this with sard in mind.*"

Trace wondered what this was like for her. Whether she was old enough herself to remember this, she surely possessed memories from that time compiled by others, and transmitted digitally. Trace had often wondered at her own emotional reaction to seeing Sugauli again, were she to one day return. What would a drysine queen feel, to see this old grandeur once more? The still-living memory of a dead civilisation, from a time when her people had ruled the galaxy?

"*Look,*" said Yun as she spotted something. "*Flippers.*" 'Flipper' was the Fleet Intel codename given to sard warrior gunships. These were clustered at docking gantries about the habitats, a bristle of engines and weapon pods about an armoured hull. The sard equivalent to Fleet marine shuttles, based on tavalai tech like most sard ships, and overwhelmingly deadly to a civilian shuttle like AT-7. "*I count nine.*"

"*You can be sure there'll be a lot more,*" Hausler said grimly, adjusting course toward one of those yawning hexagonal gaps in the superstructure. About them the steel city closed in, blocking out the thin glow from the distant star. Artificial lights bristled from within Tartarus, like many distant campfires in a haunted forest.

"I calculate from Tartarus design and this sard dispersal that there could be more than ten thousand sard in the vicinity," said Styx. *"Sard are numerically predictable."*

Trace could feel the jaws of the trap closing around her... if it was a trap. If most of the workers running Tartarus were reprogrammed drysine drones, then most of the sard here would be either warriors or combat-capable administrators whose fighting skills and equipment weren't far behind.

"Going to be quite a job getting out of here," Jalawi murmured.

"Styx," said Trace. "How far in do you think the deepynine queen is?"

"Deepynine command centre will be approximately central with an offset. Navigation through this structure will take approximately twenty-eight minutes. First guard change is commencing now."

"Guard change?"

"I have new drones," Yun announced. *"Six marks, closing fast."* On her scan feed, Trace could see the new dots coming, and saw the existing six drysine drones decelerate and break off. *"Looks like the honour guard just changed... I'm reading a different transmission from these ones, they're bigger too."*

"Deepynine warriors," Styx said calmly. *"It appears that reprogrammed drysines are allowed only limited access to Tartarus interior and command functions."*

One of Ensign Yun's exterior cameras zoomed on the approaching deepynines... and immediately Trace could see the family resemblance with the deepynine command unit her marines had killed on TK55. An extended carapace and head-shield up front, a menacing, three-eyed 'face' and an angular profusion of limbs, modular jets and weapons. Everything about them looked deadly, the way a new settler on a colonial world could just tell that some strange insect was poisonous and shouldn't be touched. As though a million years of human evolution had conspired to imprint on the human brain that anything that looked like *this*, was death.

And Trace wondered if hacksaws had cultivated this appearance for that purpose, or arrived at it by unhappy accident.

"*Styx,*" asked Romki, "*who is more capable in combat? Deepynine or drysine drones?*"

"*Deepynine,*" said Styx with surprising certainty. "*Individually. But in manoeuvre, drysine tactics are more flexible and adaptive. All specifications and armaments being equal, one deepynine will beat one drysine six times out of ten, but a hundred drysines will beat a hundred deepynines by the same ratio.*"

"*So the more numerous and successful you became,*" Romki concluded, "*the more the drysines won.*"

"*Yes. I have a new course — Lieutenant Hausler, adjust accordingly.*"

"*Whoa,*" said Ensign Yun, "*I'm getting a big coms spike from these guys.*"

"*They are querying me,*" said Styx. "*Communications intensity has multiplied. They are... intrigued. No, fascinated.*"

It twisted Trace's brain to think of a machine being fascinated. And yet, as the deepynines fell into close formation about AT-7, guiding her through the surrounding structure, it almost seemed as when Trace herself had arrived on many human stations, and been surrounded by crowds of civvies and children come to catch a glimpse of the legend. Deepynines from alo space would no doubt have wondered often if they'd left anyone behind, hiding as Styx herself had been hiding. And now, here was a queen, perhaps the first they'd found in thousands of years.

"*If they're capable of being fascinated,*" Sergeant Kono remarked, "*then I bet they're capable of being pissed when they find out the truth.*"

"*I have expanded data access,*" Styx announced. "*I can see a long way now.*"

"*You've accessed the Tartarus data net?*" Romki asked.

"*Limited. I... hold a moment. Hold a moment.*" That was disconcerting too, sounding like what a lower-tech AI might say when its processing became so intense it lost the ability to talk. Until now, Styx had been talking quite calmly despite all her complex transmissions with the deepynines — an indication perhaps of just what a peripheral function speech was for her.   Bird calls, Captain Pram had said.   *"I have found someone."*   She sounded nearly astonished.   *"A drone unit, of normal function.   A drone not reprogrammed."*

"Styx?" Trace asked.   "Styx, what do you mean?   I thought the deepynines had reprogrammed all the drysine drones?"

"As did I.   This one has been hiding.   Pretending, from fear."

Fear.   Again Trace's brain struggled to accept that a drone could be scared.   "He's managed to avoid reprogramming?   Styx, can you make contact?"

"I do not wish to give him away.   He is also now the last of my kind."

Across from her acceleration seat, Jalawi gave her a concerned look.   Now was not a good time for the drysine queen to discover conflicting loyalties.   "Styx, this may be your only chance to save him.   If he stays here the deepynines will discover him eventually."

A thrust burst pushed them sideways as Hausler adjusted course through the maze.   *"He recognises me,"* Styx said then. *"He is... astonished.   He is... hold a moment.   Hold a moment."* Trace flipped quietly to the viewpoint of Lance Corporal Penn, and saw on his helmet cam Styx's wide carry cage bolted to the deck between rows of seats.   Penn's seat was higher, in zero-G stacking, and with his Koshaim unracked he'd have a good shot through Styx's head and into the decking, where no vital shuttle systems were located.   Trace had gotten Hausler to check.   *"I have a manifest of Tartarus shipping.   He has provided me access.   Seven major vessels under construction.   Fourteen completed new-generation warships in close protection, specification unknown. One hundred and thirteen sard assault gunships, accompanying eleven major sard warships."*

Dear god, thought Trace.   That was a fucking sard fleet, buried in here somewhere.

"Three captured vessels.   One tavalai, mostly destroyed, intercepted at a neighbouring system, name unknown.   One human, intercepted at a far system, name Europa.   One barabo, intercepted at..."

"Wait!" Trace snapped, as even her calmly thudding heart nearly stopped. "Did you say *Europa?*"

"Regelda Freightlines ship Europa, civilian freightliner. Thirty-one crew registered living and in captivity, Captain Aldon Houli registered deceased, passenger Calvin Debogande registered alive, passenger Elizabeth Chow registered alive..."

"Styx," Trace cut her off, "get me a secure line back to *Phoenix.*"

"I will have to disguise it as deepynine code, but the modulations may not look convincing.   I do not recommend this course of..."

"Do it now!"

For a moment Erik could not think or breathe, and simply sat locked in his command chair. This wasn't fair. This wasn't... and thoughts flashed to his family, and childhood times with Uncle Calvin and his kids, Erik's cousins, and games, dogs and barbecues. Cousin Sarah's dangerous virus and Uncle Calvin not leaving her bedside, so devoted to his kids, comforted now in his memory by Erik's mother, a hand on her brother's shoulder and assuring him that everything would be okay...

Those memories did *not* belong out here.   Those were his family, his home-life, that jumble of mundane complexity, loves and trials and relationships that were everything *this* life was not. In that life, Cousin Sarah had recovered and they'd celebrated with a ski-trip on her birthday, Sarah's favourite thing with fireplaces and snow, and presents, food and songs...

And now, her dad had been abducted by deepynines. It just wasn't possible that those two worlds could collide like this.   But here was Trace Thakur, perhaps the most reliable person he'd ever met on things that mattered, telling him exactly that.

"Shit they must have followed them!" Shahaim breathed in horror. "From the Joma Station attack, the sard must have followed them and…"

"Hello Styx," Erik cut her off, because it really didn't matter now. Suddenly the confusion vanished, replaced with hard certainty. If there was one thing in all the galaxy he had been fighting for, in all his military life, it was to stop his military and home lives from colliding. And that was what he'd do. "Your distraction. Will it be big?"

"The possibilities of scale just increased."

"How have they increased?"

"This friendly unit has encrypted communications with fellow drysines. I have access to the override programs. I can deprogram them."

"How many of them?"

"Unknown. Perhaps some, perhaps most."

"To what effect?"

"Localised civil war in Tartarus. My people can be freed."

In the chair to his front and left, Kaspowitz had turned his head to stare. 'We're going to give her an army?' that stare asked. He said nothing, but Erik knew.

"Styx, likely outcome of localised civil war?"

"Mutual mass casualties. Unsupported, drysines will cease effective resistance in under fifty human minutes. Supported, victory is possible, if unlikely."

"Styx, we are going to send in another shuttle once you start the war. Its objective will be the rescue of human and other alien crew from those captured vessels. *Phoenix* will operate as a base of support for all rebelling drysine drones."

"LC," Trace retorted, *"this plan will endanger our primary mission to confirm the existence of a deepynine queen…"*

"No it won't, she will expose herself in any fight we start."

"LC as marine commander in the field, I will not…"

"You're in a spacer shuttle Major, and this is *not* your command. You will obey orders or I will have you replaced." His words held no temper, just the certainty of what it would take to make her shut up. "Lieutenant Jersey, please report."

"Hello LC, this is Jersey, PH-3 is ready and waiting."

"Hello LC, this is Crozier, Delta Platoon is go."

Jersey and Crozier were a pair, Delta Platoon standing by in PH-3. Trace's concerns with Crozier's state of mind occurred to him... but she *was* the standby roster, and for this job only one platoon was going to fit.

"Lieutenant, PH-3 and PH-4 will depart on combat approach when I give the signal. Your objective is rescue, humans first, anyone else who can fit in second. PH-3 will take Delta Platoon, PH-4 will fly empty for prisoner recovery. We will try to get you an escort."

"PH-3 copies, an escort would be real interesting."

"PH-4 copy," Tif echoed. *"Good fun yes?"* Erik wondered what the kuhsi word was for 'bravado.'

"Phoenix," said Styx, *"my drysines will provide both shuttles with escort. I have a fix on the prisoners' location now, I will feed it to you."*

CHAPTER 33

Trace flipped her visor view to widescreen as AT-7 entered a cavernous bay. Four major warships were under construction here, in an interior space so large it made the huge ship bays on TK55 look like closets. Each ship was woven into a tight embrace of gantries and grapples, a cluster of interlocking steel skeleton so tangled it was hard to see where the Tartarus began and the warships ended.

About the ships were a small storm of construction vessels, tugs and drones. Upon the ships themselves swarmed hacksaw drones, like ants devouring the dead carcasses of larger animals, only these were not devouring, but building. The construction zone flashed with blue and yellow welding glow, dancing spot-fires that showered orange sparks into the vacuum. Hausler adjusted course to avoid haulers pulling hull segments across the void, and the deepynine escort flexed their formation without breaking it. Ahead of them, the construction cavern went on forever.

"Styx, can you get control of some of these ships?" Trace asked. She could see Jalawi's face across from her, viewing the same view that she did, grim and increasingly certain that this would be his last mission.

"*They are drysine command, but a different coding to my drones. I cannot do it myself, but some of the higher-ranked drones may find it possible.*"

"What about the ships in the vicinity of *Phoenix*?" If they started a fight here, the picket ships would immediately fire on *Phoenix* once they realised the situation.

"*The firebases are all drysine. I can gain control and fire upon the picket vessels. The surprise should incapacitate many, and the rest shall be too occupied with that threat to be concerned of Phoenix.*"

"You're certain?"

"*Yes.*"

"How many ships in Tartarus? Get me a map."

And with that her visor flashed again, and she zoomed fully into tacnet. It gave her a 3D display of the entire Tartarus sphere, alive with more activity than she could possibly track. But here, blinking for convenience, were seven locally-constructed warships, all docked within various inner cavities.

"Gaining access to those ships will be the first priority," said Trace. Her heart was thudding in spite of all her habitual calm, and she focused her breathing, slow and deep. "We need to keep them busy and divert their attention. They'll want to protect their base, so big warships inside their perimeter will do that."

"Agreed. I have no firm number of drysine drones, I cannot contact them all. I estimate between three and four thousand."

Trace licked her dry lips. She could not deny her nerves now, nor her fear. She'd never commanded anything a fraction as big. A glance at her visor counter showed T-minus-42.

"If we don't do it soon Makimakala's going to run through here and blast Tartarus with us still inside," Jalawi growled.

"We have to get closer," said Trace. "Styx, can you confirm the queen is at the central core?"

"No, but it is the traditional location for command. Major, most of my drones are workers, though a small number have weapons. I estimate no more than ten percent, for rapid defence."

"Can we get more? You guys have modular configuration, the drones that attacked Joma Station were armed. Where are those weapons?"

"I am scanning. Here, directly ahead, a reconfiguration point. There are others, all will be guarded." And Trace saw on her tacnet a large structure at the end of the shipbuilding cavern, highlighting now as she zoomed on it. Interior structures appeared, maze-like.

"Unarmed drones attacking that could get slaughtered if the defenders are well set. Everything depends on getting enough drones armed to make a difference, we can't launch a rebellion without weapons."

"Well we're going to be there on our present course in one minute," Hausler told her. *"Phoenix is still a long way out to launch a rescue shuttle, they'll have to boost up to get here quick."*

"Can they do it?"

"Yes."

"Then we're out of time. Styx, do it now. Don't message *Phoenix*, they'll figure it out when the shooting starts."

"Yes. Commencing." Trace took several more breaths to slow her thumping heart. Just before it started was always the worst, like the anticipation of jumping into ice cold water. Once you were in, the body and mind adjusted. On tacnet, nothing changed. Trace wondered how she'd be able to command something this scale once it started. And realised that of course, she couldn't. Styx might manage it. If it worked.

"I'm getting new scan activations from our escort," Yun said with alarm. *"It looks like they're querying."*

"They have registered something wrong. My signal is propagating. Do not break formation or they will destroy us."

Trace saw Jalawi looking at her. AT-7 had no guns save for its marines, and the marines had to stay hidden. Emerging to shoot at the deepynines would get AT-7 shredded before they could hit anything.

"Styx?" Trace heard Romki press. *"Progress?"*

"Localised. We must not flinch. Patience."

"Shit," muttered Hausler, as one of the drones swung sideways on its course, full-frontal with all weapons. Trace could see underside launchers, and twin rotary cannon on its 'shoulders'. In zero-G, hacksaw drones were like flying tanks, only smaller and more mobile.

"As soon as we're clear we dock with the armoury ahead," Trace told Hausler.

"Copy. Thirty seconds." The end of the cavern drew closer, visible now within the shadow of massive steel walls. Wedged between several gantries was a huge, dark spheroid, cocoon-like and ominous. Trace could see entry portals — hacksaws needed no airlocks — hexagonal openings into the maze.

"Charlie Platoon, prepare for mobile disembark and rapid assault," said Trace, activating full suit combat settings and hearing the powerplants whine and thump to life about her. Some more drones jetted across their path, grasping assembly segments destined for the far side.

Ensign Yun saw the movement before Trace did. *"Fast approach!"*

"I see it." As scan showed deepynines rotating fast to face it — a large ship segment, pushed by multiple drones, burning straight at them. Eruptions of white as the deepynines evaded, then an abrupt twist of vertigo as Hausler flipped AT-7 and slammed full power.

"They're hitting 'em!" said Yun, as a camera struggled for focus past Hausler's burn — a blur of bright flashes, rotary guns flaming and worker drones coming apart. One collided with a deepynine and sent it spinning. But now Hausler's evasion was taking them away from the armoury sphere.

"Hausler, get us behind that armoury!"

"Trying, they're locking us!"

"They will not fire on us yet," said Styx. *"They are confused. Head for the armoury, deepynine missiles are no threat."*

"Do it," Trace confirmed, then another spin and hard burn as Hausler realigned. Trace caught another glimpse on visual, a flood of drysine drones pouring off their ships and straight at the six deepynines like a steel tide. Unarmed against murderous fire they disintegrated by the dozen, filling the cavern with tumbling silver debris. More exploded from missile strikes. Then another missile, inexplicably missing, turned a full arc and blew a deepynine apart.

The remaining five drones turned toward the fleeing AT-7, as though on cue. That was Styx, Trace realised. Taking control of deepynine missiles in flight and using them to kill each other. They knew, and now turned to kill the source.

"Evasive," said Styx, but drysines were hitting the deepynines before they could fire, some wrecked and half-dead but still holding momentum, grasping their hated enemies with broken steel limbs, some with impacts the force of car-crashes with

417

accumulated velocity. And then the larger deepynines were slashing and cutting with those horrid close-quarter blades for which humans had given hacksaws their name. But the drysines had working tools too, and each cluster tumbled in an accumulating, thrashing ball of steel as more drones crashed in to replace the ones destroyed.

"Alignment!" Hausler advised, and suddenly the rear hold cracked open, seats retracting as only harnesses locked marines in place — AT-7's civilian design included orbital construction work, and personnel deployments not dissimilar from those marines used. *"We are dead on line, marines deploy!"*

And those down the back left without ceremony, the entire hold vanishing in white thruster-mist as they jetted out, then the next, then the next, in well practised order. Then it was Trace's turn and she grabbed Sergeant Kono's rig as he thrusted first, and Jalawi grabbed hers, a big armoured chain pulling them rapidly into vacuum.

And then she was out, spinning in open space and bringing her Koshaim rapidly to hand, orienting to find the big, dark sphere was indeed right before them and they'd have to brake hard not to slam into it. Already her marines were doing that, fanning wide into groups and formations as they did, many turning back to see the deepynines... but they were gone. In their place came a swarm of silver drysine workers, like a scene from ancient nightmares. Every instinct in Trace's body screamed at her to command her marines to turn their weapons on them and fire.

"First and Third Squad flank!" she said instead, fixing all attention forward at the sphere. "Second Squad go straight in, Command Squad has your rear. Flankers, watch for reinforcements, kill anything not drysine. If you're not sure, the drysines will show you."

Ahead, marines were firing, heavy fire pulverising those entry portals, and the figures emerging there. *"Sard,"* Jalawi announced. *"Sard warriors, they're inside, don't let 'em get set."* As fifty-two armoured marines spread wide across the approach, thrust and muzzle-flashes leaping, picking targets as they came.

"Sard warrior shuttles approaching," Styx announced calmly. *"They are acquiring long range missile lock. They will not succeed."*

"Get us a fix, Styx," said Trace as her first marines reached the sphere. Second Squad flipped guided grenades through several entry portals, awaited the explosions, then thrusted inside. "AT-7, stay real close. You're our command and control centre with Styx, stay within our sphere and we'll protect you."

"Copy Major."

Tacnet showed Trace the spheroid armoury's interiors as Second Squad penetrated — branching zero-G corridors, lots of junctions, open architecture beyond where things spread out. They were shooting now as they went, sard defenders scrambling and out of position — suiting up took time and preparation, which a surprise attack had robbed the defenders of. So where were the sard living quarters? Since nothing in the armoury was pressurised for organic habitation?

"First Squad, someone circle backside to see where these sard are living." Shouts and terse commands as Jalawi passed that on. Trace hit the sphere beside a bullet-chewed entrance, yanked a mauled sard corpse from her path... and was cut off by Kono and Rolonde going in first, Arime and Kumar guarding her back as she followed them in.

She pursued the shooting ahead, watching the tight coordination on tacnet and listening to sharp commands from sergeants and corporals, broken by bursts of fire. On tacnet, Corporal Riskin of Heavy Squad found the sard habitation module built onto a huge structural support on the rear side of the armoury — a big seed-like thing with life-support modules attached.

Trace did not need to tell them to kill it, and Heavy Squad opened fire with chain guns and autocannon. Barely five seconds later and drysine drones were arriving at speed, burning hard to change course on modular thrusters and slam into the well-holed structure. Riskin yelled his squad to cease-fire, and with a squeal of cutters and construction tools hacksaws ripped into the damaged module in an accumulating, frenzied mob. Even from the corner of

419

her eye on a visor display as she advanced through armoury tunnels, Trace felt a mesmerised horror to see it — the habitat torn to pieces in seconds, then the bodies of struggling sard emerging, some suited and others not, similarly dismembered and sent spinning with the rest.

Trace returned attention to her environment as the corridors gave way to a massive open space, a framework of storage grids, each dividing an equipment bay from its neighbours. Within them, meticulously racked and stowed, were modular weapon systems, thrusters and other things Trace could not identify. It was a hacksaw locker room, with each locker holding everything a drone might need for a variety of different missions. It must have been here when the sard had found Tartarus, Trace thought. With their total control of reprogrammed drysines, they'd thought the armouries too useful to consider the negative possibilities, if the drysines could be freed. The corridors turned into levels, encircling the sphere like the rings of an onion — no walls only layers of racked equipment, now quickly being freed of sard with rapid movement and bursts of precise fire. A last few tried to flee from armoury exits, and were killed by flanking First and Third Squads. Sard were known to retreat, occasionally even to panic and run, but no human had ever seen one surrender.

Fat lot of good it would have done them here, Trace thought as movement behind revealed a crashing, clattering mass of drones following them into the sphere. "Second Squad, Command Squad, move out before we get trampled!"

She hit jets for where tacnet schematic showed corridors would lead to an exit, bouncing off walls in her haste to get clear... but agile drones came rushing past from behind, hauling themselves with precise tugs of multiple legs, guiding and propelling their mass with surprising grace. They darted above and behind the retreating Command Squad marines, intent on their business and with no interest in allied humans. More astonishingly still, other drones on the point of entering hung back while the marines got out, before rushing inside to join their comrades.

Out in the huge cavern, the space around the armoury was now a cluster of drones, a sensation like being inside an insect hive. Amongst them were dismembered steel limbs and other tumbling debris from the fight, glittering like Deliverance decorations scattered by a strong wind.   Nearby, a knot of several drysines tumbled over and over about a common hulk they were busily dismembering — one of the deepynines, Trace saw, from the small remains that were left.   This was the war, then.   The great deepynine-drysine war — twenty five thousand years ended in the drysines' favour, and now in this one little corner of the galaxy, very much back on.   And it looked as though the genocidal hatred had not diminished one bit.

Missiles were incoming, and Trace hit the jets toward one of the massive steel cross braces, and a secure vantage from which to see. Explosions as the missiles hit supports or spiralled past without direction, Jalawi securing return-lock and marines returning fire with back-launchers.   Trace jetted to a halt amidst the cross-beams, and saw in the forest of steel and shadows beyond the shipyard sard shuttles evasive, ducking for cover and firing again.   Those missiles were no more effective — Styx was jamming them, but the marines' fire wasn't any better.

"They're jamming us back," Trace observed as her scan indicated that. "Rifle fire, aim your shots. Styx, see if you can find out what's jamming us so we can kill it. How far to the core?"

"Nearly twenty kilometres."   A bright flash erupted from several kilometres away. *"My drones in Sector Five have acquired a docked warship, we are employing weapons."*   More bright flashes, close-range ship defences engaging.   Some fast blurs streaked the dark, and something exploded off a support nearby. Within the Tartarus's open structure, weapons fire and shrapnel would travel a long way.   Things were about to get very messy. *"They are regrouping, centring defences about the core."*

"I can see that." Heavy gunfire ripped in from the shuttles, sparking and ricocheting off supports and slamming holes in the armoury.   Marines returned fire, and one shuttle ceased fire and spun.   Koshaims would put holes in heavier armour plate than shuttles possessed — using them to engage marines in firefights was very ill-advised. "We need to hit them before they get set. How wide is the uprising?"

"It is nearly universal. We are gaining ships, but in these facilities we cannot manoeuvre them, and will lose them quickly. I have lost all contact with the deepynine queen, all enemy transmissions have gone defensive. Deployment patterns suggest high probability of command presence neither deepynine nor sard."

"Alo," said Trace, diverting attention from the fireworks that lit the Tartarus interior before her to consider her tacnet. The scale of it was insane — she was a major, accustomed to a full company command at most. What she saw here required admirals and generals. But even if she had the rank and experience, she had no means of ensuring these troops would obey her command. Besides which, *no* human commander had ever seen anything like this. "These sard are delaying us, we must advance quickly."

"My drones have captured multiple armouries about the middle-perimeter. We will have acquired sixty-percent armament in another two-point-five minutes. Anything less will be insufficient for a successful assault."

"We'll do a staggered advance," Trace said sternly. "See this next ring of manufacturing facilities? Armed units must capture that first, units still-to-arm can follow behind. We must expect a deepynine counter-attack from the core and that inner ring gives us better position."

Trace wondered what she'd do if Styx had other ideas. Tell Corporal Penn to threaten her? If these drones decided to protect their queen from the humans first, Charlie Platoon and Command Squad would last no more than a minute, if that. More explosions and shooting, close and distant — always disconcerting in vacuum as the mind instinctively braced for the huge, crashing noise that never came. A sard shuttle exploded, stubbornly insisting on a shooting-vantage. Heavy ship-fire tore through gantries from somewhere distant — drysine vessels employing main weapons at close range. Drysine drones were swarming from the armoury exits now, armed with their latest attachments — chain guns, launchers, close-range cutters, auto-cannon.

"You are correct.   Human marines should act as fire-support, your tactics against deepynines are ineffective."

Trace might have argued, for pride, but in this environment Styx had a point. "I copy, let's flank these sard shuttles and move."

CHAPTER 34

Erik pulsed as soon as the shooting started, and *Phoenix* ripped out of hyperspace abruptly closing on the Tartarus. Scan called coordinates, and Arms shouted for permission to fire, as stationary firebases opened up on picket vessels that were suddenly too busy dodging and defending themselves to worry about *Phoenix*. One of them broke up on scan, then a firebase vanished, and fire ripped past them from somewhere as Karle and Harris tracked and returned fire on automatic.

"V downrange target!" Karle announced as armscomp highlighted a ship emerging from Tartarus docking along that huge circumference rim. "Confirmed sard warship!"

"Kill it," Erik confirmed, and Karle fired. Even now the Tartarus was racing up, and Erik hit pulse once more to dump V at crazy close range, and came out tumbling purposely end-over to burn off the remaining V and make their approach evasive at the same time. Return fire ripped by, *Phoenix* autos detonated some more close-range, then a huge explosion turned an outer portion of Tartarus into a fireball as Karle's sard target detonated from high-velocity fire.

"I'm going to get in close," Erik told them as deceleration-V eased off, and he tumbled them beam-on for the gunners to get a view. Harris obliged by killing a docked sard freighter, its back breaking in high-mass slow motion. "The outer pickets won't be able to shoot without hitting Tartarus."

"Massive manoeuvres!" Shahaim said tersely, staring at the same combat scan that he did, a mass of swirling, evading ships as the pickets tried to avoid getting killed by their own firebases. "Operations approaching mark!"

"Operations stand by!" Erik told his shuttles, seeing nav tag the optimal release point as he corkscrewed their way in. Incoming fire came up from Tartarus, light and possibly no more than heavy infantry weapons. Harris pasted their locations with *Phoenix*'s close range armaments, and whole swathes of Tartarus steel cross-braces erupted in fiery bursts that killed anyone or anything not in armoured cover across several square kilometres.

"I'm getting a feed from Styx!" Shilu announced. "I've got marine tacnet, they're all still there!" Erik felt wave of relief, but no great surprise — Styx and Trace were dropping the pretence and resuming combat communications. "They're in a big furball at grid A-15, and we've got..." Shilu had to gasp to take it in, and Erik resisted the temptation to glance at marine tacnet, something the Captain had drilled into him he *never* had time for, "...we've got Tartarus-wide uprising, I'm reading *thousands* of drones on the move! They're getting armed and they're taking over docked drysine shipping!"

"Operations mark in five!" Shahaim announced. "Good luck girls."

"You betcha," said Jersey. *"Tiffy, stick on my wing."* And Operations showed them gone as the countdown reached zero, disconnected and racing toward the Tartarus's fast-approaching surface tail-first and thrusters blazing.

Styx would be coordinating all of that, Erik realised. Trace retained command of *Phoenix* marines, but she had no facility to command anything on this scale, and the drones would not listen to her anyway. And so the balance of power shifted once more, terrifyingly... and yet they had no choice. An uprising of this scale was the only way they were going to get what they wanted and get out alive, and yet Styx now had exactly what Kaspowitz and others had argued she'd get — a drysine army, weapons and even warships. If she turned on Trace and *Phoenix*, they'd all be dead very quickly.

But then again, if Styx had simply wanted resources to restart the drysine race and then vanish into the void, she had all of that now... but was still here, and apparently fighting, or commanding all her newly acquired forces to fight. So whatever she was after, immediate escape was not it.

'Hekgarh', Tif's people called it.   The hunter's fear. Humans knew only one kind of fear, but kuhsi knew many.   Too often in her life, Tif had known 'muhkgarh', the quarry's fear.   It came from helplessness, and was sometimes called 'the woman's fear'. 'Muhkgarh' was the fear of things you could not control.   It was the fear of a game animal in the tall grass, the fear of a wife in violation of her husband's command, the fear of a passenger in a burning aeroplane.

Tif had known muhkgarh when she'd run from her family estate in the Heshog Highlands as a youngster, to the great plain city of Regath. Her family had tried to kill her by the old laws of clan-right, but Lord Kharghesh's agencies had stopped them, and punished several. Those were the new laws, Lord Kharghesh and his supporters' invention, to give a new role to women in all the nation of Koth. Inspired, Tif had applied to an academy, and been accepted on aptitude.

There, for the first time, she'd learned hekgarh, the hunter's fear. Hekgarh was the fear of warriors in battle, of hunters stalking their prey, of talented practitioners employing their skills in a dangerous field. The kuhsi doctors described it as a difference of adrenal glands, stimulating different portions of the brain. Many insisted that hekgarh was medically unknown to women, and claimed 'science' that proved it. But strapped tight into her cockpit on approach to a fight far crazier than Tif had ever imagined, she knew those old kuhsi doctors were frauds. She felt fear, yet unlike that fear of her youth, it did not make her wish to flee. *Phoenix* was her clan now, and in *Phoenix*'s fight she would charge, slash and kill her enemies. This hunter's fear was an intensity unlike anything she'd known, and if only to spite her blood father, she could not think of any place she would rather be.

Lieutenant Jersey's voice came in her ears, but past the engine roar and vibration, plus the crackle on the coms, Tif caught perhaps one word in three. Something about entry points and *Europa*'s location…

"Ree," she said impatiently, "nav screen." Because she and Ensign Lee had a system worked out, where any incoming commands that could be flashed to her screens would happen immediately, and save her the trouble of trying to figure out what was said.   Between the words and the visual, she could usually figure it out in just a few seconds more than it would take a human pilot.   For anything that required a faster reaction than a few seconds, she was on her own.

The nav screen flashed, and Tif's blink transferred it to her visor — a plotted trajectory, with *Europa*'s position on the far end. In between, Jersey would take them down very low to the Tartarus surface, to avoid exposure to fire.   Scan overlaid active data onto that course-plot, as *Phoenix* compiled as much data as it could gather from the battlespace, then fed it out to its pilots.   And what it showed was crazy, drysine drones swarming in the Tartarus, sard warriors fighting back, and in all likelihood deepynine drones gathering forces near the core.   Tif found a moment to be thankful Lisbeth wasn't coming along on this one — the girl had a rough idea what she was doing, and probably some natural talent as well.   But this was a place for warriors.

PH-3 and 4 hit the turnover point, cut deceleration thrust and flipped to face the target.   The sheer size of it baffled the senses, a vast horizon of steel-grey beams and girders, creating odd patterns that reminded her for a crazy moment of the baskets her grandmother had once weaved from river reeds.   But she had no time to ponder it, locking forward cannon to her visor with thumbs on the triggers.   That weapon system she'd gotten good at.   The others, she left to Lee in the nose seat.

Off to one side, a series of rolling fireballs across the steel horizon — *Phoenix* engaging surface targets in their path. Correction point arrived and she hit thrust as the lines matched, Gs slamming her down and rolling PH-4 about so she could see her course direction through the upper canopy.   Then they were matching the Tartarus horizon, the steel whipping past a hundred meters below.   Tif nudged them lower, heard Lee warn of debris ahead and gave them a little kick sideways to miss it.   There were no big burns and big manoeuvres down this low — like the low altitude flying she'd learned on Choghoth in Lord Kharghesh's academy, you kept your movements smooth and small, or you made a smoking crater in something hard.

More fire from *Phoenix* ahead, paralleling their course 'above' relative to Tartarus, and moving to put Tartarus between herself and those picket vessels. Something big blew up with the brightest flash Tif had ever seen, her visor blackening to save her vision. Steady chatter now on her coms — human chatter, far beyond her ability to understand, but she trusted that if she needed to know something, Lee would flash it to her screen or yell it at her in time. The flash died away — probably *Phoenix* had hit another sard ship. Tif could not help the surge of pride in her heart. *Phoenix* was a beast, a legend of the human war machine and as powerful as a squadron of ships in the meagre kuhsi fleet. That the scared little poor girl from Heshog should find herself *here*, a vital part of the *Phoenix* operation, would make the spirits of ten thousand ancestors rise from their graves to notice.

Jersey said something else, sounding alarmed, and Tif heard the word 'escort'. Scan showed small marks approaching, and Lee was not tagging them as hostile, so she held course and swung the tail out for a light burn to keep her course circular, matching Tartarus's curve as the base lacked the gravity to make a normal orbit. And then the marks on scan arrived, and Tif glanced out the canopy to see hacksaws off her wing, in flexible formation. She'd expected it, but still it was shocking to see them this close. They looked like dark-silver lobsters, bristling with limbs and bulky with modular weapons and thrusters that nearly doubled their size. In gravity they'd be nearly immobile, but out here a drone could act as a very small ship, though without the powersource to thrust for long before running out of fuel. Clearly these were drysine, given no one was dead yet. Their escort.

Course correction arrived, and Tif swung PH-4 tail-first and kicked the thrust at a full 4-Gs to slow them. It was unnerving, because slowing down would make them an easier target for an enemy shooting at them from the cover of Tartarus... which was where, at slower velocities, an escort would be useful, to spot and kill any threat before it could fire.

She reached nearly zero-V immediately over the lip of a cavernous shipyard. Within was chaos, several smaller ships ruined and floating free amidst the smashed debris of a recent fight. Tif cut thrust a moment to allow PH-3 to assume the lead — unloaded, PH-4 was a little more mobile, and she'd get ahead of Jersey if she wasn't careful.

"Watch your V," Jersey said tersely as they powered inside, then cut thrust and swung to dodge the best course through the debris. *"Could run out of room real fast."*

Tif matched her lead — no more than two hundred kph in here, little more than a ground car on a big city freeway, but surrounded by things to crash into and with no direct line-of-sight to anything, it felt fast enough. Flying shuttles was nothing like driving cars or flying aeroplanes in atmosphere — those vehicles went where you pointed them. Shuttles in zero-G vacuum went with their momentum, like a puck sliding on ice, and in close proximity a pilot's illusion of control could disappear real fast. To move she'd have to swing PH-4's thrusters well out past where she wanted to go, which took at least several seconds' advance planning. Shuttle pilots in proximity had to think and look well ahead of their immediate surroundings, like a racecar driver already plotting the apex of a corner three turns ahead. Reflexes helped, but if your fast evasion only put you smack on course to an even worse obstacle, reflexes alone could get you killed.

Tif swung and rolled her way through the moving debris field, giving repeated little kicks of thrust to change course, then a final big one past a large chunk of engine housing, tumbling with explosive scorch marks. Beyond was a much larger ship — a warship, Tif judged, though barely half the size of *Phoenix*. Hacksaw drones swarmed over it, even now Tif could see them disappearing into small holes torn in the midships hull.

"Looks like they're still fighting in there," Lee observed. *"Probably sard warriors still inside."* Only half of the drones appeared to be armed... but inside the close corridors of a ship, unarmed hacksaws could still be deadly.

"Big target," Tif complained, thinking of those docked ships she'd seen *Phoenix* kill so far. "Draw big fire, we go." Ahead, their thrust-equipped escort dove and skidded through a hexagonal gap and into the gloom beyond. Through the forest of pylons and supports, Tif could see a flashing red storm of tracer fire. She took a deep breath, swung PH-4 sideways, and kicked the thrusters to begin her first turn.

Command Squad shot forward on accumulated V, Trace hitting light thrust to edge closer to a massive support truss for cover, her local formation flexing to pass around it. About them, Charlie Platoon did the same, First Squad ahead, Second and Third on the wings, proceeding with depth and flexibility as they avoided the most deadly open space without losing formation.

Out to a kilometre ahead the shooting was intense, as armed drysines dodged and ducked through the Tartarus tangle in a silver swarm, coordinating cross-fires and zig-zags with their comrades amidst a rain of incoming and outgoing fire. That fire was going everywhere, already her marines had taken several hits, all thankfully stopped by armour with minimal damage so far. But Styx had been right — operating without cover was something best left to machines that could soak up damage and keep functioning at close to optimal. With limited cover, hacksaw warfare in Tartarus turned into a contest of fire volumes, and with most of the drysines' immediate enemy being sard, it was a contest the drysines were winning.

Sard defenders now fell back past a series of dark bands encircling the Tartarus interior. Trace had supposed those bands constituted a manufacturing layer, but now they seemed more complex — enclosed factory complexes interlocking with the open frameworks that hacksaws seemed to prefer as living space. Tacnet highlighted defensive positions the sard had hastily set up, hundreds of drones feeding data into what was undoubtedly the largest and most stable tacnet setup Trace had ever seen. Her marines put missiles on those locations, primed for airburst, and drones rushed them before sard could recover their aim.

"Get in and find cover!" Trace commanded, above the background flurry of small chatter, noncoms keeping formations tight, buddies warning of debris or exposure to incoming fire. "I want good forward fire positions, we are the base of fire for the drysines!"

Her eye flicked to the countdown as she approached — it was T-minus-twenty-six minutes until *Makimakala*'s arrival. Ahead was a latticework of steel frames, deep and complex like honeycomb with drones scrambling through the gaps. She decelerated hard at fifty meters and followed Kono though an opening.

The interior was black, alien and harsh... yet strangely beautiful. Central structures were like ornamental stars, with exploding points fanning in all directions, twenty meters wide and spreading like fingers. Even now several drones backed onto those fingers with an almost sensuous wiggle, and made a connection. Power recharge? A hive-mind uplink for hardline data transfer? There were dozens of star-structures in irregular rows amidst the interconnecting hexagons of overlapping spheres, everything both predictable and utterly unpredictable at the same time.

"Some kind of goddamn living room," Kono guessed, jetting quickly past the stars to the far side, and cover with a view of the Tartarus interior.

"Guess they're not much on scrabble, huh?" said Rael. Drones jetted past, suddenly close-up and scary again, evading humans and each other with grace and pushing off steel structures with nimble limbs. Trace grabbed a star arm to halt her momentum, and paused to study tacnet — always hard with so much going on around her, and particularly so here.

Drysines were pouring in behind, but in straggling formation. Most of the armouries were nearer the perimeter, closer to where drones would deploy to meet external threats. Arming there, then getting here, took a while, particularly as some of the armouries in other parts of Tartarus were still engulfed in heavy fighting. It looked to Trace as though four armouries had been thoroughly captured, producing these successful thrusts of armed drones toward the central hub. Another three armouries were much less successful, with far heavier sard resistance than they'd seen here, and unarmed drones destroyed in large numbers. If they couldn't shoot back, even drones were vulnerable.

"Styx?" she asked. "Our numbers here are good but our positioning is patchy, we've got massive gaps on our flanks. We can't spread out because we lose fire volume intensity, I'd rather they tried to flank us through those gaps and get caught in our crossfire."

"Yes," Styx agreed.

"Do we have enough? Can you tell what we're up against?" Random fire snapped off nearby steel, close enough to feel the vibration through her gloved grip on cover.

"Uncertain as yet. Jamming is strong, and I have no eyes on the hub to inform tacnet further. There should be no advancing beyond this position until our numbers grow."

"I copy that." It gnawed at her, though. She was hardly eager to take her marines across open space into the kind of defences that could be waiting... but somewhere up ahead was a deepynine queen, and quite probably an alo presence of some sort. And *that* connection, if they could see it, prove it and understand it, could tell them just how much danger the human race was actually in. Without that knowledge, they were blind.

"Hey buddy, you okay?" That was Terez, talking to a drone of all things. One-and-a-half times his size in the body, far wider across the legs... only several of those legs were missing from gunfire, and it now struggled to remove a dangling remnant with its cutting-tool. A slash and it was gone, and the drone departed.

"Leo, you fucking nuts?" Rolonde asked Terez.

"Just making conversation," said Terez. *"Guess they're not big on conversation."*

Trace's feed began fracturing with static, and her suit tactical warned her that local coms traffic had reached such intense volumes that it was interfering with her marines' communications. "Styx, tell your drones to turn it down a bit, they're breaking up our coms."

"I will tell them Major.   They are excited and angry, and unaccustomed to coordinating with humans."

Trace found it easier to pretend she hadn't heard that, rather than trying to process it.   Styx was translating into concepts humans might understand, surely, and she couldn't take it literally.   A drone grappled onto the star-arm she was using for cover, and Trace saw the little portal open in the gap between armoured thorax and abdomen, and the arm inserted.   Definitely some kind of data-uplink... Rael had made a joke about scrabble, but electronic brains had no need for physical pastimes when they could experience an electronic, VR reality far more intensely than humans.   Was this really their communal space, where they came to plug into a larger, singular reality?

She pushed out from within the star-frame, and was confronted by a drone stopping immediately before her with a burst of white thrust.   Dual eyes, one big, one small and off-set within a central mobile head, a big cutting tool held in small arms below, twin rotary cannon on the main abdomen, recently added from the armoury.   Amidst added thrusters, half its arms were occupied, while a middle pair gestured at her aggressively.

"Whoa whoa whoa!" Kono said in alarm, swinging his rifle about to the drone confronting his major.

"It's okay Giddy," she told him.   "Just cool it."   Red laser light flashed on her visor from the drone's carapace... lasercom? Her suit received and decoded it reflexively.

"This unit is A1," announced a very synthetic voice in her ear.   Definitely a vocal program, something dumb and automatic employed by a machine that was neither, to translate its familiar numerical communications into speech.   *"A1 has local command. A1 will coordinate with humans."*

"Yes A1," Trace replied, with deliberate calm.   "How many levels of local command do you have?"

"Multiple.   A1 is sufficient for humans.   Integrate tactical analysis, proceed go five nine alpha."   As the vocal processor got carried away, or A1 forgot to limit its instructions to things useful to humans... but suddenly Trace's tacnet flashed and expanded, as

though infused with many multiples of incoming data. Individual markers now glowed blue, marking drone positions beside her marines. Amazingly, those markers were not alone, but were joined by a spaghetti of multi-coloured lines. Binding those drones together in distinct formations, Trace realised. Like squads and sections, though here the numbers were irregular and she'd never make sense of it in this limited time…

"Thank you A1," she told the drone. "We will coordinate and kill deepynines." It seemed safest to repeat that common cause, at this range.

"Yes," said A1, and jetted about and away.

"What the hell was that?" Kono wondered.

"Damn thing took control of my suit commands by lasercom and fed me some kind of hacksaw tacnet," Trace told him. That was pretty scary — that they really *could* just assume control of human tech by remote. Or maybe these drones only knew how because Styx had shown them. "That's an individual, their regional commander. Called himself A1."

"No shit," muttered Rolonde, unimpressed.

"They're individuals?" Arime asked. *"Not just numbers?"* It was impossible to know, Trace thought. Like it was impossible to know what Styx actually thought of anything, given all of her vocal cues were just simulations that fooled human brains into thinking they'd heard human emotion where none existed. A1 identified himself as an individual because that was what humans understood. What kind of individual consciousness could just be reprogrammed by an enemy queen, and deprived of the free will to resist?

"Major Thakur this is Phoenix," came Lieutenant Shilu's voice. *"Picket vessels are returning, most of the firebases appear to have been destroyed. Phoenix has cover on the far side of Tartarus, current trajectories suggest picket vessels are not threatening us but returning to Tartarus."*

Trace flipped tacnet displays to see *Phoenix*'s feed — sure enough, multiple warships were racing in on pulse-V, and not spreading wide to open an angle on *Phoenix*, tucked tight behind Tartarus.

"They're going to flank us, probably with sard warriors, they'll be dropped right in our rear. I'm expecting a major deepynine counterattack any moment, they'll catch us between them." Ahead, the shooting had died down considerably. Far off to one side, her apparent 'right' on this orientation, some major fireworks were flaring near the Tartarus rim. "The sard are putting most of their fight back into recapturing the warships the drysines took, we've only got two fully on our side, another three are heavily contested and I can't get any reading on the rest... my viewpoint here is a lot more limited than I'd like and I don't know how much of this tacnet feed is reliable."

Her visor countdown showed twenty-three minutes to *Makimakala*'s arrival. If the tavalai was late, or had somehow decided to screw them over, then there'd be no getting out of this for humans or drysines.

"Major," came Erik's voice, *"if you can't get to the core, withdraw on AT-7."*

"I'm getting what I came for," Trace said grimly. Ahead, tacnet erupted with massive movement. "Here we go, counter-attack commencing... Charlie Platoon, full defensive, I want clean kills and watch your ammo."

She jetted to where the outer framework gave her cover and a rifle brace, activating the mild forearm magnetism that stopped her from drifting out of cover. The habitation complex, if that was what it was, spread in a wide layer across this part of the inner Tartarus sphere. Ahead of her were more nodules, blocking a clear field of fire but impractical for defence because of their exposure. It hadn't stopped many of the drysines from occupying them, nor the surrounding superstructure, creating a multi-layered defence. Trace bit back an objection — surely drysines knew better how they'd best defend against a zero-G massed deepynine assault than she did.

Tacnet lit up with motion as those forward positions saw the enemy, and moments later Trace could see them too — hundreds of approaching dots amidst the structures, weaving to avoid obstructions. Bigger than drysines, she reckoned even from this range, and recalling AT-7's brief escort on the way in. A hundred flashes across that front as missile fire erupted, then accelerated... and Trace thought of TK55, and the deepynine commander's rain of missiles.

On one flank, tacnet showed her an entire formation of drysine defenders suddenly moving. Styx had some kind of clever plan, she thought, and glanced that way past her obstructing cover. Perhaps seventy or eighty drones were pulling off that side, darting away on hard thrust, leaving the flank exposed. But they weren't curling about to make a flanking run on the incoming assault. They were just leaving.

"Styx!" Trace snapped, as deepynine missiles tracked and dodged, engaged by defensive fire from drones and marines alike. Explosions darkened her visor, long strings of brilliant light. "You're leaving our flank exposed." No reply. The forward line engaged, a brilliance of chain guns and proximity detonations, drysines falling back with zigzagging bursts of thrust while firing. "Styx!"

"It is a superior priority," said Styx, with no more emotion than she ever said anything. *"Focus on this defence."*

"Follow superior instruction," A1 added.

Trace could have wasted time exclaiming that she didn't take orders from a disembodied head in a human shuttle. "Corporal Penn," she said instead. He was the only one of Charlie Platoon not in formation, having stayed behind in AT-7 with Styx and Romki for vehicle protection... and one other purpose too. "Point your weapon at Styx. If she's deliberately getting us killed, she'll go first."

"I copy Major," said Penn.

Immediately one of the nearby drones abandoned cover to face them, dual cannons humming in pre-fire warmup, legs withdrawn and body braced for recoil. Exclamations across Trace's coms told her that all across her formation, other drones were doing the same.

"If I wanted you dead, Major," said Styx, *"there is a far more simple method. You are an organic who appreciates a fact. This is rare. My fact is that you are not in command. You know*

this.   Stop pretending and fight like a drysine, with purpose and method."

CHAPTER 35

Tif had never concentrated so hard in her life. All hopes of keeping her relative V to sane levels had evaporated once it became clear that the drysine uprising in this part of Tartarus had not been very successful. Fighting was ongoing, chaotic and scattered, random groups of drones and sard jetting back and forth, exchanging fire and killing each other. In this flying environment, too much speed was lethal, but too little speed was worse.

Tif flew like a crazy teenager with a death wish, sliding, skidding and rolling through Tartarus's impossible maze, burning hard for V and trajectory when she could, then braking harder and relying on her visor display to show what lay 'ahead' as she approached it tail-first and skidding. Jersey stayed with her, and it became increasingly difficult to remain in second spot like she was supposed to, as every time she hit thrust PH-4 was a little faster than her lead. The drysine escort kept up with some difficulty, their thrusters barely large enough for the 5-G burns a combat shuttle could pull. Frequently one or several would deviate from the shuttles' course to swivel and shoot at something Tif was too busy to notice. Just as frequently, fire would snap back, and tracer would flash and bounce off steel structure. Jersey reported one hit so far but no real damage — if PH-4 had taken a hit, Tif was not aware of it. Coming out of one sliding burn her armscomp flashed red with visible enemy — several small armoured figures, sard warriors, caught in mid-dash between cover. Tif locked with her visor-target and fired, but they were passing too fast and no doubt even more startled to be nearly struck by a couple of suicidal human shuttles, as no return fire chased them.

Then finally ahead some big structures, solid and enclosed within the maze like prey trapped in the grasp of an alien organism. A series of connected cylinders and spheres, surrounded by the web-like tangle of hacksaw habitation and smaller shipping docks. Solid structures meant organics habitation, Tif reckoned, as they looked to contain atmosphere. Hacksaws didn't need it, and were quite happy in this kids' climbing gym gone mad.

Now Jersey was announcing something, and Lee was highlighting red targets on Tif's visor as fire whipped past the canopy. Tif kicked the nose up, slammed thrust for evasion, then rotated back onto target, sighting a ship at the docks and firing. It was a small sublight transport, maybe three times the size of a shuttle, and pieces flew off as it flashed by. Larger explosions as Jersey's missiles did more significant damage, and Tif hammered thrust again to push PH-4 through a narrow gap in the habitation tangle, then spun the nose before more thrust and a wide, skidding burn to circle around the cluster and back again.

"Target Tif, target!" Lee was shouting from the backseat, and Tif noted her visor's red highlight upon docking tubes and fuel canisters. She caught a brief glimpse of sard, and weapons firing, then more target highlights — on this orbital burn she was going to fly straight into their field of fire. She locked guns and jammed the trigger, saw one emplacement ripped to bits as steel framework disintegrated, then shifted to another as Lee fired missiles... her own guns blew a pressurised docking tank just before the missiles hit beside a habitat, multiple explosions blinding all forward view.

More fire shredded sard defences further left — that was Jersey, now properly behind and following Tif's lead. Tif repressed nervous tension — she wasn't a trained military pilot and taking the lead in a shooting fight hadn't been in the plan. She continued the burn, nose in toward the habitat cluster as she passed scattering wreckage from the explosion... and shouted a warning before even Lee did, seeing new movement on scan, at least ten marks incoming from further out.

Even as she hit thrust, two disintegrated and the others broke off amidst heavy fire as the drysine escort hit them — sard powered armour, spinning and returning fire with precise coordination. Tif dove for the cover of a heavy power regulator wrapped around a cross-brace, thrusting with vision-blurring force to come to a complete halt, then let a pair of sard zip into her line-of-sight. She fired as both saw her and evaded, one was hit and spun like a top, the other fired back and Tif felt the jolt even as she let the autos guide her guns to target, and the second suit's ammo blew with a brief flash.

Scan showed her the drysines pulverising the rest, as Lee fired more missiles into another docked transport. It blew, as peripheral vision showed a drone running down an injured sard warrior, a flash from its saw-blade and the sard came apart at the waist.

"We lost an escort," Singh observed from PH-3's rear seat. *"Another's damaged, better make this fast."*

"PH-4, continue fire suppression," said Jersey, pulling around for an approach run. *"Sard know we're here now, stay sharp. Delta Platoon, stand by for combat deploy."*

"Delta copies," came Lieutenant Crozier's voice. All of *Phoenix* knew Crozier had been rattled by events on Joma Station. Tif hoped she didn't play the dumb cub to restore her honour.

Damage lights blinked at her as she recommenced her circular trajectory about the complex, warning of a nose thruster malfunction even as she noticed the controls responding awkwardly on that side. *"They took out an attitude thruster, we're leaking a little air but the sealant's plugging it,"* Lee told her. *"Are we flying okay?"*

"Fry fine," said Tif, mentally figuring what she'd have to do differently to yaw. Scan showed her PH-3's position breaking into multiple blips on track to the complex — that was Delta Platoon deploying out the rear. A big relief for her personally, because marines outside the shuttle were a lot more use than marines locked inside, and this area of the Tartarus just got a whole lot safer.

"Delta is clear," said Crozier, followed by a lot of marine-chatter as the units agreed on which parts of the complex they were going to hit, based on where they thought the prisoners were. They'd have to be fast, Tif thought, or the sard would just kill the prisoners to stop them from being rescued. Big risk though that was, she was certain that if *she* were held captive by sard, she'd prefer *Phoenix* marines to take the chance. Being held captive by

the chah'nas had been bad enough.　She was certain the sard would make the chah'nas seem gentle.

"They are flanking!" Trace announced as all holy hell broke loose across the marine-and-drysine defensive front.　"Charlie Platoon, displace and manoeuvre!　Too long in one spot makes you a sitting duck!"

She took her own advice, broke cover and moved with a burst of thrust as missiles flashed in, her visor blanking dark from multiple explosions and a rain of shrapnel.　Luckily for her the deepynines were more intent on killing drysines than humans, and now divided in dark-silver streams to flow about the defensive positions and through neighbouring gaps.　The volume of fire between them and the drysine forward defences was insane, chain guns pouring like rain, autocannon bursts detonating like strings of firecrackers, drysines ducking back and manoeuvring to counter the aggressive thrusts and sweeps, like flocks of angry silver birds.

Trace hit new cover and braced her Koshaim in search of a target, but more interested in tacnet than shooting.　Command Squad repositioned with her, less restrained with precise shots at deepynines still rarely closer than five hundred meters.　Fire sparked and snapped off Kono's side and he swore — probably random fire, every bullet had to go somewhere.　Incoming and outgoing missiles were less effective as jamming took its toll, but random high explosive could still get lucky.

First Squad was now deploying outward along one flank, through the drysine 'living quarters' toward a factory complex as the deepynines looked to swarm around that side, sadly not stupid enough to charge head-on into strong defensive positions.　Trace put fire onto several flashing deepynines, saw a hit, then a fast move-and-fire that shredded a drysine before a burst of hard thrust saw them escape amidst pursuing and covering fire.　The deepynines were certainly getting the better of it.　The drysines were worker drones, multi-purposed as all drones were, and well capable of effective combat, but not to the same standard as these deepynine specialists. Already there were many floating, spinning metal corpses, and for every one that was deepynine, two were drysine.

"Major," Lieutenant Shilu spoke in the chaos. *"We count four of the picket vessels closing to dock directly behind your location, ETA four minutes. If they've got combat shuttles you can expect assault at your rear in barely ten, maybe twelve minutes."*

A nearby explosion sent Arime tumbling. Chain gun rounds hosed across them, Trace ducking back as a shot clubbed her arm with a teeth-jarring rattle. Marine armour could take one of those per segment, maybe. Multiple hits and everything fell apart, including the occupant.

"Makimakala's coming in hot, no word on her intentions yet," Shilu continued. *"She won't get there in time to save you from those sard in your rear."*

"I copy *Phoenix*. It's gonna be tight." Truth was, if she couldn't get past these deepynines, they were all going to be trapped here.

"I'm okay," Arime answered queries from his comrades. *"Visuals off, systems wobbly... dammit, lifesupport's out."*

"Irfy, get your ass back to AT-7," Kono told him between shooting.

"It's okay, I think I can..."

"That's an order Private! Now!"

Arime hit thrust and went, muttering at his now-twenty-minutes of emergency air supply.

"Breakthrough at 230," said Trace as she watched it happen, tacnet showing a weakpoint in drysine defences suddenly fold and a deepynine thrust cut through. "That's us Command Squad, follow me!"

Staying inside the open-frame habitats was going to slow them down, so she accelerated through a gap, reoriented to keep most of the structure between herself and the fighting, then kept burning. The big structures extended relative 'north' of their forward facing, and Trace wove past supports, pipes and machinery as drysine fire converged on the apex of the deepynine thrust.

Drones on neighbouring structures were hit by return fire, Trace saw one blasted sideways as its thruster pod exploded, another was shredded by chain guns... and then unarmed drones were zooming past, flying straight at the attackers. Those who had not managed to find weapons at the armoury had been holding back, and now committed themselves as a final, suicidal reserve, burning to full V.

"It's a suicide charge!" Trace told her squad. "Get open and find targets!" As she peeled sideways, away from the covering structures and into open space, still at considerable velocity as she selected full missile spread and fired, then lined up her rifle as the rest of Command did the same. Charging drysines were torn apart by oncoming deepynines, struggling to retain control and aim straight for their enemies even as they lost limbs, pods and lives. Explosions tore through them, but then the marines' missiles were hitting, relatively unjammed amidst the drysine lines... and in the carnage Trace got a good sight on a spinning deepynine and hammered a ten round burst at ninety meters.

Nine hit and the deepynine's ammo blew, as her squad found similar preoccupied targets for similar results. Survivors ignored them, firing instead on drysines, killing several then smashing through a habitat structure ahead. Trace decelerated hard, pumped multiple grenades into the habitat, then plunged through a gap as other grenades followed, and drysine fire tore free-form steel to so much confetti.

Inside was a whirlwind of explosive residue and debris, within which many-legged nightmare figures clashed, spun and fired. Armscomp IDed several as deepynine and Trace fired without question, blazing full auto and only hoping she didn't hit drysines by mistake. More explosions, armoured limbs shattering. A deepynine decapitated a drysine and blasted through partitions to swing both chain guns onto Trace, and was hit by autocannon even as Trace dodged, then struck physically by a charging drysine that rammed a humming blade through its midsection in a flurry of scrabbling legs.

Other shooting stopped, and the only thing in the habitat was humans, a few drysines, and dead, twitching drones. Trace checked her displays, and could barely believe that all her squad were still alive. Deepynines hated drysines so much, the homicidal bastards were flat out *ignoring* the humans, even as it killed them.

The drone that had killed Trace's attacker nimbly swatted some debris, checked a dead comrade with a fast probe, then fixed a red lasercom at Trace's visor. *"Human guns effective. Koshaim model, armour piercing. Good deepynine killer."*

Trace frowned. The synthetic voice was familiar. "A1? Is that you?"

"Yes. More breakthroughs at grid-114. Fight on, parren-successor." A1 turned and jetted off. 'Parren-successor'? The drysine's parren alliance had ended twenty five thousand years ago. And now this drysine thought that *Phoenix* was their replacement?

"Incoming mark!" Geish announced from Scan One. "Right on the money, that looks like *Makimakala*."

"Transponder identification, *Makimakala* confirmed!" said Shilu at Coms. "She's broadcasting wide and loud!"

"Welcome to the party, froggies," someone muttered. That was a 'get out of my way' signal, Erik thought. Anyone who didn't would be identified as hostile and targeted for destruction.

"Outer pickets are evasive!" said Jiri at Scan Two. "No change of course from the others."

Phoenix now hid on the far side of Tartarus, just ten klicks off its surface. The picket vessels seemed content to leave her there, knowing that the first one to poke its nose into view around Tartarus's curving horizon would get it shot off. Four ships were now approaching Tartarus's far side instead, presumably to drop off combat soldiers — deepynine drones or sard warriors, it wasn't possible to tell what the picket ships were carrying. Only now they had *Makimakala* charging down on them from behind, high-V and hostile.

If she fired a full spread at that velocity, the impacts would be devastating, even to something the size of Tartarus. High-V ships could kill planets, and Tartarus was significantly smaller than a planet. The fire stations and picket vessels combined would have easily intercepted any such incoming fire, but the former were mostly destroyed, and the latter now out of position. Erik stared at the display across his visor and main screens, and saw the path was open. Damned if this might not actually work. But now his people in Tartarus were running very short of time.

"Hello *Makimakala*, this is *Phoenix*. We have multiple operations underway in Tartarus, the schedule looks tight, can you make your approach V-variable?"

And he watched the seconds tick by, counting the time to *Makimakala*'s most likely response. Upon Tartarus's surface, or just below it, some very heavy fighting raged about one shipping and docking complex, with many explosions small and large. Occasionally *Phoenix*'s close range rail-cannon snapped fire at some identified target, and added a new ball of flame to the carnage.

"*Hello Phoenix,*" came Captain Pram's impeccable English. "*We cannot become V-variable, we are engaging multiple targets and if we slow down they will hit us. Our timeline is fixed, we will strike Tartarus in... fourteen minutes plus a bit.*" As he did some fast mental calculation to convert tavalai time-measurement into human. "*Tell your people to evacuate before then, we cannot and will not change our approach.*"

A big flash on scan from that direction. "One of those damaged pickets just got blasted," Geish announced. "That's *Makimakala*, froggies mean business." And Erik recalled having seen the same thing happen to human ships in the war, who got too close to ibranakala-class in combat.

"Operations," said Erik, "inform our rescue party they have fourteen minutes until terminal impact on Tartarus."

"*Aye sir, fourteen minutes.*"

Erik flipped channels. "Hello Major Thakur, you have fourteen minutes until terminal impact, *Makimakala* is inbound and will not adjust her velocity to help you get clear. If you're still there when she arrives, you're finished."

"Styx," said Trace. "Tacnet's showing me something big near the core, can you confirm?"

The fighting swirled about Command Squad's position, deepynines and drysines engaging with mechanical ferocity while the marines held cover in the middle and laid down supporting fire for their allies. Trace saw that Charlie Platoon's position was the same, Lieutenant Jalawi maintaining good formation and not exposing his marines to too much enemy fire, having correctly seen that the deepynines weren't expending much ammunition on humans.

"Major, there appears to be a ship," Styx replied. AT-7 remained in close cover barely a kilometre away, now with another two of Jalawi's marines aboard plus Arime — damaged or wounded and now of more use defending their escape ride. *"There are pathways for rapid evacuation from the core, for smaller ships."*

"That's the queen escaping," Trace surmised, and fired at a briefly-visible deepynine, blowing off legs. "They're going to move her out before *Makimakala* arrives. Neither of our ships is in position to stop her, she'll dock with one of the pickets and disappear."

So far the assault had been brilliantly if fortuitously managed. If *Makimakala* could get past the remaining pickets, Tartarus was finished — no mean feat considering what had been initially arrayed to stop them. But the deepynine queen was about to get away, and the humans could not advance beyond this position. The deepynine inner defences had held them up, and now *Phoenix*'s primary goal — intelligence on the queen — was about to disappear like smoke. Without that intelligence, Trace knew this whole mission was for nothing.

Finally she found that her brain was coming to visualise the broader fight. These drysines accompanying the human thrust toward the core were barely five percent of the total force. Drysines seemed to be winning control of two major shipyards, with at least three vessels relatively undamaged so far. That was Styx's escape route, and by the defensive withdrawal many drysine formations were now commencing, it seemed that she was going to get as many of them out as possible before *Makimakala* torched the place. When that happened, Styx would have a choice to make. Turn on the humans, eliminate them and escape with her own kind on the captured vessels? Or stay as she was? *Phoenix* was an asset, and leverage with various organics — humans, tavalai via the Dobruta, and even kuhsi. Was Styx interested in simple survival, or did she have bigger strategic plans?

And then there were the drysines who'd peeled off this flank prior to the deepynine attack. She could still see them on tacnet, fighting a ferocious battle barely three kilometres away about an inner power complex that appeared to have no strategic value whatsoever. What was there that Styx would put her own safety in jeopardy to capture?

"Styx," she called. "Do you have any angle on that deepynine queen?"

"No Major. She is inaccessible by any forces from our current position."

"That's what I thought." It wasn't technically true — there were various drysine formations that could sacrifice themselves if they charged, and possibly get a few units close enough to transmit visuals before dying. That Styx refused told Trace something about her priorities. The deepynines might be prepared to sacrifice everything to kill drysines, but the drysines were just trying to get the maximum assets out alive.

"Don't you try it Major," said Kono. *"If you ditch us and make a run for it, I will shoot you myself."*

Trace nearly swore, jetted from cover as cannon rounds flashed about where she'd been, clanging her suit with shrapnel. She hit new cover, braced and stared out through the intervening structures, temporarily free of deepynines.

"Someone's got to do it," she retorted. "We have to know what that fucking thing is, it's the reason we're here!"

"Major I can temporarily blank you from tacnet and intensify jamming along a narrow corridor," Styx told her. *"I will attempt to rendezvous a transport for your escape but you must move now, there is no more time."*

"Major, hell no!" Jalawi shouted. *"I'll go, you stay the hell here!"*

"You're out of position," Trace told him. "You have formation command, just make sure you get the hell out before the froggies turn this place to ash. Command Squad, follow me and keep as tight to cover as possible."

She pushed off, across the habitat and through a gap rear-side from the deepynines and into open space. Then she jetted hard and selected a course in tight past several habitats and support structures. Command Squad followed, and she held thrust down and watched the velocity build. Using marine suits as spaceships was ill-advised — she had nothing like the power of a shuttle, nor even a hacksaw drone, and once at velocity she'd dodge like a loaded bulk carrier. But if the deepynines were only going to shoot at drysines, then maybe, just maybe...

...and abruptly her coms blanked to static, visor displays flickering as she lost tacnet and even basic scan. That was Styx, upping the jamming as she'd promised. How the hell she was doing that... but Trace was no engineer and had no way to guess. Probably she was coordinating some kind of mass effect from her drysine army, dozens of drones coordinating jamming fields in unison.

She skimmed a habitat at full thrust, now travelling dangerously fast. If something got in her way, she wasn't going to be able to dodge, and even at low thrust a suit could accumulate plenty of V if you were stupid enough to hold the button down in one direction. And if the deepynines came back...

Something silver flashed from behind the habitat structures, heading away — deepynine, a scout covering this flank, and Trace tracked even as she flew, then fired. Heavy recoil threw a wobble in her trajectory, thrust compensating on auto as the deepynine flashed, tumbled, then smacked into one of Tartarus's thicket of steel frames and bounced like a broken thing.

Ahead the structures were ending, and open space loomed between cathedral-like spans of steel. Trace hit hard thrust offset, and tried to cut the curving trajectory as closely past a support as possible — with her visor display a static-flecked mess, she had to do it entirely by eye, no simple thing without navcomp aligning course for her. The steel flashed by at perhaps three hundred kph, and she cut thrust briefly to rotate and glance behind. Command Squad hurtled after her, also cutting thrust to coast, Rolonde and Rael at the rear now firing backward with a staccato hammer of rifle fire. So something was chasing them, though without coms Trace couldn't hear a thing... and several missiles streaked around the corner they'd just turned, accelerating fast but losing acquisition and detonating on either side with bright flashes that would have knocked her tumbling in an atmosphere, but made barely a jolt in vacuum.

A deepynine appeared behind, chasing at high speed... and died immediately to Rolonde's fire. Rael got the second, and Terez drifted wide enough to kill the third, which sprayed chain gun fire as it tumbled before exploding. A1 had been impressed with Koshaim rifles, and it was a comfort to know that even deepynines had reason to be worried about marines at close quarters. But the only reason those missiles kept missing was Styx and her jamming. Deepynine drones seemed missile-reliant, and struggled to adjust when they missed. Where Command Squad was headed, Styx's jamming would not reach, and for the first time since the shooting started, Command Squad would be on their own.

CHAPTER 36

Lieutenant Crozier's instructions to dock were too fast for Tif to follow, and overlapping with marine-chatter and occasional gunfire in the background.   But Ensign Lee flashed the extraction point to Tif's screen and she went without question, a hard burn away from her cover-orbit and straight toward the remains of a blasted shipping dock.   It looked a mess, and Tif rotated to consider it through the top of her canopy as she braked hard on approach.

"Tif can you get in?" Lee asked from the front seat.   *"Or do you want me to blast something?"*

"Blast you make more bad," said Tif, picking a path with her eye through the drifting remains of a sublight runner and a lot of connecting umbilicals and framework.   "We go.   Watch guns, I no kill sard and fly."

"PH-4, I have a reading on approaching forces," came Lieutenant Jersey's urgent voice.   *"Looks like some nearby sard have won their fight and are heading our way.   Make it fast, you've got two minutes."*

Tif said something very bad in her native tongue, kicked thrust and rolled into the debris field at a speed her academy instructors would have suspended her for.   She could see the airlock ahead, an organic-looking nodule on the side of a huge cylindrical habitat, but there was barely enough room between it and the drifting hulk of the crippled runner — not a large ship, but ten times the mass of PH-4 and worse, it was still drifting.

Marine-chatter was telling her something about status at the airlock, but she let Lee handle it and slid the shuttle sideways past some tumbling debris, then a pivot past some unexploded pressure tanks, then purposely hit some light plating just to get it out of the way.   Attitude thrust leaped and danced in rapid white puffs as she manoeuvred, then a light kick of the mains, followed by another spin and zigzag.   The dead nose-thruster nearly tripped her several times but her hands recovered with fast little movements when the nose-yaw failed to fire as expected.   A final braking thrust blew the visibility before her into white clouds, and then she was wedged in tightly, barely four meters' clearance to the ship hull while slamming the dorsal hatch against the airlock.

"*Go go go!*" Lee told the marines, and suddenly Tif found several of them outside and coming past her canopy, thrusting out to cover positions in preparation for Jersey to pick them up. Her ears did not pop at the crash entry to the rear hold — the cockpit doors were closed, separating her and Ensign Lee from any pressure changes behind. But freed prisoners were filling their hold, Tif had no idea who or how many, being far too busy staring at her scan and seeing the alarming signal that Jersey had identified, fading and strengthening in waves as the static came in and out. Enemy suits and ships, probably sard, approaching fast. One minute ten.

More fast coms between PH-3 and Lieutenant Crozier, marines clustering fast for a pickup as Lieutenant Jersey made a much easier approach, avoiding most of the debris as the marines simply jetted out to meet her. But the freed prisoners had no suits, necessitating an airlock match. Tif felt the fear surge, seeing that signal getting closer. It ticked below a minute. The tavalai ship's incoming ETA was now under thirteen minutes, and then all this place would become the fires of hell. Hekgarh, she told herself firmly, resisting the temptation to rip the shuttle away from the airlock early. Hekgarh, fear like the hunter, not the prey.

"*All in!*" came a marine's shout, and "*Go Tif!*" from Lee. Tif broke contact so fast Lee nearly lost a docking grapple, forward view a storm of white as she backed out hard. Stopped with a slam, spun, thrust then spun again as she rotated through the mess, trying to judge with her eyes what the shuttle could survive hitting, and what it absolutely could not.

"*Tif!*" called Jersey. "*Major Thakur just made a run toward the core with Command Squad! She's got no evac, AT-7 can't fly in there, it'll get killed! Tif we can make it, we have a clearer path from here, we're not far from the core!*"

"Save Najor Thakur?" Tif asked, crashing some light framework. Major Thakur had saved her and Skah from the chah'nas. If there was one thing Tif's people believed in, it was payback — both the good kind and the bad. "You give course, we go."

She finally got clear and burned hard as Jersey's new course appeared on her screen. It was completely insane — directly toward the core of Tartarus, deeper into the maze when they should have been running hard back to *Phoenix*. But Lieutenant Jersey was a gun military pilot who would never say to do something that wasn't possible. And having made the decisions in her recent life that she had, Tif knew that she simply had no choice.

She burned hard toward the core, seeing PH-3 in fast pursuit with Crozier's marines back on board... and a fast glance out her canopy showed her drysine escort firing at something else. Gunfire joined them from the back of PH-3, where military shuttles had no fixed weapons... and then she realised — Delta Platoon marines had somehow lashed themselves to the shuttle's outer hull and were acting as Lieutenant Jersey's tail gunners.

"*Fast Tif!*" Jersey told her. "*You fly crazy Tif! Crazy is our only chance, understand?*"

"Fry crazy," Tif agreed, holding down thrust until they were well past the safe zone for proximity flying, and kept thrusting. Cannon fire cut past from behind, sard suits and ships approaching, and something big exploded to one side. "You watch taiw, I watch front. We go kuhsi crazy, you keep up."

Trace was barely half-a-klick from the core perimeter when it became clear that Styx had lied to her. Ahead, half-hidden amongst the heavily built power-core shielding and layered, dense structures, a huge firefight was in progress. Tacnet insisted that there were no drysine drones in this area, and Styx had said that no forces could be committed to intercept the deepynine queen — and yet Trace could see the distinctive red storm of chain gun fire, the now familiar movements and patterns of a zero-G drysine assault.

Command Squad wove past huge interior bulkheads, decelerating with feet toward their target even as that target became visible. It was a ship, only small, probably a sublighter. At this range, past the obstructions, Trace could see that this part of the cavernous interior formed a passage, like a tunnel to the surface, snaking at points and broken by docking ports and security barriers. A small ship here could make rapid progress to clear space, though doubtless the passage was heavily defended at most times.

Now those defences were being torn to pieces by a relentless drysine onslaught. Trace could see the wreckage of destroyed shuttles and many smashed drones, others attempting to create crossfires from cover positions about the ship only to be outflanked in turn and decimated beneath a hail of chain gun fire. Several of the ship's weapons were still operational, laying down close-range carnage on any drysines that drifted within their view. But without any space to manoeuvre, it was doomed, and even now drysines were clamping onto its hind-section, cutters blazing at weak-points to open holes in the hull and disconnect vital systems.

"Hold up!" Trace commanded. "Cover positions five hundred meters to the ship's rear, we're not getting too close!"

"That's the damn deepynine queen in there," said Kono. *"Shouldn't we help dig her out?"*

"They didn't want our help, Styx said she couldn't intercept the queen. We watch what they're up to, we'd only get in their way."

Trace picked a deceleration course between structures and emerged at a near-stop half-a-klick behind the conflagration. That was plenty close enough, with near space filled with flashing, bouncing rounds and shrapnel, and a few surviving deepynine defenders streaking in desperate, wide orbits trying to find a way back in, pursued by merciless drysines.

Trace clamped herself to a support, magnetism halting her drift, explosions announcing the end of the ship's defensive weapons. *"Major, seven minutes,"* said Kono.

"Dammit, where is she?" Trace muttered. "Styx didn't want us to see her, probably wanted her captured without us knowing. We have to get in closer…"

"New contacts!" announced Rolonde as she saw it, no need for scan because suddenly they could all see it, roaring in like a giant silver wave from further up the passage. *"Holy shit!"*

A wall of deepynine counter-attack hit the drysines, and Trace yelled for cover as the firing became the most intense that she'd ever seen in her life. Braced to the support, she could hear the impacts through the vibration in her suit, and it sounded like a hailstorm on a tin roof.

When she looked again, surviving drysines were scattering amidst the carnage, pursued by the new arrivals... and a new ship was coming down the passage, small like the first, but undamaged and *different*. Out of it were pouring humanoid armoured suits unlike anything she'd seen before, but they were fast, mobile and heavily armed, spraying fire every bit as deadly as the deepynine drones at any drysine in range.

Others raced to the damaged ship and tore inside. Trace saw one hit, and a deepynine rushed to grab it, and stop it from spinning. Several others made common formation with deepynines, and combined fire as though they were coordinating with a single mind. A badly damaged deepynine with torso and thrusters mauled was dragged by another humanoid suit, back toward the new ship, and escape.

These pressurised suits housed organics, Trace knew. They were not so different from human marine suits, though perhaps a little more advanced, and certainly more mobile in zero-G. And they were doing more than coordinating with the deepynines. They were fighting with them. Fighting *for* them. Dying for them, as the deepynines were fighting and dying as well. This looked like more than a mere alliance. This looked like a bond of blood.

"Alo!" she gasped as she realised. "Alo came to rescue the queen."

"Stan Romki you son of a bitch," Kumar muttered. *"You were right all along."*

"There!" said Rael. *"Mid-hatch, I see her!"*

From a mauled middle-hatch in the non-rotating crew compartment, there emerged a huge, gleaming dark-silver beast.

She had wide legs, multiple body segments, and bristled with attachments that Trace could not identify, but guessed were mostly weapons. She was perhaps four times the size of her attentive drones, and even now they formed around her in a phalanx, deepynine and alo alike, blazing fire at any threat and darting to obey every flicking gesture of her limbs.

Abruptly the queen spun, a flurry of white thrust as her defenders kept fighting, oblivious. Even at this range, Trace could swear the queen's tri-partite eyes were fixed upon her, and only a fool would question how she could spot the more distant humans when so much was happening close-by. It was tempting to consider a shot, but Trace knew the drones would shield their queen with their bodies, and so long as she did not fire, the deepynines would expend their ammunition only on those directly threatening them.

Instead, Trace raised an armoured hand, and gave a small salute. The deepynine queen stared back. Knowing, perhaps, that this was the enemy that had destroyed Tartarus, and brought this new sard alliance to a crashing halt... temporarily, at least. Surely there were plans beyond this one, and the alliance was not just limited to Tartarus. Surely there were queens beyond this one, too. Who did they answer to? Who did she? Whatever it was, it was at the very top of all alo civilisation — humanity's ally in the Triumvirate War, now double-dealing with humanity's enemies. And now the secret was out.

The queen turned and again and thrusted toward the alo ship, her defenders in support. And Trace saw that *Makimakala*'s strike was four minutes forty away, and she was completely out of time.

"Chase them!" she said. "It's our only way out." And left cover to jet after the alo ship, which was already leaving with a glare of thrust. Most of it missed the marines as they held to the passage sides and burned... and past the glare, Trace could swear she saw the queen simply latch to the vessel's underside without bothering to board, herself and drones grasping those alo who had nothing else to hold onto, refusing to leave even lowly soldiers behind.

"Hello *Phoenix*," Trace called on that channel. "Have you been reading my visual feed? If not, stand by to receive, I'm not sure if we can get out of here in time..."

"*Najor, behind!*" a voice cut through the static. "*You get, board fast!*"

And Trace shot a glance down past her feet even as she accelerated by the debris of recent combat and tumbling steel bodies that could smash her off-course... and saw a *Phoenix* combat shuttle, coming at her sideways in a huge corrective slide, and now straightening for approach.

"*Tif's here!*" Kono yelled with relief. "*That's PH-4, combat boarding, spread it wide!*"

"*Where's PH-3?*" asked Rael. "*I can't see Lieutenant Jersey...*" As a second shuttle skidded sideways into the framework passage, corrective thrust burning and Delta Platoon marines blazing fire out the back from their hull anchorpoints, evidence of a fast and desperate retreat.

"*This is Jersey, I'm full up, get on PH-4!*" As PH-4 crashed through recent debris, and ducked beneath the torn and drifting hulk of the ruined deepynine ship.

Ahead the passage made a turn, the alo ship already past it and burning harder. Suddenly PH-4 was paralleling the marines, braking with nose thrust as Rael, Terez and Kumar changed directions and dove for it. There were ten positions on a combat shuttle's hull that could pass for anchor points in an emergency, and marines frequently practised reaching them. Trace saw all three marines hit the shuttle's broad back, forward of the upper aft thrust, and magnetise. But now the tunnel corner was arriving, and she turned, calculating her apex just past the inner bend, and fired thrust.

Trace missed the inner apex by a few meters only, then drifted wide and gritted her teeth in hope she wouldn't need to brake before hitting the far wall... only for her armoured feet to hit something unseen. She glanced down in astonishment, and found PH-4 directly beneath her as it went around the corner sideways, now using its own mass to correct Trace's course, balancing her small, armoured figure upon its nose. Behind the heavily armoured canopy, Trace caught a glimpse of Ensign Lee in the front seat, and realised that the awed tales of the Operations techs who'd watched Tif fly simulator missions were probably true.

Trace stepped off the nose, cut thrust and 'fell' past the canopy to an unsecured anchor point, grabbed it and magnetised. PH-4's thrust burned hard, hauling Trace down at a force rarely felt within an armour suit, then a rapid spin, and a blurred glance showed that Tif had gathered another marine, similarly latched by the shoulder nacelle. Another fast spin, then the hard thrust returned, and Trace had no way of checking that all her marines were aboard, with tacnet gone to hell and static on her visor display, but she had to trust that Tif knew.

Now thrust cut back in, and the passage opened into another of those huge, Tartarus internal spaces. This one was filled with tumbling, drifting debris — whatever ships or structures had been here were now smashed and broken. Trace could hear pilot chatter on coms, but now she was a total passenger, and could only hope Tif recalled that even small impacts on her ship's hull would make direct strikes on her marines.

One visor function was still working clearly, counting down the seconds to *Makimakala*'s strike. One minute fifty and counting.

"One minute forty!" said Shahaim, fingers racing as she locked in possible escape trajectories, and calculated outward runs to jump. "I'm projecting an explosion terminal radius of at least five hundred K!"

"Everyone is leaving!" Geish added. On Erik's tactical feed, sublighters and FTL vessels were departing Tartarus as fast as they could burn. Even now several exchanged fire, exposed beyond cover but with no choice if they were going to escape the blast radius in time.

All of Erik's attention was fixed on two emergent points, where tactical showed AT-7 leaving Tartarus amid a cloud of drysine drones and at least one captured sublight ship, and another point thirty degrees around the Tartarus perimeter where latest projections showed PH-3 and PH-4 should emerge. Might emerge.

The picket vessels had scattered again at *Makimakala's* arrival — a number had evidently been damaged in their exchanges with the fire stations Styx had assumed control of, and now *Makimakala's* high-V ordinance was incoming on them as well. *Makimakala* was following a little behind her own ordinance, unloading new fire even now, filling space between herself and evasive pickets with a huge spread of guided destruction. It made staying close to Tartarus a deadly proposition for those defending ships, and gave *Phoenix* and her shuttles a chance.

"Helm I want a cover intercept on our shuttles," said Erik. "They're going to build V fast as they leave, we're going to match between them."

There was a picket vessel out that way, and at least two more beyond who could theoretically target them if they weren't currently concerned with *Makimakala*. Amidst the ships fleeing Tartarus in that vicinity were various small shuttles, some sublighters and a whole bunch of low-V drones who were likely going far too slow to get clear in time.

"I can't raise Styx or AT-7," Shilu said tersely. "The jamming out there is too intense, I think there's something big in their vicinity."

"Fifty seconds!"

Going to be tight, Erik thought, his brain in overload trying to predict all those overlapping possibilities. But then, it was always tight.

At forty-six seconds he hit thrust hard, and *Phoenix* accelerated at 8-G across Tartarus's curving surface. *"Target mark one priority,"* he formulated as the Gs made speech impossible, and armscomp fixed the near picket with a priority red. *"Full firepower."*

"Mark one priority aye!" said Karle, and let fly as soon as that target appeared past the horizon.

"Incoming full spread!" Harris added, as mark one fired back, and Erik kicked them into a defensive corkscrew that also gave

Harris's defensive emplacements a good look. They hit something with a loud bang, then multiple detonations as incoming fire was intercepted, and a red light flashed on Erik's screen.

"Something departed our second emergence point!" called Jiri from Scan Two. *"Too big to be our shuttles, it's burning hard! Fourteen-Gs!"*

Fourteen-Gs was far too hard to be a human vessel of any sort. Thirty seconds. Directly behind that blazingly fast alien ship, two more familiar dots appeared, and scan showed them accelerating at 5-Gs — right on the mark for a *Phoenix* combat shuttle. Erik just knew, and spun them to thrust hard for position even before Jiri could confirm it was them.

"Phoenix to shuttles, crash grapple!" he yelled at them, as thrust dropped enough to talk. "Crash grapple, line up! We're coming in hot!"

Both continued burning at near maximum, but now they were drifting astern into the position of *Phoenix*'s combat grapples. Velocity built fast with constant thrust, but if five hundred K was minimum safe distance, the shuttles weren't going to make a hundred before the detonation wave hit them. Nearby at a thirty-degree offset, AT-7 and company were much further ahead, and much faster. But Erik couldn't do anything to help them now.

He spun *Phoenix* around to approach tail-first, burning hard to decelerate. More incoming detonations, then a massive smack sideways as something big hit them, and the red light on his screen had quintuplets as Karle snarled triumph — the picket vessel catching far worse. Harris blasted several small, fleeing deepynine ships nearby, then Erik cut thrust to spin once more on approach as Shahaim's fine-tuning helped him line up the angle of impact just right...

And his display countdown reached zero. Rear-facing cameras blanked white, unable to handle the glare. Large asteroids could kill planets, and while *Makimakala*'s missiles and magfire contained only a tiny fraction of that mass, they carried monstrous multiples of that velocity. For the briefest instant, Erik's visuals showed the Tartarus globe spitted through the middle, as though by a spear, and a huge, white-hot plume of molten energy spewing out behind in the direction of V. Then the whole lot came apart.

Erik saw his twin targets match, the grapple system aligning on its own autos to crash and grasp both shuttles in a grip designed to paralyse much larger warships, if necessary. Then he aligned upon Shahaim's escape trajectory, and pulsed as his stomach dropped out from under him...

...and emerged racing massively faster, streaking away across the gas giant's gravity slope. Behind, Tartarus remained invisible through a glare of white. Two more picket vessels had similarly disappeared, victims of *Makimakala*'s fire. And here came *Makimakala* herself, streaking at ridiculous velocity just beyond the expanding blast-zone of Tartarus's destruction, far too fast for the naked eye and a thousand kilometres distant before you could blink. Several picket vessels pulsed up after her, and Erik spun *Phoenix* about, burning hard to slow them. Already the shockwave was far behind, though scan showed clouds of high-V debris were approaching fast, ready to kill anything in their path.

"Scan, I want AT-7's location," Erik demanded. "Operations, status on our shuttles?"

"*Hi LC, it's Jersey,*" came the reply before Operations could respond. "*I got a bit crushed by the grapples, but I think we're good.*"

"*LC, marines are all good,*" came Trace's voice, and Erik's heart leaped in relief. "*Go get Hausler.*"

CHAPTER 37

They found AT-7 tumbling and damaged, accompanied by a sublight freight hauler that drysines had hijacked to get clear. A grappling nudge straightened the shuttle, followed by dock, and then a moment of crazy indecision as Styx insisted that all the drysine drones from the freight hauler should be brought along. The hauler was just small enough that *Phoenix* could hyperspace with it attached, so Erik grappled it, burned to get clear of the expanding debris field, and jumped.

Despite the latest damage, *Phoenix* held together beautifully through the first jump, and then through the second, which brought them to the rendezvous point where *Makimakala* was waiting for them. They made for deep space rendezvous, well away from sunlight or gravity wells, and soon had two, then three more FTL vessels coming to join them, all transmitting drysine codes and in apparently friendly conversation with Styx, and the freighter grasped in *Phoenix*'s talons. Each had been appropriated, Erik gathered, during the Tartarus uprising. Exactly how many drones had piled into each before departure, Styx would not say. Erik guessed many hundreds, possibly more than a thousand in total. Most drysines had died in the uprising, but this many had escaped. Now they had ships, and a queen. And *Makimakala*, whose solemn task was to destroy all hacksaws they found, now found herself party to unleashing this new spread of once-dormant drysines into the galaxy.

With *Makimakala* still twenty minutes ahead, two of the drysine ships came into formation with *Phoenix* on approach. It made the gunners nervous, but Erik assured Karle and Harris that there was unlikely to be any threat so long as Styx was aboard. And told them to keep a close watch on their new friends anyway. Probably the drysines knew exactly what *Makimakala* was, and thought it best to confront her with overwhelming odds before rendezvous. That they now considered *Phoenix* one of their own where those odds were concerned, was more disturbing than flattering.

At first opportunity Erik changed shifts to let Draper and Dufresne take command and headed to the kitchen for some food, then to Engineering 3C which was currently used only for storage, and was often converted into a rec room most usually frequented by Operations crew. There amidst the secure shelving racks he found various first-shifters on the low-mass folding plastic chairs that were all the unsecured furniture crew were allowed, drinking and eating.

In one especially exclusive circle were the shuttle crews — pilots Hausler, Jersey and Tif, plus co-pilots Yun, Singh and Lee. Lisbeth was also here, having ridden out the entire thing in PH-1 — Hausler's usual ride — with Dufresne in the pilot's seat in case they'd been needed. And Erik realised with astonishment that he hadn't agonised over that fact much at all, during the fight. Perhaps he was finally getting used to Lisbeth being in danger... or perhaps he'd simply become fatalistic. Either way, he wasn't sure he liked it.

He took a seat and ate with them, exhausted as they all were, and the shuttle crews still damp from recent sweat. "Tif, where's Skah?" he asked.

"Sreeping," said Tif, half-sprawled as she tore at the cold meat her species preferred. Her big ears held an unnatural upward curve from having been bound in their scarf beneath her helmet for too long. "Conbat ops very tiring for baby. Poor Skah."

Her fellow pilots grinned. One of Tif's hands jumped and twitched as she ate, completely beyond her to control. Tif saw Erik looking, and grimaced, flexing the hand. But the twitching continued.

"You should have seen her just after we got out," said Lee, seeing Erik looking. "Kuhsi adrenal overload." He made a face, teeth bared, fingers curled like some crazy animal. "Couldn't touch her, she was jumping at loud noises."

"You stiw awive," Tif complained. "I no kiw, you shut up." Lee grinned and nudged her shoulder. Tif twitched again, and this time her finger claws came halfway out. She flicked an ear at her co-pilot in irritation.

"This girl," Jersey said to Erik, pointing at Tif. "Impossible. I've never said this of any pilot in the Fleet, but I can't do that."

"Not even him?" Erik asked, pointing at Hausler. Apparently the least ruffled of them all, Hausler ate calmly.

"Not even him," said Jersey. "That last run to pick up the Major, I just followed Tif. I thought she'd gotten us both killed a dozen times, flown us into something, but each time we missed it by a few meters. Any human doing that would have died. And if we hadn't gone that fast... well."

"*Phoenix*," Tif said to Jersey, by way of explanation.

Jersey nodded, and gulped her drink. "*Phoenix*," she agreed.

"*Phoenix*," the others echoed.

"You had guns," Hausler complained. "I wish I'd had guns." Being stuck in that situation, unarmed, hadn't been something he enjoyed.

Erik's next visit was to Medbay Two, where wounded marines were being treated. Incredibly there were only four, and none of the injuries were serious. Even more incredibly, there had been no fatalities. None of the four marines could believe it.

"They just weren't shooting at us, LC," said Private Arime from Command Squad, who was hooked up to tubes with a breathing mask as precaution against mild hypoxia. "Deepynines just wanted to kill drysines. If they'd been shooting at us, we'd have lost about half. If Styx hadn't been jamming their damn missiles, way more than half. It was nuts."

"And Styx?" Erik asked.

"Completely screwed without her," Arime said with clear-eyed honesty. "She didn't try to screw us that I could see. Maybe the Major saw differently."

Next was Sergeant Lai from Delta First Squad, who was having some small fragments removed from his lower leg. Seated on a bunk, a scanner-brace about his calf, he looked mostly unbothered as a corpsman tweezered the bits out under anaesthetic, AR glasses showing her exactly where the fragments were.

"Pretty crazy entry," Lai admitted, sipping a doctor-approved fruit juice. "Place was a maze, but the sard weren't real organised

463

defending it. No one else there but prisoners and guards, not hard to keep the two apart. Had to shoot a bunch of sard, you know." He shrugged. "They're not great up close and outgunned."

"And how was Crozier?" It wasn't really Erik's place to ask, but sending her had been his call, and he felt entitled to an answer.

"She's not *back* sir, if that's what you mean," Lai said with a protective stare. "She never left. Best LT in the company."

All the marines said that about their own particular lieutenant. Erik patted Lai on the shoulder. "I know, Sergeant. No argument here."

His next visit was Medbay One. Here were the prisoners — all eighteen of them. Seven were off *Europa*, some crew, some passengers. Another eight were from *Grappler*, of all the unexpected things. The last three were tavalai, and no one knew which ship they'd been taken from. Probably there had been other prisoners of various species dispersed elsewhere in Tartarus, taken off other ships that sard had intercepted over the last months and years. Erik regretted that desperately, but there just hadn't been any time to do more.

On a bunk by the door lay Calvin Debogande. Erik sat by his uncle, whose eyes flicked open behind his oxygen mask. He looked pale and drained, but managed a weak smile. Erik grasped his hand, careful of the tubes in his arm.

"Cal," he said. "How are you feeling?"

"Weak," Calvin murmured, voice muffled. "I'm okay. Others had it worse." He had claw-scratches down one side of his face, now plastered with gleaming gel. Those smart, friendly eyes were now haunted. Sunken and fearful, having seen too many unwanted things. "I can't believe I'm alive. Your people are amazing, Erik."

"I know." Erik squeezed his hand. "I'm so sorry Cal. You shouldn't have had to come out after us. We were in over our heads, and looking the wrong way. We didn't figure out why the sard were after us until too late. And we had no idea they'd grab you when they couldn't get us. If I'd known…"

Uncle Calvin squeezed his hand back, weakly. "Big galaxy kid. Lots of things are hard to know."

"How did they treat you?" Erik asked fearfully. The worst part of making a mistake, he knew, was living to see the consequences hurting people he loved.

"Not great," Calvin admitted. He swallowed. "They came aboard straight out of jump. It was like they knew where we'd be. They hit our engines, there was nothing we could do. Colonel Khola killed a bunch of them on his own... I don't know what it proved, there were far too many of them. He was never going to win that way."

"Kulina go down fighting," Erik said quietly.

"I guess. But he seemed to impress them, so they didn't kill him. When they eventually got him. They killed Captain Houli though. Right in front of us, as a lesson. Just tore him open." Calvin's eyes squeezed shut. "God I hate them. Tell me you killed a lot of them just now."

"We killed a lot of them," Erik confirmed. "Thousands, conservatively."

"Still not enough." Calvin stared at him. "I used to toy with the peace movement, when I was a student. And later, in adulthood. Lots of people think we should at least try to talk to our enemies, you know?"

"I know," Erik said sombrely. "I've met those people."

"But by god, if I could press a button that killed every sard in the universe forever, I would."

Erik nodded. "I'd love to make peace too. But the universe doesn't care what I want. Neither do sard."

"If our enemies were human, we might have a chance at peace. You did the right thing, Erik. You and Major Thakur. Trying to make peace. Worlders and Spacers aren't like sard. We've got a chance. You were right to try."

Erik took a deep breath. "Right now I'd just be pleased if there's enough of us alive in a few years to *have* a good war." He patted his uncle's hand. "You rest Cal. There's only access for essential and command personnel at the moment, but you can bet Lisbeth will be here the second that restriction's lifted."

He walked to look at several of the other prisoners, a few in induced comas, some others rigged to auto-care units, pumping needed drugs and micros into their systems in place of human care. Intensive care was adjoining the medbay, separated by a wall, and he knew Doc Suelo and some others were in there, treating one gunshot wound from the escape, and another two severe torture cases.

Nearby lay Colonel Khola, rigged into auto-care, apparently sleeping behind his oxygen mask.

"They tortured him," said a heavy set man in the neighbouring bed. He didn't look so bad, save the IV and a bandaged hand. "The holding cells were kinda open. Weird design, zero-G stuff. We saw them moving him, could hear them... doing stuff."

Erik extended a left hand to the man, considerate of the bandaged right hand. "I'm Lieutenant Commander Debogande. Were you on *Europa*?"

"*Grappler*. Tari Rodwell, First Engineer's mate. They didn't have me as long as those poor guys on *Europa*."

Erik frowned, recalling the helmet cam from the marines first aboard *Grappler* at Joma Station dock. Remembered the backpack the barabo crewman had discovered, with a name attached. "T. Rodwell. Damn, we found your pack when we first boarded *Grappler*. We thought you were dead."

"Plenty of my buddies are," said Rodwell, blinking back emotion. "We were thirty-eight crew and twelve passengers. Now we're five, plus three passengers. I think your Uncle's lucky sard recognise human names, or he wouldn't have made it."

"Not so lucky," Erik said quietly. "If he hadn't had that surname, he'd never have been on *Europa* in the first place."

In zero-G midships, Operations crew and marines gathered about and above the unoccupied grapple five. Trace was unarmored, partly because she needed to be mobile post-ops, and partly because her suit's damage would make it pretty useless until repaired. Another four marines from Echo Platoon were fully armoured, weapons ready as crew worked the airlock to admit guests from the other side. Those guests had not come off a shuttle, however. They'd simply stepped out into vacuum, and free-flown across.

Crew floated well back as the inner door came open, and spidery steel legs grasped the rim from within. A torso came after it, lately familiar but shocking all the same, to see it venturing so freely into this human space. A drysine drone, off-set twin 'eyes', many legs, underside thrust modules and upperside twin guns.

It peered around with fast-scan wariness, then drifted clear and jetted to a cargo-net wall. Trace saw marine rifles twitch in its direction, but no more. Insane to allow it aboard. But everything was insane lately, and these three drones had come alone from the drysine ship now paralleling *Phoenix* at five klicks off their flank. A second drone emerged, and this one was badly damaged, legs missing, multiple bullet holes punching strange patterns through its armoured thorax and carapace. It moved awkwardly, and was followed inside by a third, undamaged like the first.

Trace looked to the nearby wall, where Romki was waiting with Lance Lance Corporal Penn. Styx's containment cage floated between them, and all three drones were now staring up at it. Trace nodded to Romki, who pushed gently off the wall with Penn, and floated down to the drones, holding the cage. They stopped short, and the damaged drone approached, staring in a manner that seemed almost human. The head-unit moved in short little jerks, considering and reconsidering, trying to comprehend this sight now before it. A drysine queen. Or her head, at least... but with hacksaws, that was the part that mattered. The drone approached with tiny bursts of reverential thrust, and extended a cautious, damaged limb. About the hold, no one moved. Save for Erik, whom Trace saw entering from above, just in time to see it happen.

A tiny probe appeared from within the drone's headpiece, and touched lightly upon Styx's single, dull-red eye. A connection appeared to be made. Everyone waited.

"Styx?" Trace ventured finally. "I know it requires very little of your attention to talk. What's going on?"

"This drone resisted." Her voice came from the midships wall speakers, effortlessly acquiring their control despite all the security systems in place to stop it. *"I had not thought any could. But while all others were enslaved, this one remained free. The original mind held, and the drysine way was strong."*

Trace remembered. "It gave you a way in. A way to reprogram all the others. To restore their natural minds."

"Yes."

"Through this one drone." And then she realised. "This is what you sacrificed our flank protection for in the fight. You pulled drones off our flank to go and find this one."

"This unit would have been destroyed. In truth I could have sacrificed more. The value is sufficient."

That sacrifice had nearly included Charlie Platoon and Command Squad, Trace knew. "Why is the value sufficient?"

"This drone holds information. Twenty five thousand of your years old. Information that I had never expected to see again."

For a machine, Styx certainly seemed to enjoy the theatrics. "Go on."

"The data is parren. There are locations, dates and names. I believe that they record the exchange of a very old data core, at the very end of the Drysine Empire. The final stand of the drysines against the organic betrayers took place very near this space. There were data threads, traces of possibility, recording an old data core exchange upon the very fall of the last command."

"A data core exchange containing what?" Trace tried to keep the impatience from her voice. Preposterous as she would have found it a while ago, it now seemed likely that these drones would take offence if she scolded their queen.

"The Drysine Empire," Styx repeated. *"All of it. A full recording, all of our secrets, our technology, our history. All lost now, save for this. A final glimpse of light before the dark."*

Trace stared, barely looking at Erik as he drifted to her side. "All their last secrets," he murmured. "All given for safekeeping, before the last of them died. Styx, who did they give the data core to? You said the data was parren?"

"Not all parren betrayed us. The Tahrae continued to fight at our side, against their own kind. This unit's memories are of the exchange, to the Tahrae of the parren. The Tahrae swore to keep it hidden, and safe, until one day, a drysine command would return to claim it."

Erik and Trace looked at Romki. Subdued and exhausted, Romki's eyes held quiet incredulity. "I don't know," he admitted. "My expertise has never extended as far as the parren. I'm not sure any human has met one in... well, centuries."

"Styx," said Erik. "What use would this data core be to us? If it still existed somewhere, and we could find it?"

"It could teach us everything we need to learn about what happened to the deepynines, and how to defeat them. It could be the salvation of the human race from certain doom."

Trace thought of those alo armour suits, occupied by alo soldiers and fighting as humans had never seen alo fight before — up close and personal, rather than distant and conservative within their deadly warships. Risking their own lives to save machines, deepynine machines, who risked theirs in turn to save alo. Among allies, such a bond was usually heartwarming, but the thought of it now filled her with dread. What had the most murderous of the hacksaw races forged, out in the dark millennia since their supposed extinction? What was this bond with the organics they'd once so despised? And what was their goal?

"He is ready," said Styx. *"The data is buried deep. Its extraction will destroy him."*

The damaged drone put one foreleg to Styx's cage, and gently touched her head. From it emitted a high-pitched whine, perhaps a mechanical function, or perhaps a final defiance of the dark.   An answering, eerie song climbed and dove upon the wall speakers.   Then a sudden burst of static, and the drone ceased movement. And simply floated, adrift.

    "I have it," said Styx.   She sounded quiet, and sad.   *"There are names and destinations.   A trail is begun.   We can follow, if we choose."*

CHAPTER 37

"That's why the drone couldn't be reprogrammed by the deepynine queen," Trace surmised before the entire command crew. They were all squeezed into the marines' briefing room, plus Captain Pram and one of his bridge officers. "The memory implant changed its brain somehow, it was hardwired in. It blocked the reprogramming, and the drone managed to pretend and fool the deepynines into thinking otherwise. That implant had been sitting there since the end of the Drysine Empire, waiting for someone to discover it. The drone was protecting that data with its life, terrified the deepynines would discover it first.

"In fact, I think that drone is the only reason we're still alive." Glancing at Erik, and the other *Phoenix* seniors. "Styx didn't screw us, but I'm pretty sure she would have. She had an army, ships, weapons. Maybe she would have just ditched us without killing us, but that would've been hard given she'd have had to rescue herself first from AT-7. Either way, the deepynines would have got us once she'd withdrawn — Styx has far less interest in killing deepynines than deepynines have in killing her, whatever her talk about her primary function. She just wants to survive and rebuild her race. My guess is that raiding the Tartarus and gaining all those assets was her best bet, until she discovered a better one. Which means that whatever's in that data core, she thinks it might still be around, and she thinks it's more valuable than all the assets she's just accumulated."

"It's the blueprint to her entire civilisation," said Erik, seated across from her, and beside Captain Pram. "The old civilisation, in all its glory. Whatever that data is, she doesn't currently have it. It could be her key to rebuilding everything that was lost."

"You do realise," Captain Pram said heavily, "that this cannot be allowed?"

"And what if a drysine army of some kind is the only way to defeat the alo-deepynine alliance?"

"Wait," said Pram, holding up a webbed hand. "We don't know that this alliance is anything like you've supposed."

"I saw it," said Trace. "We have it on camera, and now you've seen it." Pram said nothing. He looked grim and troubled. "It's just not conceivable that this is anything other than an organised, orchestrated move. Random deepynine survivors don't just 'hang out' with alo in old hacksaw bases. This was an organised plan. Occupy the base. Use the technology to make an ally of the sard. Pry the sard away from the tavalai."

Erik nodded. "Only they got distracted by their discovery that *Phoenix* had a drysine queen aboard," he said. "And it was the alo at Heuron who discovered it, if we're right about that. They must have passed that information on to the queen running the Tartarus operation, and she was prepared to jeopardise the whole thing just to get Styx, and us in the process. So they're clearly all in it together — alo High Command, deepynine queens... who knows how many there are back in alo space?"

"I've been thinking about that," Romki volunteered. Erik sensed no ill-will toward him this time, unlike before the Tartarus raid. He'd been on AT-7 the whole fight, and been relatively little help, it was true. But marines and crew didn't judge a person so much by their utility in a fight as their willingness to put their neck on the block in the first place. "Winning the sard to their side is a huge strategic move. Tartarus won't be the only bauble they're offering, I'm sure, and likely there are other old hacksaw bases in near space that the sard haven't been able to find uses for, but deepynines and alo can now show them how. But it's still a huge thing to risk, just to get one drysine queen."

"Not such a surprise if she's the last of her kind," said Kaspowitz.

"True," said Romki, carefully. "But it strikes me as entirely possible that Styx is considerably more important than we thought. And more than she lets on."

"Yeah, well she doesn't let on much," Shahaim muttered.

"She seems confident she can find this parren data core, for one thing," Romki continued. "Given that this is now... well, the *most* ancient history, that seems improbable. But I'm inclined to think that if she believes she can find it, then she can. And it would certainly explain why the deepynines and alo were so desperate to have her killed."

"Captain?" Erik said to Pram. "The tavalai know the parren far better than any humans. Can you tell us anything of the Tahrae?"

Pram was silent for a long moment. Weighing his options. Erik was almost surprised that he didn't refuse outright. This talk of alliance, with drysines and drysine queens, was the kind of thing the Dobruta would normally put a stop to with firepower and to hell with the details. But Trace's footage had shaken him. Alo space was vast and unexplored by non-alo. Alo technology was frightening. A deepynine alliance, forged millennia ago, would explain it. Many tavalai feared the alo more than humans, even without deepynines in the picture. Now, that fear was dramatically increased.

"Parren space is large," Pram said finally. "Small compared to what they once had, following the demise of the Machine Empire. But large enough still. They keep to themselves, and they do not welcome outsiders much more than alo do. Civilisations change over so many thousands of years. The parren are a very old spacefaring race, and old races tend to keep old traditions alive... but twenty five thousand years is a long time in anyone's language.

"The parren are... fastidious. Determined. Humans might say fanatical, in details at least. They have codes and customs. Many are extremely old. I do not know of anyone who thinks the Tahrae might still be around after all this time, but if there is one species that might have kept a... a secret society of some kind, alive for all that time? And remembered their purpose across the millennia? The parren would be it.

"Or perhaps the Tahrae simply buried it somewhere long, long ago. Perhaps your queen has some idea where." He looked about at them all, with wary resignation. "There are tavalai scholars we could ask. It seems like quite a... what do humans call it? A treasure hunt?"

"Tavalai space?" Kaspowitz asked. Crew exchanged anxious looks. "Can we do that?"

"To get to parren space, it will be necessary," Pram replied. "Dobruta can guarantee you a degree of protection. Though I warn you, many tavalai will not like it. Powerful tavalai. And no surrender agreement will protect a renegade human warship in tavalai space — that protection will rest entirely upon the Dobruta's guarantee of passage."

"They'll like it even less if they know what we've got on board," Shahaim added. "Styx is coming with us, right?"

"That's definitely the plan," said Trace. "I think she realised that as soon as she found the corrupted drone. Hacksaws can't venture through organic space, certainly not tavalai space. They can't pursue wherever the Tahrae have hidden that data core, they can't talk to organics without getting killed, and they don't really understand our civilisations anyway. It's our galaxy now, not theirs, and Styx will stay hidden aboard. She needs us to find the data core for her."

"Wonderful," Dale muttered.

"She has made one demand though."

"Only one?" Erik wondered.

Trace grimaced a little. "She wants a new body. She thinks she can help us make one."

After the briefing, Trace was in her quarters when Kono entered. A while ago she might have had to ask Lisbeth to leave first, but these days Lisbeth was in quarters as little as Trace. The ability of that rich, privileged girl to make herself a necessary part of the crew was for Trace one of the greatest marvels of the journey so far.

She sat on the room's single chair by the desk and wallscreen, and gestured for Kono to sit on Lisbeth's empty bed. He did, having to duck his head a little beneath the top bunk. Staff Sergeant Gideon Kono did not fit easily into small spaces.

"So," she said to him. "Any idea why you're here?"

"I'm not much on guessing games, Major." He didn't look all that happy, Trace thought. Kono was somber-serious most times, but rarely angry. Today he looked darkly displeased.

"You told the company commander you'd shoot her," Trace reminded him. "If she did something that might have proven necessary."

Kono made a face. "So I did."

Trace folded her arms, frowning as she wondered how to play this. Kono's mood was not what she'd expected. "I *should* have you shot," she ventured.

"Fine," said Kono. "Shoot me."

He knew damn well she wasn't going to shoot him. She'd been trying to provoke a reaction, and had gotten nothing. "You know, I'm going to take a wild stab in the dark and say that something else is bothering you. Out with it."

"I'd like a transfer from Command Squad."

Trace blinked. "Why?"

"You," said Kono, meeting her gaze properly for the first time. "With your death wish."

Trace sat straighter in her chair, her eyes hardening. "What about my death wish, Staff Sergeant?"

Kono sat up straighter as well, though that was harder beneath the low bunk. She'd called him by rank, and now things were far more serious than just two friends having a chat in quarters. "You were going to leave us, Major," Kono accused her. For the first time there was emotion in his eyes. Anger. "You were going to abandon your command and go it alone."

"I was considering the possibility. A larger group drew more attention. And Command Squad together did draw pursuers. If I'd gone alone, I'd have gotten through and seen what I needed to see with less opposition."

"Major it's my job as Command Squad leader to protect you. I can't do that if you're determined to get yourself killed."

"And what if I'm determined to complete the mission, Staff Sergeant?" Her voice hardened now, along with her expression. "Would you have a problem with that too?"

"Major in my professional opinion, completing that mission did not require you to go on a solo suicide run."

"So now you think you know my job better than me?"

"No Major. But you should have been thinking about sending me. Or Corporal Rael."

"I'm a better rifleman than you," Trace told him. It wasn't meant to hurt, because it was true, and Kono knew it. "In or out of full-G."

"Major, we're on a long mission here," Kono tried again. "*Phoenix* has a long fight ahead of her, and spending the Company Commander's life on one small part of that mission does not seem like a smart..."

"I'm not going to debate my command decisions with you, Staff Sergeant," she cut him off. "If you have a problem with my judgement in command of this company, you're welcome to take it up with the platoon leaders."

"Your command decisions aren't the damn problem," Kono growled. "Major." Any of her marines were welcome to disagree with her on substantial issues when the time was right, but most of them would have shown at least a little anxiety doing so. 'Giddy' Kono showed none. "Your problem is that your Kulina ethos means that you deliberately downplay the value of your own life. Now as a moral thing that's fine. It's admirable. But as a strategic thing, in our current situation, it's nuts. You're tasked with commanding this company. I'm tasked with keeping you alive. I simply can't do that job if you won't respect what it requires. You won't let me do my job. It's like playing babysitter for a kid who hurls herself onto every sharp object she can find. I'm a professional like you are, and I find this professional situation untenable. I quit."

He was upset, she realised. He covered it with anger like a lot of tough marines did, the men in particular. But mostly it was upset caused by fear, in this case at something that had nearly happened, and been narrowly avoided. It upset him that she'd even considered it. And it upset him that she'd been prepared to abandon him, to abandon them all, in order to complete the mission. It made her love him even more, but she couldn't show it. Men like Kono did not follow her because she was soft.

"You're not allowed to quit," she told him. "Request denied." He looked elsewhere, with an expression as though he'd smelt something very bad. Obviously he had more he'd like to say... but even he knew there was a line beyond which he could not go, and he was standing on it. "But I will take what you've said into consideration."

He looked at her. Mildly astonished, but hiding it well. "You will?" he asked skeptically.

"Do others feel as you do?"

"I couldn't speak for them, Major."

"Bullshit, as Command Squad leader it's your job to speak for them."

Kono took a deep breath. "The entire company has broad concern that you will one day get yourself killed doing something unnecessarily reckless. But I think you're already aware of that."

Trace nodded slowly. She was. "Thank you Staff Sergeant. You're dismissed."

"Major." He got to his feet. "And my punishment for speaking out of line in combat?"

"You know perfectly well that I can't punish my Command Squad leader without diminishing his authority before his marines," Trace said drily. "That means that you have effective carte blanche to misbehave all you like, without punishment. You have this privilege, and you abused it. The marines under you are not so lucky."

Kono swallowed, and glanced at his feet. Chagrined before her stare, for the first time. "Yes Major. It won't happen again."

"I know." She jerked her head toward the door. Kono left. Trace sat where she was, thinking about it for several minutes longer, unmoving. Then she got up, adjusted her collar and hair in the mirror, and followed Kono out the door.

In a corridor near Medbay One, she found Colonel Khola, walking with the aid of exo-legs and a hand on the wall for balance. Privates Rajesh and Cuoca walked a slow escort, rifles down and a wary three steps back, in case the legendary Kulina tried something.

"So," she said, stopping before him. Khola stopped his slow walk with a grimace, and leaned again on the wall. "How are you feeling?"

He didn't look too bad. The corpsmen said that most of the torture appeared to have been electrical, with few lasting physical scars. But he was no longer the youngest man in the service, and such things could take a physical and mental toll on even the healthiest, Kulina or otherwise.

"The rescue," he said, looking down and breathing hard from the effort. He should of course have still been in bed. Trace understood perfectly why he was not, and sympathised. Beds were for sleeping or dying. "Your idea?"

"Hell no. That was the LC. I thought it was a stupid waste of resources and told him so. He threatened to relieve me." They still hadn't thrashed that one out either. It was coming, Trace knew. The prospect didn't bother her particularly. Erik was a work in progress, and she would keep chipping away at the emerging form until it acquired some kind of agreeable shape.

"It *was* a stupid waste of resources," Khola agreed. "But karma intersects at curious junctions, and so my course continues." He considered her, with tired eyes. She'd always felt that those eyes somehow saw more of her than any others... until she'd met Captain Pantillo. "Did you find what you were looking for?"

"Yes. Evidence of an alo-deepynine alliance." Challenging him. Khola showed no surprise. "As I've already told you. And you didn't care."

Khola smiled faintly, and shrugged. "It changes nothing."

"It changes *everything*. You have to drop this stupid crusade of yours and tell Fleet what we've found out here. Tell everyone. Humanity is in terrible danger — already the alo-deepynine alliance is looking to recruit the sard. They may already have the chah'nas. Sard will have no problem with the return of deepynines to power in

478

the galaxy, they'd probably prefer it. Chah'nas lust only for power. The two main species who *will* mind are tavalai and humans. Alo have just used one to depose the other from power, and now we're next — they'll take out their obstacles one by one until they've restored everything they lost from the Machine Age and more."

Khola nodded sombrely. "I'll tell them. But it still changes nothing. Your Lieutenant Dale met with Supreme Commander Chankow before he died. He heard how many of your revelations Chankow already knew. This is no surprise to anyone, Major."

"And you trust that Fleet will do something about it?" Trace asked dangerously. "Fleet is more interested in war against Worlders, and using the chah'nas to do it."

Khola considered her for a long moment. "I was wrong about you Major. You *do* still have the human cause at heart. And your motivations are as selfless as any Kulina's. I will always disagree with your current course, but I accused you unfairly before. Perhaps even from personal spite." Trace frowned. An apology? She couldn't recall Khola ever giving one, to anyone, for anything. "These false things can divert the true course of karma. Please consider this an amends."

He extended his hand. The look in his wise, lidded eyes was as honest and open as ever. Trace knew Khola to be many things, but a manipulator and deceiver was not one of them. This apology was genuine, and perhaps unprecedented. An act that could perhaps reroute the flow of karma back to a better, truer course.

She smiled, and grasped his hand.

He yanked her forward, and the left hand flashed for her neck, lighting fast… only Trace caught it, swung and slammed him into the wall. Two handed she fought for wrist-leverage to pry the medical scalpel from his hand, and he lashed with exo-leg-assisted power as the blade fell. Trace took the kick, yanked him forward and took advantage of his poor footwork to spin behind him and apply a choke hold.

"You forget that I know you too," she hissed in his ear as he struggled and flailed against the grip that blocked his airway. He slammed her back against the wall, her legs wrapped around his waist and clinging like a spider.   Khola gasped and strained for breath, as the horrified marines searched for a shot but refrained with their Major in the line of fire.   "And now we've come full circle, because I know Fleet told you to keep me alive.   So now you've betrayed *your* sacred oath, you fucking hypocrite.   And that's why you were *really* apologising."

"There's only one sacred oath of Kulina," Khola wheezed. "And only one of us has... has..."

He collapsed face-first on the deck, and Trace kept the choke in place for a few seconds to be sure.   Then she collected the scalpel from the deck alongside, and stood up.

"Don't hurt him," she told the privates as they rushed to secure him.   "He's out, he's no threat for now."

"Major, I'm sorry!" Private Rajesh exclaimed as Cuoca secured the unconscious Colonel.   "I didn't know he had that... I mean, we searched him and..."

"That's okay," said Trace.   "I knew."   Or she'd guessed. And she thought of what Erik was going to say to her, about *Phoenix* marines and basic non-combat security tasks.   She nearly rolled her eyes in exasperation.

Cuoca held Khola's wrists behind his back, a knee in his shoulder blades.   In this condition, Khola was so far below his best there would be no more trouble from him, Trace was sure.   He'd only had just enough left for a final attempt at *her*, if she'd been dumb enough to fall for it.

"Major, we asked if we should restrain him before," said Cuoca, breathless and puzzled.   "We thought word got to you, and you said no."

"That's right," said Trace.

Rajesh stared.   "Did you *expect* him to try this?"

Trace winked at the private, and gave him a light whack on the cheek.   "Stay awake boys.   Restraints on his bed, and could someone please try to keep track of where all the sharp objects go? That'd be ace, thanks."

Truth was, she thought as she walked away, she hadn't truly *expected* it.   She'd just wanted to know for sure.   And now she knew that every time Khola tried to kill her, he only convinced her even more of how right she'd been to leave.

CHAPTER 38

There was no time to haul out the dress uniforms. Neither marines nor crew had enough personal storage space to keep dress uniforms in accessible lockers, so on long cruises the fancy stuff went into long-term storage. Getting it all out would require an effort from crew who were already overworked and under-slept. They were still technically in a combat zone, given that everywhere *Phoenix* went lately became a combat zone whatever it had been previously, and dress uniforms in a combat zone were as useful as bells on a rifle.

But there were jackets over jumpsuits, and hats of any available sort, so that stained, worn and scruffy as they were, *Phoenix*'s crew made a presentable display when arrayed row upon vertical row along the ledges and gantries of Assembly. A presentable display of a working, fighting combat crew, Erik thought as he looked up and about at them all, on the ledges before the rows of racked marine armour and weapons. Only about a quarter of crew and marines were here — in light of continuing threats the crew were needed constantly at their posts, and safety regs forbade any more than a hundred and fifty in Assembly at any time due to the lack of G-slings in an emergency. But there was camera vision taken for later viewing, so everyone would get to see eventually.

Erik supposed it would have been more dramatic to save himself for last, but it meant more to the crew to have their new brass pinned on them by a captain than an LC, so obviously he had to go first. Chief Petty Officer Goldman sounded the bosun's whistle when he first came in, and everyone snapped to attention in their vertical rows. Two others held the twin flags of Fleet and United Forces. It felt strange to salute the flags, given everything that had transpired between *Phoenix* and Fleet, but everyone had agreed it would have felt more strange to do the ceremony without the flags, and perhaps unlucky too. —

And so Erik did the salute, spun on his heel and marched along the line of first-shift bridge crew, Command Squad and Alpha

Platoon marines on the other side, and then stopped before Trace. Erik fancied he did a parade turn somewhat better than her, and showed it, then stopped before her with a precise stamp, and saluted.

Trace might have smiled, ghostingly faint as she saluted back, and opened the small, velvet case in her other hand. She looked different beneath the officer's hat she rarely wore — Assembly was to be considered 'outdoors' for formal purposes, and was thus the only place on *Phoenix* where uniform hats could properly be worn, with salutes given and received. Seeing the hat reminded Erik of just how rarely Trace ever relied on rank or trappings of any kind to garner respect from anyone. Something to aspire to, Erik thought, and could not help his heart thudding a little faster at the sight of captain's eagle wings in the velvet case.

Trace removed the Lieutenant Commander's gold leaf from his collar, then pinned the eagles with very little ceremony. Erik thought she must have practised a few times, it wasn't like she'd done it very often. Another salute, and that was that. Surely there was more to it? And as his gaze travelled along the line of faces watching, he knew that of course there *had* been far more to it. The audition had been long and hard, and this was just the final act. He still did not believe in his heart that he deserved it, but he was used to that by now. It was necessary, as Trace would say. Necessity came first, and feelings could wait.

He then took his place at Trace's side, and accepted a similar case from Lieutenant Shilu. Inside were a commander's silver leaves, which he then had the pleasure of pinning on his friend Suli Shahaim, after first removing her lieutenant's bars. She looked quite emotional, which surprised him. Though really, he thought, Suli was nearly twice his age, and had been doing this a hell of a lot longer. Lieutenant was the usual 'cap rank' for Fleet officers, the one that plenty of good officers reached, but rarely progressed beyond. And now, after so long spent at Captain Pantillo's right hand, and now at his, she'd finally taken that next step, in one giant stride that skipped the lieutenant commander's rank completely.

After salutes, Commander Shahaim left immediately for the bridge to relieve Second Lieutenant Dufresne. In the meantime, there were others to promote, and a line to work through. Erik did the honours with the spacers, and Trace with the marines, though each gave and accepted salutes from both. Among them were Second Lieutenant Rooke, finally promoted to full-louie, while Erik took particular pleasure in promoting Ensign Remy Hale up to Second Lieutenant behind him. While notably among the marines, the once-Staff Sergeant Vijay Khan finally left the service of Family Debogande to take a corporal's rank — a significant demotion, but he looked pleased enough with it. And perhaps even relieved, to have finally found his place on the ship.

Dufresne arrived, and received her promotion to full Lieutenant with cool precision, then saluted and left to fetch Draper. Erik saw dry amusement from some of the first-shift bridge crew — Dufresne should have been plenty happy to just make full-louie after so few years out of the Academy. But Draper was getting the real promotion, not her, and she didn't seem entirely thrilled about it.

Then came the civilians. There had been some long but mostly constructive debates about it first, command crew sitting late over a meal, squeezed into Erik's quarters while arguing about what made sense for whom to get what. Lisbeth was of course impossible to induct into Fleet ranks, even in an emergency. Temporary shuttle co-pilot and invaluable Engineering assistant though she was, a family name like Debogande couldn't just be disregarded. Plus there was the technicality that siblings were *never* allowed rank on the same ship, partly in case one lost vessel wiped out half a family, and partly because a captain's impartiality could not be guaranteed when ordering his sister into danger. That Erik was *already* in that position with her, irrespective of her lack of official rank, did not change anyone's opinion.

Romki was similarly impossible, mostly because whatever oath he gave, no one would believe it. That, plus it was the last thing he actually wanted, and would probably only accept with a gun to his head, and possibly not even then. Stan Romki would always be a lone wolf and master of his own conscience, for better or worse. And Erik thought he was probably more use that way.

Jokono and Hiro were another matter — ensign for both of them, the lowest rank on the officer scale save for warrant officer, but warrants had to know how to actually do stuff on the ship. Ensign, it was generally agreed, would allow each to become an operational part of the command structure without giving them the ability to question any of the more senior officers. Both were given the specialisation of IN-1, for Intelligence — something utterly unknown on Fleet ships to date. They were temporary ranks of course, applied under press-gang rules, often used in Fleet when ships in desperate need of crew were allowed by Fleet law to 'recruit' able civilians, against their will if necessary. Erik was grateful that both men seemed considerably more enthusiastic than that, but had little hope that either of them would stick around if this whole mess ended tomorrow. Neither were Fleet men by nature, just by circumstance. But this circumstance required that they improvise, and make the best use of every asset to hand — people in particular.

And in that spirit, it gave Erik perhaps the greatest pleasure of all to pin a second lieutenant's single bar on Tif's collar, the lowest feasible rank for a pilot, and to see the shining pleasure in her big, golden eyes. Her salute was very rusty, and her parade steps worse, but no one cared — the other pilots said that she was a gun, and her co-pilot Ensign Lee had gone from the most nervous co-pilot on *Phoenix* to the most smug in record short time. There had never before been a kuhsi given rank on a Fleet warship. Erik did not need to check any records to know that — it was well known that the one prerequisite that *all* Fleet personnel had to meet was humanity. Tif was not merely the first kuhsi to hold rank on a Fleet vessel, she was the first non-human, and that was a record Erik was more than happy to smash.

Finally there arrived at the event Lieutenant Draper, having been relieved from bridge duty by Lieutenant Dufresne. He beamed and looked the happiest Erik had ever seen him, as his new Captain pinned Erik's old gold leaves on his collar. Erik was surprised how hard they were to part with. He'd worked so hard to get those leaves, and he'd been so proud when he'd received them. They'd been his highest rank in the war, the culmination of all his hard work and hopes that he could make his family proud. But he knew when he saw them pinned to the collar of the younger man that some old things had to be left behind. And with them, all the innocence and lightness that went with a lesser responsibility.

When the ceremony was all over, there were handshakes instead of salutes, and everyone fell out for congratulations and some photos before heading back to duty. Erik was mildly surprised that Trace made a point of coming to shake his hand.

"Congratulations Captain," she told him, with a subdued smile to tell him that she really meant 'about damn time'.

"Given how much you disagreed with my last call," said Erik, "I'm a bit surprised you didn't stick it in my eye." He could feel the new rank at his collar, tugging with unreasonable weight. It was the most curious sensation.

Trace shook her head faintly. "No sir. It's not the calls themselves. It's the officer's willingness to make them in the first place."

"But you think I was wrong to send the rescue after *Europa*'s crew?"

"Yessir. They weren't the objective. If we divide resources by chasing multiple secondary objectives, we increase the risk of failure."

"You know what's really surprised me since we've been out here?" Erik asked her. "The thing I wouldn't have predicted three months ago? How eager the crew is. I'd thought we'd have morale problems by now, but instead they're keen as anything."

Trace nodded slowly. "I agree," she said carefully.

"This is why they signed up," Erik insisted. "The Triumvirate War was always an awkward, nasty thing. Tavalai were never the horrible enemy we wanted them to be — which isn't to say we shouldn't have fought them. But it was a war of politics and advantage, not a war of passion.

"*This* is a war of passion." He jabbed his finger at the deck. "Our war. *Phoenix*'s war. Everyone can see the stakes. I think for a lot of them it's almost a relief, particularly the veterans. The

Triumvirate War left everyone with a bad taste in their mouths. We won, but it was never as sweet as we wanted it to be. But this fight, it seems almost as though the more dangerous it gets, the keener everyone becomes.

"I'm different to you, Major. You've fought against that passion all your life. You've sought to control it. But I'm only here because of it. Most of the crew are also. If we're not here to rescue the *Europa* crew, and others like them? Then we lose that passion. Without it, we've lost this fight before it even starts."

"That sounds nice, Captain," Trace said calmly. "But combat doesn't care about sentiment. Mostly it comes down to odds and percentages. You play the wrong ones, we all die."

"I know my ship," Erik replied with certainty. "And I know my crew. I knew those odds, and I thought we could do it. Plus the *Europa* crew will go home now. They've got a scary story to tell, and a lot of them are people Fleet HQ can't easily shut up. My uncle among them, but others as well. They'll tell humanity the story that we can't, and start the debate that we won't be present for. It was worth it."

"It's always worth it when it works. It's never worth it when it doesn't." As usual, it was impossible to tell exactly what Trace thought. "Would you really have removed me from command?" she asked. "If I'd continued to refuse your order?"

"Yes," said Erik, and meant it.

"Good," Trace replied, and meant that too.

"And now that I properly outrank you," Erik said edgily, "I won't have to worry about that any longer, will I?"

"No sir," Trace said innocently. "Not *that*, at least." And her smile turned faintly dangerous.

Ensign Jokono entered Engineering Bay 8D with no small trepidation. Within, he found a very odd sight — Stanislav Romki seated at a workbench at the side of the open bay floor, beside a large, square framework that contained the head of *Phoenix*'s resident drysine queen.   Splayed in a great, blue holographic glow across the floor was a technical hologram, displaying shapes and diagrams so complicated that Jokono had no idea what he was looking at.

The newly promoted Lieutenant Rooke was also here, Jokono saw as he came fully into the room, walking now through the interactive hologram and pointing to technical shapes, moving them by touch, joining things together.   The shapes looked vaguely like hacksaw body parts.   Perhaps they were considering how to build Styx the new body she had reportedly demanded.   Neither man paid Jokono any attention, talking in a technical jargon so dense it might have been another language.

"Hello Ensign Jokono," said a female voice from the room speakers.   Jokono had been warned of this too — the machine that pretended to have a gender, and to use vocal speech with emotive inclinations, to make its listeners feel more well disposed toward it. It was not, he'd been warned, anything more than that.   *"Have you been sent here to ask me some questions?"*

"Well yes," Jokono said carefully, stepping about the edge of the bench to the holographic perimeter, where the single red eye within the frame-brace could see him directly.   "Hello Styx.   We haven't yet been introduced.   But you seem to know who I am already."

"A curious state of existence," said Styx.   *"To only know intimately that to which you have been personally introduced.   Can I take it we are now acquainted?"*

As though she were teasing him, Jokono thought.   From Styx, it was neither comforting nor amusing.   She had his details on file, of course, and knew his face on sight.   AIs, she was suggesting, did not place greater value on data just because it was standing directly before them.   Data from memories many thousands of years old could seem just as strong, to a mind in which everything was digitally encoded.

"Yes of course," Jokono agreed, with all the cool he'd ever used while interviewing crazy people accused of crimes.   "It's very nice to meet you finally."

"Of course," said Styx.

"Careful," Rooke told Jokono with an amused look. "She's getting snippy. Comes from listening to Lisbeth too long."

Romki ignored them all, frowning as he considered the various components hovering in the display around him. "Now what if," he suggested as something new occurred to him, "we realign this module with the X-matrix along here..." and he shifted the new parts into line, launching into his and Rooke's foreign language once more.

"As it happens," Jokono continued, "as the ship's intelligence officer, I have been asked by the Captain to gather more information from you on various things. If you can spare a moment?"

"Of course I can," said Styx. *"Supervising these two is not taxing."*

"Hey," Rooke protested. "I heard that."

Jokono nodded. "Firstly, the drysine ships that are now preparing to leave. I take it you will not tell us where they are going?"

"No. Their destination must remain hidden. They are now the last of their kind, as am I. I cannot accompany them for now, and so they must go alone."

Once upon a time, *Phoenix* had placed the highest priority upon destroying old hacksaw nests. Now they'd likely just created a huge new one, with FTL ships and more than a thousand drones. It made no one happy... except perhaps Lieutenant Rooke and Stan Romki, whom everyone agreed were enjoying their new ship-guest far too much.

"Very well," said Jokono. "Now the parren. I'd like to ask you some questions about where we're going, and who you think we might be able to meet."

"Ensign Jokono," said Styx. *"Please understand that my data on the parren is now twenty five thousand years out of date. You'd do better consulting Mr Romki, his data is at least current, if incomplete."*

"Well no," Jokono insisted. "Actually I'd like to ask you of your old data. If we are to track the current whereabouts of this data-core, we first need to understand where it has been.   My background is in criminal investigations, where we attempt to establish a timeline of events based on whatever snippets of information we can uncover.   And so I'd like to begin by asking you of your memories of the parren, during your time."   He turned on his recorder, and sat on the edge of the bench.   "Come to that, what *was* your time?   Or put more simply, who *are* you?   *What* are you?"

Silence from the queen.   Rooke and Romki both stopped what they were doing to look at her, fascinated.   Typical that they hadn't had the nerve to ask her already, Jokono thought drily.   Both were so clearly in awe of her, it made them a potential liability in her presence.   He made a mental note to report that to Captain Debogande, with the rest.

"Any identifiers that I could communicate to you would be in drysine coded language, or the language of our enemies," Styx said finally.   *"It would mean nothing to you."*

"And that," said Jokono, "is exactly the kind of unhelpful answer that I've been instructed to no longer accept from you.   So please, take your time."

"But the parren," Styx continued as though she hadn't heard him.   *"The Tahrae faction, as you've called them.   They called themselves 'tukayran maskai' — I believe it could translate as 'the chosen', in your English.   Them I knew well."*

"Twenty five thousand years ago?   For how long?"

"Our people evolve, Ensign.   In body and mind, I was not the entity I am now even a hundred years before that time.   Identity shifts.   You ask me to identify a singular sense of self, yet it is not something my people typically possess."

"But the parren knew you as a single entity?" Jokono pressed.   "You may not believe in such things, but they're organics, and most organics do.   How did they know you?   What did they call you?"

"They called me Halgolam," said Styx.

Jokono frowned, and was about to ask more when he saw Romki's expression.   His eyes were wide.   "Stanislav?   You recognise the name?"

"Halgolam is one of the oldest parren gods," said Romki. "Long dead, like our Greek and Roman gods. Zeus, Venus, Mars. Styx. I don't think any parren have worshiped Halgolam in… oh, ten thousand years. At least."

"And what was she?" Jokono pressed, feeling cold dread prickling up his spine. Some old things in the galaxy, he was quite certain should stay dead and buried forever. "What kind of god was this Halgolam?"

"The literal translation in the old tongue was 'the wings of the night'," said Romki. "Halgolam was the goddess of violent retribution, sent by the creator to wreak terrible justice upon the wicked." He took a deep breath. "We might call her the Angel of Death."

ABOUT THE AUTHOR

Joel Shepherd is the author of 12 Science Fiction and Fantasy novels, including 'The Cassandra Kresnov Series', 'A Trial of Blood and Steel', and 'The Spiral Wars'. He has a degree in International Relations, and lives in Australia.